Praise for *PopCo*

"You might say that Thomas has redefined activism for the Digital Age. *PopCo* is at heart a novel of social protest. Inspired by a venerable tradition, she achieves here a scope and a passion to match the intelligence and empathy her fiction has always had."

—*Los Angeles Times Book Review*

"Enough code-breaking tips, puzzles and graphs, charts, postscripts and appendixes to satisfy that other mathematician storyteller, Lewis Carroll."

—*The New York Times Book Review*

"Peppered with curious clues and mysterious diaries, *PopCo* cleverly combines revelations about Alice's past with a jaundiced look at the culture that created the manipulative toy empire."

—*People* (3½ stars)

"Brilliant and rebellious. Outstanding and unforgettable. I only put this book down to eat and sleep. It captivated me, pure and simple. It is a wonderfully, gorgeously original piece of work. A one-of-a-kind piece of literature. I'm eager to see what else Thomas has in store for the world."

—BookSlut.com

"It's mystery, romance, and corporate satire rolled into one—a sort of Harriet-the-Spy-meets-Douglas-Coupland with a *Treasure Island* twist."

—*Daily Candy*

"*PopCo* offers a critique on the power struggles between those who run corporations and the underlings whose ideas fuel the machine—the 'creatives,' as Thomas wryly calls them. The novel will appeal most to those who came of age in our current toy-glutted culture."

—*The Washington Post*

"Extremely ingenious. British author Thomas is without question a gifted writer, and many readers will certainly find her new work a mind-blowing experience. Strongly recommended."

—*Library Journal* (starred review)

"[An] ambitious novel, which quietly but scathingly critiques consumerist society. Thought-provoking fiction for the Digital Age."
— *Kirkus Reviews* (starred review)

"Smart, engaging. Thomas delivers a captivating heroine and a pointed cultural critique that will especially resonate with the *No Logo* crowd."
— *Publishers Weekly*

"*PopCo* is written for the cat owner, the disillusioned cyberpunk, the RPGamer; for those who embrace counterculture *and* the popular culture, for those who read *The Da Vinci Code* and wanted to hear more about the Fibonacci number . . . this is an updated *Westing Game* for the 'net generation."
— *Lumino* magazine (3 stars for art, 4 stars for entertainment)

"If *Cryptonomicon* and *Fight Club* jointly impregnated *Thursday Next*, then *PopCo* would be their unholy demon seed. Sprawling, imaginative, clever, and absorbing, *PopCo* is a thinking person's adventure tale, and will delight any reader who embraces their inner four-eyed, scholastically inclined, geeky misfit. And it has pirates! Resistance is futile. Buy *PopCo* now and accept your nerdy destiny."
— StephsBookReviews.com

"Richly allusive, freewheeling and, in the end, enormously satisfying narrative riffs on popular and corporate culture, maths and crypt-analysis, like a dreamland collaboration between Douglas Coupland, Naomi Klein and Douglas R. Hofstadter."
— *Independent on Sunday* (London)

"Ambitious, thought-provoking, fun and partisan—with an ending that gives a tick to all the right values."   — *The Times* (London)

The End of Mr. Y

Also by Scarlett Thomas

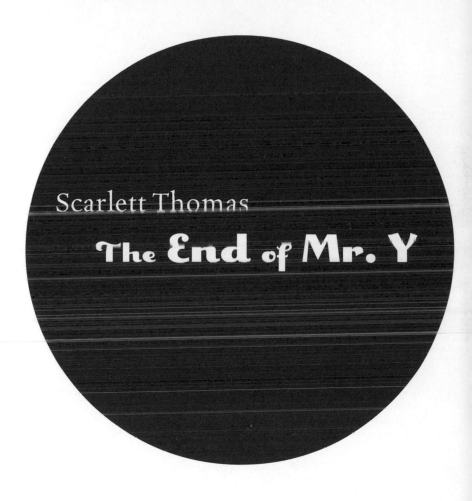

Scarlett Thomas

The End of Mr. Y

A Harvest Original • Harcourt, Inc.

Orlando   Austin   New York   San Diego   Toronto   London

www.HarcourtBooks.com

Library of Congress Cataloging-in-Publication Data
Thomas, Scarlett.
The end of Mr. Y/Scarlett Thomas.—1st ed.
p.   cm.
"A Harvest original."
I. Title.
PR6120.H66E53   2006
823.'92—dc22   2006004790
ISBN-13: 978-0-15-603161-5   ISBN-10: 0-15-603161-2

Text set in Sovereign Light
Designed by April Ward

Printed in the United States of America
First edition
K J I H G F E D C B A

For Cauze Venn

The End of Mr. Y

But what if God himself can be simulated, that is to say can be reduced to the signs that constitute faith? Then the whole system becomes weightless, it is no longer itself anything but a gigantic simulacrum—not unreal, but a simulacrum, that is to say never exchanged for the real, but exchanged for itself, in an uninterrupted circuit without reference or circumference.

Jean Baudrillard

Indeed it is even possible for an entity to show itself as something which in itself it is *not*.

Martin Heidegger

Part
One

Not only is nothing good or ill but thinking
makes it so, but nothing is at all, except in
so far as thinking has made it so.

Samuel Butler

Chapter One

You now have one choice.

You . . . I'm hanging out of the window of my office, sneaking a cigarette and trying to read *Margins* in the dull winter light, when there's a noise I haven't heard before. All right, the noise—crash, bang, etc.—I probably have heard before, but it's coming from underneath me, which isn't right. There shouldn't be anything underneath me: I'm on the bottom floor. But the ground shakes, as if something's trying to push up from below, and I think about other people's mothers shaking out their duvets or even God shaking out the fabric of space-time; then I think, *Fucking hell, it's an earthquake,* and I drop my cigarette and run out of my office at roughly the same time that the alarm starts sounding.

When alarms sound I don't always run immediately. Who does? Usually an alarm is just an empty sign: a drill; a practice. As I'm on my way to the side door out of the building the shaking stops. Shall I go back to my office? But it's impossible to stay in this building when this alarm goes off. It's too loud; it wails inside your head. As I leave the building I walk past the Health and Safety notice board, which has pictures of injured people on it. The pictures blur as I go past: A man who has back pain is also having a heart attack, and various hologram people are trying to revive him. I was supposed to go to some Health and Safety training last year, but didn't.

As I open the side door I can see people leaving the Russell Building and walking, or running, past our block and up the gray concrete steps in the direction of the Newton Building and the library. I cut around the right-hand side of the building and bound up the concrete steps, two at a time. The sky is gray, with a thin TV-static drizzle that hangs in the air like it's been freeze-framed. Sometimes, on these January afternoons, the sun squats low in the sky like an orange-robed Buddha in a documentary about the meaning of life. Today there is no sun. I come to the edge of the large crowd that has formed, and I stop running. Everyone is looking at the same thing, gasping and making firework-display noises.

It's the Newton Building.

It's falling down.

I think of this toy—have I seen it on someone's desk recently?— which is a little horse mounted on a wooden button. When you press the button from underneath, the horse collapses to its knees. That's what the Newton Building looks like now. It's sinking into the ground, but in a lopsided way; one corner is now gone, now two, now . . . Now it stops. It creaks, and it stops. A window on the third floor flaps open, and a computer monitor falls out and smashes onto what's left of the concrete courtyard below. Four men with hard hats and fluorescent jackets slowly approach the broken-up courtyard; then another man comes, says something to them, and they all move away again.

Two men in gray suits are standing next to me.

"Déjà vu," one of them says to the other.

I look around for someone I know. There's Mary Robinson, the head of department, talking to Lisa Hobbes. I can't see many other people from the English Department. But I can see Max Truman standing on his own, smoking a roll-up. He'll know what's going on.

"Hello, Ariel," he mumbles when I walk over and stand next to him.

Max always mumbles; not in a shy way, but rather as if he's telling you what it will cost to take out your worst enemy, or how much you'd have to pay to rig a horse race. Does he like me? I don't think he trusts me. But why would he? I'm comparatively young, relatively new to the department, and I probably seem ambitious, even though I'm not. I also have long red hair and people say I look intimidating (because of the hair? Something else?). People who don't say I look intimidating sometimes say I look "dodgy," or "odd." One of my ex-housemates said he wouldn't like to be stuck on a desert island with me but didn't say why.

"Hi, Max," I say. Then: "Wow."

"You probably don't know about the tunnel, do you?" he says. I shake my head. "There's a railway tunnel that runs under here," he says, pointing downwards with his eyes. He sucks on his roll-up, but nothing seems to happen, so he takes it out of his mouth and uses it to point around the campus. "It runs under Russell over there, and Newton, over there. Goes—or used to go—from the town to the coast. It hasn't been used in a hundred years or so. This is the second time it's collapsed and taken Newton with it. They were supposed to fill it with concrete after last time," he adds.

I look at where Max just pointed, and start mentally drawing straight lines connecting Newton with Russell, imagining the tunnel underneath the line. Whichever way you do it, the English and American Studies Building is on the line, too.

"Everyone's all right, at least," he says. "Maintenance saw a crack in the wall this morning and evacuated them all."

Lisa shivers. "I can't believe this is happening," she says, looking over at the Newton Building. The gray sky has darkened and the rain is now falling more heavily. The Newton Building looks strange with no lights on: It's as if it has been stubbed out.

"I can't either," I say.

For the next three or four minutes we all stand and stare in silence at the building; then a man with a megaphone comes around and tells us all to go home immediately without going back to our offices. I feel like crying. There's something so sad about broken concrete.

I don't know about everyone else, but it's not that easy for me just to go home. I only have one set of keys to my flat, and that set is in my office, along with my coat, my scarf, my gloves, my hat, and my rucksack.

There's a security guard trying to stop people going in through the main entrance, so I go down the steps and in the side way. My name isn't on my office door. Instead, it bears only the name of the official occupier of the room: my supervisor, Professor Saul Burlem. I met Burlem twice before I came here: once at a conference in Greenwich, and once at my interview. He disappeared just over a week after I arrived. I remember coming into the office on a Thursday morning and noticing that it was different. The first thing was that the blinds *and* the curtains were closed: Burlem always closed his blinds at the end of every day, but neither of us ever touched the horrible thin gray curtains. And the room smelled of cigarette smoke. I was expecting him in at about ten o'clock that morning, but he didn't show up. By the following Monday I asked people where he was and they said they didn't know. At some point someone arranged for his classes to be covered. I don't know if there's departmental gossip about this—no one gossips to me—but everyone seems to assume I'll just carry on my research and it's no big deal for me that he isn't around. Of course, he's the reason I came to the department at all: He's the only person in the world who has done serious research on one of my main subjects: the nineteenth-century writer Thomas E. Lumas. Without Burlem, I'm not really sure why I am here. And I do feel something about him being missing; not loss, exactly, but something.

My car is in the Newton car park. When I get there I am not at all surprised to find several men in hard hats telling people to forget about their cars and walk or take the bus home. I do try to argue—I say I'm happy to take the risk that the Newton Building will not suddenly go into a slow-motion cinematic rewind in order that it can fall down again in a completely different direction—but the men pretty much tell me to piss off and walk home or take the bus like everybody else, so I eventually drift off in the direction of the bus stop. It's only the beginning of January, but some daffodils and snowdrops have made it through the earth and stand wetly in little rows by the path. The bus stop is depressing: There's a line of people looking as cold and fragile as the line of flowers, so I decide I'll just walk.

I think there's a shortcut into town through the woods, but I don't know where it is so I just follow the route I would have driven until I leave the campus, playing the scene of the building collapsing in my mind over and over again until, realizing I'm remembering things that never even happened, I give up thinking about it at all. Then I consider the railway tunnel. I can see why it would be there: After all, the campus is set on top of a steep hill and it would make sense to go under rather than over it. Max said it hadn't been used for a hundred years or so. I wonder what was on this hill a hundred years ago. Not the university, of course, which was built in the 1960s. It's so cold. Perhaps I should have waited for the bus. But no buses pass me as I walk. By the time I get to the main road into town my fingers have frozen inside my gloves and I start examining roads off to the right, looking for a shortcut. The first one is marked with a NO THROUGH ROAD sign, partially obscured by seagull shit; but the second looks more promising, with red-brick-terraced houses curling around to the left, so I take it.

I thought this was just a residential road, but soon the red-brick houses stop and there's a small park with two swings and a slide rusting under a dark canopy of tangled but bare oak tree branches. Beyond that there is a pub and then a small row of shops. There's a sad-looking charity shop, already shut, and the kind of hairdresser that does blue rinses and sets for half price on a Monday. There's a newsagent and a betting shop and then—aha—a secondhand bookshop. It's still open. I'm freezing. I go in.

It's warm inside the shop and smells slightly of furniture polish. The door has a little bell that keeps jangling for a good three seconds after I close it, and soon a young woman comes out from behind a large set of bookshelves, holding a can of polish and a yellow duster. She smiles briefly and tells me that the shop will be closing in about ten minutes but that I am welcome to look around. Then she sits down and starts tapping something into a keyboard connected to a computer on the front desk.

"Have you got a computerized catalog of all your books?" I ask her.

She stops typing and looks up. "Yeah. But I don't know how to use it. I'm only filling in for my friend. Sorry."

"Oh. OK."

"What did you want to look up?"

"It doesn't matter."

"No, tell me. I might remember dusting it."

"Um . . . OK, then. Well, there's this author called Thomas E. Lumas . . . Have you got any books by him?" I always ask this in secondhand bookshops. They rarely do have anything by him, and I've got most of his books already. But I still ask. I still hope for a better copy of something, or an older one. Something with a different preface or a cleaner dust jacket.

"Er. . . ." She screws up her forehead. "The name sounds sort of familiar."

"You might have come across something called *The Apple in the Garden*. That's his famous one. But none of the others are in print. He wrote in the mid to late nineteenth century but never became as famous as he should have been . . ."

"*The Apple in the Garden*. No, the one I saw wasn't that one," she says. "Hang on." She walks around to the large bookcase at the back of the shop. "L, Lu, Lumas . . . No. Nothing here," she says. "Mind you, I don't know what section they'd have put him in. Is it fiction?"

"Some is fiction," I say. "But he also wrote a book about thought experiments, some poetry, a treatise on government, several science books, and something called *The End of Mr. Y*, which is one of the rarest novels . . ."

"*The End of Mr. Y*. That's it!" she says, excited. "Hang on."

She goes up the stairs at the back of the shop before I can tell her that she must be mistaken. It is impossible to imagine that she actually has a copy up there. I would probably give away everything I own to obtain a copy of *The End of Mr. Y*, Lumas's last and most mysterious work. I don't know what she's got it confused with, but it's just absurd to think that she has it. No one has that book. There is one known copy in a German bank vault, but no library has it listed. I have a feeling that Saul Burlem may have seen a copy once, but I'm not sure. *The End of Mr. Y* is supposed to be cursed, and although I obviously don't believe in any of that stuff, some people do think that if you read it you die.

"Yeah, here it is," says the girl, carrying a small cardboard box down the stairs. "Is this the one you mean?"

She places the box on the counter.

I look inside. And—suddenly I can't breathe—there it is: a small cream clothbound hardback with brown lettering on the cover and spine, missing a dust jacket but otherwise near perfect. But it can't be. I open the cover and read the title page and the publication details. Oh shit. This is a copy of *The End of Mr. Y.* What the hell do I do now?

"How much is it?" I ask carefully, my voice as small as a pin.

"Yeah, that's the problem," she says, turning the box around. "The owner gets boxes like this from an auction in town, I think, and if they're upstairs it means they haven't been priced yet." She smiles. "I probably shouldn't have shown it to you at all. Can you come back tomorrow when she's in?"

"Not really . . . ," I start to say.

Ideas beam through my mind like cosmic rays. Shall I tell her I'm not from around here and ask her to ring the owner now? No. The owner clearly doesn't know that the book is here. I don't want to take the risk that she will have heard of it and then refuse to sell it to me— or try to charge thousands of pounds. What can I say to make her give me the book? Seconds pass. The girl seems to be picking up the phone on the desk.

"I'll just give my friend a ring," she says. "I'll find out what to do."

While she waits for the call to connect I glance into the box. It's unbelievable, but there are other Lumas books there, and a couple of Derrida translations that I don't have, as well as what looks like a first edition of *Eureka!* by Edgar Allan Poe. How did these texts end up in a box together? I can't imagine anyone connecting them, unless it was for a project similar to my Ph.D. Could someone else be working on the same thing? Unlikely, especially if they have given the books away. But who would give these books away? I feel as though I'm looking at Paley's watch. It's as if someone put this box together just to appeal to me.

"Yeah," the girl is saying to her friend. "It's like a small box. Upstairs. Yeah, in that pile in the toilet. Um . . . looks like a mix of old and new. Some of the old ones are a bit musty and stuff. Paperbacks, I think . . ." She looks into the box and pulls out a couple of the Derrida books. I nod at her. "Yeah, just a real mix. Oh, do you? Cool. Yeah. Fifty quid? Seriously? That's a lot. OK, I'll ask her. Yeah. Sorry. OK. See you later."

She puts the phone down and smiles at me. "Well," she says. "There's good news and bad news. The good news is that you can have the whole box if you want, but the bad news is that I can't sell individual books from the box, so it's all or nothing really. Sam says she bought the box herself from an auction, and the owner hasn't even seen it yet. But apparently she's already said she hasn't got the space to shelve loads more stuff . . . But the other bad news is that the whole box is going to cost fifty pounds. So . . ."

"I'll take it," I say.

"Seriously? You'd spend that on a box of books?" She smiles and shrugs. "Well, OK. I guess that's fifty pounds, then, please."

My hands shake as I get my purse out of my bag, pull out three crumpled ten-pound notes and a twenty and hand them over. I don't stop to consider that this is almost the only money I have in the world, and that I am not going to be able to afford to eat for the next three weeks. I don't actually care about anything apart from being able to walk out of this shop with *The End of Mr. Y,* without someone realizing or remembering and trying to stop me. My heart is doing something impossible. Will I collapse and die of shock before I've even had a chance to read the first line of the book? Shit, shit, shit.

"Fantastic, thanks. Sorry it was so much," the girl says to me.

"No problem," I manage to say back. "I need a lot of these for my Ph.D., anyway."

I place *The End of Mr. Y* in my rucksack, safe, and then I pick up the box and walk out of the shop, clutching it to me as I make my way home in the dark, the cold stinging my eyes, completely unable to make sense of what has just happened.

Chapter Two

By the time I get to my flat it's almost half past five. Most of the shops on the street are starting to close, but the newsagent opposite glows with people stopping for a paper or a packet of cigarettes on their way home from work. The pizza restaurant underneath my flat is still dark, but I know that the owner, Luigi, will be somewhere in there, doing whatever needs to be done so that the place can open at seven. Next door the lights are out in the fancy-dress shop, but there's a soft light upstairs in the Café Paradis, which doesn't close until six. Behind the shops, a commuter train clatters slowly along the brittle old lines and lights flash on the level crossing at the end of the road.

The concrete passageway that leads to the stairs up to my front door is cold, as usual, and dark. There is no bicycle, which means that Wolfgang, my neighbor, isn't in. I don't know how he gets warm in his place (although I think the huge amount of slivovitz that he drinks probably helps) but in mine it's a struggle. I've no idea when the two flats were constructed, but they are both too large, with high ceilings and long, echoey corridors. Central heating would be wonderful, but the landlord won't put it in. Before I take my coat off, I put the box of books and my rucksack down on the large oak kitchen table, switch on my lamps, and then drag the space heater down the hall from the bedroom and plug it in, watching its two metal bars blush dimly (and, it always seems to me, apologetically). Then I light the gas oven and all the rings on the cooktop. I close the kitchen door and only then take off my outdoor things.

I'm shivering, but not just from the cold. I take *The End of Mr. Y* carefully out of my bag and put it down on the table. It seems wrong, somehow, sitting there next to the box of other books and my coffee cup from this morning, so I move the box of books and put the coffee cup in the sink. Now the book is alone on the table. I pick it up and run my hand over it, feeling the coolness of the cream cloth cover. I turn it over and touch the back, as if it might feel different from the front; then I put it down again, my pulse going like ticker tape. I fill my little espresso maker and put it on one of the blazing gas rings, and then I pour out half a glass of the slivovitz Wolfgang gave me and down it in two gulps.

While the coffee heats up I check the mousetraps. Both Wolfgang and I have mice in our flats. He talks about getting a cat; I have these traps. They don't kill the mice; they just hold them for a while in a small plastic oblong until I find them and release them. I don't think the system works: I put the mice outside and then they come straight back in, but I couldn't kill them. Today there are three mice looking bored and pissed off in their little see-through prisons, and I take them downstairs and release them into the courtyard. I didn't think I'd mind having mice in the flat but they do eat everything, and one time one ran over my face while I was lying in bed.

When I get back upstairs, I take four large potatoes from the box in the vegetable rack and wash them quickly before salting them and putting them in the oven on a low heat. That's about as much cooking as I can cope with now; and I'm not even hungry. My sofa is in the kitchen, since there's no point having it in the empty sitting room, where there is no heat. So, as the room starts to steam up and fill with the smell of baking potatoes, I finally take off my trainers and curl up on it with my coffee, a packet of ginseng cigarettes, and *The End of Mr. Y.* And then I read the opening line of the preface, first in my head, and then aloud, as another train rattles along outside: *The discourse which follows may appear to the reader as mere fancy or as a dream,*

penned on waking, in those fevered moments when one is still mes-
merised by those conjuring tricks that are produced in the mind once
the eyes are closed.

I don't die. But then I didn't really expect to. How could a book
be cursed, anyway? The words themselves—which I don't take in
properly at first—simply seem like miracles. Just the fact that they are
there, that they still exist, printed in black type on rough-cut pages
that are brown with age; this is the thing that amazes me. I can't
imagine how many other hands have touched this page, or how many
pairs of eyes have seen it. It was published in 1893, and then what
happened? Did anyone actually read it? By the time he wrote *The
End of Mr. Y*, Lumas was already an obscure writer. He'd been noto
rious for a while in the 1860s, and people had known his name, but
then everyone lost interest in him and decided he was mad, or a
crank. On one occasion he turned up at the place in Yorkshire where
Charles Darwin was receiving what he called his "water cure": He
said something rude about barnacles, and then punched Darwin in
the face. This was in 1859. After that, he seemed to retreat into ever
more esoteric activities, visiting mediums, exploring paranormal
events, and becoming a patron of the Royal London Homoeopathic
Hospital. After about 1880, he seemed to stop publishing. Then he
wrote *The End of Mr. Y* and died the day after it was published, after
everyone else who'd had something major to do with the book (the
publisher, the editor, the typesetter) had also died. Thus the rumored
"curse."

But there may have been other reasons for the idea of the curse.
Lumas was an outlaw. He favored the evolutionary biologist Lamarck
(who said that organisms pass on learned characteristics to their off-
spring) over Darwin (who said they don't), when even people like
Samuel Butler—once described by someone as "the greatest shit-
stirrer of the nineteenth century"—were coming around to the idea
that we are all, actually, Darwinian mutants. He wrote letters to the
Times criticizing not only his contemporaries, but every major figure
in the history of thought, including Aristotle and Bacon. Lumas became very interested in the existence of a fourth spatial dimension and

wrote various supernatural stories about it, somehow managing to upset people who did not believe in the existence of another dimension. His response was: "But they are merely stories!" although everyone knew that he used his fiction mainly as a way of working out his philosophical ideas. Most of his ideas were about the development and nature of thought, particularly scientific thought, and he often described his fictional works as "experiments of the mind."

One of his most interesting stories, "The Blue Room," tells of two philosophers who attend a party in a mansion. Somehow they get lost on their way to play billiards with the host, and end up in a blue room in the (supposedly) haunted wing of the house. This room has two doors, on its north and south walls, and a spiral staircase in the middle. One of the philosophers says they should go up the stairs, but the other thinks they should leave via one of the doors. They can't reach an agreement, and instead end up speculating about the existence of ghosts. The first one argues that, as there are no such things as ghosts, they have nothing to fear. The second agrees that there is nothing to fear: He has never seen a ghost, and therefore has concluded that they don't exist. Satisfied that there are no ghosts, and enthused by their agreement, the philosophers leave the room via the door they came in and try to make their way back to the party. However, the blue wing of the house seems to be arranged in a peculiar way. Once they leave the room they find a corridor leading to a spiral staircase. When they go down it, they end up back in the blue room. When they try the other door, the same thing happens. But when they go up the staircase, they simply find one of the doors. Whichever way they go, they end up back in the blue room.

There have been a few academic papers written about Lumas as a historical figure, and maybe ten about his novel, *The Apple in the Garden*. There have been no biographies. Back in the 1990s, a couple of Californian queer theorists claimed him, or at least his *Journals*, in which one can find, among other things, half-finished homoerotic sonnets about some of Shakespeare's male characters. But I don't know what happened to the queer theorists. Perhaps they lost interest in Lumas. Most people do. As far as I know, hardly anything has ever been written about *The End of Mr. Y.* What has been written has all been by Saul Burlem.

"The Curse of Mr. Y" was the subject of Burlem's paper at the conference in Greenwich eighteen months ago, delivered to an audience of four people, including me. Burlem hadn't then read *The End of Mr. Y,* but instead talked about the probable invention of the "curse" story. He had a rough, sandpaper voice, and a slight stoop that somehow wasn't unattractive. He talked about the idea of the curse as if it were a virus, and discussed Lumas's body of work as if it were an organism attacked by this virus, destined, perhaps, to become extinct. He talked about information becoming contaminated by unpopularity, and eventually concluded that Lumas's book had indeed been cursed, not in a supernatural sense, but by the opinions of people who wanted him discredited.

There was a reception afterwards, in the Painted Hall. It was packed in there: A popular scientist had been giving a talk at the same time as Burlem, and he was holding court in the large Lower Hall, underneath an image of Copernicus. I had considered going to his talk instead, but I was glad I'd chosen Burlem's. The other people from Burlem's talk—two guys who looked a bit like a pair of tax inspectors except for their almost white-blond hair, and a fiftyish woman with pink-streaked gray hair—hadn't hung around, so Burlem and I started on the red wine, drinking too fast, hiding away in the far corner of the Upper Hall. Burlem was wearing a long gray wool trench coat over his black shirt and trousers. I can't remember what I was wearing.

"So would you read it, then?" I asked him, referring, of course, to *The End of Mr. Y.*

"Of course," he said, with his odd smile. "Would you?"

"Absolutely. Especially after this."

"Good," he said.

Burlem didn't seem to know anyone in the Lower Hall, and neither did I. Neither of us attempted to leave our corner and mingle: I'm not very good at it and often offend people by accident; I don't know what Burlem's reason was—maybe he just hadn't been offended by me yet. The whole time I was in the Painted Hall I felt a bit like part of a huge box of chocolates, with the browns, creams, golds, and reds of the vast paintings seeming to melt around me. Perhaps Burlem and I were the hard centres that no one was interested in. No one else came to the Upper Hall the whole time we were there.

"I can't believe more people didn't come to your talk," I said.

"No one knows Lumas exists," he said. "I'm used to it."

"I suppose you were up against Mr. Famous, as well," I said.

Burlem smiled. "Jim Lahiri. He's probably never heard of Lumas, either."

"No," I agreed. I'd read Lahiri's best-selling popular science book about the end of time, and knew he wouldn't approve of Lumas even if he had heard of him. Popular science can say some pretty wild things these days, but the supernatural is still out, as is Lamarck. You can have as many dimensions as you want, as long as none of them contains ghosts, telepathy, anything that fucks with Charles Darwin, or anything that Hitler liked (apart from Charles Darwin).

Burlem picked up the bottle of wine, refilled both our glasses, and then frowned at me. "So why are you here? Are you a student? If you're working on Lumas I should probably know who you are."

"I'm not working on Lumas," I said. "I write these little articles for a magazine called *Smoke*. You may not have heard of it. I'll probably write one on Lumas after this, but I don't think that counts as 'working on' in your sense." I paused, but Burlem didn't say anything. "He's a great person to write about, though, even on a small scale. His stuff's pretty compulsive. I mean, even without the controversies and the curse it's still amazing."

"It is," said Burlem. "That's why I'm working on a biography." After he said the word "biography," he looked first at the ground, and then up at the painted ceiling high above our heads. I must have been frowning or something, because when he looked back at me he smiled in a crooked, apologetic way. "I hate biography," he said.

I laughed. "So why are you writing one?"

He shrugged. "Lumas got me hooked. The only way to write about his texts seems to be to write a biography of his life. It might sell. There's a vogue for digging up these nineteenth-century eccentrics at the moment and I might as well cash in on it. The department could do with some funding. *I* could do with some bloody funding."

"The department?"

"Of English and American Studies." He told me the name of the university.

"Have you started on it?" I asked him.

He nodded. "Yeah. Unfortunately there's only one biographical detail about Lumas that really does it for me."

"The punch?" I suggested, thinking of Darwin, imagining, for some reason, a huge splashing sound as he fell over after Lumas hit him.

"No." He looked up at the ceiling again. "Have you read Samuel Butler at all?"

"Oh yes," I nodded. "Yes—that's actually how I came to read Lumas. There was a reference in Butler's *Note-books*."

"You were reading Butler's *Note-books*?"

"Yeah. I like all the stuff about the sugared Hamlets."

Actually, what I like about Butler is the same thing I like about Lumas: the outlaw status and the brilliant ideas. Butler's big thing was consciousness; he thought it was very likely that machines would become conscious and, probably, take over the world. He said that since we evolved from organic, unconscious vegetable matter, our consciousness must at some point have emerged from nothing. If we had become conscious out of nowhere, then why couldn't machines? I'd written about that in the magazine only a couple of weeks before.

"Sugared Hamlets?" said Burlem.

"Yeah. These sweets they were selling in London. Little sweets in the shape of Hamlet holding a skull, dipped in sugar. How great is that?"

Burlem laughed. "I bet Butler thought that was hilarious."

"Yeah. That's why I like him. I like his sense of the absurd."

"So presumably you know the rumors about him and Lumas?"

"No. What rumors?"

"That they were lovers; or at least that Lumas was infatuated with Butler."

"I had no idea," I said. Then I smiled. "Does it matter?"

"Probably not. But it leads to the biographical detail I'm most interested in."

"Which is?"

"Have you read *The Authoress of the Odyssey*?"

"No." I shook my head. "*The Authoress* . . . ?"

"You must read it. It's Butler arguing that the *Odyssey* was written by a woman. It's fucking brilliant." Burlem ran his hand through his hair and went on: "Butler published his own translation of the *Odyssey* alongside it, with some black-and-white plates showing photographs he took of old coins, and landscapes relevant to the *Odyssey*. One of the landscapes, supposedly the basis for the tidal inlet up which Ulysses swam, has a man and a dog in the distance. In the introduction to the book, Butler goes out of his way to apologize for this, and to say that they only appeared when he developed the negative; that they weren't supposed to be there."

"Wow," I said, not sure where this was leading. "So . . ."

"The man in the picture is Lumas. I'm sure of it."

"How do you know?"

"I *don't* know. I don't even know if they travelled together. But the way the man appears in the developed photograph, previously unseen . . . You can't see the figure well enough to tell who it is but . . . What if it was Lumas? What if it was even his ghost, but before he was dead? I may be a little drunk. Sorry. He had a dog, though, called Erasmus."

At this point Burlem did a jerky thing with his head, as if he was trying to get water out of one of his ears. He frowned, as if considering a difficult question, and then made another face, suggesting that maybe the question didn't matter, anyway. Then he raised an eyebrow, smiled, walked over to the table, and got another bottle of wine. While he did that, I looked at the vast image beyond him, painted on the back wall. The scene showed what seemed to be a king descending from heaven, alighting on some reddish, carpeted stairs. The stairs almost appeared to be part of the room rather than the painting, and the figures in the image looked like they might be using them to step into reality; into the present.

"Lumas can drive you a bit crazy," he said, when he returned.

"I like the idea of the photograph, though," I said. "It reminds me of that story of his, *The Daguerreotype*."

"You've read that?"

I nodded. "Yeah. I think it's my favorite."

"How on earth did you get hold of it?"

"I got that one on eBay. It was in a collection. I've got almost all of Lumas's books apart from *The End of Mr. Y.* I found a lot of them on secondhand book sites."

"And this is all for a magazine article?"

"Yeah. I do it pretty intensively. For a month I'll live and breathe, say, Samuel Butler. Then I'll find some link from him to take me to the next piece. The column is called Free Association. I started with the big bang about three years ago."

Burlem laughs. "And what did that lead to?"

"The properties of hydrogen, the speed of light, relativity, quantum mechanics, probability theory, Schrödinger's cat, the wavefunction, light, the luminiferous ether—which is my personal favorite—experiment, paradox . . ."

"So you're a scientist? You understand all that stuff?"

I laughed. "God no. Not at all. I wish I did. I probably shouldn't have started with the big bang, but when you do, that's what you get. At some point I went from artificial intelligence to Butler, and now here I am with Lumas. While I'm working on him I'll probably decide on what link I'm going to follow through next so I can order all the books. I might do something about the history of photography, actually, following through from *The Daguerreotype*. Or I might follow it through to the fourth dimension, and that Zollner book, although that takes me back to science again."

In *The Daguerreotype*, a man wakes up to find a copy of his house in a park across the road, with a large group of people gathered around it. Where has the house come from? People immediately accuse the man of losing his mind and arranging to have a copy of his house built in the park overnight. He points out that this is impossible. Who could have a whole house built overnight? Also, the house in the park does not seem new. It is in fact an exact copy of the "real" house, down to some scuffing on the door panels, and some tarnish on the brass knocker. The only thing that's different is that his key doesn't work, and the keyhole seems to be blocked by something. The man initially tries to ignore the house, but soon it takes over his life and he has to try to work out where it has come from. Because of the house in the park he loses his job as a teacher, and his fiancée runs off with someone else. The police also become involved and accuse the man of all sorts of crimes. The house has some strange properties as well, the main one being that no one can get into it. It is possible to look through the windows at the things inside: a table, a vase of flowers, a bureau, a piano; but no one can smash the windows or break down the door. The house behaves like a solid shape, as if it had no space inside.

One day, when the man in the story has almost lost his wits, a mysterious old man comes to his (real) house with a box full of equipment. He tells the man that he has heard of his predicament and thinks he knows what has happened. He takes out a velvet-lined folding case and explains to the man about the daguerreotype, and how it works. The man is initially impatient. Everyone knows how daguerreotypes work! But then his visitor makes an impossible claim. If humans, three-dimensional beings, can create two-dimensional versions of the things around us, would it be too impossible to assume that four-dimensional beings could make something like a daguerreotype machine of their own, but one that produces not flat, two-dimensional copies of things, but three-dimensional ones?

The man is angry and throws the photographer out of the house, thinking that there must be another explanation. However, he is unable to find one and later comes to the conclusion that his visitor must have been right. He finds the man's card and resolves to call on him immediately. But when the maid lets him into the man's house, he finds something very strange. The photographer seems to be standing in the drawing room, holding the daguerreotype machine. But it's not the real man; it's a lifeless copy.

"You know what I love about *The Daguerreotype*?" Burlem said.

"What?"

"The unresolved ending. I like it that the man never does find his answer."

Up until that moment there had been no music in the Painted Hall, just the crackle of voices and laughter echoing around the large rooms. But someone must have remembered that they were supposed to have music on, and the first heavy notes of Handel's *Dixit Dominus* seeped into the hall, followed by the first line, with all the choral voices tumbling over themselves: *Dixit Dominus Domino meo, sede a dextris meis.*

"So," Burlem said, raising his voice over the music, "you work full time at this magazine, then?"

"No. I just write my column every month."

"Is that all you do?"

"For the moment, yes."

"Can you live on that?"

"Just about. The magazine's doing pretty well. I can afford my rent, and a few bags of lentils every month. And some books, too, of course."

The magazine started as a small thing, edited by this woman I met at university. Now there's a distribution deal and it's given away in every big record shop in the country. It has proper advertising now, and a designer who doesn't use glue to put the layouts together.

"What did you do at university? Not science, I take it."

"No. English lit and philosophy. But I am seriously thinking of going back to do science. I think I'm probably going to apply to do theoretical physics." I explained that I wanted to be able to actually understand things like relativity, and Schrödinger's cat, and that I wanted to try to revive the dear old ether. I think I was feeling a bit drunk, so I wittered on about the luminiferous ether for some time. Burlem was familiar with it—it turned out that he ran the nineteenth-century Literature and Science MA at the university—but I still went on at length about how fascinating it was that for ages people couldn't work out how light could travel in a vacuum, considering that sound couldn't (you can see a bell in a vacuum, but you can't hear it go *ding*). In the nineteenth century people believed that light travelled through something invisible—the luminiferous ether. In 1887 Albert Michelson and Edward Morley set out to prove that the ether existed, but in the end they had to conclude that it didn't. While talking to Burlem I couldn't, of course, remember the date of this experiment, or the names of the scientists, but I did remember the way Michelson referred to the lost object of his experiment as the "beloved old ether, which is now abandoned, though I personally still cling a little to it." I got a bit excited about how much poetry there was in theoretical physics, and then I went on for a bit about how much I like institutions: especially ones with big libraries.

And then Burlem interrupted and said: "Don't do that. Fuck theoretical physics. Come and do a Ph.D. with me. I'm assuming you don't already have one?"

It was the way he said it. *Fuck theoretical physics.*

"What would I do it on?" I said.

"What are you interested in?"

I laughed. "Everything?" I shrugged. "I think that's my problem. I want to know everything." I must have been drunk to admit that. At least I didn't go further and say that I want to know everything because of the high probability that if you know everything, there'll be something to actually believe in.

"Come on," Burlem said. "What's your thing?"

"My *thing?*"

He took a gulp of wine. "Yeah."

"I don't think I know what my thing is, yet. That's the whole point of the magazine column. It's about free association. I'm good at that."

"So you start at the big bang and work your way through science until you end up at Lumas. There must be a connection between all the things you've written about."

I sipped some more wine. "Lumas's ideas about the fourth dimension are particularly interesting. I mean, he didn't exactly preempt string theory, but . . ."

"What's string theory?"

I shrugged. "Don't ask me. That's why I want to do theoretical physics. At least, I think I do."

Burlem laughed. "For fuck's sake. Come on. Find the connection."

I thought for a moment. "I suppose almost everything I've written about has had some connection with thought experiments, or 'experiments of the mind,' as Lumas called them."

"Good. And?"

"Um. I don't know. But I quite like the way you can talk about science without necessarily using mathematics but using metaphors instead. That's how I've been approaching all my columns. For each of these ideas and theories, you find there's a little story that goes with it."

"Interesting. Give me an example."

"Well, there's Schrödinger's cat, of course. Everyone can understand that a cat in a box can't be alive and dead at the same time—but hardly anyone can understand the same principle expressed mathematically. Then there are Einstein's trains. All of his thoughts about special relativity seem to have been expressed in terms of trains. I love that. And whenever people want to understand the fourth dimension nowadays, they still go back to *Flatland*, which was written in 1880-whatever. I suppose you can look at Butler that way, too. *Erewhon* is basically a thought experiment intended to work out ideas about society and machines."

"So write a proposal. Do a Ph.D. on these experiments of the mind: I'd be very interested in supervising that. Work in some more novels and poetry. I'd recommend looking at Thomas Hardy and Tennyson, as well. Make sure you don't get too carried away. Set a time frame, or some other sort of limit. Don't do a history of thought experiments from the beginning of time. Do, say, 1859 to 1939 or something. Start with Darwin and end with, I don't know, the atom bomb."

"Or Schrödinger's cat. I think that was in the thirties. The bomb is too real; I mean, it's where the thought experiment becomes reality, really."

"Maybe." Burlem ran his hand over the stubble on his face. "So, anyway, what do you think? I reckon we could sign you up pretty easily. You have an MA?"

"Yeah."

"Superb. So let's do it. I can get you some teaching as well, if you want."

"Seriously?"

"Seriously." Burlem gave me his card. At the top it had his name in bold, and then: PROFESSOR OF ENGLISH LITERATURE

So I wrote the proposal and fell in love with my idea. But then . . . I don't know. When I went to start working with Burlem, he seemed to have gone cold on the idea of Lumas. My proposal had been accepted, of course—I was planning to look at the language and form of thought experiments, from *Zoonomia* to Schrödinger's cat—and everything was fine with Burlem until I mentioned Lumas. When I did, he stopped making eye contact with me. He looked out of the window, now my window, and said nothing. I made some joke relating to our conversation at the conference; something like "So, has the curse claimed any more victims, then?" and he looked at me and said, "Forget that paper, OK? Leave Lumas until later." He recommended that I start by focusing on the actual thought experiments: Schrödinger's cat, Einstein's *Relativity*, and Edwin A. Abbot's book *Flatland*. He also persuaded me to leave out *Zoonomia*, Charles Darwin's grandfather's book about evolution, and begin later, in 1859, when *The Origin of Species* was published. He also reminded me to look at some more poetry. I had no idea what was wrong with him, but I went along with it all. And then, a week later, he was gone.

So now here I am, unsupervised, like an experiment with no observer—Fleming's plate of mold, perhaps, or an uncollapsed wavefunction—and what am I doing? I'm reading Lumas. I'm reading *The End of Mr. Y*, for God's sake. Fuck you, Burlem.

Chapter Three

THE END OF MR. Y
BY THOMAS E. LUMAS

⤙PREFACE⤚

T HE DISCOURSE WHICH FOLLOWS may appear to the reader as
mere fancy or as a dream, penned on waking, in those
fevered moments when one is still mesmerised by those conjuring tricks that are produced in the mind once the eyes are
closed. Those readers should not abandon their scepticism, for
it is their will to seek to peer behind the conjurer's curtain, as it
is the will of man to ask those peculiar *whats* and *wheres* and
hows of life. Of life, as of dreams. Of image, as of word. As
thought, as of speech.

When one looks at the illusions of the world, one sees only
the world. For where does illusion end? Indeed, what is there in
life that is not a conjuring trick? From the petrifactions that
men find on the seashore to the Geissler tube recently seen at
the Royal Society, all about us seems filled with fancies and
wonders. As Robert-Houdin has built automata with which to
produce his illusions, I shall here propose to create an automaton of mind, through which one may see illusions and realities

beyond ; from which one, if he knows how, may spring into the automata of all minds and their electricity. We may ask what illusion is, and what form may it take, when it is so easy to dive into its depths, like a fish into a pool, and when the ripples that emerge are not ripples of illusion nor ripples of reality but indeed the ripples made by the collision of both worlds ; the world of the conjuror and the world of His audience.

Perhaps I mislead the reader by talking of the Conjuror in this manner. Let the creator become curator! And we creatures who live on in the dreams of a world made of our own thought ; as we name the beasts and barnacles who creep on and cling to this most precious and mysterious earth ; as we collect them in our museums, we believe ourselves curators. What folly takes light through ether to each eye from every horizon. And beyond this is not truth but what we have made truth ; yet this is a truth we cannot see.

Can this place—this place where dreams and automata are one, where the very fibres of being are conjured from memories no more real or unreal than the dream in which we may observe them, and fish with noses and jaws and skin made only of thought play on the surface of the pooled fancies of our maker— can this place be real, created as it is in Aristotle's *metaphora*? Indeed, for it is only in the *logos* of *metaphora* that we are to find the *protasis* of the past, that glorious illusion which we call memory, that curtain of destiny, drawn tightly over the conscious mind but present in every fibre of being, from sea-creature to man, from pebble to ocean, as Lamarck and E. Darwin have maintained. Can this place be real? Perhaps not. For this reason, it is only as fiction that I wish this work to be considered.

T. E. *Lumas*, July 1892

⇢⇾◉ PROLOGUE ◉⇽⇠

I see ahead a time-wrought shore;
A fishing boat lifts on a wave;

No footprints on the sandy floor,
　　Beyond—an unfamiliar cave.

Or—forest tree'd with oak and yew
A dark mare waits to carry me,
Where nothing stirs yet all is true,
　　A cabin door and here—the key!

Perhaps I'll wander in a field,
With poppy-flush on carpet green:
However thought has been concealed
　　No sleeper's eye can now undream.

In any place that I take flight
The dark will mutate into light.

I finish reading the preface at about nine o'clock. *It is only as fiction that I wish this work to be considered.* That's how the preface ends. What does that mean? Surely anyone would read a novel as fiction, anyway?

The main narrative begins with a businessman, Mr. Y, visiting a fairground in the rain. But I don't read properly now. Instead I skim the first couple of chapters, reading the odd sentence here and there. I like the first line: *By the end I would be nobody, but in the beginning I was known as Mr. Y.* I keep flicking through the book until I reach the end (which, of course, I don't read), mainly just because I like the feel of the pages, and then I turn back to the first chapter. It's while I'm flicking backwards that I see it. There's a page missing from the book. Between the verso page 130 and the recto page 133 there is simply a jagged, paper edge. Pages 131 and 132, two sides of one folio page, are missing.

I don't quite believe it at first. Who would want to rip a page out of *The End of Mr. Y* like this? Is it simply vandalism? I carefully check the rest of the book. There are no other missing pages, nor any other obvious sign that somebody wanted to damage it. So why rip out a page? Did someone not like that page? Or did they steal it? But if you were going to steal a page from a book, why not steal the whole book? It's too confusing. I shiver, wishing it would heat up in here.

Downstairs, I hear the squeal of the main door that suggests that Wolfgang is back. Then, a few seconds later there's a soft tap at my door.

"It's open," I call, putting *The End of Mr. Y* away.

Wolfgang is small and blond and was born in East Berlin. I don't think he ever washes his hair. Today, he's wearing what he always wears when he plays at the hotel: a pair of pale blue jeans, a white shirt, and a dark blue suit jacket. When I first met Wolfgang, on the day I moved into this flat, he told me he was so depressed he couldn't even get the enthusiasm together to kill himself. I became worried and started doing small, life-enhancing things for him, such as making him soup and offering to bring him books from the university library. For ages he said yes to the soup and no to the books, but recently he's been asking me for poetry: Ginsberg and Bukowski mainly.

As Wolfgang walks into the flat, I keep thinking of Lumas's words: *Of life, as of dreams.* Shall I tell Wolfgang about the book? Perhaps later.

He grins at me sadly. "Oh, well. I'm rich in one universe. Are you cooking baked potatoes for me?"

The "rich in one universe" thing is something I told him. It's what the Russian physicist George Gamow said after he lost all his money in an American casino. It means that, as usual, Wolfgang has gambled his tips away in the hotel casino. In a parallel universe, perhaps, some other version of him has won thousands of pounds.

"Mmm," I say back. "Potatoes with . . ." I look around the kitchen. "Olive oil, salt. Um . . . I think I've got an onion somewhere."

"Great," he says, sitting at the kitchen table and pouring some slivovitz. "Gourmet." This is a joke between us. *Very gourmet* is worse, and implies a meal costing almost nothing. (I can do something very gourmet with lentils; Wolfgang's very gourmet meals usually include fried cabbage.)

I open the oven and take out the potatoes. "I suppose you could say I'm rich in one universe, too," I say, through the steam and heat. I put the baking tray on the counter and smile at Wolfgang.

He raises a blond eyebrow at me. "You've gambled also?"

"No." I laugh. "I bought a book. I've got about five quid left until the magazine pays me at the end of the month. It was . . . it was quite an expensive book."

"Is it a good book?"

"Yes. Oh yes . . ." But I still don't want to tell him about it just yet. I start slicing the onion. "Oh—the university fell down today as well."

"It fell down?" He laughs. "You blew it up? No. How?"

"OK, well, it didn't exactly all fall down, but one building did."

"A bomb?"

"No. A railway tunnel. Under the campus. It all kind of collapsed inside, and then . . ."

Wolfgang downs his drink and pours another. "Yes, I see. You build something on nothing and then it falls down. Ha." He laughs. "How many dead?"

"None. They evacuated the building in the morning."

"Oh. So is the university shut down?"

"I don't know. I suppose it must be, at least for the weekend."

I mash olive oil into the potatoes and put them on the table with some olives, capers, and mustard. We sit down to eat.

"So how's life, anyway?" I ask him.

"Life's shit. No money. Too many mice. But I've got my afternoon shifts back."

"Fantastic," I say. "What happened to Whatshername?"

A few months ago some talented kid came along and took some of Wolfgang's shifts. From her point of view the narrative must have been exciting: *Teenage girl gets life-changing opportunity playing piano in public.* But it meant that Wolfgang couldn't pay his rent and his bills, so he stopped paying his bills.

"Pony accident."

I smile while he fills in the details. I'm not really listening; I'm thinking about the book.

"Oh . . . Wolf?" I say, once we've finished eating.

"What?"

"Do you believe in curses?"

He looks at me with his head slightly tilted to one side. "Curses? Of what sort?"

"Like a cursed object. Can something be cursed?"

"Now that's interesting," he says. "You could argue that everything is cursed."

I had a feeling he'd approach the question from this angle. "Yes, but . . ."

He pours more slivovitz. I get up to sort out some coffee.

"Or you might ask why curses even exist. What is their purpose? I've been wondering this myself for a long time, ever since I first saw Wagner with Catherine."

Wolf has a girlfriend who is aiming to "improve" him by taking him to the opera.

"I suppose maybe we have to start by defining 'curse,'" I say. "Is it a word or a thing?"

Wolfgang groans. He's had enough conversations with me before that have started in this way. We usually get into an argument about Derrida and différance.

"Stop. Please. Don't start hurting me with your French deconstruction. Just pretend for a minute that there is something called a curse and it exists and it is a thing. Where does it come from? That's what we need to ask."

"Do we?"

"Yes. Is it something magical, or is it a prophecy that comes true because you make it come true? Or is it even just nothing at all, just a way of explaining bad things that happen to us that are actually random. I may ask: Why do I have an infestation of mice? Did someone curse me? Or did I just leave too much food out one day to tempt them? Or is life just as simple as *there are mice*?"

I light a cigarette. "I found three today."

"Three what? Curses?"

I laugh. "No. That would be very unlucky. No. Three mice."

"And you put them where? Not in the corridor again?"

"No. Outside. In Luigi's backyard."

Wolf starts talking again about getting a cat. After a few minutes the coffeepot hisses and I pour the coffee.

"Anyway," he says, exhaling slowly as I put the cup in front of him. "This is what I am wondering about curses: Can they exist if we don't believe in them?"

I laugh. "How is that different from what I was saying?"

"It's simpler."

"Not if you think it through."

As Wolf starts talking about voodoo curses, and how they only work on people who believe in voodoo, I imagine something like a Möbius strip, the shape you get if you glue together a long strip of paper with one twist in it. You could be walking along one side of this strip quite happily forever, without ever realizing that, in a strange kind of way, you kept changing "sides." Just as this world once seemed flat, so your world would seem flat. You could walk forever and not realize that you kept going back to the beginning and starting again. Even with the twist, you wouldn't know. Your reality would change, but as far as you were concerned, you'd just be walking on a flat path. If this Möbius strip was a spatial dimension, your whole body would flip when you travelled past the twist and your heart would be on the right side of your body for a while until you looped back. I learned this from one of the physics lectures I downloaded onto my iPod. At Christmas I made myself some paper chains that were all Möbius strips. I prepared to stay in on my own all day reading and drinking wine; then Wolf came round with a huge, misshaped plum pudding and we spent the rest of the day together.

"What if it isn't people who make curses?" I say.

"Ha," says Wolf. "You think curses are made by gods."

"No, of course not. It's just a hypothetical question. Can something be created in language independently of the people who use the language? Can language become a self-replicating system or . . ." I'm drunk, I suddenly realize, so I shut up. But I do wonder for a moment about this idea, that something could emerge within language—an accident, or mistake, perhaps—and the users of that language would then have to deal with the consequences of this new word being part of their system of signification. I vaguely remember some radio documentary about the Holy Grail suggesting that the whole thing was just a mistake: a wrongly used word in an old French text.

We sit in silence for a while, and a train goes past outside. Then I start to clear the plates away while Wolfgang finishes his coffee.

"So anyway," I say to him, "you haven't said whether or not you do."

"Whether I do what?"

"Whether you actually *believe* in curses, or cursed objects."

"It's not whether something is cursed that's important," he says. "You have to find out why it is cursed, and what the curse is. Let me wash up."

"OK."

Wolf gets up, walks over to the sink, and squirts about half the carton of washing-up liquid over the plates. Then he runs the hot tap, swears a bit because the water never gets as hot as he likes, and eventually boils the kettle and tips its contents all over the dishes. I'm thinking about whether or not to show him *The End of Mr. Y.* In the end I decide that I won't. Before he leaves he gives me a look, as if his eyes are made of electricity, and he says: "You do have something, don't you? Something you think is cursed."

"I don't know," I say back. "Probably not. I'm probably just feeling a bit weird after today, with the university collapsing, and after all this cold and too much of your bloody slivovitz, and . . ."

"Show me anytime you like," he says. "My life can't get any worse. Don't worry about protecting me."

"Thanks," I say. But . . . *Shit.* What's happened to me? The last thing I'd thought of was protecting Wolf. I just wanted to keep the book to myself and, if I'm honest, stop him stealing it. As I go to sleep, with a dry mouth, and *The End of Mr. Y* under my other, empty pillow, I wonder if curses exist after all.

Chapter Four

Sometimes I wake up with such an immense sense of disappointment that I can hardly breathe. Usually nothing has obviously triggered it and I put it down to some combination of an unhappy childhood and bad dreams (those two things go very well together). And most times I can shake it off pretty quickly. After all, there's not much for me to be disappointed about. So I never got any of the publishing jobs I went for after university? Who cares. That was ten years ago and I'm happy with my magazine column, anyway. And I don't really care that my mother ran away with a bunch of freaks and my father lives in a hostel up north and my sister doesn't even send me Christmas cards anymore. I don't care that my ex-housemates all got married and left me on my own. I like being on my own; that wasn't the problem—I just couldn't afford to do it in the big house in Hackney that seemed to sprout empty rooms like baby universes. Coming here has meant that I have been able to just get on with being on my own and reading my books, so it's hardly as if I have anything to be sad or disappointed about.

Sometimes I like to think that I live with ghosts. Not from my own past—I don't believe in those sorts of ghosts—but wispy bits of ideas and books that hang in the air like silk puppets. Sometimes I think I see my own ideas floating around, too, but they usually don't last long. They're more like mayflies: They're born, big and gleaming, and then they fly around, buzzing like crazy before they simply fall to the floor, dead, about twenty-four hours later. I'm not sure I've ever thought anything original anyway, so I don't mind. Usually I find that Derrida has already thought of whatever it is, which seems like a very grand thing to say—but actually Derrida's not that hard; it's just his writing that's dense. And now he's a ghost, too. Or perhaps he always was—I never met him, so how can I be sure he was real? Some of the most friendly ghosts I live with are those of my favorite nineteenth-century science writers. Most of them were wrong, of course, but who cares? It's not like this is the end of history. We're all wrong.

Sometimes I try my own thought experiment, which goes as follows: What if everyone is actually right? Aristotle and Plato; David and Goliath; Hobbes and Locke; Hitler and Gandhi; Tom and Jerry. Could that ever make sense? And then I think about my mother and I think that no, not everyone is right. To paraphrase the physicist Wolfgang Pauli, she wasn't even wrong. Maybe that's where human society is now, at the beginning of the twenty-first century: *not even wrong.* The nineteenth-century crowd were wrong, on the whole, but we're somehow doing worse than that. We're now living with the uncertainty principle and the incompleteness theorem and philosophers who say that the world has become a simulacrum—a copy without an original. We live in a world where nothing may be real; a world of infinite closed systems, and particles that could be doing anything you like (but probably aren't).

Maybe we're all like my mother. I don't like to think about her, or my childhood, too much, but it can be summed up fairly quickly. We lived on a council estate where reading books was seen as the most disgusting combination of laziness and hubris and only my mother and I—as far as I know—had library cards. While the other kids had sex with each other (from about eight years old) and the other adults drank, gambled, bred violent dogs and mangy cats, and thought up ways to get rich and famous, my mother occasionally took me to the library and left me in the kids' area while she researched the meaning of life via books on astrology, faith healing, and telepathy. If it hadn't been for her I probably wouldn't have even known that libraries existed. That's the only good thing she ever did for me. At night she used to sit downstairs in her pink dressing gown waiting for aliens, while my dad would take me to the park and photograph me picking up aluminium benches and writing graffiti on the walls of the subway—so he could send the pictures to the local paper as proof that the council was losing the war against hooligans. My father, who was at his best when approximately 50 percent sober, and used to buy me toy cars and football stickers, believed everything was a government conspiracy. My mother believed that the conspiracy went higher than that. They taught me that everything you are told by anyone is a lie. But then it turned out that they lied, too.

It's not that I didn't enjoy hanging around with the other kids, playing chicken in the main road, stealing rich children's bikes, setting fire to things, and letting the older boys grope me for ten pence a go. In fact, I got pretty rich on the money and was eventually able to buy a bike that didn't have to be given back or dumped in the river. After that I gave up sex and rode to the library every day. That was when I got into the habit of binge-reading. It's easy to do when you spend hours of every day surrounded by more books than you can ever read. You start one, but you're distracted by the idea that you could, equally, have started a different one. By the end of the day you've skimmed two and started four and read the ends of about seven. You can read your way through a library like that without ever properly finishing any of the books. I did finish novels, though. But I wasn't one of those kids who read Tolstoy. I read the kinds of adult books that they didn't let you actually borrow.

The grammar school started off feeling sorry for me, with my secondhand uniform and my weird hair. But (thanks, Mum; thanks, Dad) I wasn't allowed to attend assembly and never believed anything I was taught, which made me stand out as one of the "difficult" children. I also had to do my own laundry after I was about thirteen, and usually I didn't bother. The other kids didn't care that my shirt collars were grubby, or that my too-short skirt hadn't been ironed in weeks. But the teachers would occasionally take me to one side and say things like "Maybe you could mention to your mother that school uniform should be . . ." My mother? You could communicate with her, in theory, but only if you had a CB radio and could do a convincing impression of something from outer space.

So I did what you'd expect and ran away to university as soon as I could. But I couldn't even do that properly. I expect that someone in my position should have sat on a coach quietly reading *Jane Eyre* and occasionally sobbing into a handkerchief as she considered the nasty stains on her life. I drove down the M4 to Oxford in a car with no tax disc, stopping on the way to have a torrid weekend affair with a biker, get a tattoo, and have my broken tooth replaced with a silver one.

I sit up in bed slowly, feeling the disappointment trickle away like puddles after a rain shower. I have an old coffee-making alarm clock that I got from a jumble sale, so I'm able to lie in bed sipping thick black coffee while this happens and the fog of sleep and slivovitz hangover slowly thins out. I think it's fair to say I hate mornings. I hate the honesty of the morning; the time before your consciousness switches on the light and gets rid of all the nasty shadows. Yuck. But my coffee's OK.

The End of Mr. Y. I take it out from under my pillow and slowly start reading from the beginning of the main narrative. I read the first line several times: *By the end I would be nobody, but in the beginning I was known as Mr. Y.* Then I read on. The story begins with the protagonist, a respectable draper, on his way to Nottingham on the train. He has some business there the following morning. Once there, he can't help but notice that the annual Goose Fair has taken over the town, and, the following day, after his business is concluded, he happens to wander past it.

There was a persistent drizzle hanging over the town, as if it were being gently smothered by a damp veil. Having no previous experience of anything like the Goose Fair, I nevertheless willed myself to avoid what I felt certain would be the most diabolical sort of entertainment, and instead resolved to find a respectable establishment in which to take tea. However, I soon found myself drawn into the fair, as if by mesmerism. It comprised side-shows and stalls with several mechanical attractions, and, fringed by the ramshackle vehicles of its considerable staff of animal trainers, performers and penny-showmen, extended to the edges of the Market Square. Once within its perimeter, it felt somewhat as though I had entered another world, one perceptibly warmer, and, once under cover of the various tents and stalls, certainly drier than the one I had just left. Curiosity's crooked finger beckoned me further. A hand-bill, tacked to a post and flapping in the breeze, informed me of the appearance at the fair of Wombwell's Menagerie, and assured me that this was the Queen's favourite exhibition. Other gaudy posters alerted me to such spectacles as the Strange Girl, the Indian Snake Charmer, The Wonderful Talking Horse, a Beautiful Serpentine Dancer on a Rolling Globe with Lime-light Effects and Professor England's Performing Fleas, including an 'entirely new and original novelty' : The Funeral of the Flea.

The breeze reduced as I proceeded further into the fair, although the air seemed to darken and thicken despite the freshly illuminated naphtha lamps which hung from the openings to the tents, and which decorated the frontispieces of the various stalls. A glance upward confirmed the appearance of the darkest rain-cloud I had ever seen. Eager to escape a thorough drenching, I looked for a covered diversion. I soon came upon a waxwork exhibition, outside which stood figures of the most unhealthy complexion I have ever seen. This seemed singularly unappealing, as did the promise of the 'living skeleton' just beyond, so I continued onwards towards a tent in which there were taking place, a young woman promised me as I walked past, marionette shows of the very highest quality. She was playing an organ ; an old, battered thing from which emanated the most harrowing bombilations. I was informed that the next show was about to start and, mostly out of pity for the girl, I paid my penny and went in.

The show turned out to be a trivial moral spectacle involving a pair of village idiots who are stuck on a country road with a donkey that will not move. At some point the devil appears and offers to help the idiots. Needless to say, the story did not end well. The tent in which this took place was made from canvas, and included a small proscenium of a somewhat mouldy appearance, made of what seemed to be packing boxes draped with two pieces of worn black velvet. The closed space soon overwhelmed me with its peculiar olfactory mixture of old snuff, tobacco, treacle, sour milk and pomade and I was pleased when the show was complete.

I left the marionette show to find that the rain-cloud was, as I had feared, spilling its contents with an alarming intensity. In my attempt to keep dry, I found myself part of a crowd that had gathered under a dirty white canopy to the left of the marionette tent. There a man was offering an entertainment which he called 'Pik-a-Straw'. He had, he claimed, various envelopes containing a secret so grave that the authorities would not let him sell them. Instead, he was selling—quite legitimately, he assured us—lengths of straw. The person to choose a long length of straw would win one of the envelopes. He who had the ill-fortune to pick a short straw would win nothing. The straws were a penny each. I observed several gentlemen and one lady approach him. Of these, the lady and two of the gentlemen drew the longer straws and were handed an envelope each. All eyes were on them as they drew out the paper from within and, after considering the contents for a few moments, made startled exclamations. I wasn't about to be fooled by such an old trick, and I felt pleased when my suspicions were confirmed by a more thorough examination of the lady in question. The mud on her shoes, combined with the redness and strength of her hands, suggested that she was either engaged in service, or she was a fair-ground girl. A wink from her accomplice soon confirmed the latter.

Having turned away from this spectacle, my eyes were soon

drawn to a far more intriguing advertisement outside a large marquee. It told of something called a Spectral Opera, featuring Pepper's Ghost and Gompertz's Spectrescope, and boasted royal patronage. It was a ghost show, the sort of entertainment I had heard men talk of in my club, but which I myself had never attended. Bowing my head under the pounding rain, I ventured out from under the canopy and towards the tent, which, after climbing several steps, I entered.

The make-shift theatre was half full and the lights dimmed as soon as I had alighted on the hard wooden bench. Shortly thereafter, the beginning of the performance was heralded by the most singularly spectral and dissonant music I have ever heard. I was reminded of a music box from my childhood, a small, silver contraption, used primarily by one of my sisters as a church organ for the extravagant funerals of broken dolls and dead mice. Soon, still bathed in this eerie music, I was able to behold a truly intriguing spectacle, as, by some ingenious science, transparent phantoms did indeed appear on the stage. There were three of them, each the height and breadth of a living man, but with flesh as pale and insubstantial as a dandelion clock. At first I half believed these to be actors in particularly perlaceous costumes ; they were of human form and did not jerk about like marionettes. Indeed, they appeared to float across the stage, with their feet never touching the board beneath them. Then, quite suddenly, a solid actor strode onto the stage and put a sword through the nearest phantom with neither resistance, nor blood. I confess that I, along with the other members of the audience, let out a gasp of horror as the sword penetrated the frail and pitiable body of the ghost. It was at this moment that my reason must have deserted me. After the show was complete, I confess I dawdled, hoping for some indication of the construction of this elaborate hoax. I did not then believe in ghosts, and I had no doubt that science and reason were behind this display of phantasmagoria, but I became frustrated that I could not deduce the method for myself.

Very soon I was left alone in the tent with a thin-framed man. He walked over to me slowly and pointed in the direction of the stage.

'It is certainly an intriguing spectacle,' he said.

'Indeed it is,' I concurred.

'And it is my guess that you are trying to find an explanation for it.'

'Yes,' I said.

The man was silent for a moment, as if he was making a calculation.

'For two shillings I will show you.'

Before I had even had time to protest at the price, I was following the man towards the stage. At first I believed that he was going to show me the mechanics of the illusion, and explain it in that manner : by a simple demonstration. Instead, he led me through a flap in the tent into a smaller canvas structure in which there was a medicine chest balanced on a small table along with a large lamp, a more vulgar example of which I had never seen. Its ceramic base seemed to combine the deep variegated reds of an old wound, and on this base were painted sickly yellow flowers of a sort, I felt certain, not known to nature. From the rim of its ceramic shade dangled several glass beads, clearly intended to refract the light in the manner of a chandelier, but in fact only managing to create an eerie spattering of shadow on the back of the tent. Beyond the table was a slab that looked like a closed coffin, but which I assumed was intended as some sort of bed.

'I don't believe I caught your name,' I said.

'You can think of me as the fair-ground doctor,' said he. 'And you?'

His manner made me reluctant to introduce myself in the proper way and so I simply suggested that he address me as Mr. Y.

I was suddenly overcome with the peculiar sensation that everyone else had gone home and that I was the only man left at the fair-ground. I could hear the many fists of rain beating on the top of the tent but fancied that I could not hear anything else from outside : no laughter or voices. Even the infernal drone of the organ would have been welcome. I suddenly felt vexed, and I did not trust this doctor. Yet, when he motioned for me to sit on the slab I did as he suggested.

'You wish to know the nature of the illusion you just witnessed,' said he. 'I can show you this, and more. But—' Here he faltered. 'Perhaps you do not have the constitution for the illumination I am about to offer. Perhaps—'

'I have two shillings,' I said to him curtly, and withdrew the money. 'Now, do as you promised.'

The doctor opened his medicine chest and drew from it a vial of clear fluid. From this vial he poured a small measure into a glass which he then passed to me. With his other hand, he motioned to me to wait. He then withdrew another object from his chest : a white card with a small black circle at its centre. He then instructed me to drink the mixture and lie down on the slab, holding the card above my face, concentrating as hard as I could on the black spot. As I did as he asked, I wondered to what kind of trickery I was being subjected. I suspected mesmerism of the crudest sort. Not for one second did I believe that the mixture would have any effect, nor was I aware that the rest of my life would be altered as a result of drinking it.

By eleven o'clock I have finished the first chapter of *The End of Mr. Y.* The winter sun is peeping meekly through the thin curtains and I decide to get up. It's freezing. I pick up my jeans from the floor and quickly exchange them for my pajama bottoms; then I put on a random jumper. As I trot down the concrete steps to get the mail, I am suddenly possessed with a feeling that I've forgotten something. Have I locked myself out again? No, it's not that. My keys are in my hand. I note the take-away flyers and taxi cards without picking any of them up, and go back upstairs. What could I have forgotten?

Porridge. Coffee. A whole day of reading ahead of me. Things could be worse. I already have the sleepy feeling I get when I'm reading a good book: like I want to curl up in bed with it and forget about the nonfictional world. At some point I still have to try to work out how to survive for the next three weeks on five pounds, but that could even be fun. Once I've had breakfast I dig out my packet of ginseng cigarettes and light one. In fact, I'm feeling pretty relaxed when the buzzing sound starts in my bag. It's my mobile phone, which is broken and can no longer ring. At first I think the buzzing represents a call and so I ignore it. But the vibrating only goes on for a few seconds and I realize it's a text message, so I go and get the phone out of my bag. There's a little picture of an envelope on the front and I press the button that metaphorically opens it.

r you still on for 2 day where shall we meet

Shit. That's the thing I've forgotten. It's Patrick. I think quickly and then text back: *Cathedral crypt 5pm*. I can't not see him. I cancelled last time, and anyway he'll probably buy me dinner. His text messages aren't very articulate when you consider that he's a professor of linguistics, but then again he's the kind of person who writes his e-mails in lowercase type because he thinks it's the done thing. I've been seeing Patrick for about the last three months, and in that time we have had sex less than a dozen times. But it's good sex; intense sex; the sort of sex you can only really get with an older man who isn't worried about whether or not you will eventually get married; the kind of sex that is had for its own sake, and not as a deposit against something one party wants to gain in the future. Patrick is already married, of course, although his wife has affairs, too, which stops me from feeling guilty about our arrangement. Sometimes I think through the logic of all this and realize that there must be young men out there—the equivalents of me—who want infrequent sex and companionship without the complications of love and commitment. Would I sleep with one of these guys if I could find one? Probably not. There's something too smooth about younger men. And anyway, older men really do know how to fuck. Crude, but there you are.

I don't think Saul Burlem was married, and maybe it's a good thing he disappeared: I did have a bit of a thing for him, after all. But it is obviously a very bad idea to sleep with your supervisor, and I could have grown to really like him, if his books and online lectures are anything to go by. I would have gone home with him on the night I met him, though, before I'd had a chance to think any of it through. Did he know that? Maybe he knew it would be a bad idea, too. After we'd talked about my Ph.D., I excused myself and went to find the loo. I was drunk and I did get a bit lost, but I wasn't gone that long. I do remember an amazing corridor, though. It was this low-ceilinged, whitewashed space that felt like the inside of an antique telescope: smooth and cold. I must have walked up and down it three or four times, wishing I had a camera, or a better memory. When I got back to the Upper Hall, Burlem had gone.

By half past four I have had a bath, got dressed again—this time with more sense of purpose—and completed a short inventory of the food items I have in the house. The list isn't very inspiring. It tells me that if I am happy to live on porridge, tinned soup, and noodles, I can do so for roughly one week. Can five pounds therefore stretch to cover the remaining two weeks? I could buy a big bottle of soy sauce for about fifty pence at the market and, say, fourteen bags of slightly out-of-date noodles at twenty pence each. That would leave a bit of change that I could use to buy a large bar of bitter chocolate. But what about cigarettes and petrol? What about coffee? I can't buy bad coffee, but I certainly can't afford the good sort. I could drink tap water and slivovitz for the duration, I suppose. And what about vegetables? How long before I got scurvy? The idea of suffering scurvy and both nicotine and caffeine withdrawal at the same time doesn't give me happy thoughts. Is it all going to be worth it for the book? Probably. I'd make the same decision again in any case.

Mr. Y, I think, smiling. *Mr. Y.*

A mouse runs across the kitchen floor and I instinctively draw my legs up and hug my knees. I've read so little about *The End of Mr. Y*. All I really know about it is the curse. It's a strange experience, coming to such an old book without the benefit of a thousand TV adaptations and study guides and reading groups. What is it about? What thought experiment of Lumas's does it represent? And what about this question of fiction? *It is only as fiction that I wish this work to be considered*. I guess I'll have to finish the book to find out what that means.

Already, though, the fiction has become blurred. Am I Mr. Y? Do I have to be for the book to work? When I was a kid I always made an agreement with myself never to identify with main protagonists, because bad things or, more troublingly, big things tended to happen to them and I couldn't cope with the feeling that these things were also happening to me, to the self that you project into fiction when you read. So I would decide on a secondary character that I would "be" for the duration of the book. Sometimes I died; sometimes I turned out to be evil. But I never had to take center stage. Now I'm older I read more conventionally. Right now I'm scared for Mr. Y/me and I feel as though it must be raining outside, even though it isn't. How does his/my/our life change as a result of drinking this potion? I remember the missing page and suddenly it means more, now that I am involved in the story. I hope I can work out the bit that's missing. And I hope that Mr Y's end isn't too painful, although I suspect it will be. Lumas's books and stories never have anything like a happy ending.

I leave the house at about twenty to five and start walking up Castle Street towards the cathedral. In this town you can see the cathedral from almost anywhere. When I was new here, I used it to navigate by. The sun has almost completely set, and the sky behind the pale gold spires is smeared with a cold, waxy pink. As on any other Saturday afternoon in winter, I walk past shops advertising the football scores, and young academics out buying a paper or something for dinner. My breath freezes in the air in front of me and I wonder when the university will be open again. I think of the free heat in my office, and the free coffee in the staff kitchen. OK—the coffee's not really free: You are supposed to pay about five pence a time, I think, but most of us just put in a pound or two when we remember. Will Patrick buy me dinner? I can't see why not. I usually insist on paying half, but I just won't today.

Only a couple of weeks ago the courtyard outside the cathedral was full of carollers and Christmas shoppers; now the space is virtually empty. The cobbles have taken on a dark, pinkish hue in the sunset and I hurry across them and through the Christ Church entrance. Then I cross the precinct gardens and enter the cathedral. I walk up the left-hand side of the nave towards the crypt and then down the stairs into its pale stone interior. I love the cathedral crypt, despite (or even because of) what happened here, which feels more like a story than a real thing. I love the soft, hollow sounds of the few people walking around, and the single candle burning in the Chapel of Our Lady Undercroft. A while ago it felt like everything in London was being blown up and the prayer desk seemed only to contain Post-it Notes asking for world peace. I would come here just to sit quietly, but I'd always read the prayers first. I remember once imagining a bomb going off in the cathedral itself. But the place is so vast, and the walls so solid, that it would surely have as little effect as a firework.

Patrick is standing by the Eastern Crypt, so I walk over to him.

"Hello," he says quietly, kissing me on both cheeks.

"Hi," I whisper back.

"This is a rather somber meeting place," he says, raising an eyebrow.

I smile. "I know. Sorry. I just wanted to light a candle; then we'll go."

I walk over to the small altar and pick a small tea light candle from the box underneath it. I put forty pence in the collection slot. I'm not sure why I am even lighting a candle: It's not something I've made a habit of in the past. There's no breeze in here, but I watch the small flame of my candle flicker uncertainly for about half a minute before it seems to decide not to go out and starts to glow, uniformly, along with the others. I look at it for a moment and then turn away, wondering what happens to all the energy generated in places like this. It's as if we make God ourselves out of all that energy. Is God made from the thoughts of people, or are people made from the thoughts of God? I'm sure I came across that idea in my research, but I can't remember where.

Chapter Five

Patrick has booked a hotel somewhere over by the ring road. We walk through town to the underpass and then, once we come out from that, down the main road towards the hotel. This is a nighttime space, with neon signs hanging off take-aways, video shops, late-night supermarkets, and nightclubs. We check in and walk up a broad wooden staircase to our room, which is airy and clean, if a bit shabby with age. While Patrick changes, I stand in the bathroom contemplating myself in the mirror. Am I cursed? I don't look cursed. I look as if I have caught myself unawares, washed out and dazzled in the fluorescent light.

Would you read a cursed book if you had one? If you heard that there was a cursed book out there and you found it in a bookshop, would you spend the last of your money on it? If you heard there was a cursed book out there, would you go searching for it, even if no one thought any copies existed anymore? I think about my conversation with Wolf last night and wonder if life is as simple as "there is a book." But again I think about stories and their logic and wonder if there can be any such thing as simply "there is a book." *Once upon a time there was a book*. That makes more sense. There is a book. And then what happens? There is a book and it contains a curse and then you read it and then you die. That's a proper story.

I come out of the bathroom and find Patrick wearing expensive-looking blue jeans and a pale pink shirt. He doesn't look bad in jeans, but I preferred Burlem's look: the black shirt, the dark trousers, and the trench coat. But Burlem's not here, and Patrick is. After flirting for a while we go for dinner and have a strange conversation about nineteenth-century poetry, during which I go on and on about Thomas Hardy, and how the best bit of his poem "Hap" is his invented word "unblooms," as in: "And why unblooms the best hope ever sown?" The whole poem is about wishing for evidence of a vengeful god—since there certainly isn't any evidence of a benevolent one—because a higher power, even a cruel one, gives us meaning in a way we can't give meaning to ourselves. This ends up with us talking about structuralism and linguistics (Patrick's specialism) and then Derrida (one of mine).

"How can you read Derrida?" Patrick asks me at some point.

"How can you not?" I say.

We've finished dinner, and I realize that I am now having the conversation as if I were a robot taking part in the Turing Test. I can probably convince Patrick that I am human and listening to him, but really I'm thinking about *Mr. Y.*

"Are you OK?" he asks.

"Yeah," I say. Perhaps I should try harder. "Have you ever listened to any of Derrida's lectures?"

"No."

"You should. I've got one on my iPod. In it, he says that praying is 'not like ordering a pizza.' I love that. I love the little image of Derrida spending an evening praying and ordering pizzas to prove they're not the same thing. Not that he would have done. I mean, I can't see him praying, or trying to prove something by experiment. I bet he ordered pizzas, though."

Patrick is grinning again. "It's unbelievable," he says.

"What, Derrida praying?"

"No. The fact that I'm about to sleep with someone who owns an iPod."

Our roles in bed are quite simple. I am the eager young student, and he is the slightly sadistic professor. We don't go so far as to actually act out our parts, and his slight sadism doesn't extend further than occasionally tying me up with silk scarves, but I like it when he tells me what to do.

By the time I wake up the following morning, Patrick has had breakfast and left. There's a card on the bedside table thanking me for a wonderful night and explaining that there's been some sort of "crisis" at home that he needs to attend to. I wish I'd brought my book with me. I have a large room-service breakfast and read a complimentary newspaper before getting up and making the most of the hot water. The water in my flat never seems to get anywhere beyond "fairly" hot, but I like water with which you can actually burn yourself.

As soon as I am washed and dressed I walk back into town and along the dilapidated city walls towards my flat. The ring road runs next to me on my left, and the landscape I can see is a confused mess of cars, shops, road signs, bollards, a petrol station, some cranes in the distance, a pub, a roundabout, and a pedestrian bridge. At some point a train goes past, emerging from behind a billboard advertising shiny cars and disappearing again behind a nightclub. Every kind of urbanity seems to exist in this space, from the city walls themselves to the remains of the Norman castle and the ugly red blocks of flats that have gone up next to it. Beyond the castle there's a subway under the ring road and if you go through it you can walk along the river towards the motorway, passing the gas tower and the encampment of homeless people who live in tents. I walked that way once, curious about the local countryside. There was a smell of gas all the way.

When I get back there's no sign of Wolfgang's bike, so it looks as if I'm going to be on my own with the mice. When I look, I've got two full traps, so I take them downstairs and release the mice out the back by Luigi's bins. Back in the kitchen I reload the traps with stale biscuits and put them back under the sink; then I put coffee on the stove and arrange all my things around the sofa: *The End of Mr. Y,* cigarettes, notebook, pen. As soon as my coffee is ready, I curl up on the sofa and begin reading where I left off yesterday morning.

The moment the liquid struck my tongue I became aware of several new sensations, including a sudden aversion to darkness and a heavy, constricted feeling. At first I felt sure that these were simply delusions occurring because of the rather melodramatic manner in which the fluid had been prescribed, and that I was simply falling prey to fancies. However, after a time I began feeling increasingly anxious and experiencing something like vertigo. Nevertheless, I fixed my attention upon the black circle, as instructed, beckoned once again by curiosity's claw. I remained convinced that, if this fair-ground doctor was, as I suspected, a fraud, then nothing he could do would cause me any harm.

After lying on the hard slab staring into the black circle for several moments I was startled to see it begin to disintegrate before my eyes. Two larger circles took its place, one pink and one blue, and these shapes then appeared to expand and contract with the soft translucency of jellyfish. I was suddenly overcome with the feeling that one has when moving downhill on a switchback ride, or in the dreams of falling that one has from time to time. It was not my physical being, however, which was descending, but rather my mind. It was as if the thinking, reasoning part of my being was closing with the finality of a heavy, locked door. In its place a small aperture appeared, growing larger and larger until it eclipsed the black circle on the small piece of card, and continued to enlarge until it was the size of a railway tunnel. I was alarmed to realise that I was now moving down this tunnel at a giddying speed.

The walls of the tunnel were charcoal-black at first but presently I became aware of various inscriptions on the walls which appeared alongside me as if drawn by light. At first these were simply pinpricks, like little stars in the firmament, and I fancied that if one could connect them, then perhaps a picture would form. There were also oscillating lines of the sort one might observe in the crude representation of a wave in the sea. For one instant I fancied I saw before me pictures of the human genitalia. There then appeared various shapes, and, despite the tremendous speed with which I passed them, I observed several circles, spheres, triangles, pyramids, squares, cubes and rectangular parallelepiped objects until these faded and the walls of the tunnel then became adorned with what appeared to be ancient hieroglyphics, which I confess I could not read. These little pictures blinked like apparitions as I passed them : I saw things that looked like birds and feet and eyes. All of these impressions appeared before me as though drawn with light.

I became aware of my anxiety paling as I continued my journey through the tunnel, and I was intrigued by the little symbols that flowed past me as if projected on a phenakistiscope. I saw many circles bisected with a cross or a line, and an abundance of other shapes including those which resembled little flags, stalks, boxes, and the reversed Roman letters g, E, r and P. I also saw what appeared to be Roman letters as if drawn in the hand of a child. However, it was clear that not all the Roman letters were present, and their expression seemed to vary between upper and lower case. I am sure I only observed the letters y, I, z, which was crossed in the French style, and l, o, w and x. Later there also appeared the upper case characters A, B, H, K, M, N, P, D, T, V, Y and X. Presently the Greek letters appeared in sequence, from alpha, beta, gamma and delta through to phi, chi, psi and omega. Then I observed the Roman alphabet in the correct sequence, from A through to Z. Still there appeared hieroglyphics here and there. The further I journeyed into this long tunnel, the more characters I perceived on the black walls, until there was more light than shade, and thousands of characters jostled before me. I saw Roman numerals and Arabic numerals and other shapes I could not discern, for they flew past me with such tremendous velocity. There were also mathematical equations. I recognised Newton's $F=MA$ but none of the others.

Presently I began to sense that my journey was almost at an end. The light on the walls of the tunnel eventually expanded so that I felt bathed in it. Indeed, for one curious second I fancied myself to be part of the light itself. I could no longer perceive anything around me but for this bright white glow. I remember quite distinctly thinking, 'That's it! The penny showman has killed me. Now I shall see what Heaven is like.' I did not think of the other place. And, after a short time, it did appear that I had awoken in a heavenly landscape. I did not find myself confronting Saint Peter, however. Indeed, there were no other beings, mortal or otherwise, to be discerned on the softly rolling meadow I saw before me. Under a bright blue but curiously sunless sky, I observed grass, flowers and trees of species to be found anywhere in the nineteenth-century English countryside. I admit that at that moment I experienced the most profound sensation of peace, which was most welcome after the creeping dread with which I had become familiar at the start of my journey.

How long had I been travelling? I had no idea. In the depths of my mind something gnawed at me with persistent little teeth. Did I have an assignment in this place? I recollected the fair-ground doctor and his strange potion, and then the reason for my journey arrived once again in my mind. I was here to see the workings of Pepper's Ghost, although I had no idea of how this could be achieved, and also felt that my appetite for solving this mystery was a very slight pang of hunger indeed in comparison with the greedy desire I now felt to solve the far bigger mystery with which I had been presented : where was I and how had I come to be there?

At the same moment that my assignment had reappeared in my mind, so a small piebald horse had appeared in the meadow to the right of my current position. The horse presently came and nuzzled at my hand, and, noticing that it was fully tackled, I understood that I was supposed to ride it. I have some experience as an equestrian and I saw no option than to insert my foot into the stirrup, swing myself onto the animal and take the harness. With only the merest of nudges, the horse moved gracefully forward. Again I had the sensation that I knew something I could not know, and fancied that the horse would take me to the place I needed to go. This sensation was a powerful one and so I let the horse trot onwards, towards the brow of a small hill. All around me was calm and tranquillity and I felt as if I could remain in this place forever and not want for anything. Yet I felt compelled to complete my assignment.

I soon became aware of several dwellings ahead of me. As my horse drew closer I saw that there was indeed a small hamlet of cottages clustered before a vast and tangled forest. I understood that I was supposed to examine these dwellings and so I dismounted from my horse and tethered him outside the first cottage. This was a dark little place, with a garden overgrown with brambles and thick, twisted trees. Even before I saw the name on the gate, I knew that this was the fair-ground doctor's house. The next place was plainer, with a whitewashed exterior and a name on the gate that I did not recognise. Something told me to enter this gate and I did so. Again, this something that seemed to speak from within my mind told me that the door would be unlocked, and so I entered without knocking, knowing that according to the customs of this place this action would not be considered aberrant.

Then I experienced the most peculiar sensation of all. Language almost fails me when I try to formulate this sensation in words. The closest approximation is this : imagine stepping not into another man's shoes but, rather, into his soul. Even as I write this, that paltry description appears feeble in comparison to the odd, but not at all uncomfortable sensation of expansion that I felt as whatever is 'I' grew, as if from a seed, into whatever was 'him' and the two of us became one. All at once I intuited what had occurred. Inconceivable and impossible though it may appear, I had entered the mind of another. I had entered the mind of the illusionist Mr. William Hardy, proprietor of Hardy's Ghost Illusion and Theatre.

I can assure the reader that the telepathic intercourse one has with another is in no way partial, vague or insubstantial. For, although I still seemed to carry with me the portmanteau of my own being, once inside this man's mind I had the palpable sense that I existed not in his place, but alongside him. Much though it vexes me to write these words, for I am a man who does not believe in ghosts, phantoms and the so-called fourth dimension of Zollner and others, I have no doubt that I shared the mind of this man. I could think what he thought, I knew what he knew, and, for the time that I remained a guest in his being, I experienced what he experienced.

He (although it seemed to me that 'I' did all that follows, I will not confuse the reader here with the first person singular or, worse, the plural) was hungry ; this was the first sensation of which I became aware. Of course, I experienced the same hunger, now that I was inhabiting the same being, and, without thinking what I was doing, I cast my own mind back to the last time I dined. I quickly perceived something reminiscent of two transparent images placed on top of one another. Of course, this does not adequately explain the sensation but words will not allow me a fuller description. I saw, or felt, myself taking luncheon at the Regency Hotel, but at the same time experienced William Hardy, who, I understood, likes to refer to himself in his own mind as Will, or even 'Little Will,' a pet name given to him by his mother, sitting down to consume a steamed meat pudding wrapped in paper. It is with some difficulty that even I myself believe my own recollection as I write these words, but I certainly experienced the illusion of being able to taste the heavy, thick suet pudding and the dense brown gravy, as sweet as the meat inside. Nevertheless, I, or he, or we, still felt hungry. The meat pie was merely a memory and Little Will wanted his supper.

Before supper, Little Will had to pack up his ghost illusion. The fair would be departing the following morning and so everything would have to be carefully disassembled and stored in a large wagon. Will found the idea of this task rather overwhelming, as did I, and I quite understood his anguish and frustration as he barked orders at his underlings, wanting them to hurry this moment and take more care the next. I understood why he felt betrayed by his assistant Dan Roper, and I instantly knew that Peter, the boy helper, was too clumsy for this task. I do not believe that I shared William Hardy's exact thoughts while the packing up process was in progress ; I was not 'mind-reading' in the crudest sense. Rather, I had access to his memories in the same way one accesses one's own memories. Images came to me as fast as quicksilver. I saw, for example, the hapless boy Peter breaking a large sheet of glass, and was aware that this event had occurred at some time in the recent past. I saw Dan Roper creeping behind a grubby fair-ground tent with a woman. Then I saw Little Will with the same woman. Of course, I did not see him from above, like an omnipotent observer. I was his eyes, ears, nose and flesh as he coupled with this woman, barely a girl, whom I now knew to be called Rose.

I confess that I almost became lost in this new world, for, given access to another man's thoughts, who would not roam endlessly within them? What anthropology or biology was this, that I was able to read another's mind as if it were a play? I sincerely believed that the entire works of Shakespeare shrank in comparison with the tragedies, comedies, betrayals and desires of this one fair-ground entertainer. Still, however, I recalled my assignment. I was here, in the mind of William Hardy, to understand the ghost illusion that he peddled from country fair to country fair.

In an instant all was clear to me. I saw the intricate placing of the large, expensive sheet of glass, polished five times a day by Little Will himself. I saw it balanced on the stage, resting against a wall or structure behind. I saw, and understood, the forty-five degree tilt. I had the most profound knowledge of the way the illusion worked, from the tilted glass to the actors underneath who danced in a projectionist's light, thus creating images, like inverted shadows, to be reflected through the glass and onto the stage. I understood Little Will's amazement when he himself first discovered the construction of these beings of light, and I recalled, as clearly as if thinking of a scene from my own past, the evening that Little Will opened the book that revealed the secrets of this illusion. I must say, however, that the sensation of reading a book in a man's memory was a queer one, and although many passages were forgotten, and therefore appeared to be missing, I was able to read the most significant sections as if the book was in front of my own face.

There is a part of my adventure that I have not yet described for fear of entirely compounding the impression that I lost my wits that day in the fair-ground tent. However, I must now relate this curiosity, and I beg further indulgence from the reader. What I wish to describe is the way in which my field of vision altered when inside this 'spirit world' of other minds. At the beginning, I confess I had no idea of how far this world-of-minds expanded, nor how far within it I would be permitted to travel. However, on that first visit I became aware of some important factors, which I will now attempt to describe. When one sees the world in ordinary social intercourse, or in the comings and goings of a typical day, one sees the world as if that world were contained within a frame. The outside world therefore is a picture on a wall ; or, perhaps, many pictures. If I were to look to my left I would see one picture. If I glanced to my right, another. A philosopher may ask if indeed there is another picture behind me, one which I cannot see, but I shall not take this avenue of enquiry for the time being.

If one accepts this way of looking at the world as a frame with perceptible edges, albeit blurred ones, then one will more easily comprehend the altered frame through which I gazed on the world of Little Will. For Little Will's frame also contained my own, superimposed on top of it. The result of this superimposition was the existence of a milky hue over all that I saw, as if I were looking through thick glass or a thin veil. Yet the peculiarities of this new frame did not end there. Around the edge of my perception of Little Will's vision was a blur similar to that which creeps around the edge of ordinary vision. But the blur around the edges of Little Will's frame was made more pronounced by the existence of layers of little pictures, like playing cards laid out in a game of Patience ; one to the right and one to the left. There was another feature of this new kind of vision which perplexed me even further. When Little Will came close to another person and regarded him, a dwelling would appear faintly behind the already milky image that I had. I understood without fully comprehending that at these moments I could, if I so wished, simply walk into that house instead of the one in which I was currently standing ; in other words, I could enter another mind. At least, this was the theory I constructed from the evidence before my eyes, but when I tried this on the boy Peter I seemed to bounce from an invisible wall and instead landed back on the small path connecting the cottages.

Again, I was overcome with a sense of peace and fullness. The hunger I had felt when joined with Little Will immediately subsided and I realised that spending time in another man's soul was terribly draining. Out on the open landscape I felt no discomfort, but I remembered the sensation of privation and desperation I had shared with Little Will. I concluded that the further adventures I so craved were best left for another visit, and so I retrieved my horse and let him take me back to the place from which I had entered this world.

The journey back through the tunnel appeared of a far shorter duration this time, and presently I arrived, if that is the right term, for an observer would not have seen me leave, on the slab in the fair-ground tent. Once more I could hear the rain on the thick canvas, and I struggled to open my eyes on the familiar world I had left behind for a time. With my eyes still half-closed, and my head thick with fancies, I asked myself whether I had concocted an elaborate dream or whether I had in fact telepathed into another man's mind, and resolved to interrogate the fair-ground doctor the instant I had fully regained my senses. However, when I opened my eyes I found myself alone in the dark. The vulgar lamp, which had been burning brightly before, was now extinguished. The doctor was nowhere to be seen. I withdrew my watch from my pocket, along with a box of matches, and, after striking a match close to the face of the timepiece, found it to be past eleven o'clock. Startled, I immediately got to my feet and felt my way out of the tent, using another match to guide me. How could I possibly have been unconscious for such a long period of time? I confess I felt frightened as I stumbled out of the large theatre tent and into the open air of the darkened, deserted fair-ground. I was determined to find this doctor and admonish him for leaving me alone and defenceless for such a long time. However, the doctor was nowhere to be seen and, now tired and desperately hungry, I made my way back to the Regency Hotel, resolving to find the doctor the next day.

Chapter Six

By lunchtime I am hungry and cold and I need to pee. From my bathroom window it looks as if the whole world is lidded with rooftops and hinged with back doors and fire escapes, as if it were one big higgledy-piggledy doll's house. I can see the top of Luigi's back room and the dark metal staircase down which you could escape if there was a fire. Below a gray concrete roof is the back door of the Indian restaurant. I can see a guy standing there, puffing urgently on a cigarette, constantly looking around as if he's about to get caught. I can see alleyways and small, uneven courtyards; but mostly there are rooftops and chimneys, red brick and concrete, and it suddenly seems more like a three-dimensional puzzle out there. How is it possible to fit so many buildings into one small space? I think, not for the first time, about how many people there must be around me all the time, even though it often seems as if I am entirely alone. I wonder what it would be like to "telepath." Would it make you feel less alone, or would the loneliness somehow become worse?

I cook some Puy lentils for lunch; then I go back to the sofa and balance my bowl on my lap as I continue reading about Mr. Y, and his search for the fairground doctor. By the time Mr. Y gets to the fairground the following day, the whole thing has disappeared, including the doctor and his curious potion. Poor Mr. Y. He was so certain that he would be able to return to this world-of-minds that he didn't bother to investigate everything while he was still inside it. He asks around and finds that most of the fairground people have moved on to a site just beyond Sherwood Forest. But when he gets to the site and finds the fairground, he can't find the doctor. Indeed, when he asks people if they have seen this "fair-ground doctor," most of them are perplexed and assure him that there is no such man.

Once he is back in London, Mr. Y becomes increasingly obsessed with the questions posed by his adventure. Had he, in fact, been given the ability to read minds (or, as he puts it, "to telepath"), albeit only briefly? Or did the doctor simply give him a strong sleeping draught? He doesn't know, and does not have any way of finding out. But he becomes inclined to believe that he did in fact read the mind of William Hardy. Indeed, he is able to locate and read the exact book from which Hardy learned of the Pepper's Ghost illusion, and finds that his "memory" of it (from reading it via Little Will) is exactly correct. Knowing that a man cannot have a memory of a book he has not read, he concludes that something supernatural happened to him that evening at the Goose Fair. But he simply does not know what this was. In the absence of any proper explanation, he does a good Victorian thing and starts labelling and classifying the parts of the new world he has encountered. The name he gives to this other world is the *Troposphere*, which he derives by taking the word "atmosphere"—a combination of the Greek words for "vapor" and "ball"—and replacing the unknown vapors with something more solid: the Greek word for character, *tropos*. It takes Mr. Y more time to conceive of a term for the journey itself, but eventually he names it *Telemancy:* tele from *telos,* meaning distant; and mancy from *manteia,* meaning divination. In his mind this was divination at a distance, and he badly wanted to do it again.

At this point in the narrative we begin to learn something of Mr. Y's business affairs. His drapery shop, located in the East End of London, used to be a very successful enterprise but now it seems to be failing, and soon he has to let several of his assistants go. A rival has set up shop just around the corner from Mr. Y, and his business is booming. The proprietor of this rival business, Mr. Clemency, is roughly characterized in the novel as a shifty, spiteful individual who seems to enjoy the misery he heaps on Mr. Y, and believes that his method of making clothes—locking his workers in a small, hot back room and paying them hardly anything—is superior to Mr. Y's old-fashioned ways. Mr. Y soon has two obsessions: Telemancy and revenge, and he thinks that if only he knew what had been in the potion given to him by the doctor, he could concoct it himself and revisit the landscape of the Troposphere. Once there, of course, he would visit the mind of Mr. Clemency. He admits, with some shame, that he intends to blackmail his rival if he can find a way to do so.

Meanwhile, his business continues to deteriorate. On top of this, his father is taken ill and his usually meek wife becomes vexed and anxious. Mr. Y can't cope with everything, and so neglects his father and shouts at his wife. He is clearly rushing headfirst down the slope of his own ruin, but he can't see this. Instead, he burns a lamp each night and reads *Materia Medica* and herbals that might give him some clue as to what the mysterious mixture was. He finds none. But the world of the Troposphere, particularly the calm landscape on which he rode the horse, beckons him like a drug to which he has become profoundly addicted.

The light is fading outside my kitchen window and I look at my watch. It's just gone four o'clock. I've got a reading lamp in my bedroom, so I go and get that and plug it in behind the sofa and then place it on the windowsill. That's better. I can aim it directly at the pages of the book. One lamp can't use up too much electricity, surely?

At about half past five I hear the sound of the door downstairs, and then the dissonant tinkle of Wolfgang's bicycle bell as it scrapes against the wall. Although I really want to finish reading my book, my eyes are hurting and I haven't spoken to another human being for hours. So when there's a faint tap on my door a few minutes later, I call out that it's open, and get up to make coffee.

Wolfgang comes in and sits down awkwardly at the kitchen table.

"Good day?" I say, although his posture should answer the question for me.

"Ha," is all he says, putting his head in his hands.

"Wolf?"

"What is Sunday for?" he asks. "Tell me that."

"Um . . . church?" I suggest. "Family? Sport?"

The coffee hisses and I take it off the gas ring. I pour a cup for each of us and sit down at the table facing Wolf. I offer him a cigarette and then light one myself. He does not respond to my suggestions, so I try to think of some more. Without meaning to, I effortlessly transport myself back to Mr. Y's 1890s world, and summon up half-finished coloring-book images of women walking through parks in hobble skirts, children playing with hoops, and vague dot-to-dot trips to the seaside involving parasols and slot machines, although I don't think they had slot machines until the turn of the century. It's an after-church, afternoon world that I can't even begin to understand. I try to think myself back out of the 1890s.

"Sex?" I suggest instead. "Reading the papers? Shopping?"

"Ha," says Wolf again, sipping his coffee.

"What happened?" I ask.

"A weekend with Catherine's family," he says, with some disgust.

"It can't have been that bad," I say. "Where did you go?"

"Sussex. Country house. And it was very bad . . ."

"Why?"

He sighs. "Where to begin?"

I think of the *Odyssey*. "Try the middle," I suggest.

"Ah. The middle. OK. In the middle, I run over the dog."

I can't help but laugh, even though this is obviously not funny.

"Is the dog OK?" I say.

Wolfgang looks sad. "He is now lame."

I sip my coffee. "How exactly did you run over the dog?"

Wolfgang doesn't drive: thus the bicycle.

"In a . . . How would you say it . . . ? What is the word . . . ?"

This is something of an affectation of Wolf's. He speaks English better than most of the literature students in the department, but sometimes he'll fish for a word like this, playing on his foreignness to add drama and, sometimes, melancholy, to whatever story he's telling. I don't dislike the affectation, in fact, I find it funny. But that doesn't mean I'm not familiar with its mechanics.

He's still at it. "A . . . like a *little tractor*."

"You ran over your girlfriend's family dog in a 'little tractor'?"

"No. Well, yes. But I mean what is the word for little tractor?"

"I don't think there is a word for little tractor. What do you do with it?"

"You cut the grass with it."

"Oh! A lawnmower."

Wolf looks at me as if I'm simple. "I know *lawnmower*," he says. "You push a lawnmower. This other thing you sit on."

"Oh," I say. "Yeah, like a lawnmower you sit on. A . . . Oh God. What do you call those things?" I think for a while. "I think they're just lawnmowers that you sit on. What did Catherine's family call it?"

"I think they called it the 'mower.' But I was sure there would be another term."

"I'm not sure there is. So, anyway, why were you on the mower?"

"The father, Mr. Dickerson, he had got it stuck and he wanted a 'big strong lad' to drive it out."

I laugh at the thought that anyone would call Wolfgang a "big strong lad." He isn't any one of those three things.

"Yes," he says. "Ha ha."

"Sorry. So, anyway, what were they like, the family?"

"Rich," says Wolf. "From carpets."

"And is there a future with Catherine?" I ask.

"For me?" He shrugs. "Who knows?" He gets up and takes the bottle of slivovitz from the shelf. He pours himself a large glass, but when he offers some to me I shake my head. "Anyway," he says, when he has sat down again, "how is your curse?"

"Hmm," I say. "Can you keep a secret?"

"You know I can. And I've already said that I don't care if I become more cursed."

"I don't think you'll become cursed just from hearing about it," I say.

"So what is it? An object?"

"A book."

"Ah, the curse of knowledge," he says immediately.

"I'm not sure if it is that," I say. "It's a novel. I think the curse might just be some superstition. But the book is very rare and potentially very valuable—although my copy is damaged, so it's probably actually worth nothing."

"And you bought this on Friday?"

"Yeah. With, basically, all my money."

"How rare is it?"

"Very rare." I explain to him about there being no known copies anywhere in the world, apart from the one in the German bank vault. "Even with the damage, it's still a pretty amazing thing to have. It's by that author I'm studying: Thomas Lumas. I could be the only person in the world to write a paper on the actual book rather than the mysteries surrounding it. I must be one of the only people to have read it in the last hundred years." Just as I'm getting excited about it, Wolf interrupts.

"And the curse is what?"

I look down at the table. "The curse is that if you read it, you die."

The book is still on the sofa where I left it, and I notice as Wolf's gaze travels around the room and then rests on it. He gets up and goes over to the sofa. But instead of picking up the book, he simply looks down at it as if it were an exhibit in a museum. For a moment I imagine that he's much more frightened of curses than he has let on, and this is why he doesn't touch it. But then I decide that it must be simply a respect for the age and rarity of the object. Wolf isn't scared of curses: He's said so.

He comes back to the table. "What's the story about?"

"It's about this man called Mr. Y, who goes to this Victorian fairground," I begin. I tell Wolf the story as far as I know it, ending with the last scene I read, where Mr. Y's wife has implored him to stop spending all night poring over medical textbooks. Mr. Y tells her to mind her own business and go to bed. This she does, and he resumes his reading.

"What does he think the mixture might be?" Wolf asks me.

"So far he has no idea," I say. "He thinks it might be based on laudanum, which is opium in alcohol, but isn't sure. He knows it's active as a liquid, so he has ruled out nitrous oxide—laughing gas—and chloroform, both of which you have to inhale. Other candidates include ether, a substance made from sulphuric acid and alcohol, and chloral. He's also trying to obtain more exotic herbals from further afield, and concocts a weird theory about some foreign witch doctor giving the information to the fairground doctor. But if this is true then the mixture won't be something he can concoct from ingredients to be found in any Victorian pharmacy. This basically throws him into total depression. But after a while he comes to the conclusion that it can't have been an exotic mixture. For two shillings it was unlikely to have included Peruvian tree bark, African snake venom, unicorn blood, or whatever. He works out that for two shillings, the mixture must have contained relatively cheap ingredients. But what?" I shrug. "Even if the ingredients aren't exotic, they could be anything."

"And you have no idea yet?" Wolfgang asks.

I shake my head. "No. But I'm looking forward to finding out, if you ever do get to find out, that is."

Wolf lights a cigarette and falls into a deep contemplation of his glass of slivovitz. I consider telling him about the preface to the book, and the hint that there could be something "real" about it, but I don't. Instead, I get up and rinse the coffee cups while Wolf drains his glass and gets up to go.

"I can do something gourmet tonight if you like," he offers.

I am tempted. What I've got here is at best "very gourmet," but I do want to finish the book.

"Thanks, Wolf," I say. "But I think I'm just going to keep reading."

"And complete the curse?" he says, with a raised eyebrow.

"I really don't think there is a curse," I say.

By eight o'clock it's freezing and I have to switch on all the gas rings. I am nearing the end of the book and it seems clear that Mr. Y is well on his way towards bankruptcy and destitution as the result of his obsession with the Troposphere and the method by which he might return there. He has taken to experimenting with various drugs and potions and lying there on his couch gazing at a black dot, but none of the drugs he has tried have worked. At every corner he is assaulted by advertisements suggesting cure-all panaceas like Dr. Locock's Pulmonic Wafers, and Pulvermacher's Improved Patent Galvanic Chain-Bands, Belts, Batteries, and Accessories. What was in the wafers, and could the fairground doctor's vial of liquid have contained it? And what about Pulvermacher's electrical objects? Perhaps the fairground doctor had in some way electrified whatever fluid he had concocted. Mr. Y realizes that there is no way he'll be able to find the concoction by chance. The only way he will ever be able to revisit the Troposphere is by finding that doctor and persuading him to tell him how.

By the beginning of chapter 12, Mr. Y has discovered that many of the people who travel the country with fairs in the summer end up in London in the winter, exhibiting their sideshow horrors in run-down shops and backstreet houses. As a last resort, Mr. Y has taken to spending his evenings, and much of his money, touring these establishments, trying to find some clue to lead him to the fairground doctor.

My search continued into November. The weather had turned bitterly cold but I kept at it every night, even as I began to doubt that I would ever find my man. It seemed to me that London had become a sort of Vanity Fair, with many of the establishments in the back streets of the West End—and beyond—dressed up with gaudy crimson hangings and advertising, by way of vast painted representations and pictorial facsimiles, such unsavoury offerings as the Bearded Lady, the Spotted Boy, the Giantess of Peru and various other mutants, savages and freaks of nature.

Although most of these establishments remained open all day, I had discovered that it was in the evening and night-time hours that one should expect to encounter the fullest range of their offerings. And so it was that I would venture out after supper every evening and pay my penny at the doors of establishments both gaudy and drab, populated by crowds of people or empty. In every place I asked the same question, and in every place I received the same response. No one had ever heard of the fair-ground doctor.

November grew older and greyer, and each night it snowed a little more. I decided to confine my investigations to my own locality until such time as the weather improved, although I confess that by that time there was barely a waxwork or living skeleton in London that I had not already seen. However, I had been told of a new premises on the Whitechapel Road, opposite the London Hospital, formerly the site of an undertaker's, and, previously to that, a drapery business with which I had been familiar. So, after a small supper of bread and dripping, I set off on foot towards Whitechapel Road. My journey took me past the Jews' Burial Ground and the back of the Coal Depot and then along the southern side of the workhouse behind Baker's Row. Not for the first time I experienced the direst of premonitions that, if I did not succeed in my undertaking, my own family would be forced inside such an establishment. I did not imagine worse, because I knew of no worse.

I followed the railway line down towards the London Hospital, looking behind me all the time for the thieves who dwell in areas such as this. I was not carrying very much money with me but I had of course read the horrible stories of the new breed of East End thieves who, if they find you with only a few pence, will easily kick out one of your eyes—or worse—as thanks for it. The snow fell softly on me as I walked through the smoky air, with coal dust from the depot mingling with the smog already thick around me. I coughed a little, and rubbed my hands to keep warm. I thought then that if I were fully in possession of all my senses I would surely not have been out on a night such as this one. Yet on I walked.

As I turned into Whitechapel Road, my eyes almost immediately fell upon the establishment of which I had heard. The upper part of the house was adorned with a large sheet of canvas, on which various entertainments and spectacles were depicted, including yet another Fat Lady, along with the World's Strongest Woman and various other oddities. It is alarming how one so quickly tires of these sorts of spectacles, especially when one visits these establishments with such regularity as did I over those months, and if one chances, as I did, to observe the dreary reality behind the lurid and gruesome teratology presented by the showmen. Once, early on a Saturday morning, I happened to walk past an establishment I had visited two or three nights previously. There, in an overgrown garden, I observed the 'amazing' bearded woman, who by evenings was a sombre, backlit, half-human spectacle, pegging out her washing and engaging in an argument with an African 'savage' who was to be found after sunset adorned with a straw skirt, golden tunic and hoop earrings, and who apparently made only the utterances 'Ug, ug', but was at that moment wearing the rather less exotic outfit of shabby stockings, corduroy britches and a grey cloth cap, and was demonstrating an advanced grasp not only of English, but of its myriad vernacular words and expressions. I also once chanced upon the Boy With the Gigantic Head, a child of perhaps twelve or thirteen years, outside of his darkened room, and removed from all costume, lime-light and painted advertisement. He was no longer a gaudy freak but clearly a sick child who required medical attention.

Feeling rather half-hearted, I paid a penny to enter the Whitechapel establishment. On the ground floor, and requiring no further payment, were the usual trivial spectacles of ships-in-bottles, shrunken heads and the like. There were also various waxworks of prominent political figures, and a scene depicting the glories of Empire. There were also, seated at small card-tables, various scoundrels engaged in the dark art of hiding the 'Lady' from those gentlemen who would find her for a shilling, and other similar forms of petty embezzlement. As I left this room and made towards the stairs, a young girl attempted to entice me into a back-room in order that I might have my fortune told by a Madame de Pompadour. I assured the woman that all the possibilities of my fortune were already well-known to me and proceeded up the stairs. Here I found a troublesome display indeed : eleven waxworks, each depicting one of the victims of the Whitechapel Murders. I confess I had to avert my gaze after briefly regarding a mutilated copy of Mary Kelly lying on a bed in a chemise with thick wax blood coming out of her neck. However, something about this gruesome little scene—something beyond the basic horror of the spectacle—troubled me as I walked into the next room and beheld a red-headed young woman lifting weights with her long plait of hair. Presently I returned to the waxwork exhibition and regarded the scene of Mary Kelly's demise once again. And, sure enough, there it was. The gaudy red lamp that I had last seen in the fair-ground doctor's tent was now serving as a prop for this morbid tableau.

I immediately strode over to a woman sitting in an old armchair in the far corner of the room. I presumed that it was she who was keeping watch over the waxwork display. I stood facing her for some seconds before she looked up from a costume in her lap, onto which she was sewing sequins over frayed and greying sections of material.

'Can I help you?' she said to me.

'I wish to enquire after the owner of that lamp,' I said to her.

'You mean that poor girl Mary Kelly?'

'No,' I said, quickly becoming exasperated. 'No, a gentleman. A fair-ground doctor. Perhaps he is engaged here?'

The woman looked down at her embroidery. 'Sorry, sir,' she said. 'I don't think there is anyone of that description here.'

She then briefly flashed her small eyes at me and I understood what she wanted. I found a shilling and showed it to her.

'Are you certain you do not know him?' I asked.

She eyed the shilling and then reached out and took it from me.

'Try the fortune-teller downstairs,' she told me quickly, in a half-whisper. 'The man who owns that lamp is her husband.'

Without hesitating further I made may way down the stairs and, full of impatience, burst into the fortune-teller's salon. There sat a bony, pale woman, with her hair arranged in a colourful scarf. Before she even began to speak, I addressed her directly.

'I am looking for your husband.'

As she began assuring me that she had no husband and that I could pay her directly for her services, which were of a most superior nature, there suddenly came a blast of cold air into the room, and the fair-ground doctor entered.

'Mr. Y,' he said. 'How pleasant.'

'Good evening, Doctor,' I said.

'I understand that you have been looking for me,' he said.

'How—' I began, and then stopped. We both knew the effects of his medicine. I quickly worked out how this present fortune-telling act worked. The doctor presumably read the minds of all the people to enter the establishment and primed his wife with their biographies, ready for her to exploit them. Therefore, I reasoned, he had already read my mind and knew what I was looking for. I guessed that there was a chance he would give it to me—for a price.

'You want the recipe,' he said to me.

'Yes,' I said, but hesitated to tell the doctor just how much I longed for it.

'Very well. You can have it,' said he, 'for thirty pounds and no less.'

I cursed my own mind. This man, this back-room showman, already knew that I would give everything I had for another taste of his curious mixture, and, of course, he planned to take everything I had and no less.

'Please,' I said. 'Don't take all my money. I need to buy cloth for the shop, and to pay the wages of my assistant. There is also medicine for my dying father—'

'Thirty pounds,' he said again. 'Come here to-morrow evening with the money and I shall give you the recipe. If you do not come I shall regard our business as concluded. Good evening.'

He showed me the door.

The following evening I withdrew the money from its hiding place and carefully stowed it inside my shoe, lest the East End ruffians take it from me. With a heavy heart, and a profound uneasiness, I made my way back to the establishment opposite the London Hospital. The previous evening I had witnessed only a young man playing the Pandean pipes outside ; today, the girl with the organ was in attendance as well, her instrument wailing and buzzing with the same bombilations I recalled from the Goose Fair. I strode past all this, past the boys selling plum duff, the pick-pockets and the vagrants, and into the House of Horrors, paying another penny for the privilege.

I feared that the so-called doctor may have disappeared again, but the promise of thirty pounds must have been sufficiently enticing for him, as he greeted me as soon as I stepped into

And this is the place where the ripped-out page would have been. My eye keeps falling on the single sentence on page 133, the next existing page:

And so, in the freezing cold of that late November night, I walked away, each footprint in the snow a record of a further step towards my own downfall, the oblivion that faced me.

What am I supposed to do now? There is one chapter left, starting on page 135. Do I read it, and disregard the fact that what must be the crucial scene between Mr. Y and the fairground doctor is missing? Or . . . What? What are the other options? It's not as if I can just go to a bookshop tomorrow and buy a replacement copy, or simply read the page. This book is not on any library record anywhere in the world: It doesn't even exist in rare manuscript collections. Is this page lost forever? And why on earth would someone have removed it?

Chapter Seven

Monday morning, and the sky is the color of sad weddings. I'm going in to the university, although I'm fairly sure it's still shut. But perhaps they'll have the heating on, anyway. And, as long as our building is still standing, there'll be free tea and coffee. Will our building be OK? It had better be, because I need to try to break into Burlem's computer. He's the only person I know who has ever seen a copy of *The End of Mr. Y* and maybe there'll be something on his machine that will tell me where his copy came from, or whom I could contact to arrange to look at the missing page. I didn't read the last chapter in the end last night. It wouldn't be right without the missing page. Instead, I listened to Beethoven's Ninth Symphony on my iPod and wrote out everything I thought about the bulk of the novel I had read. I didn't get into bed until about three A.M., so I am not at all awake today.

I have never walked up to the university; I don't even know the right way. All I do know is that it is a steep climb, and I don't want to go up the way I came down on Friday because I am convinced that the right way must be shorter than that. So I do the only thing I can think of and go to the Tourist Information place by the cathedral. There's no one there apart from a woman with a gray perm and thin wire glasses. She is busy arranging a display of cathedral mugs, and I have to stand there for a few seconds before she notices me. It turns out that there's a free map of walking routes around the city, so she gives me one of those and I start following it immediately, walking around past the cathedral walls until I see a sign for the North Gate. I follow the sign and walk past some terraced houses and a noisy mill race opposite a pub where my map tells me to turn left, then right. Then I walk over a bridge and past some stinging nettles up a hill until I come to a footpath, which takes me through a tunnel under the railway: a strange cylindrical space with smooth, graffiti-spattered walls and round orange lights set to come on as you walk underneath them (at least, this is what I assume; perhaps the effect is actually the work of a poltergeist, or simply due to the fact that the lights are broken). I walk along the edge of a shabby suburban park, the kind of place where kids play football and dogs fight on a Saturday afternoon, then down an alleyway, across a main road, past a hairdresser, and into a housing estate. I think students live here, although it looks like the kind of place you'd come to only when you'd retired or given up life in some other way. All I can see as I walk up the hill are cream-colored bungalows and front gardens: no graffiti, no playgrounds, no shops, no pubs. The whole place has the kind of stillness you'd expect just before the world ended.

On days like this I do not feel afraid of death, or pain. I don't know if it's the tiredness, the book, or even the curse, but today, as I walk through this housing estate, there's a feeling inside me like the potential nuclear fission of every atom in my body: a chain reaction of energy that could take me to the limits of everything. As I walk along, I almost desire some kind of violence: to live, to die, just for the experience of it. I'm so hyped up suddenly that I want to fuck the world, or be fucked by it. Yes, I want to be penetrated by the shrapnel of a million explosions. I want to see my own blood. I want to die with everyone: the ultimate bonding experience; the flash at the end of the world. Me becoming you; you becoming we; we becoming forever. A collapsing wavefunction of violence. On days like this I think about being cursed and all I can think is *Now, now, now*. I want that missing page.

Soon I find the beginning of the pathway up to the campus. Weather-beaten gates stop cyclists from zooming straight upwards, not that anyone would be zooming up here: It's virtually a forty-five-degree angle. Tired though I am, I do feel a bit like running, just to get this hyped feeling out of my system. But I don't run. I walk through two sets of these gates and then past a patch of woodland on my left, where I'm hidden from the pale sky under the thin fingers of the winter trees. As I near the top of the hill, it starts to rain a little, and in the distance I can see yellow construction vehicles trundling around the collapsed Newton Building like toys in a nursery. I get to my building and the crazy feeling starts to seep away. I realize that the walk has taken more then half an hour. I wish I could liberate my car for the way back, but I was going to put petrol in it on the way home on Friday and I can't afford to do that now.

The English and American Studies Building is still standing, and isn't locked. That means someone must be in. Mind you, someone usually is. Even on Sundays I rarely have to unlock the door myself, although I did have to when I came here on Boxing Day. Even though there must be someone here, I can't sense anyone as I walk down the long corridor. It's not just that I can't hear the hum of electricity, or the monotonous sound of stressed-out fingers hitting cheap keyboards. I just can't feel the presence of anyone down here. I go into my office and find that the heating is on, although I am actually too hot from walking up the hill. I go to open the window and I see that the rain has hit the pane in these spattered patterns: broken diagonal lines that look somehow deliberate, and remind me of the pictures in my books of photographs from particle accelerators. I start up my computer and go up the stairs to the office to check my post.

Mary is in there, talking to the secretary, Yvonne.

"I suppose most people don't check their e-mail at home," Yvonne is saying. "I mean, on Friday they were talking about shutting down campus for a week. I'd be surprised if you saw people in here before next Monday. I suppose some might come in on Friday, out of curiosity. But of course the academics don't all come in during the vacation period, anyway."

The department used to be run by senior academics, who rotated the role among them. Now it, like most other departments in the university, is controlled by a manager brought in specifically to run the budget. Mary has somehow adopted the air of an academic, perhaps hoping this will make us trust her. But she doesn't really know much about academic life, and I often overhear Yvonne filling her in on what sort of things the academics traditionally do.

Mary looks pissed off. "So who is here?"

"Max is in. Oh hello, Ariel. Ariel's in."

Mary and I both know that my being here is of importance to nobody. I'm teaching one evening class this term and that's it. I don't have any admin responsibilities and I am not a member of any committees. I'm simply a Ph.D. student, and I don't even have a supervisor anymore. So I'm surprised when Mary looks at me as if I'm someone she needs to see.

"Ah, Ariel," she says. "My office, if you've got a moment."

I wait for her to walk past me into the corridor and then I follow her around the corner to her office. She unlocks the door and holds it open for me while I walk in. I don't think I've ever actually been in Mary's office before. She's got two of what they call the "comfortable" chairs set up facing a low, pale coffee table, so I sit at one of these and she sits at the other. I'm glad the days of having to face your boss across a desk are over. You can't do that kind of thing with computers in the way. Everyone faces walls or screens in offices now.

Mary doesn't say anything.

"Did you have a nice weekend?" I ask her.

"What? Oh, yes, thanks. Now." She goes silent again, but I assume that she's about to say whatever it is, so I don't attempt any more small talk. "Now," she says again. "You're in quite a big office on your own, aren't you?"

Damn. I knew this would come up one day.

"It's Saul Burlem's office," I say. "I've just got a corner of it, really."

This is a lie. Once Burlem had been gone for a couple of months, I cleared the surface of his desk, moved his computer to the coffee table, and made myself a large L-shaped arrangement out of his desk and mine. I've filled all the shelf space with my books, in case I ever have to do a runner from the flat in town, and generally populated the office with moldy coffee cups and all my research notes. I have a whole drawer full of things I believe might come in useful one day. There are three small bars of bitter chocolate, a Phillips screwdriver, a flathead screwdriver, a socket set, a spanner, a pair of binoculars, some random pieces of metal, several plastic bags, and, most worryingly, a vibrator that Patrick sent me through the internal post as a risqué present.

"Well, it's quite clear that Saul isn't coming back to us for the foreseeable future, so that means that a large portion of your space is unused?"

I can't do anything else but agree with this, at least as a theory.

"Right," says Mary. "Look. All heads of department have agreed to provide temporary office accommodation for the members of staff who have had to leave the Newton Building. It's going to be a squash for most of us but still, it has to be done. We've agreed to take four. Two are going to share the Interview Room, and two are going to come in with you. OK?"

"OK," I say. But I must look horrified. I love my office. It's the only really warm and comfortable space I've got in the whole world.

"Come on, Ariel, I'm not asking you to leave your office or anything like that. Just to share it for a while. You'd be sharing it anyway if Saul was around."

"I know. Don't worry. I'm not complaining or—"

"And we all have a responsibility for refugees."

"Yes, I know. As I said, it's fine." I bite my lip. "So . . . Who are they? Do we know yet? I mean, do I know who I'm going to be sharing with?"

"Well." Mary gets up and picks up a sheet of paper from her desk. "You can choose, if you want. There's . . . Let's see. There's a theology lecturer, a postdoctoral fellow in evolutionary biology, a professor of bacteriology, and an administrative assistant."

Well, I'm not having a bacteriologist in my office, although he or she would probably find a lot in there to study. And I fear an admin assistant might take the same view of my office as a bacteriologist.

"Um," I say. "Can I have the theology person and the evolutionary biologist?"

Mary writes something on her sheet of paper and smiles at me. "There. That's not so bad, is it?"

I leave Mary's office, wondering if she speaks to everyone as if they are children. I do try to like her, but she makes it difficult. I think she's been to some management training that tells you how to "empower" staff and let them feel that they've made the terrible decision that, after all, they're going to have to live with. Oh well. I still haven't even checked my post, so I go into the office to do that.

Yvonne already knows about the new office arrangements.

"I'll come down later and help arrange the desks," she says to me. "And Roger will be in with another desk as well, and some more shelving. We're going to put Professor Burlem's computer into storage, and any bits and pieces from his desk, so if you could maybe start sorting those out . . . ?"

There is no post for me, in the end.

When's "later"? Whenever it is, it leaves me less time to get into Burlem's computer than I'd thought, especially now they're going to put it in storage. I lift it back up onto the desk and plug it in and switch it on. This won't be the first time I've tried to get into it, although the first time was really just a halfhearted attempt to see if there was any clue to where he'd gone. Then, as now, I was confronted with the log-in screen that asks for your user name and password. I know his user name: It's sabu2. But I have no way of knowing his password. The last time I did this I pretended I was in a film and confidently typed in several guesses before realizing that it was a stupid idea. This time I am going to use a more sophisticated hacking technique. And I learned in a book last year that the most sophisticated hacking technique doesn't involve guesses, algorithms, logarithms, dictionary files, or letter-scrambling software. The most sophisticated hacking technique is where you simply convince someone to give you the password.

Who knows our passwords? Computing Services definitely do, but does Yvonne? I think for a minute. Yvonne can't have our passwords, but what if she needed to get one for some reason? Presumably she'd just get in touch with Computing Services. It can't be that big a deal: Everything here officially belongs to the university anyway, including all the files on our computers. And Burlem has disappeared, so . . . Could I just ring up Computing Services and pretend to be Yvonne? Probably not. She probably rings them all the time. They'll know her voice. Um. I think for a minute; then I run my fingers through my tangled hair a couple of times, set my expression to "very worried," and go back upstairs.

"Ah," I say, as soon as I walk in. "Yvonne?"

She's drinking tea. "Yes, Ariel? What can I do for you?"

"Um, I'm having a bit of a problem. A huge problem, actually, and I don't quite know what to do about it."

"Oh. Anything I can help with?"

"I don't know." I frown, and look down at the brown carpet. "I think it might be hopeless, actually. But . . ." I sigh, and run my fingers through my hair again. "Well, you know how Saul's computer is going into storage later on today?"

"Yes?"

"Well it's got a document on it that I need, and I don't know how to get it. I don't think I can. Saul's not here, and I don't have the password anymore. I used to have it, of course, but I've forgotten it and . . . Oh. How can I explain this? Basically there's this anthology that someone at Warwick's putting together, and I was supposed to finish the, er, bibliography for Saul and e-mail the document over to them. It doesn't have to be there for another month, which is why I wasn't too worried about it. But I was just starting to pack the things away for storage, like you asked, and then it just came to me." I shrug. "I suppose I really need some sort of miracle or something. I don't suppose you'd know how to get a document from a computer with no password, would you? I mean, you're not by any chance an experienced hacker in your spare time?" I laugh. As if any of us would ever hack into a computer.

Yvonne sips her tea. "Well, you have got a problem, haven't you?"

"I know. I think I was just putting the whole thing off until I could just get in touch with Saul. I thought maybe he'd get in contact nearer the deadline, but of course he won't know that his computer's going to go into storage and . . . God. Sorry to bother you with this, but I thought if anyone would know what to do it would be you."

I'm being careful not to mention the word "password" too much. I have a feeling that if I make this the problem it will sound a lot more dodgy than simply "I need a document and I don't know how to get it." And I think joking about hacking helps, but it is a risk.

"Have you tried Computing Services?" she asks.

"Not yet. I just thought they'd basically tell me to go away. I mean to them I could be anybody. And it is a bit of a weird thing to ask for. I mean, obviously you understand, but I'm not sure they would."

"Do you want me to give them a call?"

"Oh, would you? Thanks so much, Yvonne."

"I'll authorize the new password request and get one of them over to sort it all out for you. When Professor Burlem comes back he'll need to set a new password, but his old one will have expired, anyway. I don't know when they'll be able to get over to you, but do you want to let me know when they've been and we'll come and do the desks then?"

By twelve o'clock the technician still hasn't come and I'm beginning to feel hungry. If I could get hold of a bread roll I could make a chocolate sandwich (which wouldn't be the worst lunch I've ever had) but who knows if the canteen is even open. I try to open the university Web site so I can log on to the Intranet and see which of the various restaurants and cafeterias are open, but all I get is an Error 404 message instead of the front page. No wonder no one's here. Anyone who'd logged on to the university site to see whether it was open again would surely have feared the worst from this. I sigh. Even chocolate on its own wouldn't be the worst lunch I've ever had—in fact, it's practically gourmet—but some bread to go with it would be great, and the rolls in the canteen are only ten pence. I write a note for my door and pin it up. BACK IN FIVE MINUTES. I just hope he doesn't come and go away again.

The Russell Building is, like the Stevenson Building on the west of the campus, built in the shape of a four-petalled cyber-flower with a small set of cloisters in the middle. I haven't spent much time in the Stevenson Building, because the students all say that it is exactly the same as the Russell Building but "the other way around," which sounds impossibly confusing, especially considering that the Russell Building is confusing enough on its own. I only seem to get lost in the Russell Building at the beginning of the academic year, when all the new students are around and everybody seems confused, and it's as if the confusion leaks out of everyone's minds and infects everyone else.

Now I go out of the English Building through the side door, and under the walkway that leads to one of the Russell side doors. I go up some concrete steps, and then down some more, until I come to the mouth of a long, white corridor with a worn tiled floor and white-washed walls. When the students are around this space seems almost normal but now it feels like the medical wing of an abandoned 1960s space station, or someone's idea of one. They keep broken university furniture in one of the rooms along here. I can hear my footsteps as I walk, and for the first time ever I get the sensation that there could be no one in the whole building apart from me.

The tables in the dining hall are laid out in a geometric pattern that seems accidental until you go up to the Senior Common Room and look down. From up there you realize that the long tables all point towards the cathedral, which is itself framed in the large windows at the back of the hall. It all makes sense, from up there, the whole thing, and you feel as if you are part of one picture, and nothing on the per-fect line joining you with the cathedral really exists. You're in the dark, and the cathedral is framed in a rectangle of light. One time I had to go into this dingy room off Reception to search the slide projectors for a transparency I'd left behind after a seminar, because this librarian was basically going to kneecap me if I didn't get it back. As well as my slide (*The Runner* by Vittorio Corona) I found another one in the box: It showed the cover of Baudrillard's *The Illusion of the End*. On the way down to the canteen I held it up in the only light available: the win-dow at the back of the hall, and that's when I saw what it was. The slide was all melted on the back but not the image: The image was perfect. But when I tried to pick out some of the detail I realized I was looking at the cathedral through the slide, and the two images became one. After that I fell in love with the slide and took it back to my office and tried to find a way of projecting it onto my wall. But I couldn't work it out and I don't know where the slide is now. I read more Baudrillard after that.

Today the tables are there in their usual formation but there are no jugs of water and no people and the whole thing is, as I had feared, closed. I could go to one of the other buildings but it seems pointless for a bread roll, so I walk back to my room and eat two bars of chocolate on their own. Then I have a coffee and a cigarette and settle down to wait for the technician. I try not to feel sad that this is possibly my last day alone in my office, but it is difficult. I suppose I won't be able to talk to myself in here anymore, or smoke out of the window, or fall asleep under the second desk. Will the new people want the blind set at a different angle? Will they want to bring potted plants? It's all too much to think about.

To pass the time, I open up the Internet browser on my machine and do a search for the word *Troposphere*. I don't expect anything to come up but then I find out that it does exist. It's a part of Earth's atmosphere: the place where most weather takes place. Could Lumas have missed that? I assumed the word was made up. I do the search on the OED instead, and find that the earliest use of the word was in 1914. So Lumas invented it first, but no one took any notice. But then why would they? It's only a novel, after all. After I've read the whole entry I do a search for *The End of Mr. Y,* just to see if there's any information online that I haven't seen before.

When you search for *The End of Mr. Y* on the Internet, you usually get three links. One is an old abstract of the paper Burlem gave at the Greenwich conference. Another is a thread from a discussion board on a rare books site, where someone has left a request for the book and no one has replied. The third is a little more mysterious. It's basically a fan site, with a black background and some Gothic flourishes, and as far as I know it used to have quite a lot of information on the book. There was a page on the curse, and another page speculating about why there are almost no copies left in the world. The author of the

Web site seemed to have concocted a conspiracy theory that the U.S. government had tracked down and destroyed all the known copies, including the one in the German bank vault (which, according to this guy, had once belonged to Hitler). He didn't say why this would be so, but hinted at some powerful secret that no one knew. I think the real story is simply that there were not very many copies of the book printed in the first place, and when a book has over a hundred years to fall into obscurity, it's pretty easy for it to simply disappear. Anyway, about six months ago, or maybe a bit more, the Web site closed down. I check it today and it's the same as it was last time I looked at it. There's no error message or anything, but the front page simply says, "They shut me up and I went away."

Today I am intrigued to see that there's a fourth link to a page containing a reference to *The End of Mr. Y.* It's a blog called "Some Days of My Life," and when I click on the link I am taken to a pink and white screen with various journal entries. I scan up and down but can't see the reference. I use Find instead and then I see it. It's the entry for last Friday.

> Had to work in the bookshop again today (thanks a lot, Sam) despite humungous hangover. Spent the day dusting books which was oddly therapeutic. Had no customers apart from this student who came in and paid fifty quid for a book called "The End of Mr. Y," which I've never heard of but must be pretty rare. Maybe I'll go into the secondhand book business. How about it, Sam? We could be partners and give up crappy college and make fortunes out of people who are prepared to pay £££ for old books. How hard can it be?

There's a knock at the door and I immediately close down the browser.

It's the technician. "Ariel Manto?" he says, looking at a piece of paper.

"Yes," I say.

"Come to set a new password," he says.

"Oh, yes. Great," I say. "It's this machine over here."

I try to absorb myself in something else while he tinkers around with the system, thinking that the less fuss I make about it the less suspicious the whole thing will seem. So I don't try to explain or justify why I need the new password on the machine; I just let him get on with his job while I make a start typing up my notes on *Mr. Y.* Ideally, I'd like to write a whole chapter on *The End of Mr. Y* for my thesis. It would be easy enough to write, considering my obsession with the book, but it would also make a great article or conference paper on its own. The only problem is that I'm not sure in what way I could argue that it is a thought experiment.

Thought experiments or, in German, *gedankenexperiments*, are experiments that, for whatever reason, cannot be physically carried out, but must instead be conducted internally, via logic and reasoning, in the mind. There have been ethical and philosophical thought experiments for hundreds, if not thousands, of years, but it was when people began using these experiments in a scientific context that they were first given the title "thought experiment," a literal translation of *gedankenexperiment*, although Lumas had always referred to them as "experiments of the mind." The luminiferous ether is the result of a thought experiment of sorts, which postulated that, if light is a wave, then it has to be a wave *in* something. You can't have a wave in water with no water—so where was light's "fluid"? So people invented the luminiferous ether as an answer, only to discard it again when the Michelson Morley experiment proved that, sadly, there was no ether.

Edgar Allan Poe used the principles of the thought experiment to solve the Olbers's Paradox, and, some people believe, to more or less invent big bang theory a good hundred years before anyone else. His "prose poem" "Eureka" sets out his various scientific and cosmological thoughts, but Poe was no experimental scientist and so these theories came in the form of thought experiments, or, perhaps, something close to the way he described infinity, as the "thought of a thought." His Olbers's Paradox solution is one of the most elegant thought experiments in history. In 1823, Wilhelm Olbers wondered why we see stars the way we do in the night sky. At the time, most people believed the universe to be infinite and eternal. So if the sky was infinite, surely it would contain an infinite number of stars? And if there were an infinite number of stars, then our night sky should be white, not black. Olbers thought it was all down to dust clouds, and wrote, "How fortunate that the Earth does not receive starlight from every point of the celestial vault!" Edgar Allan Poe thought this through and decided that a simpler and more plausible solution for the "voids which our telescopes find in innumerable directions" was that some of the stars were simply so far away that the light hadn't had time to reach us yet.

Perhaps the most famous thought experiment in history is when Einstein wondered what would happen if he could catch up with a beam of light. Einstein worked out that if he could travel at the speed of light then, logically, he would see the beam of light as if it were motionless, just as if you are in a train going at the same speed as another train moving alongside you, you see the people inside it as if they are not moving. So, what would light look like if it seemed to be at rest? Would it look like a frozen yellow wave? A paint spatter of particles? And what if you could look at yourself in the mirror while travelling at the speed of light? You'd seem invisible. Maybe you'd even *be* invisible. Einstein realized that there could be no such thing as an electromagnetic field that stood still. Maxwell's equations, which seemed to imply that you could, in theory, catch up with a beam of light, also showed that light was not something that could be stationary. So one of those points had to be wrong. It would be interesting if it was the other one, and you could catch up to light *and* see it frozen, but, for various reasons that I need more physics lectures to understand, it isn't. Einstein's theory of special relativity states that no matter how fast you go, light is always travelling relative to you at c, the speed of light. It doesn't matter if you're travelling at one mile an hour or a thousand miles an hour. The light you see around you is always going faster than you, and it's always going at c. If you were travelling at half the speed of light, it wouldn't seem to you that light going in your direction was therefore travelling half as fast. It would still appear to be going at the speed of light, c, relative to you.

"Let us suppose our old friend the railway carriage to be travelling along the rails with a constant velocity, v," says Einstein in his book *Relativity*. He then goes on to explain that if you walked along the carriage in the direction of travel, you'd be going not at the speed of the train, nor at the speed you were walking, but at the sum of the two. If the train was going at one hundred miles an hour, and you were going at one mile an hour, you'd actually be moving forwards at a velocity of one hundred and one miles per hour, relative to the embankment you were passing. Similarly, if I were to drive on the motorway alongside the railway line at, say, eighty-five miles per hour and this train passed me, it would appear to me to be going at fifteen miles per hour relative to me; and you, walking inside it, would seem to be going at sixteen miles per hour. If you looked out of the train and saw me driving along, I would appear to be going backwards. All this is Newtonian relative velocity and it does not apply to light.

Einstein's equations, the end result of his original thought experiments, show that matter and energy are different manifestations of the same thing, and that if you tried to approach the speed of light you'd just become heavier the closer you got as your energy converted to mass. He also showed that space and time are essentially the same. For Lumas, the fourth dimension was a space containing beings, or, at least, thought. For H. G. Wells it was a greenish otherworld containing spirits. For Zollner it was a place full of phantoms who seemed to like nothing better than helping out magicians. But for Einstein, it wasn't a place at all. But it wasn't simply time, either. It was the fourth dimension of space-time: not just the clock, but the clock ticking on your wall, relative to you.

The technician clears his throat. "Almost there," he says.

"Great. Thanks," I say back.

Sometimes I wonder what it would have been like to be Einstein, sitting in a stuffy patent office looking out at the trains and the railway track. There's something romantic about it, of course, in the way only other people's lives can be. I briefly look up from my notes and out of my big, steel-framed window. Something comes to me, suddenly, some weird Lumas connection, and I look back down at my notes. I write:

> Metaphor (as in Lumas preface) . . . Trope . . . (Troposphere!—weird) Ways of thinking about the world. You can't use trains as metaphors if there are no trains. Cf. différance. Can a thought exist without the language with which to have the thought? How does language (or metaphor) influence the thought? Cf. *Poetics*. If there was no evening no one would think it was like old age.

"All right," says the technician. "All set. If you just want to come over here and type in the new password . . ,"

He gets up and moves to the other side of the room while I sit there and try to think of something. I should just use my own password; that would be simple. A few possible words go through my mind. But something makes me calmly type *hacker* into the box. It comes up as six little stars and I hit OK and then tell the technician I'm done. He comes over and does a couple more things and then restarts the machine.

"All done," he says, and leaves.

I have moved the mouse about a millimeter across the desktop when the phone rings. It's Yvonne.

"Has that technician been yet?" she asks.

"Yeah," I say. "He's just gone."

"You got your document all right then?"

"Er . . . No. Not yet. I've literally only just logged in."

"All right, well, you sort it out and I'll be down in ten minutes to do the desks. Roger's here now, but I'll just give him a cup of tea and we'll hang on for a bit. You're all right to wait ten minutes or so, aren't you, Roger?" I can hear a muffled "Yeah, if there's a biscuit as well" in the background. "OK, Ariel, see you soon."

Ten minutes. Shit. I'm not going to be able to investigate Burlem's machine in ten minutes. OK: plan B. I take my iPod out of my bag and connect it to the back of Burlem's machine. I pray (to what? to whom?) that it won't reject the connection, and in a couple of seconds it's appeared as the F Drive. Fantastic. Now all I need to do is transfer the contents of Burlem's "My Documents" folder over and . . . There. That took about twenty seconds. Would he have hidden any information anywhere else on the machine? I metaphorically poke around for a bit but a few clicks on folders tells me that he doesn't use anything apart from "My Documents" for his files. I'm not completely satisfied, but that will have to do. I double-check that the files have copied OK; then I unplug my iPod and shut the machine down just before a knock on my door tells me that Yvonne has arrived.

Chapter Eight

Yvonne is upset about the number of books in the room.

"What do you think, Roger?" she asks.

"Well," he says. "You're not going to fit any more shelves in here."

"No. That's what I thought."

While they're having this conversation, I'm clearing out Burlem's desk drawers, something I should have done much earlier. I've already filed a few loose documents relating to his Literature and Science course, and now I'm on to the general debris. There's a teaspoon, presumably stolen from the kitchen, which I hide before Yvonne can see it. There's a bag of filter coffee, unopened, which I also hide, thinking something along the lines of "finders keepers" but also that Burlem probably wouldn't mind me having his coffee in an emergency. But there's nothing else of interest in Burlem's drawers: just lots of pencils and board pens. Oh! And an electric pencil sharpener. I'm having that as well.

"What do you think, Ariel?" says Yvonne.

"Sorry?" I say. I've been so carried away with looting Burlem's drawers that I've somehow managed to tune them both out.

"We're just saying that Professor Burlem's books might as well go in storage, too. If I bring down some boxes, do you mind packing them up? We'll finish the rest tomorrow morning."

————

By four o'clock I've packed most of the books. Or, at least, I've packed most of the books that I think I won't ever want to use (mainly literature classics that I also have copies of, also in this room), and I am alarmed to see that they have only filled two of the five boxes I've been given. The shelf space they've left behind is minimal at best. I look again. There's no way I'm sending all Burlem's theory books into storage. I need all those. And the Literature and Science textbooks have to stay because I'm teaching the course in a couple of weeks' time. What about the nineteenth-century science books? I suppose I do have a lot of them at home. Shit. What am I going to do?

While I'm contemplating the situation further, the phone rings.

"So . . ." It's Patrick.

"So." I say back, playing along.

"Guess what I've got?"

"What have you got?"

"Keys."

"To?"

"The Russell study bedrooms. So I was thinking . . ."

I laugh nervously. He wants to fuck on campus. That's new. There's something in his voice I haven't come across before. He sounds bitter, as if he was angry a while ago but now he's resigned to whatever it is.

"Patrick," I say, as though I'm about to explain to a kid that you shouldn't play with matches. "What if . . . ?"

"There's no one around," he says. "Why don't you bring that thing I sent you?"

Can I tell him I've got to pack boxes instead? Probably not. What about investigating Burlem's computer files? I open my desk drawer and look down at the object he wants me to bring. And then that's it. Desire bites me hard and I feel its warm poison creep through my body. I ignore the fact that Patrick's voice is weird, and that this is a stupid idea, and, after agreeing to meet him in a remote corner of the Russell Building, I pick up my bag and go over there, looking behind me a couple of times in case anyone is watching. I'll do the boxes later. And how long can this take? A quick fuck might be just the thing to break up the afternoon. And other people have tea breaks, don't they?

Afterwards, at six o'clock, still sitting in the small, slightly sordid room after Patrick has left, I wonder if the reason I tend to say yes to everything is because I deeply believe that I can survive anything, but I'm still looking for the definitive proof. It turned out that Patrick's voice was odd because his wife is in the process of leaving him—not because she found out about me, but because she has fallen in love with one of her toy boys. Patrick had been angry; that was clear. And it wasn't as if he'd called me up so he could take it out on me—he's usually a nice guy. But once we were in the room his fantasy world somehow collided with the violence and anger he'd built up in the real world and made everything more intense, more desperate, and a lot darker than usual. Had he known that this was the turn it would take? He'd asked me to bring the vibrator he'd sent, after all. But he'd also brought rope (not the usual silk scarves). But surely he hadn't meant to go as far as he did? Did he want me to tell him to stop? I don't know why I didn't. Except . . . I didn't tell him to stop because I didn't want him to stop, because, well, maybe I like the darkness and violence, too. Maybe I need darkness and violence like food, like cigarettes. Maybe . . . Maybe I should stop thinking about this.

After a couple more minutes I leave the room and, after walking down a dingy hallway with posters telling the students not to leave their windows open because pigeons fly in and lay eggs, I descend the steep staircase to the main part of the building. I walk through the white corridor under the white lights only to find the side door won't open. They don't usually lock it this early. Shit. I kick it a couple of times but it definitely is locked, so I have to walk all the way around again, my eyes moving nervously like a thief's, knowing that if I bump into anyone now it will look odd, and I can't even claim to have been to the vending machines because I'm not carrying any sweets or crisps. Am I walking strangely? After what I've just done it wouldn't be surprising. But the porter just nods at me as I escape through the main entrance and I glance blankly back at him. Back in the English Building I go and make coffee in the small, deserted kitchen, and then I take it down to my office, first ignoring the fact that I am now very hungry, and then deciding to eat the last chocolate bar.

I sit cross-legged on the floor for a while, just looking at the boxes while I drink my coffee and eat the chocolate. Then I examine the small rope burns on my wrists and ankles. There's something interesting about the grazed areas of flesh; something pleasingly symmetrical about them. But I probably won't see Patrick anymore. I'll do anything once for the experience, but that doesn't mean I'll necessarily do it again—even if at the time I enjoyed it. For a moment I think about Yvonne, who is probably at home now making tea for the kids in a bright kitchen with yellow lights everywhere and a dishwasher and a big TV ready to pump out brightness for the rest of the evening; I wonder at what point my life swerved to avoid that, and if that life would have been nicer than the one I've got.

It's dark outside the window as I start putting more books into boxes. They are dusty from being on the shelves for so long, and my hands are soon almost black with the grime from them. Ignoring this, I fill the first box with as many of Saul Burlem's nineteenth-century science books as I can bear to part with, although it takes a long time because I keep stopping to touch the pages, and to read the odd line here and there. I linger for longer than usual on *Transcendental Physics* by Professor Zollner. Burlem's copy of it is a small brown hardback from 1901. I randomly open it and read a short section about Kant, God, and the fourth dimension, which is opposite a picture of some knots. Another plate, farther on, shows a small, freestanding table, with a wide, solid top and bottom, with two solid wooden loops encircling its thin single stem. It's clear that if the table and loops are both solid wood, the loops would have had to have always been there; but they haven't been. They've been conjured onto it somehow. I turn the page and read about the strange lights and the smell of sulphuric acid that preceded these loops being placed onto the leg by unseen, possibly higher-dimensional forces.

Somehow I manage to clear one whole bookcase via this method of selecting a book, reading a bit, then, slightly sadly, placing it in the box. After that, I try to arrange all my books, plus the ones I'm "borrowing," onto one bookcase, but they won't fit. I look again at

Burlem's books. If I boxed up his four volumes of the 1801 edition of *Zoonomia*, Erasmus Darwin's book, that would leave a bit more space, especially if I boxed up some of his Aristotle as well. But *Zoonomia* is one of my favorite of his books, and one I was definitely planning to use for the Ph.D. Except . . . Actually, I won't be using it anymore, since Burlem persuaded me not to include it. I remember his words. *Forget about* Mr. Y. *And forget about* Zoonomia, *as well*. He said 1801 was too early and that I should stick within my time frame. Well, I suppose if I change my mind there is a copy in the library. So they're going in the box. I have to stand on a chair to reach them and I try not to get too absorbed with touching their wide green spines, then opening them and running my fingers over the thick, pulpy rag paper that still seems to contains tiny bits of tree. Perhaps it's because it's the end of a strange day, or because my arms are tired, but I'm not as careful with the books as I usually would be, and the thick pages flap about as I lift each volume off the shelf. In fact, the volumes don't seem to be in the best condition, because as I take Volume IV down, one of its pages actually falls out and flutters down onto the carpet like a leaf.

When I get down off the chair and pick up the page, I see that it isn't the right size, or thickness, for *Zoonomia*. It doesn't have that blotting paper feel, or the thick black type with the long letter *s* that looks like an *f.* In fact, I realize, it's not a page of *Zoonomia* at all. The small, thin typescript is familiar to me, however, as is, in some unconscious way, the jaggedness of the tear in its edge. It also has a very faint crease: the result of having once been folded into four. This isn't a page that's simply fallen out of *Zoonomia*. This is the missing page from *The End of Mr. Y.*

For about five whole minutes I just stand there looking at it; not reading the words, just touching the paper and allowing the circuit in my mind to be completed. The book was Burlem's. The whole box of books from the shop was Burlem's. And it was Burlem who, for some reason, tore out this page and hid it. It must have been him. He must have left the page here. No one else has a key to this room except me, and if someone else had taken the page out of the book, surely they'd have hidden it in their own things, not in Burlem's. And I don't actually know anyone else who has ever even heard of *The End of Mr. Y*, except Burlem. But why would he hide a page of a book? And how on earth did the rest of the book end up in an auction? I can't work out how all these things could possibly fit together. Apart from anything else, the book would have been so valuable whole that it must have taken something mind-boggling to make him remove a page. And why not simply put the whole book on the shelf?

Forget about Mr. Y. Sorry, Burlem. That's not going to be possible now.

And, I now wonder, did he really want me to forget? He connected these two things: *Mr. Y* and *Zoonomia*, because he knew he'd left the page there. He connected them in language long before I connected them in the real world.

I can't read the page here, although it is difficult to stop myself. Instead, I tuck it carefully inside the Zollner book, which I've decided to take home with me, and, as quickly as I can, I finish packing the boxes and leave.

An hour later, after a cold, dark walk down the hill, I sit down on my sofa in the kitchen with a large cup of coffee. This feels like a ritual, but perhaps it should be a ritual. I never thought I'd read *The End of Mr. Y,* and then I found a copy of it in what appeared to be the most improbable circumstances. I never thought I'd find the missing page, but now here it is. And every one of these events is connected. But not by luck: It's pure cause and effect. The only piece of luck involved in all of this was the university starting to collapse and creating the cracks of chaos out of which these things could emerge. Of course, I still have no idea of what happened to Burlem, but I know that whatever happened to him is the real cause for what's happening to me now. Why did he disappear? It must have been something very bad if whatever it was meant that his most precious book ended up in a box in an auction. And the books in the box are definitely his: I flicked through them as soon as I got in and found some marginal notes in his pointy, up-and-down handwriting that proved it. I take a big gulp of coffee and, as a train clatters underneath my window, I read the first line on page 131, the remainder of the broken-off line on page 130.

the darkened room with its single lamp. I bade him good evening.

'Good evening to you, Mr. Y,' said he, a cold smile spreading itself thinly across his face. 'Shall we immediately begin this business? I trust you have the money?'

I reached down and withdrew the money from my shoe, almost losing my balance as I did so. This had the effect of thinning the doctor's smile yet further.

'I must say your purse is a little queer, Mr. Y.'

'This is all the money I have,' I told him. 'I was not about to allow it to be stolen.'

'Indeed not,' he replied.

Presently he motioned for me to sit down at the table, and he took the opposite side, as if a consultation were about to take place. I handed the money to him and felt a profound sense of emptiness puncture my soul. Would this fellow even give me what I wanted? I have to confess that at that moment I half believed that the next thing I would see would be a puff of smoke, and then the trick would be complete. However, there was no puff of smoke and the doctor continued to regard me across the table.

'I have transcribed the recipe for you,' he said. 'It is quite simple and requires no special preparation. The ingredients are common, as you will see.'

I realised then that he was holding in his left hand a sheet of tattered blue note-paper. There was the information I had been searching for all this time! I did not understand why this man was sitting there in this pose, simply holding on to this knowledge, this most precious thing. Why did he not simply give me what I had paid for? All at once I felt some demon seize possession of me, and I was overcome by an urge to reach across the table and rip the paper from his hand. I confess that

I further imagined wrestling him to the ground and taking back my money. Yet all this only happened in my mind, and in reality I did nothing but sit there meekly awaiting my prescription.

'This mixture,' I said. 'It will have the same effect as . . . ?'

'You wish to know if the mixture will enable you to telepath?'

'Yes,' said I. 'If that is indeed what took place in Nottingham.'

The doctor's thin smile returned.

'This mixture will most certainly enable you to telepath, if that is all you require of it.'

'If that is all I require? What in heaven do you mean?'

'The mixture will take you on many curious journeys, Mr. Y, I can assure you of that.' For a second or two the doctor looked as if he might continue in this portentous vein, but then something queer seemed to happen to him. His whole body appeared to grow limp, like a marionette placed in a cupboard after a performance, and for a full minute he did not move ; nor did he say anything else. When he did come back to life it was with a little jerk, as if someone had once again taken hold of his strings. He looked at the piece of note-paper in his hand as if puzzled by it and then, without saying anything else, he handed it to me.

I had only the merest opportunity to glance at my treasure before he rapped the table twice with the knuckles of his left hand and made to stand up.

'Well, then, good evening, Mr. Y. You have what you came for.'

I hesitated, understanding that this would be my only chance to ask the question that so burned on my lips.

'Before I leave,' I said, 'I have one question to ask of you.'

The doctor lifted one eyebrow in response but said nothing.

'I wish to know how many other people have this recipe,' I said.

'You wish to know how valuable is this knowledge you hold in your hand,' said the doctor. 'You wish to know how much power you now possess, and how it has been potentially diluted among the rest of the population. Well, I can answer your question quite easily. You are the only person to whom I have sold this recipe. Not everyone is as willing as you were to lie in a tent and imbibe a stranger's medicinal concoction simply for the purpose of knowledge. For pain relief, this is common. For pleasure, also. But you can rest assured, sir, that you are my only customer to date.'

I had more questions, but the doctor made it quite clear to me that our business was concluded and I walked out into the cold, murky hallway. In a parlour on my right I saw a child trying to light a fire. The result of this was a low, persistent, hissing noise and enough smoke to make my eyes sting. When I was certain that no one was looking, I rubbed the grime from my eyes and briefly examined the document in my hand. It only contained four lines, written in an untutored, unorthodox hand, in pale violet ink.

Make the tincture in the following way—:
Combine one part Carbo Vegetabilis, that is, vegetable charcoal, in
the 1000th centesimal homoeopathic potency, with 99 parts holy
water in a glass retort or flask and succuss the mixture ten times.

FD 1893

Then I slipped the blue paper into my shoe and made my way for the door.

I finish reading the missing page of *The End of Mr. Y* with a dry mouth and my heart beating as if it's trying to get out. I just can't believe it. I immediately reread the page, trying to re-create the sensation I felt when I got to the recipe, rather in the same way you queue up to take a fairground ride that has just terrified and excited you. But it doesn't quite work in that way. This isn't a ride you can take again but one, I am guessing, that is simply impossible to get off. And then I find that I can't sit down anymore. I get up and pace the room, feeling as though I should do something bigger, much bigger, to express the emotion I feel, but not knowing what that would be. Laughter? Tears? My brain is hysterical but I don't do anything to show it in the end; I just pace and smoke and think. I think about the strange preface, and all the hints that *The End of Mr. Y* contains something real. I think about the trouble someone, probably Burlem, has taken to conceal this page, which contains nothing of any interest apart from the instructions for making up the tincture. I think of Lumas's strange allusions to telepathy, and I remember this section about the "automaton of mind."

As Robert-Houdin has built automata with which to produce his illusions, I shall here propose to create an automaton of mind, through which one may see illusions and realities beyond; from which one, if he knows how, may spring into the automata of all minds and their electricity.

And when I'm certain that I understand why the page is important, and the potential reason it was hidden, I sit down and finish the rest of the book, distracted by my own desire to find the ingredients and make up some of this tincture for myself.

Part Two

The matters of which man is cognizant escape the senses in gradation. We have, for example, a metal, a piece of wood, a drop of water, the atmosphere, a gas, caloric, electricity, the luminiferous ether. Now, we call all these things matter, and embrace all matter in one general definition; but in spite of this, there can be no two ideas more essentially distinct than that which we attach to a metal, and that which we attach to the luminiferous ether. When we reach the latter, we feel an almost irresistible inclination to class it with spirit, or with nihility. The only consideration which restrains us is our conception of its atomic constitution; and here, even, we have to seek aid from our notion of an atom, as something possessing in infinite minuteness, solidity, palpability, weight. Destroy the idea of the atomic constitution and we should no longer be able to regard the ether as an entity, or, at least, as matter. For want of a better word we might term it spirit. Take, now, a step beyond the luminiferous ether—conceive a matter as much more rare than the ether, as this ether is more rare than the metal, and we arrive at once (in spite of all the school dogmas) at a unique mass—an unparticled matter. For although we may admit infinite littleness in the atoms themselves, the infinitude of littleness in the spaces between them is an absurdity.

Edgar Allan Poe, *The Mesmeric Revelation*

As material things prove all to be connected and parts of one thing; as the pebble at our feet and the most remote and profitless fixed star are still united, so "Does it rain, my dear?" and the most dreary metaphysical enquiry are still closely connected.

Samuel Butler, *Note-books*

Chapter Nine

You look in the mirror and this time it tells you that yes, you are cursed.

The sun is only just rising by the time I get to the university library on Tuesday morning, about five minutes before it opens. I'm a little mind-numbed by the experience of walking up the hill in the weak gray light, smothered by the winter sky and my own breath, which is itself a winter sky in miniature. For the first time ever I walked along listening to my iPod, and the music I felt most fitted this experience of walking up a hill at dawn, on my first day as someone who may be cursed, was Handel's *Dixit Dominus*, the same piece that was playing the night I met Burlem in Greenwich. I both love and hate this piece of music, and while it plays it feels as though it's something that's crawling on me, on the inside and the outside surfaces of my skin.

Patrick may think I am tremendously postmodern because I have an iPod, but I still prefer libraries to the Internet when it comes to research. And although I know what holy water is, and where I am likely to get some, I have no idea about the other ingredient in Mr. Y's recipe: Carbo Vegetabilis (or vegetable charcoal). Well, OK, I understand that vegetable charcoal implies burnt wood or vegetation, but what is a homoeopathic potency? I guess the Internet probably would tell me this quickly, but it may not tell me accurately. I also need to know what a nineteenth-century writer would have meant by it: Who knows; the term may not be in existence anymore, or it might mean something different now. Look at how the word "atom" has changed over the centuries. I have definitely decided that I am going to make this tincture and try it out. Even though this morning I was slashed into consciousness by that jagged honesty you sometimes get when you wake up, and something inside me told me to stop. But why should I? And it's not as if this mixture can do me any harm. Charcoal isn't poisonous, and neither is water. And it seems to me that this recipe is a part of the book, and that, for whatever reason, Lumas intended the reader to try it out.

The History of Medicine section of the library turns out to be on the fourth floor, beyond the religion and philosophy books, in a little corner by some stairs. There is a whole section on homoeopathy: lots of aged hardbacks with muted binding in dark green, dark red, and gray. I pick up a thick green book and see the title, *Kent's Repertory*, and the publication date, 1897. I sit cross-legged on the faded carpet and flick through it, intrigued by the odd format that I don't understand. The book seems to contain lists of symptoms, grouped under headings such as "Sleep," "Eyes," "Genitalia," and "Mind." I flick to the "Sleep" section and find a curious poetry there in a section entitled "Dreams." I read down the page and see one-word, or occasionally, one-sentence entries saying things like *serpents, sexual, shameful, shooting, skeletons, smelling sulphur* and, farther down, *stars falling, stealing fruit*, and *struck by lightning, that he was*. After each small piece of text are letters I don't understand, but that look like abbreviations. Under the entry "dreams, snakes" there are a lot of these: Alum., *arg-n.*, bov., grat., iris., kali-c., *lac-c.*, ptel., *ran-s.*, rat., sep., sil., sol-n., spig., tab. I don't know why some of these are in italics, nor what the abbreviations mean.

I flick backwards in the book to the "Mind" section and, under "Delusions," find some very odd entries, including the delusions *alive on one side, dead on the other* and the more vague *fancy, illusions of.* In the "Genitalia, Male" section I find references to erections that can be "impetuous" or can only happen in the afternoon, or while coughing. I like this, but I don't understand it, so I close the heavy volume and browse some of the other books on the shelf. It's strange: I always thought homoeopathy was some kind of cranky herbalism, but looking at all these books makes me realize just how seriously some people must take it, or, more accurately, must have taken it around the turn of the century when most of these books were originally published. All the authors have very grand or strange names: Constantine Hering, MD; John Henry Clarke, MD; William Boericke, MD; and even some women, including Margaret Tyler, MD, and Dorothy Shepard, MD. They all have those letters after their names, implying that all the important people who practiced homoeopathy at that time were doctors. Eventually I have amassed a pile of books from 1880 until the early 1900s; I take these to a small table and start trying to understand it all.

After two hours' solid reading I go outside for a cigarette. The sky is now a uniform, artificial blue, and for a second it feels like something has been deleted from it. A gray squirrel runs along the grass in front of me, its sleek body rising and falling like a wave. My eyes follow it as it runs up a tree and disappears. Beyond the tree, and far down the hill, the small city shimmers in the false, low light. The cathedral dominates the view as usual, and in this light it looks sepia-yellow, like a JPEG of an old photograph. As I inhale smoke in the cold air I think about what I have learnt this morning. Homoeopathy seems to have been invented (or, perhaps, discovered) by Samuel Hahnemann in 1791. Hahnemann was a chemist who had written treatises on syphilis, and poisoning by arsenic. He was unhappy about contemporary medical practices, especially bloodletting. Hahnemann believed that King Leopold of Austria had essentially been murdered by his doctors, who had bled him four times in twenty-four hours to try to cure a high fever. While he was translating Cullen's *Materia Medica*, Hahnemann had an amazing moment of insight. Cullen said that cinchona bark cured malaria simply because it was bitter. But Hahnemann happened to know that poisoning by cinchona bark produced symptoms similar to those produced by malaria, including internal dropsy and emaciation. He realized that the thing that cured malaria also *caused* very similar symptoms. Could this be true in other cases of diseases and medicines? Could it be, he wondered, that like cures like?

This was his first eureka moment. It led, eventually, to the development of a whole new system of medicine with the motto: *Similia similibus curentur*—let likes be cured by likes. Hahnemann's second eureka moment was when he worked out that it is the small dose that cures. It's all very well giving someone some cinchona bark to cure their malaria, but since the bark is poisonous, it generally harmed the person as well. Curing poisoning with a poison didn't sound like a very sensible idea, so Hahnemann experimented with dilutions of cinchona bark, and found that you could dilute the crude substance quite a lot and still get a reaction. Later, the nineteenth-century homoeopaths worked out that the more dilute the dose, the more effective the medicine: Approach the infinitesimal, and you approach something very strange, and very powerful. Paradoxical, but there you are. Paradox never stopped the quantum physicists, or Einstein.

It's freezing out here, despite the blue sky, and as soon as I have put out my cigarette I go back into the library and up to the fourth floor to continue reading. I get the first book I looked at back off the shelf and reexamine it. I now understand that this is something in which homoeopathic physicians look up symptoms and find the common substance listed under all of them. Those funny little abbreviations relate to homoeopathic substances, it appears. Ars. is Arsenicum; bry. is Bryonia; carb-v. is Carbo Vegetabilis. Once I understand how the system works, I am tempted to start looking up all my own strange symptoms—waking early; craving salt, cigarettes, and alcohol; liking transgressive sex; preferring my own company to that of others—but I don't have time. My wrists and ankles have matching rope burns that glisten on my skin like little pieces of melted plastic. Should I try and find something to cure them? That might be quite quick. Maybe not, though. I almost like them.

I yawn and don't bother to cover my mouth: No one's been up here all morning. I still don't know what Carbo Vegetabilis is, nor what the thousandth potency might be, so I flick through the pile of books on the desk until I eventually find two helpful documents. One is a short biography of Dr. Thomas Skinner, a Scottish homoeopath who visited the United States in 1876 and developed something called the "centesimal fluxion machine" for making what the book describes as "potencies in excess of the thousandth." After a lot more flicking and reading I come across the next helpful document. It's a reproduction of a 1925 catalog entry from the Boericke & Tafel Homoeopathic Pharmacists of Philadelphia, and it explains, in great detail, exactly how homoeopathic medicines are (or were) made. The process sounds crazy. It seems that a substance (cinchona bark, arsenic, sulphur, snake venom, whatever) is steeped in "the finest spirits, made of sound grain," and then the medicine is made by taking one drop of this "mother tincture" and combining it with ninety-nine drops of alcohol, then succussing (shaking or pounding) the mixture ten times; then taking one drop from this new mixture and combining it with ninety-nine new drops of alcohol, and so on. The thirtieth potency, apparently common in homoeopathic prescribing, is made by doing this thirty times. The thousandth potency, therefore (which they call the 1M potency), is made by doing this one thousand times. At least, I think I've got that right. It sounds impossible. I read it again. Yes. That is right.

Shit. Do people even make this stuff anymore? Is there still such a thing as Tafel's High Potencies or the Skinner Machine? Am I going to have to go out and find some charcoal and start messing around with pipettes and slivovitz (does that count as the finest spirits? Probably not). Could my wrists even cope with all that shaking? I don't have bionic arms, and I have absolutely no stamina. Once I rubbed out the pencilled-in marginalia from a hundred pages of a book that I wanted to photocopy (long story) and afterwards it felt like I'd been wanking off a giant for a hundred years.

I'm still thinking about this, and wishing there was a way of finding some sort of Victorian pharmacist to help me, when someone taps me on the shoulder. Even though I thought I was alone in here, I don't jump. In fact I am so absorbed in this new problem that I vaguely shrug the hand away from my shoulder and keep reading. I can already sense that it's Patrick, anyway. I can smell his woodsy aftershave, and the lemony scent of his clean clothes. He touches my shoulder again and this time I have to respond.

"Hi," I say without really looking up.

"Hello," he says, hovering behind my right shoulder. "What are you reading about?"

"Nineteenth-century homoeopathy," I say, turning my hand over so it rests on the book, rather than holding it open. I don't want him to see my wrist.

"Gosh," he says. "Was homoeopathy around then?"

"I think it was its heyday," I say.

There's a long pause. I wish he'd go away.

"Ariel," he says.

"What?"

"Can I buy you a coffee to say sorry?"

I sigh. "I'm quite busy doing this."

"Ariel?"

I don't respond. He stands there behind me silently and I don't know whether to turn and look at him or just to continue with this and hope he'll just get the message and leave. I'm not quite sure exactly what message I want him to get. Something like *Leave me out of your fucking family shit*. After I've ignored him for a while he comes closer and looks down at the book in front of me, in the same way that people look at photographs in a lonely room.

"OK, I'll leave you to it," he says, without moving. "Hey," he puts his thin finger down on the textbook in front of me. "Phosphorus; I've taken that."

I look up. "You've taken homoeopathic medicine?"

"Yes, of course. I'm not sure it worked, but . . ."

"Look. Maybe we should have a quick coffee," I tell him. "But you'll have to give me a few minutes to finish up here and check out some of these books. Say outside in five minutes?"

"Wonderful."

Shelley College (named after Mary, not Percy Bysshe) has a Fibonacci staircase, a 1960s chandelier, and a bistro called Monster Munch. Monster Munch is the only bit of the college I don't like. It's all done out in clean orange and pithy white curves and edges, with new-looking pool tables and a plasma screen. I prefer the decrepit little bar in the Russell Building that has stand-up ashtrays and chipped particleboard tables. The students don't like the Russell Bar, which means it's usually empty. Occasionally they'll go in there to revise, or to curl up on one of the stained old sofas with a hangover, but not that often. Anyway, you can't smoke in Monster Munch. You can only do shiny things in Monster Munch; you have to be a shiny, clean person in here: The fluorescent lights and the mirrors on the walls prevent you from being anything else.

I sit on a stool at a small white table by the window and pull the arms of my jumper down to cover my wrists while Patrick gets coffee for both of us: some sort of frothed milk thing for him, and an Americano for me (they call it "black coffee" in Russell). I have my pile of homeopathy textbooks in front of me, and they look wrong in here, as do I. The mirrors reflect the unhealthy tone of my skin, pale against my red hair, and the fraying on the bottom of my jeans that I didn't think was that noticeable. I put on this black jumper this morning without even thinking about it, but now I can see how thin the wool has become, and how smudged it makes me look. If it wasn't for my hair I'd basically resemble a bad-quality photocopy.

Patrick puts my coffee in front of me and looks out of the window.

"Wow, you can see a long way today," he says, sitting down. The sky is still a hyperreal blue.

"Yeah, but you can't see the cathedral." All you can see from up here are fields with nothing in them and, farther away, strange industrial towers.

"Do you have to be able to see the cathedral?"

"I think so. I mean, it's the only thing to look at, isn't it? From up here."

"Maybe." Patrick digs around in his froth with a thin silver spoon. I notice that his hands are shaking slightly and there's a slight reflection on his forehead from a thin sheen of perspiration. "So."

"So," I say back. "Are you . . ." What do I say? I was about to ask if he's feeling any better, but then I realize that this is an absurd thing to say, because I don't really care how he's feeling. The ellipses hang in the air for a moment, and then Patrick fills in his own question and answers it.

"Yes. Emma's back. I'm . . ." He prods his froth some more. "I'm sorry if I seemed to be in a rather strange mood yesterday. I wonder if you'll ever forgive me."

"It's OK," I hear myself saying. "It's not as if I said . . . You know, I mean . . ."

"No, but, I shouldn't . . ."

"I mean, maybe we should try to avoid . . . In future . . ."

Monster Munch is not the kind of place to have this conversation. This is a post-midnight, post-watershed, jazz-bar conversation, and we're trying to have it in a place that looks like it's already been censored.

"Anyway," I say.

"I'm really sorry."

"It's OK."

I think about Frankenstein's monster, the fictional character who indirectly gave his name to this place. *She was there, lifeless and inanimate, thrown across the bed, her head hanging down, and her pale and distorted features half covered by her hair . . . The murderous mark of the fiend's grasp was on her neck, and the breath had ceased to issue from her lips.* That's what Victor Frankenstein's creation did to his fiancée, Elizabeth. Maybe this is the place to have this conversation after all.

"You . . . ," I begin, at the same time that Patrick says, "I . . ."

"You first," he says.

"No, go on."

"No, really."

"I just . . . I don't want to be a stand-in for your wife. Especially not when you're angry with her. That was never the deal."

"No. I'm sorry. It won't happen again."

We're silent for a couple of moments. I sip my coffee and vaguely wish I could have a cigarette. Two women walk in and order juice from the bar and then come and sit at the table behind ours.

"So how come you took homoeopathic medicine?" I ask Patrick. He shrugs. "Someone suggested seeing a homoeopath a while ago." "What was it like?"

He sips his coffee and I notice that his hands are not shaking anymore.

"It was interesting." He frowns. "They ask you lots of odd questions. They want to know what foods you crave, what you dream about, what you do for a living, and how you feel about it. It's like seeing a therapist in a way."

I saw a therapist once. A gym teacher saw the scars on the tops of my legs and made me go to the doctor. The doctor referred me to some teenage unit at the local hospital. I remember watching a soap opera in the waiting room, which, as well as the smeary TV screen, had green plastic chairs and posters about AIDS. The guy who saw me was a young, moon-faced man with glasses. I told him how amazing it was to be able to give yourself pleasure through pain, and how I knew cutting was addictive but I wasn't addicted yet. I laughed through an account of my childhood. Through all this the therapist simply looked at me in a puzzled way, and a week later I got a letter saying they didn't have the facilities to help me "at this time." I still remember the boxy, thin-walled little room, though. It smelled of smoke, and I noticed a silver foil ashtray on the table by the box of tissues and the vase of plastic blue flowers. That was the moment it occurred to me to try smoking. That eventually replaced the cutting, but I still have the scars. Patrick likes them.

I sip my coffee as Patrick keeps talking about the homoeopathic interview.

"I don't know why they need that level of detail about your life," he says, and laughs briefly. "I only went there with headaches and insomnia."

I finish my coffee. "So you ended up with phosphorus?"

"Yes. Now I think about it, I haven't had any headaches since, although I still don't sleep well."

"Do you actually believe in it?"

"Mmm. I don't know. I saw a documentary that said the remedies are just placebos, and there's nothing in them that can have any effect on anything. They actually dilute the remedies so much that, in chemical terms, all that is left is water. Apparently, homoeopaths argue that water has a memory, which sounds pretty wacky."

"So what did the medicine look like?" I ask him. "Where did you get it?"

"Oh, the homoeopath gave it to me. She had this huge wooden cabinet . . ." Patrick opens his arms about three feet wide and, with one finger pointing up on each hand, tries to show the scope of this thing. I notice that he doesn't look at his hands as he does this, but at the wall behind me. It suddenly occurs to me that when people describe size this way, they're relying on perspective to help them. He's not saying, *It's this big.* He's saying, *It would look this big from here if it was over there.*

He goes on, "It had all these little drawers labelled alphabetically. She opened one of them up and there were lots of little glass bottles inside, each containing tiny white sugar pills. She explained to me that the medicine is originally a liquid, but that the little pills absorb it and make it more convenient to take. Sorry. This must be boring."

"No, I'm really interested. I just had no picture in my mind of what any of this stuff actually looks like." I try to run my fingers through my hair, but there's some huge tangle at the front, so I try to tease it out as I speak. "So, do you have to get these pills from a homoeopath?"

"Oh no." Patrick laughs. "Don't you ever go into Boots? They sell homoeopathic remedies everywhere now. You can get them at any health food shop as well. I get Nux Vomica for indigestion. You just buy it over the counter."

"Hmm," I say. "That's interesting. I never realized it was so mainstream."

"It's big business now," he says. "I've got some Nux in my office if you want to see what the tablets actually look like."

"OK."

Most people's offices tend to be a mess. I've seen people who seem to be trapped in their rooms, still working at eight P.M. because perhaps there really is no way out across towering piles of old journals, books, and printed e-mails. Patrick's room, on the other hand, is large, square, and spotless. It doesn't exactly have the shine of the Monster Munch bistro, but you can see why he likes having coffee there. He has an L-shaped desk arrangement similar to mine, but his tables are larger and one has a glass top. The glass-topped one faces the door and has nothing on it apart from a heavy translucent paperweight and a white lamp. The other one faces the window and has nothing on it apart from his computer, and looks as if it's been polished recently. The room is so large that there is also space for a coffee table and four comfortable chairs.

He shuts the door behind us and walks over to his desk drawer.

"Here," he says, taking out a small brown glass bottle and offering it to me.

I put my library books down on the coffee table and take the bottle from him. The label says *Nux Vom 30. 125 tablets*. An instruction on the side tells you to take a tablet every two hours in "acute" cases and three times a day otherwise. I unscrew the cap and peer inside at a pile of tiny flat tablets, pure white like miniature aspirins.

Now Patrick is locking the door and closing his blinds.

"How forgiven am I?" he says.

"Hmm?" I say, looking up, but he has already grabbed me and is kissing me hard. "Patrick," I say, once he stops. But what am I going to say next? Despite—or, weirdly, because of—yesterday, a familiar sensation trickles through me and instead of talking about how this isn't a good idea, I allow him to remove my jumper and pull down my jeans and knickers and then bend me over the glass table, holding me by my hair. My breasts press against the cold glass, and, while Patrick fucks me, I wonder what they look like from underneath.

"God, Ariel," he says afterwards, wiping his cock with a Kleenex as I pull my jeans back up. "I don't know if you bring out the best or the worst in me."

"I think it's the worst," I say, smiling.

He smiles back. "Thanks for forgiving me."

I laugh. "I'm not sure if I have yet." I pick up my books and head for the door. "Oh well. Guess I'd better go and see what my new room-mates are like."

Patrick throws the Kleenex away. "Roommates?"

" 'Refugees' is what Mary's calling them. People from the Newton Building. I'm sharing my office with two of them."

"Oh. Bad luck." Patrick leans against the glass-topped desk and looks at me. "Well, you're always welcome here."

"We'll get caught."

"Yes. Probably." He sighs. "Back to hotels then."

"We'll see." I soften this with a naughty smile, since something's just occurred to me. "Oh, Patrick?" I say with my hand on the door handle, as though it's an afterthought.

He's fiddling with the buttons on his trousers, making sure they're done up.

"What?"

"I've left my purse at home. You haven't got like a tenner lying around, have you? It's no big deal but I've got to put some petrol in the car on the way back. I'll give it back to you tomorrow or something."

He immediately reaches for his wallet and pulls out a twenty.

"Don't worry about it," he says. And then, just as I'm leaving, and in a lower voice: "There's always more where that came from."

As I leave, I wonder if that was better than stealing from the tea and coffee fund in the kitchen, or worse.

Chapter Ten

There's a young woman in my office. She's about my age, or a bit younger, and has thick black glasses and short, blond, curly hair. She's putting books on one of the shelves I cleared. Around her feet are about five other boxes with all kinds of things spilling out of them: mainly books, but also CDs, a small stereo, a plush green frog, and a scrunched-up lab coat.

"Hi," I say, walking around the boxes. "I'm Ariel."

"Oh my God. I'm so sorry about this. I'm Heather." Her accent is Scottish, possibly Edinburgh.

She grins at me, puts down the book she's holding, and holds out a hand for me to shake. I put my own pile of books on my now single desk and take it.

"Seriously," she says. "I'll be out of your hair as soon as possible. It's so nice of you to offer to share, though. I do really appreciate it."

"Er . . . That makes me sound like a better person than I am," I say. "Not that I wouldn't have offered. But I was originally sharing this office with my supervisor and he's not around at the moment, so, well, it's logical for me to share, really. My head of department suggested it, though."

"Well, just, thanks so much. I mean, you could have said no."

I couldn't have said no, but still.

"I'm just going to check my e-mail," I say, sitting down at my desk. "But I can give you a hand in a minute if you like."

"No. You're all right. I'll try not to make too much of a mess, though. I don't want to completely ruin your office."

"Honestly," I say. "It's fine."

Heather has already set up her computer on the desk that is now facing the window. The theology guy is therefore going to have the one behind mine, facing the other wall. Heather's computer has got a large, flat-screen monitor, which appears to have gone on standby. I press the buttons to turn on my computer and then I get up and start picking my way through the maze of boxes to go upstairs to check my pigeonhole and get a coffee from the kitchen.

"Do you want a coffee or anything?" I ask Heather as I go.

"Really? Oh, no. I couldn't ask you to make me coffee as well as everything else."

"It's no trouble. I'm already making myself one."

"Oh, OK. But only if it's no trouble. I probably need some to keep me going."

"I know the feeling," I say.

Once I'm back at my desk I immediately start searching the Internet for homoeopathic remedies. From what I can make out they cost about three or four pounds a bottle. I could order them online, but I don't have a credit card so I'll have to go into town. I'm feeling so hungry that I think I might pass out, but I don't think I'll waste any of my money in the canteen. I think I'll finish my coffee and then liberate my car, go home, and have some soup and a bath. Then I can go out and find the Carbo Vegetabilis. There's a huge Boots and two or three health food shops in town, and if these medicines are as ubiquitous as Patrick says I shouldn't have any trouble finding what I need.

While I'm doing this, Heather finishes putting her books on the shelves.

"Oh dear," she says.

I glance up and see her looking at the shelves. "Is everything OK?"

"Oh, sorry, I don't want to disturb you if you're working."

"I'm not," I say. "What is it?"

"I haven't left any room for the other guy."

We both look at the shelves. She really has managed to fill a whole bookcase to the extent that there are even books lying on top of other books and volumes poking out awkwardly as if the other books are trying to eject them. Even the green frog is there, looking squashed. She bites her lip, clearly genuinely worried about this. Then she catches my eye and we both laugh.

"Oh well," I say, shrugging.

"Maybe he won't have many things. I only have mine because everything was in storage. My office was going to be redecorated over the holidays. I suppose if he has, I can always put some of mine back in boxes." She walks over to my desk and looks at my pile of homeopathy books. She touches one of them as if she thinks it might be contaminated, and then she takes her hand away. "You're an English lit person, aren't you?"

"Um, yeah. Sort of."

"Why the homoeopathy books?"

"Oh, I always have weird books. I'm doing a Ph.D. on thought experiments. I think the department wants to kick me out, actually. It's all a bit too scientific, even if I do look at poetry and stuff as well."

"Thought experiments! How cool."

"Yeah. It is fun. You're an evolutionary biologist, aren't you?"

"Yeah, I've got a postdoctoral fellowship in molecular genetics, so it's kind of evolution from the beginning of time, or at least the beginnings of life, which gets pretty crazy. I get to teach a few of the kids—that's what my old supervisor calls the students—in term time, but mostly I'm making these computer models. Actually, do you want to see something cool?"

"Yeah," I say. "What is it?"

"Look." She touches the mouse on her desk and her flat screen jumps back into life. Suddenly I can see white numbers and letters covering the whole black screen, all changing, like numbers on a stock exchange or information on a computer matrix, as if there should be a *tick-tick-tick* noise at the same time. "It's working out the origins of life," she says. Then she laughs; it's the kind of high-pitched laugh that ideally needs more people in a room to absorb it. "That sounds a bit mental actually. Sorry."

"Wow," I say, staring at the screen.

"Yeah. Well. My research proposal made it sound a lot more boring than that, but that's essentially what I'm trying to do. It's all about looking for LUCA. Or actually looking beyond LUCA, since no one really believes in LUCA anymore."

I'm still staring at the screen, but Heather now turns away. There's a pencil on her desk and she picks this up and starts playing with it, leaning against her desk with her back to the monitor. The numbers and letters keep changing and repeating in front of me. It's the kind of thing you could watch for ages. You'd watch it all night and then close your eyes and see thousands of letters and numbers still crazily scrolling in the darkness. "What's LUCA?" I ask.

"The Last Universal Common Ancestor."

"Like . . ."

"The thing we all descended from."

"Aha," I say. "So this program on here. What's it doing?"

Heather runs her hand through her hair. "God—there's a question," she says. Then: "Oh, hello."

A male voice says, "Hi."

I turn around. There's a guy standing in the doorway holding a small box. He's got shoulder-length black hair and he's wearing haphazard layers of black, gray, and off-white clothes. Under his black thigh-length cotton jacket is an open gray shirt. Under that there's a thin black sweatshirt. Under that there seems to be a white T-shirt. Despite all these clothes he is thin and angular-looking with a slightly pointed nose and high, corpselike cheekbones. He also has about three days' stubble. He's young, probably in his early thirties, but his brown-black eyes look millions of years old.

"Hi," I say back. "You must be . . . ?"

"I'm Adam. Apparently there's a space for me to work in here?"

Heather immediately takes charge, pinging around the office like a squash ball.

"Hi, Adam. I'm Heather. This is Ariel. Here's your desk and your notice board is right here and I'm so sorry but look at what I've done to the shelves already . . ." I'm vaguely aware of the high-pitched laugh again, and Heather saying something else. I'm not sure if Adam's listening to her at all: His eyes are locked on mine. I have no idea why, but I have an urge to walk across the room and merge with him: not to kiss, not to fuck, but *to merge*. It's ridiculous—he's way too young for me. I think he's going to break this deep, infinite stare any second, but he doesn't. Could this go on forever? No. Suddenly I think about Patrick and everything else to do with my sordid past and I rip the moment in two by turning around and looking at my computer screen instead. For the first time I notice all the dust around its edges. Everything seems dirty. I look back to Adam again, but now he's busy reassuring Heather about the shelves.

"I really don't have anything," he's saying. "Look."

He's showing her his box. Inside are three blue pencils, a university diary, a red notebook, and a Bible.

"You do travel light," Heather says.

Adam shrugs. "You keep the shelves. I'm just grateful for the desk."

He sits down at the desk and starts up the computer. Heather keeps talking to him and from listening to their conversation I learn that Adam is working on nothing more exciting than planning some MA seminars for the coming term. I'd usually find this kind of conversation boring, but Adam's voice is so mesmerizing that I can't help but listen. I can't place his accent. First I think it's South London; then I revise it to South London with a hint of New Zealand. Then I revise it further to New Zealand with a hint of Irish. Then I give up and start thinking again about going home. I can't develop feelings for a guy who carries a box around with a Bible in it, especially not when I can still feel Patrick's spunk dribbling down my legs. Oh, I'm so gross. I get up and start putting on my coat.

"So," Heather's saying. "I think we should all celebrate." She's looking at me. "Ariel? Oh, are you off? What do you think?"

"Huh?" I say, putting the homoeopathy books in a bag to take home with me.

"Dinner, my house tonight? I was thinking that I can tell you about LUCA and Adam can tell us about how God made Man and we can all get really drunk. Well, we can. I'm guessing Adam doesn't drink. What do you think, Adam?"

"I'll come only if I can drink," he says.

I smile at Heather. "Er, yeah. It does sound good."

"Fantastic," she says. "Seven? Here's my address." She scribbles something down on a piece of paper and gives it to me.

This time when I get to the Newton car park there aren't any men standing around and all the yellow tape has torn and is flapping loosely in the wind. Beyond that, the broken building stands unevenly with scaffolding half-erected around it. My car is the only vehicle now parked here and I'm glad I can take it away. I always expect my car to be warm when I get into it but as usual it's refrigerator-cold, slightly damp, and smells of cigarette smoke. Still, it starts first time.

The traffic's heavy going into town, and as I approach the level crossing I see the lights start to flash and the big gates slowly come down. Shit. That means I'm going to be stuck here for about ten minutes. There's a bus in front of me, sticking out at an awkward angle and half-blocking the other side of the road, and the few cars that got through before the level crossing went down start trying to maneuver around it. There's a bakery on this side of the road, just beyond a pub, so I get out of the car and go to buy some bread. There's a woman in the bakery who smiles at me as if everyone I've ever known has just died. On my way back I realize the reason for the awkward angle of the bus: It's a white van, parked on the curb outside the pub. The lettering on the side of it says SELECT AMUSEMENTS. After a couple of seconds a man comes out of the pub wheeling an ancient-looking fruit machine with wires hanging out of the back. He leaves it on the pavement while he opens the back doors of the van. As I walk past, I can see six or seven other upright machines inside, all with tarnished buttons, each presumably bearing the fingerprints of thousands and thousands of people. There's a second man in the back of the van polishing one of the machines with a white cloth. Once he sees that his colleague is back with the new machine, he stops doing this and jumps down to help lift the machine into the back of the van and then strap it in. For a moment I suddenly think the machines are alive, and these men are taking them prisoner. Then the gates come up, the traffic starts to move again, and I jump back in my car and drive off. I get to the filling station without any problems and buy five pounds' worth of petrol.

I rent a parking space from the Chinese restaurant around the back of my flat and luckily today no one else has parked in it by mistake. After I've had some soup, I go and get in the bath with two of the homoeopathy books: *Kent's Lectures on the Materia Medica* and a rather strange-looking volume called *Literary Portraits of the Polychrests*. I'm going to read about Carbo Vegetabilis, then I'm going to go and buy some. It doesn't matter how dirty I am, or that I want to pretend there's nothing wrong with me, or that I desperately want to see Adam's face again, or that I should think about getting back to my thesis and my new piece for the magazine. This is my mission. This isn't real life. Real life is letting men fuck you over their desks (and enjoying it, which is somehow the worst thing). Real life is regularly running out of money, and then food. Real life is having no proper heating. Real life is physical. Give me books instead: Give me the invisibility of the contents of books, the thoughts, the ideas, the images. Let me become part of a book; I'd give anything for that. Being cursed by *The End of Mr. Y* must mean becoming part of the book; an intertextual being: a book-cyborg, or, considering that books aren't cybernetic, perhaps a *bibliorg*. Things in books can't get dirty, and real life is, well, eventually it's dust. Even books become dust, like the crumbled remains H. G. Wells's Time Traveller finds in the museum. But thoughts are clean.

Before I start reading I think an experimental thought, just for a second. What if this *is* real life? What if I am cursed and I'm going to die, just like Lumas and everyone who read *The End of Mr. Y* in the 1890s? If I really thought this was real, some survival instinct would make me stop doing it, surely? But if it's not real, why am I bothering? I pick up the first book, *Kent's Lectures*, and start to read about Carbo Vegetabilis.

We will take up the study of Vegetable Charcoal—Carbo-veg. It is a comparatively inert substance made medicinal and powerful, and converted into a great healing agent, by grinding it fine enough. By dividing it sufficiently, it becomes similar to the nature of sickness and cures folks.

The Old School use it in tablespoonful doses to correct acidity of the stomach. But it is a great monument to Hahnemann. It is quite inert in crude form and the true healing powers are not brought out until it is sufficiently potentized. It is one of those deep-acting, long-acting antipsoric medicines. It enters deeply into the life, in its proving it develops symptoms that last a long time, and it cures conditions that are of long standing—those that come on slowly and insidiously.

What follows is basically a long list of symptoms that can be cured by this medicine in homoeopathic doses. Not much of it seems particularly interesting or gives any indication as to why this would be the "special" medicine chosen for Lumas's concoction. I read of sluggishness, laziness, and vomiting of blood. Then I read down the page and learn that people who need Carbo-veg are also cold and cadaverous. I close this book and pick up *Literary Portraits of the Polychrests*. The flap informs me that it should be possible to "read" or decode characters in literature in the same way as one reads a person with an illness. I can see how that would work: all those little symptoms I read about before, all the emphasis on knowing whether someone feels worse at eleven A.M. (sulphur) or four P.M. (lycopodium). I open the *Portraits* book and read the following:

Carbo-v is known as the corpse-reviver—and any practicing homoeopath will tell you why. When a patient appears to draw his last breath, this is the remedy that must be given in the highest possible potency. 1M or 10M is usually sufficient to bring about a revival, or, indeed, to aid the patient in his passing.

After an introduction, this chapter then lists the various famous literary personages who, in the author's opinion, would require this remedy. Mina Murray and Jonathan Harker get a few pages to themselves, and the author spends a long time considering the dying character in Edgar Allan Poe's short story "The Mesmeric Revelation." Then, of course, there's a section on Elizabeth Lavenza from *Frankenstein*. The section ends with this:

Is it any wonder that it is carbon that holds this mystique? Carbon is nothing less than the compression of life itself, which becomes the fuel for our furnaces and machines that themselves provide the fuel for life. Carbon, to which all living things eventually return (ashes to ashes, dust to dust), must be the most mysterious of all substances and in that respect the alignment with death is unavoidable. But carbon is also life. It is the beginning of life and its end. In potency it retains not physical substance but energy, which is meaning. And the meaning of carbon is both simple and complex. Life. Death. The limit of all things.

As I get out of the bath, damp and clean but not perceptibly warmer, I feel my mind tick-ticking like the screen on Heather's computer. The *corpse-reviver*. Now that at least does sound interesting. And all that stuff about carbon being the essence both of life and death. I remember there was something interesting about carbon in Jim Lahiri's popular science book, so, with my dressing gown on, I go into the kitchen and put on some coffee while I search my shelves for the book. Eventually I find it and it tells me what I remember reading.

In the furnace of the big bang, hydrogen was the first element to form from the hot plasmic soup of electrons and protons. It's a bit of a no-brainer: All you need for hydrogen is one electron and one proton. The mass of this hydrogen isotope is one—because it has one proton (electrons don't really have any mass). In the incredible heat, hydrogen isotopes with masses two (deuterium—one proton and one neutron) and three (tritium and trialphium) also formed. Then helium, with mass four. But there is no stable atom with mass five. Because there is no atom with mass five, no one understood how carbon could ever have been made. Each new element is made from fusing the elements that came before it, but you can whiz hydrogen and helium around in a cosmic blender for as long as you want and you won't make carbon.

That is a problem, because if you can't make carbon in this way, then the rest of the periodic table looks impossible as well. But because the most usual mass of carbon is twelve, you'd have to get three helium atoms to collide at exactly the same time, at a vast temperature, in order to create it. It looked like it was impossible that this ever happened. Then the cosmologist Fred Hoyle reasoned that carbon had to exist since he was made of it, and worked out exactly how the "mass-five crevasse" could be jumped. In response to all this, George Gamow wrote a spoof of Genesis, in which he had God creating all the possible chemical masses but forgetting to create mass five in his excitement.

> God was very much disappointed, and wanted first to contract the Universe again, and to start all over from the beginning. But it would be much too simple. Thus, being almighty, God decided to correct His mistake in a most impossible way. And God said: "Let there be Hoyle." And there was Hoyle. And God looked at Hoyle . . . and told him to make heavy elements in any way he pleased.

Now, of course, carbon is the basis for life and, as the homoeopathy book pointed out, the inevitable outcome of death. So if you were going to create a mysterious concoction of any sort, carbon wouldn't be a strange inclusion at all—especially if you diluted it so that it didn't even exist anymore; so it was simply a memory.

I get to the health food shop at around half past four but although Patrick was right and they do have a homoeopathy section, there's no Carbo Vegetabilis. After trying Boots and Holland & Barrett I am feeling less confident about this mission. Boots didn't have Carbo Vegetabilis at all, and Holland & Barrett only had it in a 6C potency, about 994 times less dilute than I need it. It's gone five by the time I drift into the little shop by the Odeon cinema. I've never been into this place before, and I don't even know what it sells. When you walk past, it looks as if it is simply a door with no shop behind it, but if you look more closely there's a glass display built into the wall next to it. Inside the glass display are a couple of jars of what look like herbs, a copy of the Tao Te Ching, and a pack of tarot cards. The name of the shop—*Selene,* Greek for "moon"—is on the door, along with a faded sign in an ornate script inviting you to "come in and browse." I am hopeful that the shop may have homoeopathic medicines, though, since the woman in Holland & Barrett told me to come here.

As I open the door, something inside tinkles feebly. Beyond the door is a thin wooden staircase, and I walk up in the semidarkness. At the top of the stairs I find another door, this one with frosted glass panels, and I open this and walk into the tiny shop where I find a thin bald man sitting behind a desk reading a book. The shop smells strongly of sandalwood incense and is arranged in a small rectangle with the desk on the near left-hand side. The desk looks like something a nineteenth-century architect might have used: It's large and broad with what seem to be many drawers in it; each is only a couple of inches high, but about three feet wide. There's no cash register. Behind the desk is a frayed and curling poster in a script I can't understand, and next to that there's a wooden purple door covered with an orange bead curtain.

The man doesn't acknowledge me but I start drifting around the displays, anyway. The far left-hand side of the shop has a wobbly set of wooden shelves containing little brown bottles of homoeopathic remedies. I find Carbo Veg, but this time it's in the potency 30C. I sigh and walk around to the right, past plastic tubs containing crystals, and rows and rows of big penny-sweet jars of herbs. Underneath the herbs there's a small, dusty display of glass jars and vials, some stoppered with cork; others with simple screw-tops. I pick up a glass vial to use for the holy water. I can't see any other homoeopathic medicines anywhere. I walk over to the counter and wait for the man to look up.

"I'm looking for a homoeopathic medicine," I say.

"Over in the corner," he says, and goes back to his book.

"I know," I say. "I need it in a higher potency, though."

"Oh," he says. He looks at his watch. "We're actually about to close, so . . ."

"So you don't have any higher potencies?"

"We do," he says. "But we can't sell them over the counter."

I frown. "What, do I need a prescription or something?"

He shakes his head. "You pay for a consultation." He sighs. "Which remedy did you want?"

"Carbo Vegetabilis," I say, blushing as the unfamiliar word comes out.

"Sorry?" he says.

"Carbo Vegetabilis. The corpse-reviver. At least, that's what people seem to call it. I found it in one place but not in a strong enough potency."

"The corpse-reviver? Where did you get that?"

"Oh, a book," I say.

So much for trying to sound like I know what I'm talking about.

"Well, I've got it in everything up to 10M," he says.

"I want 1M," I say. "The thousandth potency. That's right, isn't it?"

He frowns again. "You know that higher potencies can be dangerous if you don't know what you're doing?"

I don't say what I'm thinking, which is: *But it's just water.*

"Yes," I say. "I know. It'll be fine."

"All right," he says. "But I'll have to give you some sort of consultation. What seems to be the problem?" He yawns while I say something about a headache. He lets me go on for a while and then, while I'm still talking, he opens up one of the big drawers and takes out a brown bottle.

"Yeah, yeah. OK. I prescribe Carbo-v," he says. "That'll be eight pounds. That's for the consultation. The remedy is free."

"Thanks," I say, taking the bottle. I pay for the "consultation" and the glass vial I picked up before. Then I leave.

Chapter Eleven

Somehow it's gone six o'clock by the time I'm back out on the freezing street. The light from car headlamps hangs mournfully in the thin mist and people are walking along wearing thick hats and gloves and carrying briefcases, or plastic bags full of lumpy shopping, or both. I decide to go home now and try to pick up the holy water on my way to Heather's instead. The cathedral is on my way to her house, anyway.

Wolfgang's bicycle is in the hallway when I get home. My hands are frozen, even though I kept them both clenched in my pockets all the way back, one holding the glass vial, the other holding the Carbo Vegetabilis. The first thing I do is hide the remedy in an old sugar tin at the back of one of my cupboards; I'm not entirely sure why. Then I put the glass vial on the table and run both my hands under warm water, trying to wash away the cold. I put some coffee on the stove and then go into the bathroom. I try brushing my hair but it's too tangled, so I stick it up in a band instead. I look at myself in the mirror and, as usual, wonder to what level I am cursed. Common sense says that curses don't exist. But then I think that later tonight I am going to make Lumas's concoction, drink it, and see what happens. My reflection doesn't seem to react to this thought, except I think I can sense a mild disappointment in my eyes. When the concoction fails to have any effect, then what? Then it's back to real life and real work without even an office to myself anymore. I put some face powder on my already pallid face and then apply some pale pink lipstick. I don't think I'll get changed again. The jeans I put on earlier are clean, if a bit washed-out and frayed, and all my jumpers look more or less the same, anyway.

After I've had my coffee, I wander down the hallway and bang on Wolfgang's door. He answers it almost immediately and invites me in to his kitchen. Neither of us has a fitted kitchen, just a couple of shelves and cupboards. Wolfgang's shelves are all crammed with nuts, seeds, and dried fruit in clear packets. His cupboards only contain alcohol, and that's why I'm here. As I walk in I realize that the kitchen smells cleaner than usual. Usually it only contains one Formica-topped table and one chair, and if I come to eat here I have to bring my own chair. This evening, however, there are two chairs and there is a little pot of flowers in the center of the table.

"Do you think this is an inviting space?" he asks me.

"Yes, of course," I say. "Especially with two chairs. Is Catherine coming round?"

"Catherine? No. I have finished with Catherine. I'm expecting someone much more special than Catherine."

"Your love life moves quickly," I say.

"Ha! Yes. Quickly and unexpectedly."

"OK. Well in that case I won't keep you . . ."

"You were not coming for dinner? Because as you know, any other night . . ."

"No," I say. "Don't worry. Although I wish I was looking for somewhere to have dinner. I'm actually about to go and meet the people who've taken over my office." I shake my head. "I don't know why I'm going, really."

"Ah," he says. "Then, if it is not one of my gourmet dinners, presumably you want something else?"

"Mmm. Yeah. I was wondering if you had any more of that dodgy wine."

Just before Christmas Wolfgang acquired about thirty bottles of Bulgarian red wine from person or persons unknown and he was selling it to me at a pound a bottle. I haven't bought any for a couple of weeks but I need to take a bottle over to Heather's and I don't want to pay a fiver in the supermarket when I've now only got about ten pounds left in the world.

He shakes his head. "Dodgy? How can you say my wine is dodgy?"

I laugh. "OK, then. Your totally legal wine."

His eyes flit horizontally to one of the cupboards. "I have a few bottles left."

"Can I have one?"

"Of course." He pulls one out of the cupboard. The label is written in Bulgarian, which does make it look pretty authentic and, dare I say it, expensive. "So how is life?" he asks, handing it over.

"OK," I say, giving him a pound coin. "Weird. Oh—did I tell you I finished the book?"

"The cursed book?"

"Yeah."

"And this recipe was there? You have the ingredients?"

I don't ask why on earth Wolf would make the accurate assumption that, once I knew these ingredients, the next thing I would do would be to track them down.

"No," I lie. "Sadly, it wasn't there."

"So what happens to Mr. Y?"

"Pretty much everything he feared would happen. There is one good thing: He makes up the concoction and takes it, and it does transport him back to the Troposphere. But it's all horrible. He enters his wife's mind and discovers how unhappy he has made her. Then he enters his business rival's mind and realizes he will never defeat him. Just before it becomes clear that he and his wife are going to have to go to the workhouse, he discovers a bit more about how the Troposphere works. You can in fact jump from one person's mind to another, just as Mr. Y thought. And by doing that you can travel across memories. . . . It's a bit like surfing, although Mr. Y gives it his own term: *Pedesis*."

"Across memories . . . ? So perhaps like time travel?"

"I think that was the implication."

I remember the penultimate paragraph of the book.

I had not found happiness, or, indeed, my fortune, within the shadows of the Troposphere. Yet within it I felt something of what a bird may feel skimming in the air : for the time I roamed within this new world I knew I was free. And although in the world of flesh I had failed, in the world of minds I flew, perhaps not as a bird flies, but as a man moving fast over an infinity of stepping stones, each new stone providing a platform from which to jump to many others. As I became accomplished at this method of leaping further inside the world of minds, moving with the lightest and quickest of steps, with the ease of the surf on moving water, I decided to call this movement Pedesis, from the Greek πήδησις. This river with its stones, like the landscape with its dwellings, flowed forwards—yes—but also backwards. And so I have decided to take flight, pedetically, into the mists of time. Thus I arrive at my story's end, for, this evening, at midnight, I plan to embark on this journey into the very depths of the Troposphere. I doubt that I will ever return to complete my story, so far will I be from its beginning.

"So what actually happens to Mr. Y?" Wolfgang asks. "In what sense does he meet his end?"

"Oh, he vanishes into the Troposphere."

"What, in his body?"

"No." I shake my head. "They find his body later."

Wolf's eyes open wide. "He dies?"

"Yes," I say. "There's an 'Editor's Note' at the end that explains how he was found, cold and dead, on the floor of his cellar. He had locked himself in and taken his last journey from there. His wife thought he had gone missing, and then discovered the locked cellar door and alerted the police. He had starved to death."

"And the author of this book, he died, too?"

"Yes."

"It is a good thing you don't have these ingredients then, isn't it?"

"Mmm."

Sometimes at night the cathedral gates are like an open mouth: an exclamation of surprise in a street crowded with old lopsided buildings, patched up and filled in over the years like teeth. Tonight the mouth is closed. The big wooden gate is up and there's a sign telling visitors that the precinct opens again tomorrow morning at eight thirty.

No holy water tonight then. No Pedesis.

But I know it's not real, so perhaps I'm just putting off knowing for sure. I could have gone to the cathedral earlier, after all. So it's real life again for the evening, but real life with an implicit promise of something else, something fictional. Another night of that isn't bad, although now I see the closed gates, I wish I had the holy water: I wish I had something dangerous to do later on.

I walk on along the twinkling, frosty pavements, using my new map to find Heather's street. It turns out to be in a side road just behind the cathedral: a small yellow-brick terrace with a black door. I knock twice with the silver knocker and then take a step back to wait for her to answer.

"Ariel, hello!" she says, when she opens the door. "Thanks so much for coming. Is that wine? Fantastic—I need as much as possible after the day I've had. How are you? Oh, sorry: Here I am, chatting away on the doorstep. Come in."

The door opens from the street right onto the sitting room. It's the kind of house lots of young academics seem to have before they get married and have children: pine floorboards, rugs, lots of bookshelves, framed Picasso prints, autumnal throws over the sofa and chairs, a coffee table with coffee-table books, and several lamps. It's what my place would probably look like if it had heating and no mice and I could be bothered to inhabit more than one room. I can smell garlic cooking, mingled with something in an oil burner; some combination of peppermint and lavender. The house is warm. Jazz is playing on a small speaker system. There's no sign of Adam.

"White or red?" Heather asks. "Oh, and make yourself at home, by the way. Put your coat anywhere—it's always a bit of a shambolic mess in here."

Why do people always say their houses are messy when they're not?

"Er, red, please. Your place is lovely, by the way. I love that print."

"Oh, it's cool, isn't it?" Heather says over her shoulder as she goes into the kitchen for my wine. She comes back and gives it to me in a huge glass with a silvery pink stem. "I love Picasso."

"I particularly like that one," I say, gazing up at it. "I like anything to do with four dimensions. It's kind of an obsession."

"Four dimensions?" she says. Then she groans. "Go on, tell me what I've missed. I never appreciate art properly: I just think, *That's a pretty picture* and then hang it on my wall. This is what happens when you're a biologist. You need humanities people to explain real life to you."

I laugh, and, after reassuring Heather that I only know a tiny bit about the cubists and the futurists, and not much else about art, say something about the way the woman's head could be said to be moving through time, or that, alternatively, a fourth-dimensional being is viewing her.

"Wow. That's so cool. I like *The Scream* best. But I thought it would be a bit studenty to have it on my wall, so I went for something a bit more sophisticated. I so love *The Scream*, though. It's how I feel most days."

"Why?"

"Oh, um . . ." There's a knock at the door. "That'll be Adam, I hope, and not some mass murderer." She laughs. "Hang on."

For no reason I'm aware of, my hands start to shake. I put my wine down and then pick it up again. There's a sharp blast of cold air as Heather opens the door and greets Adam. He looks exactly as he did earlier; the only difference is that his hair seems scruffier.

"Hi," he says to me, taking off his coat.

"Hello," I say back.

Heather tells him to put his coat anywhere and repeats her apology about "the mess" and then goes into the kitchen to get a glass of white wine for him. We stare at each other without moving or saying anything.

"So," she says, coming back. "I'm doing pasta and roasted vegetables. It's just simple—I hope that's OK with you, Adam."

"Yeah, thanks," he says, taking the wine while still looking at me. I'm looking right back at him, but this time he breaks the moment and focuses on Heather. "That sounds perfect."

Adam settles into a corner of the big sofa across the room from where I'm sitting. Without looking at either of us, he leans forward and examines the books on the coffee table. Once he's looked at them all he picks up a large hardback book called *Weird Fish* and starts flicking through it. None of us says anything for a couple of seconds. Heather must have her music on shuffle, because once the jazz track stops, a mournful acoustic guitar tune begins and a guy starts to sing about being alone in the small hours of the morning.

"Better put the pasta on," says Heather.

"Well," Adam says, once she's gone, "how's life?"

"Fine, I think. How about you? Are you settled in OK?"

"Yeah. And thanks for sharing your office with us."

"It's OK. Anyway, as I was telling Heather before, I didn't exactly have a choice."

"Ah. Right. So we were foisted on you?"

"Yeah. But I don't mind at all. Really."

Small talk, small talk. And now he's back to flicking through the pages of the book on his lap.

Heather comes back in.

"So, how's the world of religion?" Heather asks him. "How's life with God?"

"How should I know?" says Adam.

"Aren't you religious?" she says. "I thought . . ."

Adam smiles. "I'll give you the short answer: no."

"Oh, come on," says Heather. "What's the long answer? Oh!" Something in the kitchen has just gone "ding" and she jumps up to go and deal with it. "Sorry—it's my pasta, I think."

Adam gives me a look as if we're both about to rob a bank together. He also looks as if he doesn't really want to.

"Saved," he says.

I smile at him. "It's a shame, though," I say. "I would have liked the long version, too."

"Oh . . ." He sighs and runs his fingers through his hair.

"Hey—it doesn't matter," I say. "I'm only playing around. You don't have to tell me anything."

"I'd rather look at fish, to be honest," he says.

I smile. "Yeah, I think I know what you mean."

"They are weird, these fish. Have you seen them?"

"No."

"Come and look."

As I move onto the same sofa as him I'm reminded of all the times I've been with a man and chains of lies have led us first to the same house, then the same sofa, then the same bed. *I'm tired. I'm cold. Come here, I want to show you something.* It always ends in fucking. I'm sitting only a couple of inches from him now, but, of course, Heather's in the kitchen. I pull down the sleeves of my jumper to cover my wrists.

"Look," he says, pointing.

The book is open on a full-page image of a transparent fish. It looks like a used condom with red teeth.

"Yuck!" I say. But I actually quite like it. "Does it have a name?"

"I don't think so. Look at this one."

Adam turns the page and leans the book towards me. There's what looks like a fish, but instead of a normal fish "face" with bulging eyes and a little mouth this thing seems to have the head of a stone monkey, as if someone just slapped two things together—the fish body and the monkey head—as a joke, or even as an accident.

"What would you call that?" I say.

"I don't know. Monkey Fish? Pretend Monkey Fish?"

He turns the page and there's another picture. It looks like a worm with a disembodied vulva coming out of it. I want to laugh but I don't.

"Orchid fish," he says. And then we're called into the dining room to eat.

"So please tell me you don't approve of teaching creationism to kids," Heather says to Adam about five minutes after we've started eating. "Or whatever they're calling it now: intelligent design."

We're eating pasta and roasted vegetables, as promised, with a large salad. Until this new conversational segue, Heather had been talking about her problems finding any decent men at the university. The pasta is almost as impossibly bouncy as she is, and the white spirals slither off your fork if you aren't careful. The vegetables—cherry tomatoes, mushrooms, aubergines, and roasted onions—have been coated with olive oil and lemon juice and they've got that sticky, almost caramelized texture. There's garlic bread, too, and I'm eating as much as I can. In fact, until this moment I'd been much more interested in the food than in the conversation. I tend to hate dinner party conversations, but even I can see that this one could get interesting.

"In what sense?" Adam says.

"As part of science courses," Heather says.

"Aren't creationism and intelligent design different?" I say.

"Not really," she says. "Intelligent design claims to be scientific but it's not: After all, it deals with things you can't ever know."

"The intelligent design people are the ones who say that evolution is too complicated to have happened all by itself, aren't they?" I say.

"Yeah," Heather says. "Like, *duh*. Just because they don't understand it . . ."

"I wouldn't teach religion as science," Adam says. "But we do teach parts of science in our religion courses, if that's any help."

"Like what?" Heather says.

"We teach creation myths," says Adam. "And we include the big bang."

"How precisely is the big bang a myth?" Heather asks.

"It's a story," Adam says. "Just like the story that the world hatched from a giant egg, or that God said *Let there be light* and there suddenly was. They're all just stories about the genesis of the world—

none of us was there to gather the actual facts, so we have to conclude that the whole thing is unknowable."

I think about saying something about Alexander Pope's lines on Newton:

Nature and nature's laws lay hid in night;
God said "Let Newton be!" and all was light.

Then I think about saying something about thought experiments. Then I think about time and the universe, and I'm about to say something about that, but Heather's faster.

"We are of course still part of the big bang," she says. "So we're observing it all the time. We are 'there' right now." She grins. "I'm no cosmologist or astrobiologist, you understand, but that part of it is blindingly obvious, especially if you've read Jim Lahiri. By the way, help yourselves to more wine and everything."

"I enjoyed the Lahiri book," I say, pouring more wine and taking another slice of garlic bread. "I liked that bit about how the universe contains its own past and present—and, possibly, future, although I didn't completely go along with all that speculative stuff—and that since everything in the universe was originally part of the primordial particle, we could be said to have been 'there' at the beginning."

"Not that I want to cause a row or anything," Adam says, smiling. "But I can't agree with big bang theory any more than I can agree with people who think the world is held up by giant turtles."

"But you can't not agree with big bang theory!" Heather says.

"Why not?"

"Well, it's not an opinion; it's a well-established theory, with plenty of evidence. It's certainly not something you can choose to agree or disagree with. You could try to disprove it, but that's something different."

"So you can form an opinion on, say, creationism, or whether or not there's a God, but I can't form an opinion on whether the universe started as an unimaginably small speck that, for no reason at all, simply exploded?"

"OK, I admit that the beginning bit is pretty far-fetched," Heather says.

"And there is the problem of what came before the beginning," I say.

"Yes, yes," says Heather. "But you can put all that to one side and look at all the evidence for the big bang. The simplest bit to understand is the expanding universe. Once you realize that everything in the universe is moving, and every piece is moving farther away from every other piece, then you realize that, well, yesterday, all the pieces were a bit closer together, and the day before that, a bit closer still. Rewind the tape to the beginning and you see that logically everything must have been lumped together."

"But as a tiny speck . . . ?" says Adam. "Everything's not getting bigger, is it?"

"It depends how you define 'big,' " says Heather. "The universe is getting bigger, but it doesn't have more matter in it. That's the other thing—the universe is a closed system with the same amount of matter that never changes."

"Unless you listen to Stephen Hawking circa 1980," I say.

"I could never get my head around all that black hole stuff," says Heather. "But anyway, Adam, you have to agree with the reverse tape scenario."

"Do I? Oh, can I have some more vegetables, please?"

"Only if you agree with me," says Heather, laughing.

"Oh, well in that case . . ." Adam holds up his hands as if to stop something big from crashing into him.

"No, I'm only kidding. Here . . ." She pushes the dish of vegetables towards Adam. "But I still don't see how you can disagree with scientific fact."

" 'Fact' is a word. Science itself is just a collection of words. I'm guessing that truth exists beyond language, and what we call 'reality.' It must do; well, if it exists at all, that is."

"Come again?" says Heather, frowning.

"Aha," I say, nodding and raising an eyebrow. "He may have you there."

"It's all just an illusion," says Adam. "Creation myths, religion, science. We tell ourselves how time works—so, for example, you can imagine running your tape-of-the-universe backwards and be sure of what you'd get in this portion of time we call 'yesterday'—but yesterday only exists because we made it up: It's not real. You can't prove to me that yesterday even happened. Everything we tell ourselves to believe is simply a fiction, a story."

"Well," says Heather, "you can't argue with that—which makes me suspicious. And anyway, if all reality is just an illusion, then why do we bother?"

"Bother what?"

"Trying to work it all out. Trying to find the truth."

"You can try to find the truth outside reality," Adam says.

"By doing what exactly?"

Adam shrugs. "Meditation, I think. Or possibly getting very drunk."

I was going to say something pithy about Derrida, but Heather looks genuinely upset now so I decide not to.

"Meditation isn't science," she says.

"That's the point," says Adam.

"For God's sake," she says, slightly breathlessly. "All that woolly, superstitious stuff . . . No offense, but you just need words and logic to do science. I teach this evening class on the scientific method for adult returners and I always give them the example of the spiders' webs outside the room I teach in. Basically there's this long passageway outside the classroom with these orange lights attached to the wall. The lights are always on. In the evening you can see the spiders' webs stretched over the lights, and you can see all the crane flies and other night insects that get trapped in them. You could look at that and think: *Aren't the spiders clever because they know to build webs where the other insects will fly because they're attracted to the light.* Or you can go one step further and realize that you can only *see* the webs near the lights and that's why you have assumed those are the only ones. A poet might stand there and dream about the cunningness of spiders. A scientist would record exactly how many webs there are, and where, and conclude that some of them are built over the lights just by chance."

"But all of that just proves what I'm saying," Adam says. "I wouldn't conclude that the spiders intended to use the light to help trap the insects. I'd assume that I could never understand what the spiders were doing and why, because I'm not a spider."

"But scientists have to try to understand things. They have to ask why."

"Yes, but they'll never get a proper answer," Adam says.

"Anyway," I say, in a louder voice than I intended. "Er . . . Anyway, I was just going to say that this stuff about science and language is really interesting in relation to something I read about the big bang. It's a bit complicated, but it shows that if you start with a few basic assumptions about the big bang, then logic takes you to a situation where we're either living in a multiverse, or a universe created by God. There's really no other option."

"My head's going to be wrecked by the end of tonight," says Heather.

"Just drink more wine," says Adam, smiling at her.

I've just finished the last piece of garlic bread and Heather and Adam have both put down their knives and forks. I pick up my bag and take out a packet of cigarettes.

"If you're into all this meditation, are you supposed to drink wine?" Heather asks.

"Oh, I do it very rarely," says Adam.

I don't know if he means meditation or drinking and although I expect Heather to ask him, she doesn't. Instead, she picks up a stray rocket leaf and puts it back in the salad bowl.

"Do you mind if I smoke?" I ask her.

"No, not at all. I'll open the back door though, if you don't mind."

She gets up to do that and Adam and I briefly start making movements towards clearing the table before she tells us not to fuss and just leave it all.

"No, come on," she says. "Tell me about this whole God-or-the-multiverse thing."

"OK," I say, lighting my cigarette. "Sorry—do you have some sort of ashtray? I can go outside if you want . . ."

"No, I'll get you a saucer."

"God or the multiverse," says Adam softly as Heather gets a saucer. "Hmm."

"Are you both familiar with basic quantum physics?" I say. "Not the really hardcore stuff, but the kind of thing you'd find in a popular science book. You know, the wavefunction and probability and that sort of thing."

Adam's shaking his head. Heather cocks her head to one side as if she's trying to make the information roll down a hill in her mind and come to rest in a place she can access it.

"I should know it," she says. "I think I did know it once. But you ignore all that stuff when you're working on the molecular level. It just doesn't have any perceivable effects so it can be disregarded."

"I'm afraid I'm completely in the dark," says Adam.

"OK, well in a nutshell—and I warn you, I'm doing a humanities Ph.D. so you could probably get this from a more reliable source— quantum physics deals with subatomic particles, in other words, particles that are smaller than atoms."

Adam now frowns. "Call me nuts, but I'm having this odd sensation as if I'd seen one of these particles once or something," he says. "Maybe I'm drunk. I must have learnt this at some point and then forgotten it. Anyway, despite all that, my brain is begging me to ask you: What on earth is smaller than an atom?"

"Oh, well, everyone knows that an atom is made up of neutrons, protons, and electrons," says Heather.

"And those parts are all made up of quarks," I say. "Apart from the electron, which is indivisible—or at least people think it is. People thought the atom was indivisible a hundred years ago, and before that they didn't think it existed, so it's not as if we know everything."

It's cold with the back door open; Heather gets up and takes a small cardigan from the back of a chair and puts it on.

"I think we're pretty sure about the electron," she says. "Brrr. It's cold."

Adam and I exchange a look.

"Anyway," I say, "quantum physics deals with those tiny particles of matter. But when physicists first began theorizing about these particles and observing them in action in particle accelerators and so on, they found out that the subatomic world doesn't act the way we'd expect."

"How?" asks Adam.

"All that common sense stuff—the past happening before the future, cause and effect, Newtonian physics, and Aristotelian poetics—none of it is applicable at a subatomic level. In a deterministic universe, which is the sort Newton thought we lived in, you can always tell what's going to happen next, if you have enough information about what went before. And you can always know things for sure. It's either day or night, for example: It's never both at once. On a quantum level, things don't make sense in that way."

"This is the stuff that does my head in," says Heather.

"Yeah, it's weird," I say. "It's like . . . there are particles that can go through walls just like that. There are pairs of particles that seem to be connected and stay connected in some way even when they are separated by millions of miles. Einstein called it 'spooky action at a distance' and rejected it completely, as it seemed to suggest that information could travel faster than the speed of light."

"And nothing can travel faster than the speed of light," Heather says. "I'm with Einstein on that one."

"Anyway, one of the weirdest things about subatomic particles is that something peculiar happens when you observe them. Until they are observed, they exist in a smeared-out state of all possible positions in the atom: the superposition, or the *wavefunction*."

Adam's shaking his head. "You've lost me, I'm afraid," he says.

"OK," I say. "Imagine that you are out on a walk and I don't know where you are. You could be at the university, in the park, in the shop, in a spaceship, on Pluto, whatever. These are all possibilities, although some are more likely than others."

"All right," says Adam.

"Well, conventional logic tells us that you are definitely in one place or another, regardless of whether or not I've seen you there, or know for sure that you are there. You are somewhere, I just don't know where that is."

Adam's nodding and, for a second, I imagine a life so normal that I could be with someone like him, perhaps sharing a house like this, and have such a mundane, but somehow amazing, thought: *Is he in the shop or is he at work?*

"Anyway," I say, "obviously you're standing in for the particle in this example . . . Well, quantum physics says that when your situation is unknown—so you could be in the shop or in the park for all I know—you actually exist in all places at once until someone finds out for sure by observing you. So instead of one clear 'reality,' there's a smear. You're in the shop *and* the park *and* the university, and it's only when I go out looking for you and see that you're in the park that all the other possibilities melt away and reality is set."

"So observation has an effect on reality?" says Adam.

"Yes—well, in this way of looking at it. This idea that all probabilities exist as a wavefunction until an external observer looks at—and therefore collapses—the wavefunction is called the Copenhagen interpretation."

"Are there other ways?"

"Yes. There's the many-worlds interpretation. In a nutshell, while the Copenhagen interpretation suggests that all probabilities collapse into one definite reality on observation, the many-worlds interpretation suggests that all the possibilities exists at once, but that each one has its own universe to go with it. So there are, literally, many worlds, each one with a tiny difference. So in one universe you're in the park and in another you're at work and in another you're on the moon, or at the zoo or wherever."

"Those are the only two choices, right?" Heather says. "Like most people believe in one or other of those two?"

"Yeah, I think so," I say. "I think most people favor the Copenhagen interpretation, though."

"So how does this relate to the big bang?"

"Well," I say. "If you imagine the primordial particle: the thing that went 'bang' fourteen billion years ago . . . That particle should be just like any other particle. It would have its own wavefunction—a series of probabilities about where it was and what it was doing. So what we know of quantum physics suggests that unless an external observer showed up and observed the exact state of the particle, its wavefunction would not collapse. In other words, it would exist in a state of all the different probabilities at once. It would be both fast and slow, moving left and right, here and over there all at once. An observer external to the universe must be God. So perhaps God collapsed the wavefunction that became the universe. In other words, out of *all probabilities* God collapsed the original particle into one universe, in which we now live. That's the Copenhagen interpretation applied to the original particle. If you reject that, you're left with the many-worlds interpretation, which would suggest that there is no external observer and no collapse. Instead, all the probabilities exist 'out there'—every possible universe you could think of exists alongside this one: some hot, some cold, some with people, some without, some that create their own 'baby universes' and some that don't . . ."

Heather groans. "I knew there was a reason I'd forgotten this stuff."

"What if you reject this quantum physics?" asks Adam.

"Then I guess your CD player and credit cards stop working."

"I don't have a CD player or a credit card."

I grin at him. "Yes, but you know what I mean. Real technology is built on quantum physics. Engineers have to learn it. I mean, it is nuts, but it works out there in the real world."

"God or the multiverse," says Heather. "Which one would you choose?"

"I'm not happy with either of them," I say. "But probably God—whatever that actually means. Call it the Thomas Hardy interpretation: I'd rather have something out there that means something than feel like I exist in a vast ocean of pure meaninglessness."

"What about you, Adam?"

"God," he says. "Even though I thought I'd given all that up." He smiles without showing his teeth, as if doing more with his mouth would break his face. "No, it does make sense: the idea of an external consciousness. I prefer that anyway, given this choice."

"Oh well, I'm on my own then with the multiverse," says Heather.

"You're never alone in the multiverse," I say.

"Ha ha," she says. "Seriously, I can't believe that God made life, not with the research I'm doing. I mean the evidence just isn't there. And I get so many threatening letters from creationists that I just can't align myself to them in any way."

"I don't think this means aligning yourself with creationists," I say. "Surely some external being could have sparked the very beginning of the universe and then everything else just evolved as scientists think it did."

Although as I say this I think: *via Newtonian cause and effect*, and I realize that this is at odds with the idea of a quantum universe, and I suddenly don't know what to say.

"What is your research exactly?" asks Adam.

"Looking for LUCA," she says. "Well, that's how the headlines put it whenever science journalists write about it. LUCA stands for Last Universal Common Ancestor. In other words, searching for the mother of us all."

"She's got this computer model," I say. "You have to see it next time you're in the office. I didn't understand it when I looked at it, but it still gave me the shivers somehow."

"The universal mother," says Adam. "Interesting."

"Don't tell me—you're thinking like the Garden of Eden, with . . . ," she begins.

"No, no. The great mother. The beginning of everything. *The Tao is called the Great Mother: Empty yet inexhaustible, it gives birth to infinite worlds*. That's from the Tao Te Ching."

"Oh," says Heather. "Well, that's just as bad. Who wants pudding?"

Chapter Twelve

After pudding—baked apricots with honey, cashew nuts, and brandy—
and a long conversation about LUCA, and some other entity called
FLO (the first living organism), Adam and I thank Heather and leave
together, trying not to slip on the frosty pavement.

After we are out of earshot of the house, Adam laughs.

"What?" I say.

"Well, I didn't like to say, but I'm not sure I care about which type
of bacteria we evolved from."

"Biologists do always tend towards the most depressing explana-
tions for things," I say. "I wasn't convinced by Heather's reaction to
my idea about machine consciousness, either."

"No. She likes the status quo, I think."

"I think so, too. But I don't see what's wrong with the argument.
At some point animals evolved from plants and conscious life was
formed. What is consciousness? Obviously it's made from the same
quarks and electrons as everything else, perhaps just arranged in a different way. But consciousness is obviously something that can evolve.
Samuel Butler said as much in the nineteenth century. If human consciousness could evolve from nothing, then why can't machine consciousness do the same thing?"

There are obvious objections to this idea, some of which Heather
did point out. For example: What if consciousness can only exist in or-

ganic life-forms? But what is an organic life-form? Machines can self-replicate. They're made from carbon. They need fuel, just like we do.

"Unless consciousness isn't made from matter," says Adam.

"Yeah, well that's possible, too," I say. "But I do sometimes wonder: If a computer read every book in the whole world, would it eventually start to understand language?"

"Hmm," says Adam. Then, after a long pause: "It's cold."

"Yeah. I'm freezing."

It's almost silent as we walk towards the city center. It's past midnight and as we approach the cathedral the only sounds I can hear are the distant humming noises of trucks outside shops; the creaking sound of men unloading blouses and sandwiches and packaged salads and coffee beans and newspapers so they can appear in the shops tomorrow, as if they came to be there by magic.

"Do we know each other?" Adam suddenly asks.

I pause, and then say: "In what sense?"

"I mean I thought I knew you when I saw you earlier today."

I take a deep breath: cold air in my lungs. "I thought the same thing."

"But I don't know you. I'm sure of it."

"Well . . ." I shrug. "Perhaps we did meet before and forgot."

"I wouldn't forget. I wouldn't forget meeting you."

"Adam . . . ," I start.

"Don't say anything," he says. "Just look."

We're just walking past the cathedral gates. If you stop and look up where Adam's pointing now you can see Jesus looking down on you, carved in stone.

"It is amazing," I say, without thinking. "Even if you don't believe in all the rest of it, Jesus is a remarkable figure." Then I laugh. "That sounded so stupid and banal. Sorry. I'm sure no one even disagrees with that."

"You'd be surprised," Adam says.

"Oh," I say, suddenly remembering standing in the same spot earlier on, but looking at the gates, rather than up at Jesus. "Do you know anything about holy water?"

"That's a strange question."

"I know." We start walking again, turning off down a small cobbled street towards my flat. It occurs to me that maybe we are going to go back to my place and sleep together; maybe I could do that. But instead of my usual excitement I feel something else: the same feeling I got when I looked at my computer screen and saw how dirty it was earlier on. I'm dirty, and I'm busy doing something to help me escape. But we're walking on towards my flat, anyway.

"What do you want to know?"

"Um, well, all sorts of things, but mainly where I would get some."

"Get some?" I can't see his expression in the darkness but I can hear the frown in his voice. "Are you a Catholic?"

"No. I'm not religious at all. My mother believed in aliens."

"Ah."

"Yes. But why do you ask?"

"Only Catholics have holy water. You'd find it in any Catholic church."

"Not in the cathedral?"

"No. Not usually."

"I was sure I remembered fonts in the cathedral. I was going to go there before, but it was all locked up."

"There are fonts. But they're empty. The Anglican Church gave up on holy water centuries ago."

"Oh. So, presumably if you want to get holy water from a Catholic church you have to go in the day?"

"No. Not always. You . . ." He pauses. "Do you want to get some now?"

"Maybe. Yes. Maybe. I don't know."

"Can I ask why?"

"Probably best if you don't. It's, well, something you probably wouldn't approve of. Have you ever heard of the physicist George Gamow?"

"No. While you tell me about him shall we walk the other way? I'll show you where to find holy water."

"Really?"

"Yes. I've got a key to St. Thomas's. This way."

I follow him across a car park and through a small passageway onto Burgate. Burlem's house is just across the ring road, past St. Augustine's on a leafy residential road. I wonder what the house looks like now. I imagine it all boarded up and then realize that's silly: People don't board up houses nowadays. Maybe Burlem sold it. Maybe he's even there? I did go and knock on the door last year, but no one answered. Adam and I turn left and walk past the comic shop: a whole window display of superheroes and villains; good guys and bad guys. As we walk I put Burlem out of my head and instead tell Adam about George Gamow and how, when he was a kid, he once kept a Communion wafer instead of swallowing it and put it under his microscope to see if there was any difference between it and a normal wafer. I tell Adam that what I want with the holy water is somewhat similar to this—basically an experiment not at all in keeping with the spirit of Catholicism. Then we're at the church.

"I'll understand if you don't actually want to let me in now," I say.

"No. I like the sound of your experiment. And it doesn't matter to me, anyway."

Inside the church doors it's dark and smells of incense and cold stone. We don't go right inside: It turns out that the holy water is in a little font just inside the entrance. I notice that Adam crosses himself in front of an image of the Virgin Mary. I take out my vial.

"I'm sure this isn't something you should be letting me do," I say.

"It's only water," says Adam. "There are no rules to say you can't take some away with you. And like I said, all of this doesn't mean anything to me anymore."

But he doesn't watch as I dip the vial into the font. Instead he walks beyond me and starts fiddling with leaflets and copies of the *Catholic Herald*. There's a poster on the wall with the words *Shrine of St. Jude* on it. Adam lifts his fingers to it and touches it briefly. I don't think he realizes that I'm watching him. I look away.

"Can I ask why you have keys to the church?" I say to him as we leave.

"Oh, I'm a priest," he says. "Or, at least, I was. Can we go back to your place?"

Through someone else's eyes my kitchen must be a dark, fetid, oppressive space that smells of garlic and cigarettes. There's also a cursed book on the mantelpiece: a slim, pale volume that you don't even notice, if you are someone else.

"Sorry," I say to Adam, as we walk in.

But I'm not exactly sure what I'm sorry about. The thick gray dust on the top of the door frame? The broken arm of the sofa? The burn marks on the old kitchen work surfaces? The peeling green lino? I don't even see those things when I'm on my own. I want to open a window, but it's too cold. I want to turn on all the gas rings like I usually do, but I don't.

"Sorry it's so cold," I say.

"My place is freezing," says Adam. "I live on campus."

"Do you? Where?"

"I've got a room in Shelley College. It's tiny and smells of macaroni and cheese all the time. This is luxurious—believe me."

"Would you like some coffee?" I ask him.

"Just some water, please, if that's all right."

I fill a glass with tap water for Adam and then put on coffee for myself. A train goes past outside and the thin sash window rattles gently. I see a tiny movement in the corner of the room—there and then gone, like a phantom particle. A mouse.

"I like this place," Adam says, sitting down on the sofa.

When my coffee's ready I sit down on the old sofa next to him. I don't think I've ever actually sat on this sofa with another human being. It feels a bit like sitting on a train, our backs facing the direction of travel, both being careful not to let our knees touch.

"What's the Shrine of St. Jude?" I ask him.

"Oh, that. You noticed."

"I just saw it on the wall in the church. I've heard the name before: *St. Jude*. What's he the saint of?"

"Lost and hopeless causes. The shrine's in Faversham. I go there whenever . . ."

"What?"

"Just whenever things go wrong. You're not asking me the obvious question."

"What obvious question?"

"About me being a priest."

"I'm not very good at asking those questions," I say.

There's a pause. I should say something else; I know that it's my line next. And I do want to know. Usually I would want to know everything about being a priest and how it's possible to be a priest and then not be one. I want to ask why he still crossed himself in the church, for example. But now I've got the holy water and the Carbo-veg and it's just like those days when I kept a razor in a box and I just wanted everyone to go away so I could do what I wanted, on my own.

"Do you mind if I smoke?" I ask Adam.

He shrugs. "It's your flat."

"Yeah, I know, but . . ."

"Honestly. Don't mind me."

He sips his water while I light up. I see the slight shake of his left hand holding the water, and then I look away, my gaze moving over the scarred kitchen surfaces: the time I burned the rice; the time I scalded myself; the time I cut my finger.

"What was it like?" I ask, forcing my thoughts to stop. "Or even what *is* it like?"

"What?"

"Being that religious; I mean, being religious enough to be a priest."

He puts his water down and sits forward, leaning his elbow on his knee and propping up his face with his right hand. He uses his forefinger to draw around the edge of his face, as if he was blind and wanted to know what his own face looked like.

"I've been thinking about this," he says. "I've been trying to put it into words but I didn't have anyone to tell and . . . Now I've met you I think maybe you'll understand. In fact, I know you will."

"Why do you think that?"

Now he puts both his hands over his face and lets his head drop into them.

"I don't know."

"Adam?"

"I'm sorry. I'm not even sure I want to talk about what you want to talk about. I didn't even stop being a priest because I wasn't religious enough . . . I was just being stupid back at Heather's. I didn't lose my faith because I wanted to have sex with little boys or old men or young women or anything like that. I studied the Tao Te Ching—years ago, now—and decided to follow The Way alongside being a priest. It's not unusual—lots of people do it. But it undermined my faith. I just wanted to desire nothing, but that was something that I desired, obviously, and it almost drove me mad. And then I couldn't stop thinking about paradoxes. I thought about the virgin birth and the mystery of faith and everything else. I didn't hate the paradoxes—they're the basis for the church, after all—but I started wanting more of them. I wanted to see what a pure paradox would look like. Eventually I realized that I simply needed silence, so I joined a silent order for two years and thought about nothing. Then I stopped. I can't explain this very well . . . And you're right. Why am I telling you this? Where have I seen you before? Shit. I should go."

"Adam . . ."

He gets up. "I'm sorry for barging in here. This isn't the right place for me."

He's right. I fuck old men and become obsessed with curses and rare books. He needs someone more sensible than me to talk to. I look at his old clothes and messed-up hair and imagine his dark, strong forearms. I wonder if he's ever even been to bed with anyone?

I take a deep breath. Why am I always the wrong person?

And, without either of us seeming to do anything, we're now pressing against each other, kissing as though it's midnight at the party at the end of the world. I feel his cock get hard, and I push myself against him. This feels different. There's something real about this that I thought I'd forgotten.

"I'm sorry," he says after about twenty seconds, pulling away. "I can't do this."

"I don't know what happened there," I say, acting as if I agree that this is a bad idea. I can't catch his eye. I turn towards the stove, as if I've got something important to cook. Can you have a disappointment cake? A rejection cake? An unhappy birthday cake?

"I'm sorry," says Adam, behind me. "I'm . . . I shouldn't drink. I'm not used to it."

By the time I say sorry, he's gone. I'm a fucking idiot. Or am I? When attractive young guys offer me something, they always take it away again pretty soon afterwards, so it's probably best that this never happened. What's a man like Adam going to get from me, anyway? If you're someone like Adam, you can sleep with anyone. If he had a shower and put on a suit or something, well, I can't imagine any woman turning him down. With someone like Adam, it doesn't matter about my iPod, or my smooth neck, or my tits that have not (yet) sagged. I don't have cellulite, and men over the age of fifty therefore feel lucky to sleep with me. What have I got that Adam could possibly want? In the sexual economy, I've got millions in the offshore account called "Older Men," but I think I'd get turned down for an account anywhere else.

I used to have a black marker pen, but I don't know where it went. It was a big, phallic, chemical-smelling thing, and I used it to write the number of this flat on one of the bins in Luigi's backyard. But that was, what, a year and a half ago? It's not in the kitchen drawer, and it isn't in the cup of pens on the shelf. Damn. The closest thing I can find is a black Biro. I do have a white piece of cardboard, however. It's the backing from a cheap pair of fishnet tights I bought from the market last spring, and it's been lying on my chest of drawers since then. So I draw the black circle on the card: It takes five minutes just to color it in.

I also have a black mark on my arm; the place where I dug the pen in experimentally to see what it would feel like; to see if it would be like it used to be.

The holy water looks murky in the glass vial. I get the page from *The End of Mr. Y* and lay it on the kitchen counter to check the instructions. OK, so I have to mix the Carbo-veg into the holy water and succuss the mixture several times. That's just shaking, surely? I seem to remember from the homoeopathy books that it is. As I reach up to the cupboard to get the Carbo-veg out of the sugar tin, the single page from Lumas's book floats onto the floor. I pick it up and note that the edge is now slightly damp. I remember seeing some Sellotape in the kitchen drawer, so I get that out and spend the next few minutes carefully repairing the book, matching up the jagged tear in the page with the jagged tear left behind between pages 130 and 133. You can see the join, obviously, but the page is now part of the book again.

I remember that you're not supposed to touch homoeopathic medicines, so I tip one of the pills onto a metal spoon. It makes a tiny clinking sound. Then I unplug the cork from the vial and put the pill inside. It bobs on the surface for a second and then sinks, the water becoming cloudier as it begins to dissolve. My heart's a little rubber ball bouncing against my rib cage. I don't know why I'm nervous: All I'm doing is adding a little sugar pill to some water. Still, I stand there shaking the mixture for several minutes and then, remembering something I read earlier on, I give the vial a couple of little taps on a tea towel folded up on the work surface. I look, and see that the pill has completely dissolved into the water. So now I'm going to drink it.

Am I? Is holy water sterile, or even hygienic? How many people's fingers have been in it? Probably not that many. Come on, Ariel. But . . . Does the priest put it out at night, or in the morning? This is stupid. Cross with myself for caring about anything as banal as how many people's fingers have been in the water, I uncork the vial and force myself to drink a large mouthful. There. Now I don't have to think about it anymore. I take the piece of cardboard and lie down on the sofa, drunk and tired and now feeling a little sick.

Black dot, black dot. A smear. And then I'm asleep.

I dream of mice. I dream of a mouse-world, bigger than this one, with a faint voice saying to me *You have choice*, or something like that, all night long.

I don't wake up until gone ten o'clock, shivering in my jeans and jumper on the sofa, with hard winter light glaring at me through the kitchen window. I must have dropped the piece of cardboard as I fell asleep, because it's on my stomach now. In daylight it looks pathetic: a scribble on a cheap, floppy bit of off-white card. I should have done better, really, but I was quite drunk. So it didn't work. Or it didn't work because I messed it up. How long do you keep trying, though, before you realize that you've been fooled by fiction (again) and it's the familiar, disappointing world that is real? *You have choice.* I have the choice to stop obsessing about being cursed. I have the choice to stop drinking concoctions suggested by rare books. I could try to sell the book, presumably, even though it is damaged? But even as I think this I know that nothing would make me give it up. So I'll keep the book, but go back to normal. I'll write something about curses for the magazine. I'll get on with my Ph.D. A chapter on Lumas about the blurring between fiction and nonfiction, and the thought experiment that becomes a physical experiment. A trick that makes you see the world anew . . .

Except I don't feel like I'm seeing the world anew. I feel like I haven't even been to sleep. And my stomach hurts, like period pain but slightly higher up. That water must have been contaminated. Maybe I should eat something. Maybe that will help.

There's still some soya milk in the fridge, so I put porridge on the stove, and coffee. As I go to the bedroom for a different jumper I realize how cold and tired I really am. I think I need a scarf as well. As I pull the thick black sweater over my head and wrap a long black woollen scarf around my neck, I look out of the window. There are little icicles hanging off the inside window frame: the kind of detail you vow to recall for people at some point in the future when your life is sorted out and you want to tell an anecdote about how poor you were that winter, and how dismal your flat was. But every day I grow less and less confident in that future. I'm not sure I want it, anyway. *Ha ha, when I was poor. Ha, ha, have you seen that play? Ha ha, I know this is really bad, but I've actually been thinking lately that it might make sense to vote Conservative.* I want to swerve to avoid that life at all costs. Maybe I'll just live like this forever. So I'm not that interested in the meaning of the icicles. *There are icicles*. I smile briefly, even though no one's looking, and wrap the scarf around my neck one more time.

I walk back down the long hallway, and into the kitchen, through the wooden door that's thick with decades of gloss paint. Then I have an odd feeling that the door is much too small or I am much too big. It feels exactly like déjà vu, as if I'm about to shrink and look up at a door that is a hundred times my size, rather than a foot or so taller than me. But it doesn't happen; it just sits there in my mind: a parallel thought; perhaps something that's happening to some other me, out there in the multiverse. The sensation reminds me of the time someone gave me mushroom tea without telling me and I spent the whole evening watching this pink and cream suburban sitting room grow and shrink around me. I remember the TV being on in the corner; some Saturday night game show where loud, happy, healthy families competed against one another to win a new car or a holiday. At one point the TV towered over me, as if I could walk inside the screen. But the image I remember most vividly is when the room shrank to the size of a sugar cube. I was looking down on it, on the room I was in, but I wasn't inside the room anymore. Afterwards I asked my friend how he thought that could have worked. Where was I if I wasn't in the room? He just smiled and said, "Inside a bad trip, man." What an idiot. I close my eyes and open them again. The door's normal. I really must have drunk too much last night.

After breakfast I consider going in to the university but instead decide to stay here. OK, so the heat costs money here, but as long as I use the gas it should be OK, at least for a day while I try to get my thoughts together. Did I throw myself at Adam last night or did he throw himself at me? I can't be in a room with him today, anyway. It's still so cold, so I switch on the oven and then sit on the sofa with my knees pulled into my body, smoking and thinking about what to do next. I could write something, but I can't. I could read something—but what do you read after *Mr. Y*? I could just sit here all day and wait for the curse to hit me. But there is no curse. The only curse in my life is me.

You have choice.

What was going on in my dream?

While I'm cleaning my teeth, shivering in the damp bathroom (by far the coldest room in the flat), I remember that the marker pen is in the bathroom cabinet. Of course. I bought that weird shampoo that came in an unmarked bottle and I wanted to write on it in case I bought something else from that market stall and became confused. It's the kind of thing I do when I should be working: write labels on shampoo bottles; iron jeans; think about seagulls. I don't think I really cared about the shampoo: It was just something to do. I open the cabinet and there it is, a thick black pen lying there alongside some old paracetamol and a broken hairbrush. As soon as I open the door it rolls out and I catch it before it falls in the sink. OK.

Ten minutes later I'm sitting on the sofa again, this time with a fresh cup of coffee, a cigarette, and a perfect black circle on the back of a perfect white card. I went through all the random mail from downstairs until I found a birthday card, probably about a year old, inside a pale blue envelope. *Happy 20th, Tamsin,* it said. *We'll come and see you soon.* It was signed Maggie and Bill. But that bit's in the bin now. I've got the other bit: a rectangle of card with a Victorian pastoral scene on one side, and bright white nothingness on the other. Well, now it's bright white nothingness with a small black circle in the middle of it, perfectly filled in.

I stub out my cigarette and drain the last of the coffee, turning the card over and looking at the Victorian image again. It's dated 1867, and it's called *Summer Landscape,* although its colors seem autumnal. It looks like such a peaceful place: red earth carpeted with thick grass and canopied with emerald and bronze trees; a path by a river where you could walk in complete silence. I turn the card over and there's the circle again. Circle. Soothing landscape. Circle. Soothing landscape. I know which one makes the best birthday card. Right. Are you supposed to wait fifteen minutes before doing this? The homoeopathy books I read yesterday all said that homoeopathic medicines should be taken on a clean mouth, fifteen minutes after eating or drinking. But that's OK. If it doesn't work then I can blame the coffee and start again later. As long as I keep doing it wrong I'll have something to do all day. Then, this evening, I can admit that my adventure is over and go back to normal life. Maybe I'll reread *Erewhon*. That usually cheers me up.

So I pick up the vial and give it another little shake. What the hell—I bang it hard twice on the side of the sofa. I suppose I've probably done too much successing now, but surely that makes it more potent, not less? I think back to the homoeopathy books and remember that if I were to take a drop of this mixture and put it in some water and shake it some more, the result would be stronger than this mixture, even though scientifically speaking it would be more dilute. How does that work? Come on Ariel; stop thinking about it and just get on with it. It's just you and the liquid. OK. I drink it: a large mouthful. Then I lie down on the sofa and stare at the black circle, concentrating as hard as I can. And this time, I do not fall asleep: I watch as the black circle splits into two, and I try not to blink as it kaleidoscopes around on the sheet, lifting and turning.

And then, in an instant that feels thinner and sharper than the edge of a razor, I'm falling. I'm falling into a black tunnel, the same black tunnel that Mr. Y described in the book. But I'm not falling down, if that makes any sense: I'm falling along, forwards, horizontally. The walls of the tunnel pass by as if I were in a car, but I'm not in a car. Wherever I am it's completely silent and I have no bodily sensations at all. I'm fairly sure my body is here with me, but it has no feelings and no desires. I'm not even sure if I'm wearing clothes. Only my mind feels alive. I see—although it doesn't feel as if it's actually through my eyes—almost exactly what Mr. Y saw: black all around suddenly pinpricked by little lights that turn into wavy lines that seem to go on forever. Then a huge penis, drawn in the same style as that on the Cerne Abbas Giant, but rendered here in light. There's also a vagina, which looks less familiar, and then it's gone. Then I seem to be moving faster. I see the birds and feet and eyes that Mr. Y saw, but to me they look like Egyptian hieroglyphics, the kind of thing you learn about in primary school. Then I see many letters: Greek, Roman, and Cyrillic. I don't recognize all of them, but after a while they organize themselves into alphabets and there are several minutes where nothing seems to change in the tunnel. Could I stop this experience if I wanted to? I'm not sure I could. Can my mind even handle this experience, whatever it is? I've never much liked hallucinogens because of the lack of control you have, and the fact that you have to finish the trip; you can't just switch it off. Now I'm here and I know I can't switch this off. I could go mad. Maybe I have just gone mad. Maybe this is what it's like crossing from sanity into madness, and maybe I'll never escape. As I think, I begin to feel sick, so I try to stop thinking and instead just look at the walls of the tunnel again.

The alphabets look more familiar, and now include numerals, although in patterns I don't immediately recognize. Odd combinations of Roman numerals that I don't understand are interspersed with sequences beginning 2, 3, 5, 7, 11, 13, 17, 19 and 1, 1, 2, 3, 5, 8, 13, 21. At least, I assume they are sequences, but soon they dissolve into long lines of numerals that look like cosmic telephone numbers. In places I can see equations, but they only flicker and then disappear. I'm sure I see Newton's F=MA, and, later, Einstein's E=MC^2. I can see mathematical symbols that I don't understand, as well as those I do: the = and + signs, and later various pieces of set notation like I {1, 2, 3, . . . 100}. Then more series of numbers that go on for minutes and minutes. I see sequences that don't make any sense at all, such as: 1431, 1731, 1831, 2432, 2732, 2832, 3171, 3181, 3272, 3282, 11511, 31531, 31631, 32532, 32632, 33151, 33161, 33252, 33262, 114311, 117311, 118311, 124312, 127312, 128312, 214321, 217321, 218321, 224322, 227322, 228322. At first I think they must be dates, but then the numbers get too big again. Then something else happens, something not described in Lumas's version of this: The letters from the alphabet all disappear and turn into numbers, and then the numbers, apart from 1 and 0, disappear as well until I am left with millions and millions of 0s and 1s waterfalling down the walls around me.

01110111011010000110000101110100011101000110 10 00011001010110011001110101011000110110101101101

0010111001101100111011011110110100101101111001100
1110110111101101110011101110110100001100001011
0100011101000110100001100101011001100111010101
1000110110101101101001011100110110011101101111101
1010010110111001100111011011110110111001110111101
1010000110000101110100011101000110100001100101
0110011001110101011000110110101101101010010111001
1011001110110111101101001011011100110011101101101111
1011011001110111011010000110000101110100011101
0001101000011001010110011001110101011000110110
1011011010010111001101100111011011110110101001011
1110011001110110111101101011100111011101101000011
0001011101000111010001101000011001010110011001
1101010110001101101011011010010111001101100111101
1011110110100101101110011001110110111101101011001
1101110110100001100001011101000111010001101000
0110010101100110011101010110001101101011011010100
101110011011001110110111101101001011011100110011
1011011110110111001110111011010000110000101110
0011101000110100001100101011001100111010101101010110
0011011010110110100101110011011001110110111101101110110
1001011011100110011101101011110110111010

Chapter Thirteen

I'm standing in an impossibly dense, thin street, with tarmac under my feet. Ahead of me there's a grubby tower block that may have been shiny once. On either side of me tattered shop fronts display postcards, newspapers, shoes, cameras, hats, sweets, sex toys, and rolls of fabric, but none of them looks open. I think it's nighttime here: The sky is hard to pick out but the light is artificial and I can see something black above me, although there are no stars, and there is no moon. All around me, broken neon signs crackle like acne scars. Two or three of them flicker in sexual colors: rouge, flush pink, powder white, but the rest of them just look like they may have last worked a long time ago. The space above the shop fronts is tangled with dim sodium lights, street signs, corrugated iron shutters, and windows of what seem like hundreds of apartments and stock rooms. There are signs everywhere, sticking out at right angles from the buildings like Post-it Notes in an old book. But I can't read them.

Can I move forwards in this space? Yes. I can take a step, and then another. I can see an alleyway off to my left: another impossibly thin space. At the end of the alley I can vaguely pick out what looks like a steel fence with barbed wire curled on the top of it. There are fire escapes everywhere: zigzags and spirals leading up and down tired brick walls. A blue light dances in an upstairs window: a television? So there is life here beyond me, although I don't feel particularly alive. I don't feel hot or cold, alive or dead, drunk or sober. . . . I don't feel anything. It's actually pleasant, not feeling anything, although of course it doesn't directly feel "pleasant." It doesn't feel like anything. Have you ever not felt like anything? It's amazing. Perhaps I feel so calm because there are no people here. I've been in spaces like this before—Soho, Tokyo, New York—but there were always too many people shopping, camera-clicking, talking, running, walking, hoping, wanting. I get claustrophobic in big cities, overwhelmed by all that desire in one small place, all those people trying to suck things into themselves: sandwiches, cola, sushi, brand labels, goods, goods, goods. But there's no one here. There's a bus stop, but no buses; road signs but no traffic. I walk on, and I can actually hear the dull thud of my footsteps on the hard street. A turning on the right leads to a small square with a gurgling fountain in the middle of it. Here I see shadowy coffee shops with their tables and chairs crowding the dark pavements, and a couple of small city trees growing out of concrete blocks. I don't want to get lost, so I soon come back to the main street, unsure about what to do next. I turn around, everything jumbling in my vision.

Where do I go? I think.

And then a woman's metallic voice informs me: *You now have fourteen choices.*

My image of the street in front of me is overlaid, suddenly, with a console image: something like a city plan on a computer screen in my mind. A few areas flash briefly in a kind of pale computer-blue color, like war zones on a map of the world. These are the choices, I understand. But . . . ? I don't actually understand anything about what's going on. The nearest "choice," if that's what this means, is the third floor of a block right next to where I started. I walk a few paces and start climbing the zigzag fire escape, the rubber from the soles of my trainers hitting the metal with a hollow, clanging sound. Soon I come to a green door with peeling paint. I push the door and it opens inwards. What do I do now?

You now have one choice, says the disembodied voice.

I'm inside.

———

You now have one choice.

You . . . I'm standing still on four bent legs and—oh shit—I'm trapped. All around me are thick, blurry plastic walls and I can't move. I can go forwards a bit, and backwards a bit; I know that, but I am still at the moment. Fuck. I can hardly breathe. I keep blinking because my vision doesn't feel right: Everything outside of my prison looks brown and warped, and there are reflections everywhere. And I'm hungry; a hunger of a sort I've never experienced before, from a place in my stomach that I don't recognize. Whatever I am, this is a kind of hell: This is a feeling you could have in a nightmare for only one or two seconds before you woke up screaming. I can't move. I can't turn around. My arms/legs/wings are pushed into the sides of my body. I think I have a tail but I can't move it. It's pinned down by something. And I think I'm probably going to die here, on my own, unable to move even my head. Come on, Ariel. You are still Ariel. Yes, Ariel plus . . . What? Who am I? Into whose mind have I telepathed? I—or at least "we"; I'm having the same problem Mr. Y had—want to scratch. I want to eat: I know that's why I came into this box. There was something sweet and crumbly which I did eat, but not recently. But almost as much as that, I want to scratch. I love it when my sharp foot rubs against my ears, taking away the itch, and I'd give anything to be able to do that now (not that I understand the economy of hope). I've tried—in fact, I keep trying. Why can't I move? I, Ariel, can see the Perspex walls, but the other "I" doesn't know what's going on. This being—the other I—panicked, hours ago. She couldn't do what she always does in these situations, which is to try to run fast and look for somewhere dark and soft to hide. But it's hard to think of this being, this thing I am now part of, as "she." My fur ("*My* fur"? Well, that's how it seems) smells of fear now: a damp, sweet, biscuity smell. And I know this smell from the others, from the ones who return with teeth marks in their bodies.

Zoom out. Maintain third person. For God's sake, Ariel, you are not a mouse. But I am. I know how to groom my fur. I have been pregnant a number of times (I don't think she can count, but I can. I'm not sure if she has language, but I have. I can count things in memories perhaps she doesn't even know she has). I remember the aching feeling of giving birth, like pushing on a new bruise. I know I am going to die here, but surely I can't know what death is? Only elephants understand death. . . . Where did I read that? I've got no idea how long I've been here, but I want to get out. *Let me out!* I try to scream but all I hear is the fast breath of the mouse, her heart beating instead of mine.

What do I do now? I know how to make myself calm in these situations. I've stood on crowded tube trains and in lifts thinking *Not long now,* and *Breathe.* But my consciousness has merged with this one and I know, because she knows, that this is danger; that it is imperative to escape now. But we can't move. Shit, shit, shit. How do I get out of here? Where's all the information Mr. Y said he saw on the edges of his vision? As I think that, something like a computer desktop snaps into focus. Now I can see what the mouse sees—a vast chamber warped by the plastic and browned by its tint (although she doesn't understand that, and believes she is somewhere she has never been before because even the scent is different in this plastic box)— but with an overlay: a console on which I can make choices. It's hard to describe what this looks like, since I have no idea how it works. It feels like a computer desktop but everything on it is unfamiliar. I don't know how to navigate it. But it does seem that when I call for it, it will come. And presumably it will get me out of here.

In the top right-hand corner of my vision is a blue square that twinkles when I look (think?) at it. The rest of the "screen" is layered with small milky squares, each one very faintly showing a landscape I don't recognize. It's like a hundred science documentaries playing on the same screen. What are these images? As I glance over each one it becomes momentarily brighter, like a link on the Internet, and I realize (I don't know how) that I can choose to jump into one of them: presumably to perform what Lumas termed *Pedesis.* But I don't want to do that. I need to get out of here—out of the Troposphere—and release the mouse from her trap. I look over the milky images again. One of them intrigues me more than the others: The landscape seems extraterrestrial. But—oh no—the moment my thoughts rest on it and I think *This looks interesting* something begins to happen. I'm blurring—that's the only verb I can think of—out of this reality and into another one. I think *Stop! I didn't mean it!* But it's too late.

At least I'm not trapped anymore.

Now my paws pad over a cold, hard surface. I feel my back end sway as my paws touch the ground top-right; back-left; top-left; back-right. I have a tail that I can move! This seems both familiar and unfamiliar to me: something I've always had; something I once had a long time ago. The pale concrete below me (and I feel myself putting my own word on that, *concrete*) is ice-cube (ditto) cold, and I walk faster on it because of that. But I am warm enough. I have only just left my nest and the memory of so much fur, and the smell of my family (I'm translating as I go, here, and "family" is the closest I can get to this memory sense of togetherness and connectedness) soothes me like hot syrup (ditto). I am a mouse again (I think). But I am free.

There's something between my back legs: familiar to this mouse but not to me. It feels odd, like my tail, but while my tail is like an extra limb, this new thing feels powered-up like a clitoris, but there's more of it, and it extends from my stomach to somewhere outside of me. It tingles now as hot liquid comes out of it and hits the concrete. And I'm thinking that this will keep others away, and I've always done it because of this. My fur twitches with abstract nouns, an untranslatable, nonhuman sense of pride, property, future planning, and a constant, musky desire for violence—my claws in the backs of my small, pale rivals, ripping their flesh—and sex. Perhaps that's what I live for most of all: the way my brain trembles and softens as this clitoris-like cock moves in and out of the warm, tight hole in another being, and the feeling of oozing sweetness that eventually spreads in my stomach, back, legs, and throat, so sweet that I fall over, clutching her, she, whoever. I have desires—perhaps that's all I am—but I don't seem to dwell on them. My mind isn't equivalent to *I want, I want*. It's more like *I've got, I've got*. Only one thing is bothering me, as I wander around this space, with its bins on wheels that are bigger than me. *Where is she?* One down. One missing. One gone. I might not be able to count but I can certainly subtract. It's not fucking good.

Even I'm shocked at the idea that a mouse would swear until I realize that these are my thoughts merged with his: his feelings in my language. I should be trying to get out, but the feeling of being here, being him, is almost addictive. Everything about him is charged. Even his/my whiskers vibrate with electricity and anticipation, like live wires coming out of my face. He's moving now, so much lighter on his feet than I ever can be on mine, and it's like being on a fairground ride. We move over the concrete towards the other bin and I know where I'm going but at the same time I don't know, and every movement is a surprise. It's like being the driver and the passenger all at once. And there's something so sure about these movements, and the sensation I'm now feeling: the sensation of biting into a stale piece of bread, marinated in rain—a piece of bread I recognize as being stale because I threw it out, but which now seems delicious: a savory taste, like Marmite on toast.

But I do have to get out of here. This mouse is fine, but the other one isn't. She's in a trap I set and I have to get her out of it. I think *Console!* like I'm playing Space Invaders or starring in an SF film and yes, the thing appears, filming over my vision. I plan to ignore the milky images but then two things happen at once: In the vision behind the console—the mouse's vision—I see an orange blur, like a smear of marmalade; and in the console I see one square in which the image displayed is not like an alien landscape, one square in which there's a gray mouse sitting by a bin wheel eating bread. That's me. Something is looking at me.

Now it all becomes confusing. My mouse has seen the orange cat and it's as if we've both had an injection of icy cold water and gone onto high alert. It's fear, but a kind of fear I'm not used to. Death, death, death is coming. Fuck. My whole insides have turned to this icy mush and I have to run; I have to hide. . . . But hang on. The icy water is solidifying. I'm freezing into place. I know (some level of knowing that I haven't experienced before) that I have to keep still now. And I, Ariel, want to just get out of here but some instinct I didn't know I had—some mouse-instinct mapped onto my own—sees that there's also a doorway (gray, official) hovering over the cat. It makes me focus on the milky square with the statue-mouse in it, the square belonging to the cat, who is looking at the frozen sugar-mouse, whose terror I can feel in the tiny trembling in my own/our own body, and I think *Switch! Switch!*

And now I'm blurring again, into something bigger. My tail now feels lighter, and I flick it around as I crouch here, crazy with anticipation, my thin tongue licking my sharp teeth. This is going to be fucking fun, and I'm not even sure I can wait before I pounce. I move my bottom around in a repeating arc, balancing myself. Now? No. Wait. Need the right moment, totally the right moment. I've done this thousands of times before, and I could never, ever get bored with it. I don't plan my attacks in any detail but when I remember them they are like bloody ballets, with me as the director, poking the dancer with my paw, making the food dance, making it pirouette on broken legs, because I like food that moves. I do eat that brown shit in the plastic bowl but I don't enjoy it: It tastes like death. I only eat it to survive because half the time I have to wear a fucking bell that scares the food away. But I can take the bell off if I work long enough at it, picking away with my precise claws. So I have no bell and now there's food in front of me. I anticipate the way the warm blood-gravy-liquid will taste in my mouth once I've torn the furry coating off this thing shaking in front of me, trying to appear still. I remember the taste. . . . Oh God. Oh *yuck*. It's like hot Bovril mixed with iron tablets and rust. And now I'm thinking that must be disgusting really, but the synapses (or whatever) in my mind and the cat's mind are now jumping up and down like kids in a junior debating society. After a couple of seconds I'm almost convinced that blood is delicious after all, but whatever is left of me that is human and vegetarian thinks, *No!* I can feel this thought blending with the cat's thoughts and so, when the mouse decides this is the moment to leg it under the bin, I hesitate. And my cat-mind does a diving backflip, just for a second, but it's enough to fuck everything up. There's a voice in my mind telling me not to do it. I don't understand this. I don't have concepts like *Why?* in my language. This is like a headache, some memory of a white room and a table and being held down by my neck as something sharp jabbed into me. Well, no one's holding me down now.

Fuck off, passenger.

No.

You're like a flea inside my head.

Well . . . Maybe you're right. Why save the piece of food, anyway? What is "saving"? Nothing makes sense. . . . Ariel: *You are not a fucking cat.* You were that mouse. You remembered your nest. But I'm not a mouse, either. And now I want to taste its blood.

XXXXXXXXXXXXXXXXXXXXXXXXXXXXXXXXXXXXXXXXXXX

A buzz in my head I don't recognize. A chemical stronger than fear.

I'm moving forwards slowly now. The food has moved under the bin. New strategy. *Not* Game Over. I crouch and my back is a perfect curve: one shoulder slightly higher than the other, my left paw in front of my right. I'm going to crunch your skull, and I don't care how long I have to dance with you first. I'm . . . You've gone. Where are you? Where's my fucking food . . . ?

The mouse has gone. He's safe. My mind now has a celebration party and a funeral going on in the same room.

Console. Now I really have to get out of here. The thing comes up in my vision again, jerking as my hitchhiker consciousness bobs up and down with the cat, padding towards the wall, and then—wow—jumping up onto it. God, I liked that. But I have to get out of here. I've saved one mouse but there's still one more to release. I glance around at the desktop space again, ignoring the milky images in the center. The only thing left is the blue object/image, and so I direct my thoughts at it. *Quit now?* says the female voice I recognize from before. *Yes,* I think. *Yes, yes, yes . . .* A door appears in front of me and I am me again, twisting the knob and walking through on two heavy legs, with no tail. But I don't recognize this place. I seem to be in a long corridor with gray carpet and beige walls. Oh shit. Where's the fire escape? How do I get out?

I walk along the blank corridor, past notice boards with nothing pinned on them, past bright white office doors, until I reach a lobby with four lifts in a row. There's nothing on these walls except for one safety image: a green stick man and a green stick man in a wheelchair both moving towards a bright white exit. The stick man is winning. Not knowing what else to do, I press the button to call the lift. Instantly, all four sets of doors open. I smile at this. Is there really no one in this place apart from me? A whole city to myself—if I even am in the same city I started in. But I can't stay: I have to get back. I randomly take the third lift along from the left and press the G button. It drops down faster than I would have liked but I don't feel sick. I still don't feel anything. Once I'm on the ground floor I find a set of revolving doors that takes me back out onto the street. And then I see something odd: a small white business card lying there on the ground. It wouldn't look odd in a normal city, lying on a chewing-gummed pavement amid all the old crisp packets, fag butts, receipts, and torn pieces of newspaper. In a normal city you wouldn't notice it. But here it really stands out. I bend down and pick it up. The name APOLLO SMINTHEUS is written on it in brown ink. There's nothing else. I pick it up and put it in the pocket of my jeans.

I'm on a deserted main road lined with quiet office blocks. There are signs for subways but there's no traffic, so I walk across the road, climbing over the barrier separating the two carriageways. Now, I could go left or right or straight on, down a smaller road. Something about the smaller road seems familiar, so I walk onwards, afraid but not actually feeling fear, like I'm watching myself in a film, until I recognize the alleyway on my right with all the fire escapes. That alley was on my left before. Now I see. Somehow I ended up in the large building I was facing when I first arrived here. So presumably all I need to do to get back is to keep walking onwards, onwards down the road and then—yes—into the tunnel with the zeroes and ones and all the letters of every alphabet I've ever seen. Then I open my eyes.

Back on the sofa. I'm alive. I'm home. I'm human. I feel cold. I need to pee. The sense of disappointment I often get when I wake up from normal dreams has now mutated into something else: the disappointment of being me, here, now.

My overwhelming thought: *I want to be back in the Troposphere.* And a weaker thought: *But you wanted to get out.*

Strange how I keep thinking about drugs, but that's the connection Mr. Y made as well. This time I'm remembering a bathroom, a long time ago. In fact, it must have been just before I went to Oxford. I was in a bathroom in Manchester with a big guy who gave me a tiny little pipe, coated in green enamel. I remember sucking on the pipe and feeling something I'd never felt before: complete contentment, something similar to how you feel just after an orgasm, but more— where the whole world is a big soft duvet and you're just about to go to sleep, and you feel as if nothing will ever hurt you again. I sucked this stuff into my lungs and it tasted like ammonia. And I asked the guy what it was.

"Freebase," he said. "Like crack cocaine. You'd probably best not do it again; it'll boggle your head."

In the same way that I immediately wanted to have another go on that pipe, I now want to get back to the Troposphere. So maybe that's the curse.

Muddled thoughts, muddled thoughts. It's quite obvious that I've just been asleep again. I can't have been in the Troposphere. It's a fictional place, a place from a book. But I still get up from the sofa and, before going to the loo or anything like that, check the mousetrap under the sink. And I feel sick. There she is, the being whose memory and thoughts I shared, trembling in the little box, her tail caught in the catch. I don't think I ever really looked at the mice in the traps before, or even thought about them very much apart from trying to remember to release them outside as quickly as possible. But now I'm looking. Whether it was "just a dream" or not, I know exactly how she feels in there. I undo the box, my hands fumbling on the catch, trying to free her tail as gently as possible.

"I'm sorry," I say to her. "I'm so sorry."

I gently place the box on the floor and she walks out backwards, slowly at first, with her nose twitching. I expect her immediately to become a gray streak across the floor as she runs for cover, but instead she sits there looking at me, scratching—I know how much she wanted to do that—and then just sitting there, her tiny black eyes locked on mine. I recognize this stare from somewhere, and I return it instinctively. We stay like that for a full minute and I'm sure she knows. I'm sure she knows, on some level, that I was in her mind and that I understand her. She's not afraid of me. Then she does go, scuttling away under one of the cupboards. I check the other traps and find them empty. Then I throw them all away.

There's something wrong with the light. It takes me a while to realize—I go to the bathroom and pee, and spend about four or five minutes looking at myself in the mirror, wondering what someone else would find out if they got inside my head—but as I come back into the kitchen and put on some coffee, I notice what it is. It's dark already. Then I look at the clock and see why. It's four o'clock. That's odd. I took the mixture at about eleven, I think. And I was in the Troposphere for about half an hour, or at least that's how it felt. Maybe I am losing my mind.

I check my jeans pocket. There's no business card there.

I look out of the window: There is no cat.

But I will look up Apollo Smintheus later, to see if it's a real thing.

The oven must have gone out while I was lying on the sofa, and now I'm shivering in the cold. I remember the way it was in the Troposphere: the no-feeling of the place, the lack of any temperature. I want that back. But if I can't have that, I want to be hot, hot, hot. I turn on more of the gas rings and stand as close as I can to the stove. Soon my coffee's ready, but I don't go anywhere with it. I just stand by the stove shivering and thinking. I should be warming up by now. Am I ill? Has that mixture affected me in some deep way? Is it fucking up my whole system?

And then I think that if I really have just travelled through some strange other dimension, into the minds of mice (and a cat) and out again, that would probably make me feel a bit weird. I mean, surely that would make anyone feel weird? This thought makes me smile, and then laugh. Only I could telepath into the mind of a sex-obsessed mouse and then a psycho cat. This would be a good story to tell, except that I don't tell stories, and no one would believe it, anyway. I stop laughing. Everyone else who has ever done this has died. If you added that to the story, then no one would laugh.

There's a buzzing from my bag. A text message.

It's Patrick. *4give my persistence*, it says, *but i need u again asap.* Oh Christ.

After checking through all my encyclopaedias for references to Apollo Smintheus, I eat dinner early—a bowl of rice with the last of my miso. There's something wrong with my flat this evening. It's not just that time has passed too quickly: It feels empty, cold, and dirtier than usual. Not bothering to worry about the electricity, I switch on the big kitchen light and the lamp, and I put on the radio while I'm eating. I don't usually listen to the radio at this time of day and I have no idea what kind of thing is on. I want something comforting: half an hour of eccentric people talking about travel books, for example, or gardening. Instead of that I find a religious discussion program. Looking at the clock I guess that it has been on for about ten minutes already. There are about four different voices, including the presenter.

– . . . but Mantra II shows that the patients who were prayed for did not do significantly better than those who were not.

– I disagree . . .

– (*Laughter*) Come on. You can't disagree with scientific findings. It's there in black and white in the *Lancet*.

– For those who don't know, Mantra II—Mantra, I believe, standing for Monitoring and Actualization of Noetic Trainings—was a study concluded earlier this year. It set out to discover whether or not prayer significantly helped a group of heart patients. The group of patients didn't know whether or not they were being prayed for. The external prayer groups ranged from Christian, Muslim, Jewish, and Buddhist. . . .

– Mantra II is not the only study in this area—I feel I have to point this out. What about Randolph Byrd's classic 1988 study? Or William Harris's Kansas City study of 1999. In Harris's study, conducted in St. Luke's hospital, the prayed-for group did eleven percent better than the group who were not prayed for. Scientists have been researching this question for decades. They keep researching it because it has absolutely *not* been made certain that intercessional prayer does not help people. In fact, it is quite clear that prayer has some effect, although we are still a long way from knowing what that effect might be.

– Certainly, what I have observed in my practice is that prayer *does* have effects in the world. Coming back to Mantra II . . .

– But this is all ridiculous! Where is the proof? In the Harris study you mention, Roger—and which I looked at closely in my book—even the researchers themselves admitted that there was only a probability factor of 1:25 in the study. In other words, there would be a one in twenty-five chance of the result they obtained appearing on its own, by accident, by chance. That's certainly not enough to convince me. The Lottery would not be profitable for very long if all it had were twenty-five numbers and you only had to pick one of them!

– As I said, coming back to the Mantra II study—and I suppose this is relevant to the Harris study as well—you have to ask who is looking at the data and how they are interpreting it. . . .

– Oh—so it's a conspiracy now? The researchers have "hidden the truth"?

– No, of course not. But perhaps something like prayer can't be understood in studies with data and graphs and probability factors. How do you even begin to measure something like this? For example, what is "one unit" of prayer?

– There is an interesting ethical question here about God, I think. Regardless of how we interpret the data from studies like Mantra II, we have to ask: Supposing prayer did help people—what sort of a God would only help the people who asked, or who had other people to ask for them? Surely this implies an inequality of treatment of people by God, even though we are apparently all God's children, all equal in his eyes?

– Yes, that's an interesting question. Perhaps the whole concept of prayer is in itself a paradox. Perhaps you can't pray to a God who treats all equally. Perhaps then prayer becomes a redundant idea. If God loves all people equally, presumably one should not have to remind him to care? There should be no logical reason for intercession.

– I agree that this is a profound point. However, you can ask: What if it isn't God? What if the success of prayer actually reveals something about the power of thought? Can thought actually influence matter?

– Like spoon bending?

– Yes. (*Laughter*) I suppose you could look at it as being a little like spoon bending.

I finish my rice and light a cigarette as the discussion goes on in the background. At least the voices are there, reminding me that there is a tangible world beyond this room, beyond my mind. Where the hell did I go this afternoon? And, I can't help thinking now, how long before I can go back there? Maybe I should try again as soon as possible, and see if a) the place is as real as it felt this afternoon and b) whether, if it is real (whatever reality is in this context), I can navigate it with more success than I managed the first time.

A train rattles past and I wonder where it's going. I haven't been out today.

I smoke another cigarette and try to get warm, but it doesn't work. I should probably try to get back into the Troposphere for that reason alone: At least I won't be cold anymore. If only I didn't think the events of today point towards me being mentally ill (empathizing with mice—I think that's a tick in the box)—and if I wasn't so bloody cold—then this would be, unequivocally, the most amazing day of my life. So I'll do it again. I'll find out if it's real (although I will try to avoid cats). And then what? Freak out? Celebrate? Have a nervous break-down? There is no obvious logical thing to do before, during, or after this situation other than stop everything I'm doing right now and allow there to be no more before, during, or after. But that's the one thing I will not do. I have to try to go back.

As I settle back onto the sofa with the paraphernalia of my new addiction—the card with the black circle and the vial of liquid—there's a knock at the door. Is it Wolf? Ignoring it, I sink back into the sofa, vaguely thinking about how I never did get onto a psychiatrist's couch, and I drink more of the mixture and hold up the card over my eyes.

The tunnel.

The road.

Console.

Chapter Fourteen

You now have twenty-seven choices.

Why is it different from before? At least I'm in the same place, on the same deserted street, looking at the same signs. All but one of them are still in the language I can't read. One is now illuminated and readable. MOUSE 1 is what it says. I really must be going mad. But in here, in the Troposphere, going mad doesn't seem like something that should worry me. Like the fear I had last time—the fear that didn't feel like fear—the worry is there but it doesn't feel like anything. There's no quickened heartbeat; no sweat. I'm watching myself in a film again. I'm playing myself in a video game. So I've got twenty-seven choices. I still don't know what that means. And to be honest I'd be happy just staying out here on this nowhere road, feeling this blissed-out nothing. Could I be happy not knowing? No. I have to find out how this thing works. What is the Troposphere? The blurred console is like a translucent map over my vision, showing me which places are "live": which places I can enter. At least, that's what it seemed to mean last time. Last time the closest place I could enter was the apartment now marked with the MOUSE 1 sign. Now one of the shops just a few doors down the street seems to be highlighted. It's a little music shop with a piano in the window. In my mind I ask the console to close and it flickers out of my sight. Now I can look at the shop properly. There's the piano: a small black upright thing with sheet music propped up on the holder. I look more closely and see that the title is in German. The sign on the door is also German: OFFEN. I open the door and a small bell tinkles. I expect to see the inside of the shop but, of course, I don't.

You now have one choice.

You . . . I'm now someone else: someone human and male. I'm sitting in a café, waiting. I don't need to translate this person's thoughts: It's a strange sensation, actually being someone else, but that's how it now seems. It's certainly easier than being a mouse, or a cat. I can . . . I can speak German. I'm even thinking in German. I know how to read music. I . . . OK, Ariel, just go with it.

So I'm sitting in a café looking at the dregs in a white cup smeared with old gray cappuccino froth, and I'm pissed off, but that's nothing new. How could he do this to me again? *Again*. The word makes me want to weep. I can feel it on my skin, in my cheeks, and running down my chest: little bugs of failure crawling on me, and they're all repeating that word: *Again*. He said it would be soon. Now it looks like never. It must be because of something I didn't say. It must be because of something I didn't do. The idea that this would have happened anyway is too repellent. It must be this shirt. He said he liked the blue one, so why am I wearing this red piece of crap?

At this point the waitress comes over and, just as Lumas suggested, a faint outline of another shop appears over her body, and I realize I could step into that doorway instead of remaining "here"— whatever, in this context, is "here." Shall I try that? What about when Mr. Y did it and got bounced back onto the Troposphere? I try to call up the console, but it doesn't come. I'm not trying anything without that to guide me. And I'm not sure I want to leave this story now, anyway.

But I do want the console. I call it again.

It doesn't come.

At least I spent fifteen more minutes with him. But what's fifteen more minutes of memories against a lifetime of being together? The future I should have had. I should have said that to him. I know he wants this as much as I do, but he's a coward after all. Maybe I should have said that. *Robert, you're a coward.* Maybe I'm the coward. I couldn't say something like that to him. Imagine his face if I said something like that. He'd storm out. He'd say I'd crossed the line. Stupid English expressions. *Crossed the line.* What line? Where? Oh, yes. The line that you drew between me and everything I want to say and be. The line between "normal" life and the other one, the other choice. You could have crossed that line. You promised to cross that line. *You promised me. You promised me. You promised me.* And I've been so gentle with you over these last few weeks, talking when you needed to talk, kissing away your tears when I actually wanted to be sucking your dick. I've done everything you wanted.

I see him walking in an hour ago, already ten minutes late, as if I didn't have anything else better to do (but I haven't, Robert: The only thing I want to do is be in love with you).

"I couldn't get away," he said. "The kids were creating."

Another stupid English word. Creating what? Shit? Works of art? Both?

His kids. They're across some other line altogether. But I've pretended to be interested in them for long enough. All right. Well, I was sort of interested. I imagined weekends with them at some point in the future, when Whatshername had gotten over everything. Trips to the park. Big ice creams. It didn't exactly compute, but I could have programmed myself to do it. I would have done that for you, Robert.

The table in front of me is a little piece of art in itself. What would you call it? *After a Small Treachery.* I like that. *The Dregs of Betrayal.* Two cups, two saucers, one man. You'd look at this and you'd know that two people were here a while ago, but one has gone. One has a meeting, an arrangement, a life. The other is me and I have nothing in the world apart from this coffee cup. Perhaps you even saw him leave, the one with the thinning hair and the black jeans. An hour ago he was walking in and there was nothing on this table apart from the red-and-white checked plastic tablecloth, a laminated menu, and a pepper pot (but no salt). He made his excuse and sat down, and I could see him shaking.

"Coffee?" I said. And I wanted to slap him, this shaking mess. I wanted to tell him to be a man. If I wanted to fuck girls for the rest of my life I wouldn't be doing this, would I?

A waitress came. They all speak French here, or at least, they affect convincing French accents, so he said, "Café au lait," in a stupid English-French accent, and then added, "Merci."

What an idiot. And now? Now I want to piss on his face. I want to drown him in my shit. I want to take pictures of him drowning in my shit and send them to his girlfriend. I want to write a concerto all about him drowning in my shit and play it at his funeral, and out of a permanent speaker system at his grave, so all his relatives will have to listen to it forever.

But I was still hopeful when he looked at me across the table.

"How have you been?" he asked me, as if I had cancer.

(You're the cancer, Robert, you miserable little tumor. You've given me cancer of the heart.)

"How do you expect?" I said.

I think what I meant to say was: *Fine. Great. My life is full of pink balloons.*

Well, that's more attractive, isn't it?

He lit a cigarette with shaking hands. I taught him to smoke, of course. I taught him to smoke, and I taught him how to drink, and I taught him how to fuck me. I showed him what I'd suspected: that two men are more powerful than the cancelled out yin-yang of cock-and-cunt. We discovered it together: the beauty of the male body. Don't you remember, Robert? I even bought you a reproduction of Donatello's *David* when I could hardly afford food. In return you bought me a bust of Alexander the Great.

And you said you'd move in with me.

Sitting at the table just over an hour ago, he didn't look like someone who was about to leave his wife and move in with me. On the other hand—I suppose he would be upset if he had just left his girlfriend (they're not married, despite the two kids). *Maybe that's it*, I thought. *Maybe he's upset because he's told her and he's going to have to come back to my flat tonight and I'll give him vodka for the shock and suck his cock so hard that he'll never leave me again.* I just wanted the chance to convince him it should be me. I see Robert as a fish with the hook still in his mouth. If she tugs it, he goes back: I know that for sure now.

Robert's sitting there with the cigarette, frozen in time. My mind won't play this memory like a film: It pulls me around like an Alsatian, making me go here and there. . . . And now I'm thinking I should write a guidebook for others in my situation. Or . . . Yes. A Web site. I could send her the link, just so she knows.

Howtotakeitupthearse.com

Probably exists. And that's not what I want, anyway.

Robertisabastard.com

Not general enough.

Whenstraightmenpromisetogogayandthendonot.com

He sipped his coffee. I was facing the door; I'd placed myself there like a little welcome mat (another fucking stupid English invention) waiting for him to wipe his feet on me. So he sat there sipping his coffee, looking beyond me to the wall, covered in postcards from Paris, and I just watched people leave like bacteria looking for a new host to infect. No one new comes in at this time of day; it's as though the place has taken an antibiotic.

"Are you OK?" Robert asked me.

"I'm confused."

Last night he was due to come over to my flat to celebrate the beginning of our new life together. I'd finished my relationship with Catherine, and all that remained was for him to leave his girlfriend. He didn't come. Instead he phoned me at midnight and in a stupid whisper said that everything was too complicated and that he'd meet me here tomorrow. I said I'd bought flowers. He said he had to go. I suggested coming to my place rather than here—after all, this place is virtually next door to my flat. He said it wasn't a good idea.

So there we both were. And I knew he hadn't done it.

"You haven't told her," I said.

He was still shaking. "I did tell her," he said. "I did it last night."

"Oh my God," I said. "I didn't know. Sorry. Shit. Are you all right?"

I leaned across the table to touch his arm. Obviously he was now forgiven. He had done it. He had told her. Well, that was what I'd wanted. Actually it was what we'd both wanted. But where did he go last night? Just as I started wondering about that, he moved his arm away from my hand.

"Don't."

"Robert?"

"I told her. I told her I was leaving her."

"But that's good, isn't it? Unless . . . Well, obviously you will be upset, but I can help you with that. It's all going to be all right now."

"I'm so sorry, Wolfgang. I've changed my mind."

Microwave my fucking soul, why don't you?

"I told her. I said, 'I'm leaving you,' and she said, 'No you're not.' Just like that. She knew something had been going on. She's not stupid. We're . . . Oh God, I don't even know where I am, I'm so tired."

"We're what?" I said. "What were you going to say just then? 'We're . . .'"

"We're going to have another go."

This idiot makes a relationship sound like a children's spinning top. *Oh, I'm just going to have another go!* But I didn't say anything, and so he just went on and on talking about how he thought he was gay, perhaps, or at least bisexual, but now he wasn't sure. He said he thought he was probably bisexual but that really meant that he could stay with his girlfriend, and after all, they did have two kids and she was right when she said that he should think of them rather than just following his cock.

Console!

Console?

Console?

Shit. I've got to get out of here. I had no idea that this is Wolf's mind, although I suppose I could have read the fucking clues. Oh God. Oh God. I can't believe I'm intruding on his life like this. I shouldn't know any of this. I had no idea. Oh, Wolf . . . I'm so sorry. Where's the waitress gone now? I can't look around, unfortunately: All I can see is what Wolf sees, and he's just looking at the table. No doors. No milky images.

Console?

But it doesn't come. I'm stuck.

Now he's getting up to leave the café. But he's still not looking at anyone.

And I recognize the way he feels. It would be what, seventeen years ago now. . . . Christ, that makes me feel old. I was in love, totally, innocently, in love, for the first and only time, with a guy who was doing a degree in town when I was doing my GCSES. He had dark shoulder-length hair and drove a little blue Mini. Just seeing it parked in the university car park would give me a little buzzing thrill, like touching the heart of the fake guy (or the guy-shaped hole) in that Operation game. Then he dumped me because I was too young, and I spent a year or so semi-stalking him (including once leaving an amusingly shaped cactus on his front doorstep) before I decided to just give up on love altogether.

Wolf's not doing any stalking, though. Wolf's going to get drunk. We're going to get drunk. . . .

I'm going to get drunk.

It has started to snow. The bacteria-people on the pavement crush the flakes into instant slurry; it's exactly the consistency of the lemon-ice drinks Heike's mother used to make for us when we came back in the afternoons in our Pioneer uniforms. But the stuff on the pavement is dirty and brown. And that's it: life expressed in one moment. You start with pure crushed-ice lemon drink and you end up with a shitty mess. This is what you become. And I know where I'm going now, so I walk through the brown sludge on autopilot, not crying. I'm not crying yet.

But it will be OK. If you drink enough bourbon your humanity starts to melt away. By three o'clock this morning I won't care. Perhaps in an hour I'll be anesthetized enough to stop thinking about when I am going to cry. There's an icy wind along with the weak snow, but I can't be bothered to do up the buttons on my coat. I think I left my scarf behind at the café. Good. Maybe I'll freeze to death. Picture me frozen to death in the park, brokenhearted on a bench. Robert will read about it in the local paper and . . . Here's a sadder picture. I die as before on a park bench, etc., and the fucker *doesn't even* read about me. I could die and no one would notice. My neighbor Ariel might notice after a few days. Catherine won't care now, though. She didn't say anything after I ended our relationship. She didn't even cry. She didn't tell me I'd made a mistake. She didn't implore me to stop thinking about men. This almost makes me go straight to the park and undo all the buttons on my hateful red shirt, but, despite what I tell everyone, I'm no suicide.

There's some business guy walking towards me, holding a newspaper over his head to stop the snowflakes touching his bald patch. *Hey, idiot! Have you ever sucked someone's cock? I have.*

Then again, it's more common than people think. He's probably done it, too.

(A door hovers over the man, but I hesitate; then Wolf looks away and it's gone.)

I want something to hurt. I want physical pain, not this mental shit. This would be an excellent time to go to the dentist. *Hello, Herr Doktor. Do whatever you want. . . .*

I could headbutt a lamppost. I could try to find some queer-bashing football hooligan to kick me in the head while I lie on the ground in the recovery and/or fetal position. I'm walking towards the Westgate Tower, the tight arsehole at the center of this city. I used that description once and whoever I was talking to was shocked. "But have you never watched a bus try to squeeze through it?" I said. "They all look like they need lubricant." Ha. If I want to get in a fight I'm on the wrong side of town. I could go back towards home and then hang around near the kebab shop and wait for a gang of "youths." What would I do? All I'd have to do is stare at one of them. I wouldn't even need to call him a poof. You know who I really want to get beaten up by? I want to get fucked-up by faggots who'll fist you afterwards. I want something to hurt more than this hurts.

Console?

Console?

Still nothing. And all Wolf's looking at is the pavement.

We walk onwards, towards St. Dunstan's. Eventually we come to a door I've never noticed before. Well, I've simultaneously never noticed it and at the same time I realize I come here quite often. It leads downstairs to an underground wine bar. And I sit there until closing time, drinking Jack Daniel's, eyeing up every guy who walks past me. I think that one of them will react. One of them will want to fight me or fuck me, but I might as well be invisible. Maybe I am. Maybe I'm invisible. At last orders I go up to the bar for three more drinks.

"Am I visible?" I say to the bartender. "Can you see me?"

The wankers throw me out. And I'm not drunk enough yet. I go to the hotel.

The manager tonight is this ex-bouncer called Wesley.

"Hey—you're not on tonight," he says to me.

"Drink," I say. "I only want a drink."

My insides are volcano-hot. I need to do something about it. I think about explaining this to Wesley, but he simply says, "OK. Just a couple, though, mate."

Melissa's playing the piano tonight. I sit in the booth right next to it and eyeball her enough to make her play three wrong notes in a bar. Well, I think they were wrong. The whole world seems the wrong way up now. Why am I here? Oh yes. That bastard Robert. Perhaps when I get home he'll be waiting there for me with a little suitcase, dabbing at his eyes with a balled-up handkerchief.

In my dreams. Or, as Ariel says, in another universe—maybe the one in which I am also rich. That's the other thing: After tonight I will be so broke. I wonder if she'll lend me money? No. Didn't she say that she spent it all on that book? Could I steal the book? She said it was one of the rarest books in the world. . . . What would I do? Go in there for a drink before bed and leave the door on the catch as I leave. Then I could go back in and . . .

You bastard, Wolfgang. You're her friend.

The piano's so shiny it looks as if it might just walk out of here on its four legs. Am I going to throw up? Steady, steady. I'll go for a piss. That'll help.

I'm on my own in the fluorescent toilets, pissing into the ceramic urinal, when this guy walks in. He'd probably look more attractive in a photo-fit than in real life. Maybe he is a photo-fit. His huge eyebrows don't seem to go with his tiny slug-pellet eyes. Or maybe it's the nose that seems slapped on, or as if someone just punched him. He comes and stands next to me and takes his cock out, but he doesn't start to piss. He glances at me; down at my cock, and then up to my eyes. I look at his cock. He looks at my cock again. Is this some sort of secret code? Before I know what's happening, we're in one of the cubicles. I'm down on my knees on the slimy, tiled floor as he fucks the inside of my mouth. All I can taste is cold piss.

When it's over he calls me a bitch, and then leaves. I think of Donatello's *David* again and that's when I cry, after I've thrown up in the toilet behind me: Jack Daniel's laced with sperm and only the memory of coffee. Women are easier than this. I'll find a woman who will help me. I'll . . . Oh God. I don't ever feel like having sex again in my life. But you can't get anything without sex, or the promise of sex (unless I've got that wrong and I actually mean violence, but I'm a little drunk). Maybe I'll try hanging myself, at least for some sympathy. Is it easy to get it wrong?

The next few minutes are confusing. Wesley—I'm sure it is him—comes in just as I'm unbolting the cubicle. He drags me down the corridor into the kitchen, where I manage to put my elbow in an ice-cream tub full of prawn cocktail before he presses my face down onto the stainless steel counter.

"Don't you ever do that in my fucking hotel again, you fucking faggot," Wesley says. I genuinely have no idea what he's talking about. I don't think he's firing me. I think this is the equivalent of the first formal warning. Something hurts: my arm behind my back. "Fight back, pussy," he says, jerking me backwards by the collar.

I laugh, forgetting "pussy" in this context does not mean "cute cat."

"Are you laughing at me?"

I spin, see a fist, and then everything goes black.

Console?

Nothing.

On the way home I try to get run over. I even walk through the Westgate Tower, on the road, muttering, *Arsehole, arsehole,* but the traffic just slows behind me, as though this is a funeral procession rather than just a drunk who needs a kicking. In the park I try abusing a couple of kids on a bench but they just look upset and run away. I think I might have forgotten where I live, but then I'm there, and there's my bicycle.

I spit on the ground twice before walking in. Two guys in a black car give me dirty looks before driving off and parking around the corner. Maybe they're going to get out and come and beat me up. Do I still want that? But nothing happens: It just looks as if they've gone to sleep.

Sleep. That's quite a good idea. Maybe I'll just go to sleep and not wake up. I wonder if Ariel has sleeping pills. Unlikely. Shall I go and see her now? Am I in a state? Objectively, would I seem "a state" if I were to knock on someone's door now? Actually, I don't think I've got the energy to even get up the stairs. It looks quite comfortable on the concrete. I think I'll just . . .

"Oh. Um . . . I'm sorry."

Who said that? Oh . . . Some guy is walking down the stairs. Wow! Check out the cheekbones. But—ouch. He's all bruised. Has Ariel been to bed with him? I'd go to bed with him if I were her. He looks like she would if she were a tall man with dark hair. It's a man-Ariel, a he-Ariel. Why is he here? Is he actually Ariel in disguise? Why would she be in disguise and putting on a different accent? He's sorry. He's sorry because I'm just settling down to sleep where he wants to put his feet. I don't understand what's going on. This is too complicated. I think I'll just go home to bed.

"*Excusez-moi,*" I say, in French, to fool him. I start to get up.

"Do you need a hand?" he says.

"*Nein, danke.*"

Yeah. I'm multilingual. Now that's funny.

(My mind isn't in a much better state than Wolf's and it's as if the drink has affected me, too. But I'm still thinking *Adam. What's Adam doing here?*)

"Are you Ariel's neighbor?"

"Si," I say, laughing. *"Ja."*

He runs a hand through his messy hair and sighs.

"I have to find her."

"She lives up . . . In the clouds." I meant to say "upstairs." This is so funny.

"I know where she lives. She's not answering the door."

"She's out . . . With the bastards . . . With the wank, work . . ."

"With the what?"

"Dinner. With people from the office. Or was that yesterday? I'm sorry . . . I'm a little drunk. You see, something queer and most tragic occurred this evening and . . ."

"Look, I'm sorry, mate. If you can't help me then don't. But don't waste my fucking time, OK? This is pretty serious. Her life is in danger, if that means anything to you."

"Danger? From a cock?"

"What? For fuck's sake, pull yourself together."

"Danger. Danger! Ariel's in danger? We must help her. Where are the grenades?"

"Oh, never mind."

"I'm sorry I'm like this. Please, let me help. She's my friend, you know."

The other man sighs. "There are two men, all right? One is wearing a black suit and one is wearing a gray suit. They both have fair hair, like yours, or a bit lighter. One of them has a little goatee beard." This guy's gesticulating at me as if he could conjure up these men by drawing them in the air. "I think they're driving a black saloon. Have you seen them?"

"Who? Are they here? No. I don't know. There's a black car . . ."

"Where?"

"What?"

"You said something about a black car."

"Did I? I'm sorry. I can't remember."

"Look, I think these men have guns. They're very dangerous. They've been to a bookshop and got information about Ariel. She bought a book that they want—that's as much as I've been able to work out."

"Oh, that. Well, Ariel won't sell the book. Never."

"What book is it?"

Don't tell him, Wolf. Don't tell him.

"It's a . . . Oh. There's a voice in my head saying I can't tell you."

"What is the book?"

I shake my head. "No. Sorry. Herr Doktor's orders."

I can't understand all the voices in my head. One's telling me not to explain but another one's telling me that I should go and get the book now. And—*ouch*—not even sell it myself but give it to the nice man when he asks for it. . . .

A doorway, kind of churchy, flickers around Adam's body. *Switch!* I command. *Switch!* I have to find out what's been going on. I start to blur, just as I have done before, but instead of blurring into Adam's head I seem to be falling, but not downwards. Before I can work out what's happening, or how it's possible to fall in a direction other than down, I land just outside the music shop. I'm back in the Troposphere, lying on the tarmac, looking up at the flickering neon signs and a black, starless sky. It's as if someone's switched everything off: the throbbing of Wolf's head, the smell of damp in the concrete passageway, the cold, the traffic sounds from the street outside the flats. As before, it's almost completely silent in the Troposphere. There are no noises at all: no birds, no traffic, no people. The only sound I've ever heard in the Troposphere is the sound of my own footsteps. Did the lifts make a sound? I can't even remember.

I have to get out of here now and find Adam.

Why would men with guns be looking for the book? I don't know Adam very well, but it was clear that he believed what he was saying and that he was trying to help me. Has he led the men to me—the men in the car? Or am I somehow dreaming all this? I'm bothered by what Adam said about the girl in the bookshop. He obviously didn't know what had happened, or why, but I can work it out. It's logical: If you want *The End of Mr. Y,* you keep searching for it; I know that. These guys must have Googled it and found an intriguing new link—a girl saying she sold it in a secondhand bookshop. So they find the shop, go there, and ask her about whom she sold it to. She remembers nothing, I'm guessing, except that I'm a young woman doing a Ph.D. at the university. So what happens next? The men go on the university Web site and search for "Lumas." And they find it there under my research interests on the "Staff" pages. And they realize I'm the one who bought the book. So they come looking for me. . . . And I'm not hard to find. No one based in a university is hard to find. You could come at it from all sorts of different angles, and there I'd be: Ariel Manto—my alias, my pen name, the name I gave myself when I was only eighteen and I didn't want to be me anymore. *Ariel Manto. Research interests: Derrida, Science, and Literature, Thomas E. Lumas.*

The Ariel part is real at least. And yes, it was the poetry, not the play.

The syrupy stillness of the Troposphere won't let me panic, so I calmly get up off the pavement and turn towards the exit, part of me just wanting to just stay here, where they can't get me. A city all to myself seems better than men with guns. But then I think of myself as I must be in the real world, so zonked out on my sofa that I can't even hear the door. Come on, Ariel. Get out and run. Talk to Adam and do whatever you have to do, but if there are men with guns involved you'd better run. Get out and run. Get out and run. Get out and . . .

There's a tinkling behind me.

And a creaking: a long, high-pitched arc of a sound. I turn around. This is all wrong. I should be on my own in here. I should be . . .

It's a door. It's a door opening. The door to the music shop. Oh fuck. And one—no, two—two men are coming out, walking into the Troposphere like aliens walking off a spaceship. They're just as Adam described: one man in a gray suit and one in black. They both have blond hair. But there's something slightly cartoonish about them. As if they've been chroma-keyed onto the background. They've got—huh?—*children* with them as well. Two young boys, both with the same blond hair as the men, perhaps lighter.

"There she is," says one of the men, the gray suit, his mouth not quite moving at the same time that his words come out. "She's already figured out how to get in."

American accent. Shit. Can I run, and lose them in the alleyways? Something tells me this isn't a good course of action.

"Don't worry about it," says the other one. "We can deal with this one fairly easily." Then he says to me: "Get out of the way. Come on. This isn't anything to worry about. We're just going to let the kids fuck you up a bit; find out where you put the book. It won't hurt while they're doing it."

The kids dance forwards like two marionettes. Their skin is the refrigerator-pink of raw meat. One is dressed in a cowboy suit; the other is wearing a blue cape.

"Let us in," sing-songs one of them, like he's an extra in a Dickens adaptation.

"We want to play," says the other one.

They both have sarcastic eyes, so pale they're almost white.

"Get out of the way," says the black suit again. "Let the kids have their fun."

Get out of the way? I don't think so. But I don't want these freaks—the men or the kids—near me, either. I'm walking backwards, as all four of them walk towards me. I stumble over something: I think it's one of the stand-up signs from outside one of the shops, but it actually turns out to be a rack of newspapers and postcards. I find my balance again quickly and kick the rack into their path. The children see it and jump over it. But the men don't seem to see what I've done.

"Whatever you think you're doing," the gray one says, "it's over. Come on. Move now. We just need to get past. Ouch! Shit, what the hell's that? Come on. You're just going to make it all worse. It doesn't have to be difficult, you know."

They want to get into my mind . . . ? How? Think, Ariel. Where are they now? OK. They're in the Troposphere, just like I am. Come on. Work it out. To go back into myself, I walk down that road behind me until I get to the tunnel. So I have to stop them going there. It might not be correct, but it's the best I can do.

Help me, I think. But nothing happens. Or maybe something does. There's now a steel bar lying on the tarmac. I bend down and pick it up.

"Who are you?" I ask them.

They keep walking towards me, taking up most of the thin street between them.

"We're just here to get the book," the gray one says.

"You just need to cooperate a little," says the other one.

"Although if you don't . . . Well, we don't really care what we have to do to get the book. You know how you've been lurking in your friend's mind, just watching? That's Level One. Once the kids are in your mind they're going to turn it into spaghetti."

"*On top of old Smoky . . .*" sings the first kid.

"Get away from me," I say. "Fucking hell. Get away from me . . ."

I swing the steel bar at the gray-suited man, the one closest to me. He doesn't react until it thwangs him hard across the side of his head: It's as if he can't see the steel bar at all. Just like the newspaper rack.

"You little cunt," he says to me, swaying and clutching his head. Then: "Martin—she's got a weapon."

"You know what to do," says the other guy. "We may as well finish her here and then we'll go to her apartment and get the book. I'll bet you anything it's just there sitting on a bookshelf or something."

One of the little boys is picking his nose and, presumably, watching to see what the adults do next. The other boy, maybe slightly older, looks at me.

"When I do get into your mind, I'm going to wee on your memories," he says. "And then I'm going to poop all your other thoughts out of your eye sockets. I don't have any empathy. So you can't stop me."

I see myself in some asylum, dribbling. *What happened to her, then? Oh, she went mad. First she thought she could practice telepathy, and then, for no reason, her brains just packed up. Turned to spaghetti, just like that. It's sad. She was working on a Ph.D. before it happened.* And I'll never, ever, be able to tell anyone what happened to me. I'll have no memory. I'll . . . OK. Now I am afraid.

Console?

The thing appears. Now the two men and the boys are highlighted red. Danger. Yeah—I think I got that by myself. The small crowded street behind them appears in a kind of grayed-out black and white. That's new.

You have no choices, says the woman's voice.

How can I have no choice?

Nowhere is open now.

OK. Tell me what I can do. Are there any options?

You can quit by exiting.

I don't want to quit. These psychos will enter my mind if I do.

You have no choices.

So is that it then? Basically quit, and then die?

You can choose to play the Apollo Smintheus card.

What?

Danger approaching . . .

The console is right. The black-suited man is approaching me with . . . Ouch. Oh shit. I thought you couldn't feel pain in here. Oh fuck. It's like period pain in my head. It's toothache of the brain . . . I fall to my knees. *OK,* I tell the console. *Play the Apollo Smintheus card.* Do it now. *Do it now.* Oh God.

Chapter **Fifteen**

How much time has passed? I don't know. But the men and the two horrible little kids haven't moved forwards any more, and now there's something, or someone, standing next to me. I'm still down on my knees on the black tarmac, holding my head in my hands, pressing in my fingers, trying to make the pain go away. I was so wrong about the Troposphere. I thought you couldn't feel anything here, but the pain here is more intense than anything in the real world. It's the worst form of pain as well: not the sharp sting of a knife, a tattoo, a cat scratch. Are headaches ever nice? I don't think so. And this is the worst headache I've ever had; something's wringing out my brain as if it's a wet dishcloth. I don't seem to be able to close my eyes, although the flickering neon in the street is making me dizzy. In fact, the flickering neon is now breaking up around me. Everything's breaking up and turning into some kind of gray static: the shops, the apartment blocks, the street itself. The Troposphere is fizzing and popping as though it's being broadcast on the wrong frequency.

The silence around me is already too loud, and so when the fizzing and popping actually turns into a crackling noise, like fire in a dry forest, and the two men start saying things like *What the fuck is that thing?* I just want to die quickly so I can't feel this anymore. The "thing," still standing next to me, is wearing a long red robe and black boots, but I can see that under the robe he is an animal: a mouse-hybrid of some sort, with gray fur on his legs. I can't do more than register that before the image begins to break up like everything else. Now all I want is for this to happen quickly, for everything to shut up and go away.

Apollo Smintheus, if that is who this is, says something in a language I don't understand, and the pain goes and the static goes, as though my channel has been retuned, crisp and clear. I stand up, wobbling slightly. Apollo Smintheus is taller than me: He must be eight feet tall, standing on his hind legs. He has a quiver full of arrows slung across his shoulder. His pointed mouse-face is covered in gray fur, and he has whiskers. He's probably the most bizarre entity I have ever seen. But when he speaks now, it's English with an American accent.

"Well," he says. "I've never seen this before. Who are these people?"

"I don't know," I say.

"They are the bad guys, though?"

"Yes. If you can help me . . ." I feel like crying. "Please . . ."

"OK. Don't worry."

He starts speaking in the other language again. At the same time, he takes his bow and loads it up with an arrow from his quiver. He fires one arrow at the gray-suited guy, who seems to deflect it somehow. I can't understand all of what happens next. The kids hide behind the legs of the men; then something seems to come towards Apollo Smintheus—some ball of yellow light—but he simply raises his arm and reflects it back towards the man in black. He falls to the floor now, clutching his head the way I was before. The two kids look at him, and then each other, and then turn and run away down the street. Now Apollo Smintheus loads up another arrow and fires it again at the man in gray. It sticks in his neck, but no blood spurts as the man stumbles, sees what's happened, and then takes hold of the arrow with both his hands and pulls it out, leaving a gaping hole with skin-flaps, like some piece of gross-out porn from the Internet.

As he starts speaking, I can see his voice box move.

"You fucker," he says, thickly. "Why are you fighting for her?"

"Oh, she asked me if I would," Apollo Smintheus says.

"What on Christ's earth did she do to get the attention of a god?"

"She did it the old-fashioned way. She helped a mouse," Apollo Smintheus says, loading his bow again. "Now, as they say in Illinois: *Go to hell, fuckface.*"

Illinois? A god? This must be a dream. Nothing like this happened to Mr. Y. This must be the effect of TV and cinema and—not that I've played them often—video games on my weak mind. This is truly crazy. But I have to say I quite enjoy it now as Apollo Smintheus fires arrows into the two blond men as if they're 2D practice targets pinned up in an archery range. They're not dead, yet, but they are down. What do you have to do to kill someone in here? Apollo Smintheus now walks over to them and, after pulling a coiled rope from under his robe, binds them tightly together. Then he walks back towards me, muttering something. And, as he mutters in this odd language, a cage starts to form around the two men: like a bell-shaped birdcage made out of silvery wire. By the time he returns to my side and turns around, the men are imprisoned and unconscious, like something from a fairy tale.

"There," he says.

"Thank you," I say. "Thank you so much. I . . ." I look down the street. There's no sign of the caped-kid or the cowboy-kid. "What about those children?"

"You don't need to worry about them. Coffee?" says Apollo Smintheus. "We can go to my place and I'll explain. Sorry. I'm being rude. I can bring my place here, obviously. But perhaps you want to conjure yours up?"

I don't know what he's talking about so I just nod. "Your place," I say.

Apollo Smintheus starts incanting again and, between the music shop down the street and what seems to be a pool hall (which I never noticed before), an archway opens up. It's like an adult, live-action version of the mouse-hole from Tom and Jerry cartoons. I'm not sure I can take much more of this. If this is all going on in my imagination then I'm much more warped than I ever would have thought. I may need medication.

"This way."

We walk through the archway into what can only be described as a mouse burrow fused with a minimalist Manhattan apartment. The space is white, and it would be light and airy if it was ever daytime here, and if there weren't coarse brown blankets tacked over the large windows in the back wall. There are thick pine shelf units around the walls, but they're all empty. There's nothing on any of the tables. The floor seems to be tiled with polished dark parquet blocks, but you can hardly see it for all the sawdust. In the corner of the room there's a nest: lots of white fluff rolled into a ball. Apollo Smintheus leads me through this room and into another one. This one is more like an eighteenth-century parlor, with an open fire and two rocking chairs.

"Please, sit," he says. "I'll make coffee."

I expect him to take an old-fashioned kettle and hang it over the fire, but he doesn't do anything at all. Nevertheless, when I look down on the table, there's a mug of steaming black coffee sitting there on a wicker mat.

"So," he says. "You're not a god."

"I don't think so," I say. I want to smile but I'm still feeling shaken and freaked-out after my encounter with the two men—and the fucked-up children. "Those guys . . ." I say. "They're not dead, are they?"

"No. You can't kill things in here."

"How long will they stay there in the cage?"

Apollo Smintheus rocks in his chair. "As long as I've got the energy to keep them there. And, also, as long as I want to keep them there. What did they do to you? Why were you fighting?"

"They said they were going to go into my mind and fuck it up," I say. "Or I think they were going to send those boys."

"Oh dear."

"Yeah. I . . . I think you saved my life."

"They can't really do anything to you in here," Apollo Smintheus says. "But I assume they were on their way to your . . ." Now he says a word in the strange language again.

"My what?"

"What would you call it? My Illinois friends obviously don't have a word for this. The portal into your consciousness. Do you have a word for that?"

I shake my head. "No. This is all absolutely new to me. I'm still not sure I'm not dreaming."

"Well, you know the thing I mean."

"Yes. And that's what I was trying to defend. I think. It's all so confusing."

"So. How did you all get here?" he says. "You're not supposed to be here."

"Sorry?"

"You're not a god. You're a physical being. How did you get here?"

"I read a book. It had instructions . . . That's what those men want, by the way. The book."

It should be warm in here with the fire, but I don't feel anything above or below body temperature. I pick up my coffee and the outside of the mug does feel hot, but somehow the heat doesn't travel into my hands. I take a sip. It's the most delicious coffee I've ever tasted but when I swallow it, it doesn't actually go anywhere. I don't feel anything in my stomach at all.

Apollo Smintheus frowns. "Why do they want this book?"

I take another sip of coffee. "I don't know. I mean, they obviously already know how to get in here, so they can't want the instructions. It doesn't make any sense."

"They don't want you to have it. They want to stop people from coming. Hmm. I'd guess that'll be it. Not a bad idea. It's not good for people to come here. You're the first I've actually seen, but you're not the first I've heard of. I do approve of you coming and helping mice, obviously. That's why you got whatever you got that enabled you to call me."

"It was a business card."

"Oh." He smiles. "Very classy."

"I have to ask. Why shouldn't people come here?"

"This dimension . . . I think that word is right. It's not something you can ever understand. Tell me what you see in front of you now."

"Um, a table and a chair with you sitting on it. A fire. A . . ."

"None of those things are there," he says. "Apart from me. And I don't see any of what you see."

"What do you see?"

"Nothing you have the words for. And, out of interest, what am I?"

"You're . . ." What's a good way of putting this? "A mouse-person."

He laughs. "A mouse-person. Do I even have fur?"

"Yes."

"What color?"

"Gray."

"Do I have the bow and arrows?"

"Yes."

"Am I wearing anything?"

"Yes. A red robe."

"A red robe?" He laughs. "Where did that come from? I don't wear that in any of the pictures."

"What pictures?"

"You know who I am, presumably? You looked me up?"

"Yes. You're Apollo Smintheus. God of mice."

"Were there pictures?"

"Yes. Some coin . . . It wasn't very clear."

"I am, of course, not a mouse. Not usually."

"Oh. Sorry . . ." For some reason it seems right to be sorry; sorry for what's in front of my eyes.

"I am an incarnation of the Greek God Apollo. Or, at least, I was. I've been evolved since then. Or—what do the boys say?—*upgraded*."

I put down my coffee. The sensation of drinking something that isn't really there is weird, like bulimia. This can't really be happening. It's all too odd.

"I'm very lost," I say. "Are you saying that you are something other than what I see in front of me?"

"Oh yes. Like this whole place. It's different for everyone. Well, every human. You must know that."

"I'm afraid I don't know anything."

"Then why did you come here?"

"The book . . ."

He shakes his head. "What did it promise you? Money? Power?"

"No." I shake my head. "I don't really know why I did come. It didn't promise anything really, except knowledge. I think I just wanted to find out if the place was real."

"And now you know. Will you be coming back?"

"To be honest I don't know what I'm going to do. I think I'll have to find a way to escape from those men. If that means using this place then . . ."

"You can be sure they'll be using it to find you. And they'll be using the . . ."

It's that strange language again.

"Sorry?" I say.

"The children you saw. They'll be using them as . . . Now I can't find the word in your language. I'm coming up with *hitchhiker, piggyback*, and *infect*. The children aren't projections of entities from your world. They're beings who only exist in this world, like me."

"So they're gods?"

"No. They're something else." He smiles, and his whiskers twitch. "I'm guessing that they are attached—in the way of a hitchhiker, piggyback-rider, or a virus—to those men. They won't go into your mind on their own. They'll go where the men go."

"Are you sure?"

"As sure as I can be. I can find out more for when you return, if you like."

"So I won't get into trouble then, if I come back?"

Apollo Smintheus smiles. "Trouble from whom?"

"You. The other gods. I don't know."

He starts laughing. "Oh dear. That's funny."

"Why? I don't understand."

"We can't stop you doing anything. This is your world, not ours. We're part of it, but humans made it. All I'm saying is that we do our work best here, and you're better off staying in the physical world. But that's only advice. You can ignore it."

"If I ignore it, will anything bad happen to me?"

"I doubt it. You'll probably need to use this space, anyway, if you want to defeat your enemy. But you'll need to answer an important question."

"What's that?"

"Well, if they're the bad guys, are you one of the good guys? And if so, what do the good guys stand for? If you're going to fight them you need to work out why you're fighting them."

"I don't think I have any choice. They're going to kill me."

Apollo Smintheus looks away from me for a second, as if he's wondering whether or not to tell me something. He sips from his coffee cup and then puts it down on the table.

"Well, you should understand that you can use me for help as long as you've got the card. And as long as I have the energy."

"How long will I have the card for?"

"Who knows. Probably a few days, in your time. Maybe less."

"Right. Thanks. And what do you mean about your energy?"

"If they pray, I survive. If not, I go to sleep. It's not death, exactly, but I can't do anything very impressive."

"Who are *they*? Mice?"

"Ha! No. Mice can't make gods. They wouldn't want to. No, I'm talking about the boys in Illinois. They're the ones who keep me going. There's a small club of them. A little . . . A *cult* is what you'd call it, I guess. The Cult of Apollo Smintheus. They have a Web site." He yawns. "I'm actually getting a little tired now. I'll have to tell you about them next time."

"OK. Sorry. I'll get going." I stand up, and the chair carries on rocking a couple of times, as if it remembers me sitting in it. "I know this is an awful question . . ."

"Go on."

"Well, do you have any estimate about how long you can keep those men here? I'm assuming that while they're here they can't pursue me in the real world . . . Is that right?"

"Yes, that's right. Well, if you go now and I can focus all my energy on it, I can certainly keep them here for . . ." He screws up his eyes. "This is a more complicated calculation than you'd think . . . Um, about another three or four hours, your time."

"What do you mean, 'my time'?"

"I'll have to explain when you come back. I need some rest. I'm not the most powerful god around. With only six people in the world seriously praying to you . . . Well."

"Thanks again," I say. "You really did save my life."

Back out in the Troposphere it's started to rain. That's odd. There's never been weather in here before. It beats down on the tarmac like percussion, and then rushes down the gutters with a *shhhh* noise. The men are still unconscious in their cage, but I keep my distance as I walk around it. I have to get away from them. I saw what they could do to me, and, if they could get into my mind with those horrible kids, I think that would be it. That would be the end of me.

It seems to take ages to get through the tunnel this time, as if there's a wind blowing me the other way. What would the men see, if they went into my mind? Presumably they wouldn't go down this tunnel: I understand that this is my way into and out of the Troposphere. I wonder if I have a little shop and what's in the window. Do I decide, or do they? And what were they seeing in the Troposphere? From what Apollo Smintheus said, they wouldn't have seen what I saw—and it was certainly clear that they missed the newspaper rack and the steel bar. But those boys: They did see what I saw. He's right: It is hard to understand. But surely it can't be impossible to understand?

I pass the wavy lines and the pinpricks of light. Nearly home. Nearly . . .

Oh fuck. I come to on the sofa and everything feels different. I don't know what's happened to me. My mouth is so dry that I couldn't speak if I wanted to. Shit. I sit up, but I feel as if I've got the worst flu I've ever had. Water. I need lots of water. Somehow, I get up and make it to the sink. I drink three cups of water and then immediately throw them up. I drink two more and throw up again. I know I need fluid, so I force myself to drink another cup of water, slow sips this time. God.

What's happened to me? I thought the Troposphere was some sort of "dream world" in which you can't get hurt. My eyes sting. The light coming from the window is laser-beam strong, and I move across the room and shut the curtains. There's bright white snow all over the rooftops outside, the sun glaring off it. Hang on. Why is it light? Why is there sun? It wasn't just nighttime in the Troposphere (where it's always nighttime anyway); it was nighttime when I left Wolf's mind, not that long ago.

I look at the clock. It says it's two o'clock. It must be afternoon if it's light.

But I took the mixture at five o'clock in the afternoon.

I run my tongue over my dry mouth. I feel dizzy. I know this dizziness: It's because I haven't had a cigarette for hours. Jesus. Have I been lying on the sofa for twenty-one hours? No wonder I feel ill. Is this dehydration? Or is it part of the same madness that means I imagine that I can travel through other people's consciousness? The same madness that means I believe two men are after me with guns?

The thing is, I don't feel mad at all.

Adam. I need to find Adam and find out what—if anything—happened yesterday (or whenever: Fuck knows what day it is—I could have gone back in time for all I know). And I make a deal with myself right now. If the men are real I'm going to drive away somewhere where they can't find me. But if they're not, I'm going to go straight to the university medical center and see if I can get myself sectioned. I guess that in either case I'll need to take some things with me, so, after taking *The End of Mr. Y* from the mantelpiece, I go into the bedroom and put it into an old holdall before covering it with clothes. What else do I need? My laptop. A big knife, just in case. Obviously I need the rest of the holy water mixture, and the bottle of Carbo-veg so I can make some more. I don't really have any food that's transportable, so I'll have to worry about that later. Once I have packed my bag, I wash quickly and go to leave the flat. There's an envelope by the door with my name on it. Someone must have slipped it underneath the door when I was out cold on the sofa. It's from Adam. *Urgent,* it says. *I need to talk to you.* OK. There's a local phone number, but now I'm paranoid and I don't want to use a phone for communication. I'll just go to my office and hope he's there.

My car, like everything else, is covered in snow. Large white flakes are still falling from the sky, and the street has that muffled, secretive sound that snow produces, as if the whole world is talking under its breath. There's an old piece of cardboard balanced on a bin out by my car, and I use it to scrape most of the soft snow off my windscreen. The ice underneath is more of a problem. I don't have a scraper, and the cardboard is now floppy and wet. In the end I put the heater on full and let the engine turn over for a few minutes until it starts to melt. I still can't see properly by the time I set off, but I have to go. I have to find out if I am mad or in terrible danger. I wish there was a third option, but there doesn't seem to be.

The university campus is bisected by a main road that unintentionally (or so I have always assumed) separates the arts buildings from the science labs. Usually at this time of day the road is clear: a ribbon of black tarmac with only the odd car or cyclist trundling down it, maybe leaving early, or even driving from Shelley College, on the far east side of the campus, to Hardy on the west. Today the road isn't black: it's a mixture of white ice and old gray sludge, and it is completely clogged with snow-smeared cars, all with their windscreen wipers going. And all over campus little groups of students seem to be making snowmen. What's going on? Where's everyone going? And what has happened to lectures and seminars? I can't sit in a traffic jam all day looking at fat white blobs that—and this is a tick in my "madness" column—seem possessed, as if they have come to take over the world. Not today, *please*. Just let me get to Adam.

As I whisper this to myself, and as I repeat the word "please," I suddenly wonder whom I'm asking, to whom I'm praying. I thought I was doing OK, but suddenly I'm having trouble breathing. Come on, come on. I hit the steering wheel a couple of times and then run a hand through my hair. It's damp with sweat, even though it's freezing outside. The traffic going this way is much worse than on the other side of the road. In fact, after a white university truck goes past, there don't seem to be any cars coming the other way. The turning I need to take for the Russell car park is about fifty yards ahead on the right. Fuck it. I crunch the car into gear, pull out, and start overtaking the long line of cars. People glare at me. Just as I approach the turning, traffic starts coming from the other direction. Well, they'll just have to wait. Except they don't. Even though I'm indicating right, and it's quite obvious what I'm trying to do, the first car just drives towards me, the driver gesticulating and flashing his lights, as if this is the most aberrant thing he's ever seen. For God's sake. I can't move forwards now that this car is blocking my way. To my right, there's a triangle of grass with one featureless snowman standing on it. There aren't any students around. I swerve off to the right and drive across the grass, hitting the side of the snowman and making it tip over and then crumble to the ground. I imagine the pissed-off driver of the other car, and what he would think of that maneuver, but I don't look around to see. I think this counts as an emergency, anyway. Now I'm on the road to the car park, and my way is clear, although there is a long line of cars trying to go the other way. I recognize several people. There are Lisa and Mary. They don't see me. Oh, and there's Max. I slow up as my car passes his, and roll down my window. He does the same.

"What's going on?" I ask him.

"University's shutting for the afternoon," he says. "We had an e-mail advising us to leave. Are you just on your way in?"

"Yeah."

"Well, I'd turn around if I were you. It's only going to get worse."

I park haphazardly, unable to see the white lines marking out the parking bays and not caring at all about what anyone thinks about where the bonnet of my car is in relation to the boot and the buildings next to it and the five other cars that are still here. Who actually gives a shit about how precisely you're able to put a vehicle in a white box drawn on the ground, anyway? Car parks seem to me like collective statements of sanity. *I'm sane: I'm inside the lines. Me too! Me too!* I am not inside the lines anymore. I skid on the ice as I run into the English Building, hoping that Adam hasn't yet left.

The door to my office is unlocked, but there's no one there when I go in. I close the door behind me. Heather's computer is switched on, and I can see the cascading numbers of her LUCA model trickling away. I didn't realize how psyched up I was, but when the door opens again, I jump and let out a little yelp.

"Ariel?" It's Heather, holding a cup of coffee.

"Sorry," I say. "Wow, I'm not used to there being other people in here. Um . . ." I need to say something normal. "Thanks for dinner the other night, by the way. It was great."

"Oh, thanks," she says. But her eyes are saying something else. "Are you OK?"

"Yes, of course."

"Did the er . . . Those guys find you?"

"What guys?"

"The American policemen."

Policemen? Those guys are official in some way?

"Sorry?" I say, deadpan.

"They were here looking for you yesterday. They were actually quite vague about who they were—I'm just assuming they were police, since they acted like it. I thought Adam came to tell you. They wanted to confiscate your computer, and get all your files from Personnel, too. Yvonne wasn't happy about it, so they ended up having to try to get some sort of fax through from their offices in America to the dean. Apparently they've had to investigate someone else from this department before. They said they never found him, but they would have done if the university could have given his details to them sooner. Anyway, the fax didn't come yesterday and they went away in the end, saying they'd come back today. They weren't particularly nice. Ariel, what on earth has happened?"

"I don't know," I say. "I'm . . . I didn't see Adam. I had no idea . . . Do you know where he is now?"

"No. But he left you a note."

"Has anyone read it?"

"No. He told me to hide it, so I did. But I didn't feel comfortable about it. He's left his number, too."

She scrabbles around on her desk until she finds a scrap of paper with an 07792 number on it. It seems strange—I wouldn't have thought Adam would have a mobile phone. I'm not going to call the number, anyway: Who knows who could be listening in? If those men are official in some way then I'm more fucked than I'd thought. I'm certainly not phoning anyone, and I'm not using any cashpoints (not that I've got any money to draw out). I've seen enough of those action films to know the drill. The only trouble is that when I watch action films I usually feel the excitement and fear at one remove, as a spectator. So the hero might die, and you might think *No!* but you don't really care. It's just a story—and you know the hero won't usually die in a story, anyway. But I am aware that I'm not in a story, and that if someone really wants to shoot me, or get into my mind, or whatever, there's no scriptwriter who's going to make it all right for me in act 3. I'll be dead in act 2 and it's not as if Aristotle's going to come along and say it's all wrong.

And it looks as if I'm not mad. Not only is this definitely happening to me: It happened to Burlem as well. He's surely the "other person from the department" whom the men came to investigate. He's the last person who had the book. So I'm certainly not going to the medical center. I'm going to see if I can speak to Adam, and then I'm going to find Saul Burlem. I'm going to find him, find out everything he knows about what's going on—and then I'll work out what to do next. I guess he must have an excellent hiding place if he hasn't yet been found, but then he doesn't have the book anymore: I do.

"Have you got the note?" I say to Heather, trying to stop my voice from shaking.

"Yes. I think so. It's here somewhere."

Eventually she picks up a small blue envelope and gives it to me.

"Thanks."

"Ariel . . ."

"What?"

"Do you think those men are going to come back? They really freaked me out."

"I don't know."

"I mean, I know we're really just guests here in your office, and what you do is your business, and I don't want to intrude or anything but . . ."

"What?"

"Well, it's not very nice having the police turn up. If you are in trouble, don't you think maybe you should sort it out?"

Fuck off, Heather.

But I actually say: "I'm not in trouble. And I'm going to stay with my aunt in Leeds, so I won't see you for a while. Say good-bye to Adam for me—and enjoy the office space."

Maybe she'll send the psychos to Leeds, but I'm not counting on it.

Chapter Sixteen

Dear Ariel,

I spent most of the night banging on your door, and then all morning worrying that I led those men straight to you. You haven't phoned me. I hope you are all right.

In case no one else has told you, the men said they were from the Central Intelligence Agency. I think that's crap—but who knows. They wanted your address, but I didn't give it to them. Now they're in my dreams. Not that it means anything: I had a nervous breakdown a couple of years ago, which has left me odd, vulnerable, and liable to have nightmares.

I'm not feeling so good right now, so I'm going to the shrine to try to get myself back together. If you can, I think you should come, too. I can't tell you everything now, but I can tell you everything when I see you.

If you think this is paranoid rambling, please ignore it. I can get paranoid sometimes.

Your friend,
Adam

It's half past three and almost completely dark by the time I get to the Shrine of St. Jude. I didn't have time to stop for directions or anything like that, so I simply drove around Faversham and waited for something to happen. Eventually I saw a chipped little sign saying ST. JUDE'S SHRINE and now here I am, outside the Church of Our Lady of Mount Carmel. I think the shrine's inside. I'm estimating that I need to get away from here in the next half hour or so and go somewhere completely random to collect my thoughts. So I haven't got long.

There's no one in the church when I walk in, probably looking insane, with my tatty old bag slung over my shoulder. The whole place smells dusty, like incense. I notice the holy water in a font on my left, and although it reminds me of everything I've done, and everything that's going wrong, I dip my finger in it and touch my forehead. As I do this I remember playing Dungeons & Dragons on a couple of rainy lunchtimes at school. In some versions of the game you could go to a town and get holy water to cure all but the most serious ailments, and increase your health. In other versions you could use it as a weapon against evil spirits or the undead. But no one ever said you could drink it and go to another world, or that this might, in fact, be a bad idea. I walk farther into the church. It's a small, cold, calming space, with oak-panelled walls and hard wooden benches for pews. A sign directs me down some stairs to the shrine.

And—oh—it's so warm going down the stairs. Hundreds of candles are burning down below: There are several stands containing small tea light candles and a whole table covered with big candles in church-blue plastic holders, each with a picture—although I can't see what the pictures are. Once I'm down in the shrine it's actually hot, and I unwind my scarf. There's still no one here. On my right, and surrounded by many more candles, is a statue of what I assume must be St. Jude. The wall behind him is part mosaic, and part blackened brick. The statue is rendered in gold: a bearded man standing with his staff. There are bars separating me from him, and so for a moment he appears to be imprisoned. Of course, looking at it from his perspective, I'm the one in prison. I wander around the room. On one side are the prayer requests on yellow Post-it Notes. *Please help my aunt who is in so much pain. St. Jude, please intercede for my son Stefan, who is only nineteen. Don't let my brother die. Please bring my son back from war.* The requests are signed by people from Mauritius, Poland, Spain, Brazil. . . . All over the world. A sign explains to me that St. Jude is the patron saint of lost and hopeless causes. St. Jude seems to be the saint you come to when all others have failed. Then, on the other side of the room, a printed leaflet explains to me that St. Jude is a controversial saint, and may not even exist.

I've never prayed before in my life. But now, after lighting a candle and adding it to one of the blazing racks, I move back to the shrine and kneel in front of it. Once I'm there, I still don't know what to do. Thinking something like *Oh please, St. Jude, help me and don't let those men ever find me* seems silly. Something tells me I should not pray for myself; I should pray for another person. But whom do I have to pray for? Even the last person I slept with doesn't matter to me. I care more about the anonymous son from the yellow Post-it Note coming back from war. Instead of praying for anyone, I just gaze at the statue until its edges start to blur. *Who are you?* I think. *What do you do with all the energy that comes together in this place?* Because there is an energy here: It's crackling around me with an intensity that a million of these candles couldn't match. What is it? Is it my hope? Other people's hope? Simply the power of prayer? I feel St. Jude looking at me, and I think that if he were really there he'd be telling me to stop speculating and asking unanswerable questions.

But I'm not sure I can do anything else.

In the end I pray for meaning. I pray for the limits of reality to become clear. For a world—and a type of being—that makes sense. I pray for a life after death that is not like this life. I pray for the end of mystery. What would a life be like with all the mysteries solved? If there were no questions, there'd be no stories. If there were no stories, there'd be no language. If there was no language there'd be no . . . What? I'm just thinking about Adam, and what he said about truth existing beyond language when I hear voices coming down the stairs: one female and one male. For some reason I feel embarrassed praying on my knees, so I get up and pretend to look at the candles. I know I have to go soon: I look at my watch. It's quarter to four. I feel so tired, though, as if I haven't slept for days. And it's icy and dark outside.

"Yes, we've managed to get the shrine functioning again—at last."

"It's amazing. I was afraid the last fire would be the end."

I recognize that voice, although it sounds tired, and almost broken.

"It's never the end for St. Jude. He has so many loyal supporters."

Poor Apollo Smintheus, I think, with his cult of only six people.

"It's . . . Oh. Ariel! You're OK."

"Hello, Adam."

"Maria, this is Ariel Manto. The one I told you about."

Adam looks terrible. What's happened to his face? His right eye is swollen and bruised like a piece of rotting fruit. And he's wearing the same clothes I saw him in on Tuesday. Where are we now? Thursday. I think it must be Thursday. He's with a woman of about sixty or so. She's wearing a long brown skirt and a purple blouse. Her gray hair is mostly covered with a brown head-scarf, but a few silvery wisps fall down the side of her face. Her brown eyes somehow look younger than his.

She holds out her hand. "Hello, Ariel," she says softly. "I'm glad you got here safely. Adam has told us about your troubles. We made up a bed for you in the guest wing of the priory just in case you did drop by. You can rest here for as long as you need to."

A bed? In a priory? But I can't stay here. I have to go.

"That's very kind of you," I say, for some reason using the "polite" voice I use only to speak to schoolteachers, traffic wardens, and similar authority figures. "But I think I really am in terrible trouble and I don't want to involve you." I look at Adam, and point vaguely at his bruised face. "It's already gone too far. They did that to you, didn't they?" Adam nods. I continue: "Those people . . . I don't really understand what's going on. I just came to say thank you to Adam. And sorry."

"How about some tea?" says Maria, as if I haven't just suggested that they are all in danger as long as I stay here. "We can go to the priory kitchens."

Adam looks at me. "They can't get you here," he says.

I sigh. "You can't be sure about that." And I'm not sure about anything. I'm not sure about him. What has he done to make me trust him? Is there anyone in the whole world I would actually trust? I think of my mother, and the time that I tried to tell her that I was cutting myself. I had it all planned out. I was going to tell her about how I started plucking my eyebrows because the other girls at school did, but that I found it was so cathartic that I couldn't stop. Then there was that evening in the bath where I realized that if I kept on plucking I'd end up with no eyebrows, but I hadn't given myself enough pain, not enough *catharsis*. So I took Dad's razor and stuck it in my leg. "Not now, Ariel," she said, settling down with her CB radio. "The world doesn't revolve around you, you know." Perhaps Burlem. For some reason I think I trust him.

Maria starts walking up the stairs.

"Why don't you show her the secret passage?" she says to Adam. "There's no point going outside if there are dangerous men around. I'll see you over there." Then she looks at me. "We've been through worse than this, dear."

Once the sound of her footsteps has gone, I look at Adam again. Shadows cast by hundreds of candles bounce off his sharp features and seem to rest on the softer, broken part of his face.

"I'm so sorry," I say. "I do have to go."

"Ariel . . ."

"If I told you half of what's been going on, you wouldn't believe me. But the short version is that they can get me *anywhere*. This sounds mad." I sigh, frustrated that there's no way to explain this. "Basically if they can get near to me, they can get to me. Getting near to me is enough. I know I'm not making sense, and even I don't know how it works . . . But I think that my only hope is to go far, far away, as fast as possible."

"I'm sure you're safe here. At least come for tea. I'll explain."

"I haven't got much time before they follow me here."

"Do they know you're here?"

"They'll find out. Heather'll tell them."

"I told her not to read my note."

"But she probably did, anyway. I just can't take the risk."

My voice is rising in pitch as I speak, and it gets to a point where I realize that the next thing for me to do is cry. But I can't cry. If I cry then it's over. All the adrenaline will wash away and I think adrenaline is all I've got left. I don't have any money, and I don't even have much petrol in the car. But I can steal petrol: I've done it before. And I've got enough money to live on chips for a few days. As long as I get away, everything might still be OK.

I start walking up the stairs.

"Ariel? Ariel! Please. You're safer here, trust me."

"You can't know that."

"I know more than you think."

I hesitate.

"They didn't follow me into the university chapel," he says. "I don't think they could. And I haven't dreamed about them since I've been here. Come on. I'll explain downstairs."

He takes my hand and leads me away from St. Jude and into a room full of St. Jude–related merchandise. I'm not sure why I'm doing what he says, but I actually feel too weak to do anything else now. In this little room there are many unlit versions of the big blue candles, as well as postcards, pendants, lockets, prayer booklets, and little brown pots with white lids. Adam's hand feels cold in mine. He stops by one of the stands and, with his free hand, picks up one of the little brown pots.

"Here," he says. "You might need this."

I look at the label. OIL BLESSED AT THE SHRINE OF ST. JUDE, it says.

"And one of these." Adam now gives me a small blue pendant. It has a picture of St. Jude on it.

"Thanks," I say. And of course usually I'd say that I don't believe in lucky charms and snake oil, but I think homoeopathic remedies and holy water fit into the same kind of category, and look where they've got me. At the moment I need all the help I can get, however implausible it may seem. I take my hand from Adam's and put on the necklace. "Do I need to pay for these?" I ask.

"I'll do it for you later. Don't worry. I've been outside God's economy for quite a while now, but even I still understand it doesn't run on our money. OK. Now hang on a second . . . In fact, can you grab and light one of those candles?"

He bends down and releases a catch that I can't even see on the floor. It's a trapdoor. I take a big candle in a blue holder and light it with my cigarette lighter. I notice that my hands are shaking, and then I realize that my legs feel light and wobbly, as though there's an electric current going through them. I don't feel at all well. My head . . .

Instinct makes me try to grab Adam's shoulder. I just want to put my head down on it for a second: I think this might make everything better. Then my head fizzes with what feels like bubbles of air.

"Adam," I say. But before he can reply, everything goes silent, and it's as if I'm being dipped, headfirst, into a giant tin of black paint.

When I wake up I'm lying on a small, firm bed that's been severely made up with crisp white linen and brown blankets. My bag is lying on the floor by a cupboard. There's a small bedside table with a copy of the Bible on it, and one wooden chair. There's a window to my right, but the curtains are drawn and so I have no idea what time it is. Then again, you can't tell the time that easily from winter skies. In winter, there's no difference between five in the afternoon and five in the morning.

There's no one here in the room apart from me. What happened? Did I faint? I suppose I haven't eaten for a couple of days. The Troposphere just seems to suck all your life away. Everyone else who has ever read *The End of Mr. Y* has died. And Mr. Y himself starved to death. I can now see why. But none of this affects the part of my mind that is almost aggressively demanding to be taken back there *now*.

I'm still in the clothes I was wearing when I came here: old gray jeans and a black jumper. I'd like to change but I don't have anything more presentable, so maybe I won't bother. Instead of changing I sit there brushing my hair, trying to get every knot out of it. It takes about fifteen minutes. Then I look at the burns on my wrists: They are little silvery-red scabs now and I resist the urge to pick them off. No one comes into the room. What do you get in a priory? Friars, I think. I don't imagine that any friars are going to come in here. But Maria and

Adam. Where are they? Somewhere a bell chimes. One, two, three, four, five, six, SEVEN o'clock. Oh shit. The men will definitely have been released from their cage in the Troposphere by now. And they're not in my brain. *Yet*. At least it doesn't feel like they're in my brain. How would I know? I tie my hair into the kind of plait I think religious people might approve of and wash my face in the hand basin. There is no mirror here. Am I going to make it through another day? Who knows. I should find Adam and Maria. I open the door softly and walk out into a dim corridor. There's a yellowy light at the end of it, and I can hear the sound of women's laughter and the vibration of pan lids. I can smell food, as well: something hot and savory. It must be the kitchen. That was where I was going to have tea before I fainted; if that's what did happen to me.

My legs still feel weak. Am I going to faint again? No; come on. For God's sake, Ariel, it's just walking. But I think I need a rest. I lean on the wall for a second, breathing as if I've just run a marathon rather than walked about fifteen steps. What is wrong with me? Maybe I'll just close my eyes for a moment.

"Ariel?"

Somehow I'm now slumped on the carpet and Maria is standing over me, holding a blue-and-white checked tea towel. Her small face crunches into a frown.

"I think you should be back in bed."

"I'm sorry," I say. "I don't know what's wrong with me."

Those men could come now and they could do whatever they wanted. I wouldn't be able to stop them. Maybe it would be better that way: Get it over with. Would I prefer for them to finish me off in the Troposphere or out here? Apollo Smintheus said you can't die in the Troposphere, but perhaps there are things worse than dying. So I could just stay here and wait for a clean death. But they never said they were going to kill me. They just want to send me mad and take the book.

Maria helps me up and in a few minutes I am back in the bedroom.

"Maybe you should change out of those clothes," Maria suggests. "Get your night things on."

"I'm OK. I think I just need to lie down for a minute." I don't actually have any "night things" with me. When I packed I wasn't thinking about anything relaxing like going to sleep; I was just thinking about running away.

"You don't want to get into bed like that," Maria says. "I'll get you something to wear."

Half an hour or so later I'm lying in bed in a long white cotton nightdress thinking about going back into the Troposphere. I'm trying to work out whether it will kill me if I just go in for a little while and try to find Apollo Smintheus. Before I got back into bed I opened the curtains and looked at the sky for a while before closing them again. The sky was screen black, and snowflakes were falling with the same rhythm of the cascading numbers on Heather's LUCA program. When will she work out where I've gone? Will she tell the men?

Just after the church bells ring for eight o'clock, there's a knock at the door.

"Come in," I call.

It's Maria again. She's holding a large, thick, brown dressing gown.

"Can you face some supper?" she asks me.

"Yes," I say. "Thanks. You're being very kind."

If I eat, then I can definitely go back into the Troposphere.

"You don't have to get dressed. You can wear this."

I should get dressed, but I can't. I'm sure I'll get my strength back after eating, though. I'll get my strength back and go to the Troposphere. Or should I leave first? I imagine parking in some anonymous rural lay-by, reclining on the backseat of the car, and knocking myself out with the mixture. What would happen then? Would I freeze to death? Maybe I'll just stay here tonight. This bed is so warm and clean that I don't even want to get out of it now. But I should go and eat.

The kitchen is a long, narrow room with a large porcelain sink at the far end, work surfaces along the right-hand wall, and a long pine table running down the middle. To my left, there's probably the largest fireplace I've ever seen. There's no fire in it, though. Instead there's a fair-sized cooking range, with two large silver pans on it, steam coming from both of them and disappearing up the gray stone chimney.

I walk to the table and the wooden floorboards creak under my footsteps.

"Sit down, dear," says Maria. "Adam will be along in a minute."

I pull out a chair and slump into it. I feel like shit.

"No one's come looking for me, presumably?" I say.

"No, dear." Maria smiles a young smile. "And we've got a lookout just in case."

I imagine a friar with a telescope. But it's probably one of the kitchen women on an extravagant kind of neighborhood watch. Both images seem comical to me, and the atmosphere here is just safe enough that I manage to smile back.

"Thanks," I say.

Now Maria goes over to the range. "Vegetable stew and dumplings?" she says.

"Yes. Thanks so much," I say.

I've already started eating when Adam comes in and sits down opposite me. Maria puts a plate of the same stew in front of him, although I notice she gives him two more dumplings than she gave me. There's a jug of water on the table, and I refill my glass for the second time and drink. I need fluid and calories: Then I can spend all night in the Troposphere if I have to. I'm not sure when I'm going to sleep, though. Perhaps I should try to divide my night into half sleep and half Troposphere. But I still don't know how time works when you're in there.

"Hi," says Adam. "How are you feeling?"

"I'm OK," I say. "Sorry I fainted on you."

"I tried to stop you, but you just went down," he says. "But you didn't bang your head or anything like that."

Maria takes off her apron. "I'll be next door if you need anything," she says.

The bruised part of Adam's face is exactly the same color as stewed blackberries. The eye on that side is almost entirely closed.

"It's not as bad as what happened to you," I say. "I'm so sorry about that."

He shrugs. "Oh, well. These things happen."

"Yeah, but they don't, though. Not really." I breathe deeply and take another sip of water. "Things like this shouldn't happen. Not in real life."

"Yeah, but what's real life? Honestly. It's fine. It's over."

"But what if they come here? We'll be fucked." I realize I've sworn out loud in a priory. "I mean . . . Sorry about my language. But you know what I mean."

Adam smiles now. "It's only language," he says. "Just don't do it in front of the friars. They'll get confused." Smiling obviously hurts him a little. He winces now. "Ouch," he says.

"So what exactly did happen?" I say. "I mean, they obviously beat you up. But why?"

"I wouldn't tell them where you live."

Shit. How guilty is it possible to feel?

"But why were they asking you? I don't understand."

"They'd interviewed Heather already, and when she couldn't answer their questions she sent them to find me. They seemed to assume that we knew a lot about you, even though Heather kept telling them we'd been sharing an office for a total of two days. So she told them I'd gone to show a new sessional teacher around the university, and they caught up with me at the chapel. The woman I was showing around—her children's school had phoned and said they were shutting because of the snow, and she'd left about five minutes before. When I walked out of the chapel I ran straight into these two blond men.

"I asked if I could help them, then they asked me who I was and I told them.

"'We'd like to ask you a few questions,' one of them said.

"I agreed, obviously—there was no reason not to—and invited them into the chapel. It was absolutely freezing and snow was settling on their hair and eyebrows. I was going to suggest making them hot drinks in the chapel kitchen. One of them looked around, as if he wanted to find some other building to go into, but as you know, there's nothing around the chapel. Then they said that they'd rather talk to me outside. I remember wondering what was wrong with the chapel. For some reason I thought about bombs and terrorists, and I thought that maybe the men were here to evacuate the building or something. I asked them if everything was OK. Then it all got confusing.

"'Since we've got to stand in the freezing cold, we'll make this quick,' one of them said. 'Where is Ariel Manto?'

"'I don't have any idea,' I said. 'Why?'

"'We need to find her. It's a matter of international security,' said the other one."

I've been eating while Adam talks. Not the most dignified of responses to what he's telling me, I know, but I just have to keep forking in the calories. But this bit makes me stop and frown.

"'International security'? What does that mean?"

Adam sips his water. "I don't know," he says. "I didn't get the chance to ask. The next thing that happened was that I tried to invite them into the chapel again, and this seemed to make them angry. They swore at me and said to just tell them where you were or something bad would happen to me. They were saying, 'You fucked her and you don't know where she lives?' And I was thinking, *What?* Then I realized that Heather probably thought we'd gone off and had sex the other night. Anyway, they kept asking me really crude, sexually explicit questions about you. At that point I realized that these men were dangerous and I decided not to tell them anything. I realized as well that they didn't need to ask me where you lived: They could just go and look it up in Personnel. So I told them again that I didn't know anything. Then they threatened me. They said something like 'Tell us, or take the consequences.'" Adam shrugs. "I thought to myself that they couldn't do anything to me except hurt me, so I simply braced myself for what came next." He points at his face. "This is the result."

"I can't apologize enough . . . ," I begin.

Adam now smiles, but mainly with the bottom half of his face. "Well, that's not even the strangest thing that happened, though. To begin with, they did start hitting me. One of them grabbed me and pinned my arms back while the other one punched me in the face, I don't know . . . Three times? Maybe four. It reminded me of being at school on a lunchtime punishment, and this guy seemed to think he had all the time in the world to just keep on hitting me. He'd hit me, then pause, then blow on his hand because it was so cold, then hit me again."

"My God," I say.

"Then the man who was holding me said, 'This isn't working. This is some religious guy who probably thinks he's Jesus or something. We could crucify him and not get any fucking information out of him.' The other one then said something like 'Well, the Romans didn't have these, did they?' And then he took out his gun. I must admit that he was right: I did become a lot more frightened then. I struggled and the man holding me slipped on the ice and released his hold on me. Not knowing what else to do, I half ran, half fell into the chapel and shut the door behind me. I kept thinking of St. Thomas, and I tried to reconcile myself with the idea of death. It was easier than I'd thought. I knew I *was* probably going to die, although I was equally aware that it would be absurd to be shot dead in the university chapel. Instinct made me hide under one of the pews, but I knew that the next moment the door would open and they'd come in and shoot me. There was nowhere else for me to go."

I have stopped eating now. This is insane. "Then what happened?"

"The door opened—I think they kicked it—but they didn't come in. For about five minutes or so they stood outside calling in to me. They were just swearing, trying to get me to come out. They went into great detail about the things they'd do to you if I didn't come out—but I just blocked out what they were saying and, for the first time in years, I prayed. I heard them argue about their guns and about what they should do next. At one point one of them told the other to 'Just go in there and finish him off.' But the other one said he was crazy if he thought he was going to go in there and lose something . . . Something I didn't understand." Adam sips some more water. "Anyway, this is why I thought you'd be safe here. I got the impression that they felt that they couldn't enter religious places."

"But what happened after that? Did they just go away?"

"Yes. Well, eventually. It felt like hours, but it must only have been about five more minutes or so. Neither of them was willing to go into the chapel, and I wasn't going to come out. I don't think they fancied a siege in which they had to stand in the snow for days while I lived on Communion wafers and wine inside."

"I think this is probably the bravest thing I've ever . . . ," I start.

"Don't flatter me," he says, holding up his hands. "After they left I was shaking so much I couldn't stand up for about twenty minutes. Then, when I did get up, I drank all the Communion wine. I'm not brave."

I should argue more about this. But something's bothering me.

"That thing you said before. Something you didn't understand. What was that?"

Adam has picked up his fork and is now eating his stew as calmly as if he'd just told me the football scores, not a story about escaping from men with guns.

"Sorry?"

"You said that when one of them said the other should go into the chapel he then said he was going to lose something if he did. Can you remember what it was?"

"Um . . . Yeah. It was an acronym, I think. Three letters."

"Sorry. There's no reason why you should remember what they are."

"No, I do remember. The letters were KID. 'I'll lose my KID.' That's what he said. But it doesn't mean anything to me. Does it mean anything to you?"

I shake my head. "No. I don't know why I thought it would."

Chapter **Seventeen**

After we've finished eating, Adam comes out to the cloisters with me so that I can have a cigarette. The cloisters here consist of a small grassed quad—currently iced with snow—contained within four thin gray stone walkways. As Adam explained, it's like being outside inside, or the reverse. When I asked, he said he wasn't sure if smoking was actually allowed in the cloisters but that no one really bothered the guests here, anyway. So now I'm standing here drawing toxic smoke into my lungs, thinking about the cloisters in Russell College, and how people only use them to smoke in: Most of the students wouldn't think cloisters were for anything else.

"You're quiet," says Adam, leaning against a stone pillar.

"I just feel so out of place here," I say. "As though I'm going to be struck down any minute for smoking or swearing. Or worse—for caring about stupid things like being struck down for smoking and swearing when really I should be feeling guilty about your face, and the fact that my being here puts you all in danger and . . . And as well as all that, I've got to work out how to get away, and where to go."

"You could just stay here," Adam says.

"I can't," I say. "There's someone I need to find."

But I don't tell him who, and I don't tell him how I'm planning to find him.

"Is this connected with the book?" he asks.

I nod. "Yeah."

"I suppose I can't ask you about the book?"

"No. It's probably better that you forget there ever was a book."

Adam shrugs. "Oh. Well, I'm glad I saw you again, anyway."

"You can't be," I say. "Look at what's already happened to you."

"But I don't mind that," he says, looking away from me. "At least pain is real."

"I know what you mean," I say, after a pause.

"Do you?" says Adam.

"Maybe not," I say, blowing smoke out into the cold air. "But I have . . . I don't know. I have an odd way of looking at things. It's yet another reason I feel out of place here . . . And with you, actually." I clear my throat, and it feels as if my words are being swallowed back along with all the phlegm and junk. Everything I want to say (and also don't want to say) contracts into one sentence: "I've done a lot of bad things."

"Everyone's done a lot of bad things."

"Yes, but there's a difference between forgetting to buy your grandmother a birthday card and the kinds of things I've done. I . . ."

"Whatever you've done doesn't matter to me."

I can't explain my sexual deviance to Adam, so I throw my cigarette butt into the snow in the quad, where it sinks like a monster's eye. "I'm a self-destructive person," I say. "Or at least that's what I am in magazine-speak."

"Self-destructive," Adam says. "That's an interesting term. I suppose I'm self-destructive, but in a more literal way. It's what the Tao asks you to do: to destroy the self and get rid of the ego."

"So being self-destructive can be a positive thing?" I say. "That is interesting."

"Well, since I lost God . . ."

"You lost God?" I say, half my face dimpling into a smile. "That was careless."

Shit. This isn't the time to make jokes. Ariel, for God's sake, don't be offensive now. But Adam just looks at me for a second and then, suddenly, he walks the couple of paces towards me, pushes himself against me, and kisses me hard. I kiss him back, although I know we can't do this here. His lips press against mine with a cold urgency, and then he's using his teeth: biting my lip, almost tearing my flesh. I pull away.

"Adam . . ."

"Sorry. But you do things to me."

I look at the ground. "I don't mean to."

"Yes you do."

"No. Look—I know what you mean. I usually do mean to do things with people or even, as you put it, to people; but not you. You're different."

"What, because I managed to lose God? Or because I ever had God at all?"

"I am sorry I interrupted. What were you going to say?"

He sighs into the air: a frozen cloud of uncertainty. "I was going to say that I lost God, and then I lost myself. You know how religion usually helps people find themselves, and find God? I managed to lose everything. I thought that was the point. All the books I read about losing desire and losing the ego . . . The whole thing was soul-destroying, literally. Nothing prepared me for it. Nothing prepared me for what it would be like to be aware, objectively, of religion without being a part of it. The Bible just became a book, like any other book. I could still read it and make opinions about what this or that bit meant, but I couldn't believe in it."

"Soul-destroying. Like *self-destructive*."

"Yes. I experienced being truly selfless and it was fucking terrifying."

"Adam . . ."

"Connecting with other people; losing yourself in them; becoming 'at one.' It's hell. Who said that hell is other people?"

"Sartre."

"He's right. I didn't realize: Ripping out your soul and offering to share it around isn't at all like giving Communion, or taking some old clothes to the charity shop. It's like going into the park at night and taking off all your clothes and waiting to be pissed on."

I think about Wolf, and his useless attempts to get beaten up.

"People can't be all bad," I say.

"That's not what I'm saying. I . . . I don't know what I'm saying. This is what I wanted to explain to you the other night, but I'm not doing a much better job now. I told you I've had a breakdown?"

"Yes. I'm sorry. I . . ."

"It's part of the same thing. The self destructs; the self breaks down. It's about exploding the self until there's nothing left anymore. But I couldn't do it. I completely failed. I broke down, sure, but then before I'd even had a chance to look into the abyss and see what it was like I started putting myself back together again. I tried being 'normal': drinking and swearing. It was quite fun. But now I'm not sure who I am. I use this word 'I' and I don't know what it means. I don't know where it begins and ends. I don't even know what it's made of."

"Ah. Well, I can help you there," I say. "Everything in the known universe is made of quarks and electrons. You're made of the same stuff I'm made of, and the same stuff the snow is made of and the same stuff this stone is made of. It's just different combinations."

"That's a beautiful idea," Adam says.

"It's true." I laugh. "I don't usually say that. But it's as true as anything can be."

Once I did a class with my students about working with meaning. It's supposed to be the little introductory session I do to get them thinking about Derrida. We do Saussure and all that basic stuff, and then I show them a photocopy of Duchamp's *Fountain*—the urinal that was voted the most influential piece of art from the twentieth century—and ask them if it's art or not. In this particular class most of the students started arguing that a urinal couldn't be art: Two or three of them became quite angry about it, and started talking about Picasso, and how their children could draw better pictures; and the recent Turner Prize–winning installation with the light going off and on . . . I'd thought that it would be quite an easy class. All I'd wanted to demonstrate was that something that is called a "urinal," which we understand to be something that men piss in, is only different from something that is called a "painting," which we understand to be paint on canvas, because we make it different in language. And

whether or not we choose to group either of these things in the category "art" depends on how we define art. But the students were having trouble getting it and I became frustrated with them. I remember
thinking, *Fuck you. I'd so much rather be at home right now, drinking coffee in my kitchen.* I explained to them that everything in the
whole world is made up of exactly the same quarks and electrons.
Atoms are different. Sure, there are helium atoms and hydrogen atoms
and every other sort of atom, but they're only different in the number
of quarks and electrons they have and, in the case of the quarks, which
way up they are. I explained that, therefore, the urinal could, in a very
real way, be said to be the same as, say, the *Mona Lisa.* I told them
that what they thought was reality was all relative to the position from
which they were looking at it. Under a powerful enough microscope,
the urinal and the *Mona Lisa* would look identical.

It's not just space and time that are fucked up. Matter is energy,
but more than that: Matter is already gray sludge; we just can't see
it. Now I think of the Troposphere and I wonder what that is made
of and, even if it's only in my imagination, what my imagination is
made of.

Adam comes back to my room with me. I immediately get on the bed,
but he paces around for a while, peeping out of the curtains, then picking up the Bible and putting it back down. I think he's going to sit on
the wooden chair but eventually he comes and sits on the bed next to
me, with his head resting against the headboard about two inches
from mine.

"So if we're all quarks and electrons . . . ," he begins.

"What?"

"We could make love and it would be nothing more than quarks
and electrons rubbing together."

"Better that that," I say. "Nothing really 'rubs together' in the mi-
croscopic world. Matter never really touches other matter, so we could
make love without any of our atoms touching at all. Remember that
electrons sit on the outside of atoms, repelling other electrons. So we
could make love and actually repel each other at the same time."

I hear his breathing take on a slightly different rhythm as he puts his hand on my leg just where the material of the dressing gown is hanging slightly open.

"And what would you call that? I mean if it's just atoms repelling each other then it can't be worthy of note, really. I mean, why should anyone mind?"

"Adam . . ."

"What makes it real at all?"

For a moment I think about pain again: about forcing friction; forcing atoms to exchange electrons; forcing something to become real. But this is about something else; something beyond that.

"Language," I say. "Everything from the existence of the word *real* to the existence of the word *fucking* to the existence of the word *wrong*."

I place enough emphasis on the word *wrong* that he takes his hand away from my leg. I close the gap created by my dressing gown and cross my ankles. I know why I can't do this, but reason isn't the same as desire, and I am aware of my blood pumping purposefully around my body, preparing me for something that can't happen: Adam's lips on mine; his dark, hairy chest pressed against my smooth, pale breasts; penetration; oblivion. It's like starving and feeling you have to eat. I'm starving and someone's just presented me with a bowl of food and told me that I can't eat it; that it might be poisoned.

Adam gets off the bed and walks over to the window. The curtains are still closed but he doesn't open them; he just stands there looking at the beige fabric. He sighs.

"This language stuff is what you study, isn't it?"

"Yeah."

"It's very different from theology."

"Is it?" I say. "Some of that stuff you were saying the other night at Heather's . . . It made me think about Baudrillard and his idea of the simulacrum: a world made up of illusion, of copies of copies of things that don't exist anymore; copies with no original. And Derrida's différance and the way we defer meaning rather than ever really experiencing it. Derrida talks about faith a lot. He wrote a lot about religion."

"It's still not fun, is it? It still has the power to tell you what to do. It's like: Nothing means anything but you still have to follow the rules. I want something that tells me I don't have to follow the rules."

"Oh, well, maybe then you're back to the existentialists. I think they have more fun. Although the problem there is they don't really know they're having fun."

I think about Camus and *The Outsider.* I think about the scene where Mersault drinks coffee in the funeral parlor and the way that this is used, later, as evidence that he is a bad person. Having sex in a priory would therefore make you what sort of person?

"So Derrida is not an existentialist?"

"No. But it all comes from the same background: Heidegger; phenomenology."

"And what does that say about life?"

"What? Phenomenology?"

"Yeah."

"Um . . . This is all stuff I'm still thinking about, and the way I understand it might not be quite right, but basically it's to do with the world of things: *phenomena.*"

I think back to Lumas's story "The Blue Room," about the philosophers trying to establish whether or not ghosts exist. It reminds me of the time I was first trying to properly understand phenomenology (a process still not complete). I'd been reading Levinas's *Discovering Existence with Husserl*—Husserl was Heidegger's mentor—and I was trying to come to grips with his work, but it was very difficult. I was lying in the bath, trying not to get the book wet, and, as a thought experiment, asking myself the old question: "Is there a ghost in this room?" I reminded myself that if I were a rationalist, I could answer *no*, quite confidently, as long as I had already established that ghosts don't exist using logic and a priori statements. You can be a rationalist with your eyes shut. *I know ghosts don't exist, so there is no ghost in this room.* If you're a rationalist, and you've made your world out of a logic that says that when things are dead they are dead and that's it, then you could be there in a room full of screaming ghouls and still conclude that there is no ghost in the room. If I were an empiricist I'd look for evidence from my senses: I would see that there was no ghost in the room and conclude that if I was not experiencing it, then it wasn't there. I'd got all that. But phenomenology, it seemed to me, wasn't interested in whether or not the ghost was there. Phenomenology seemed to be asking, *What the fuck is a ghost, anyway?*

I try to summarize this for Adam.

"Basically, phenomenology says that you exist and the world exists but the relationship between the two is problematic. How do we define entities? Where does one entity stop and another begin? Structuralism seemed to say that objects are objects and you can name them anything you like. But I'm more interested in questions about what makes an object. And how an object can have meaning outside of the language we use to define it."

"So everything's just language in the end. There's nothing beyond words. Is that the main point?"

"Kind of. It's not just words though. Maybe 'language' is the wrong term to use in this context. Maybe 'information' is better." I sigh. "This is so hard to put into words. Maybe Baudrillard does it best when he talks about the copy without an original: the simulation. Like, you know the way Plato thought that everything on earth was a copy—or a shadow—of some 'ideal object.' Well, what if we've created a world in which even that shadowy level of reality isn't the final copy? One in which anything that was ever 'real' is now gone, and the copies that referred to things—in other words the language, the signs—don't refer to anything anymore? What if all our stupid pictures and signs don't make reality at all? What if they don't refer out to anything else, but only inward towards themselves and other signs? That's hyperreality. If we wanted to talk about it in Derridean terms we could talk of a world that constantly defers the real. And it is language that does that. It promises us a table, or a ghost, or a rock, but can never actually deliver one for us."

"Isn't it depressing?" Adam asks.

I laugh, but it sounds hollow in here. "Surely no more depressing than your idea that everything is an illusion?"

"But I was talking about an illusion that covers something up.

Some definite reality. You're talking about a world where nothing is not an illusion."

"Well, maybe I do want to believe that there's something outside the simulacrum. I don't know. But it is exciting to think about it. Like finding out that everything is just quarks and electrons. I find it exciting because everything you learn about the basic units of things—language, atoms, whatever—you find that they are absurd. That stuff I was telling you the other night about quantum physics: It's so crazy it can't be true. And then what you were saying about truth existing outside reality: I found that exciting as well. There's always another level that we just *don't know*. The scientists have it down to the quarks and electrons, and the various weird variations of them that come down in cosmic rays and so on, but they don't know if that's it, if they have found indivisible matter—what the Greeks called *atomos*. It could even be that there's infinite divisibility. And there are still these big questions that no one can solve: What came before the beginning and what will happen after the end. The fact that these big questions still exist is exciting. No one really knows anything very important—and there's still such a lot to know."

"So now we're back to religion."

"I thought you said religion was part of the illusion. I mean, it's made of language like everything else . . ."

"But faith," he says now. "What's faith made of?" Adam touches the curtains but doesn't open them. "But you can't base anything on faith. Nothing based on faith is true."

"Isn't it? You could argue that we all have faith. We have faith in language, for example."

"Faith doesn't always pay off, though, does it? You don't always get back what you want."

He turns and looks at me. His face is pale and I remember what he said about not feeling "so good" at the moment. But he's still probably the most attractive human being I have ever seen, and for a second I can't believe he is here in this room with me, with his long, unwashed hair and his old grayscale clothes, like there's so much more to him than flesh, so much more than just atoms. How easy it would be to just close my eyes and let him in. But then he'd go away again and I'd be left with what I'd done. I don't want him to go away. I can't have sex with him, so I'm going to have to keep him talking. And then maybe we could just go to sleep in each other's arms? Don't be stupid, Ariel. Here that would be as bad as fucking.

"You could say we have faith in a shared culture," I say.

"Based on what?"

"Shared language. I mean, we do share a culture, and that culture is made up of things that we've broken down and labelled, like the way the nineteenth-century natural scientists classified everything. Of course, people still debate all those classifications. Are two similar fish actually one sort of fish or two? Is everything different from everything else or the same?"

He's looking at me with the most sulky expression I've ever seen, everything on his face pointing downwards, including his gaze, which now drifts to the floor. But I'm still thinking that I want to drown in him; I want to drown in a pool of sulky, pissed-off Adam. I want him so much more now that he's cross with me for not agreeing to sleep with him. It's as if the lines of force between us have become elastic, and they're trying to contract. Are we different from one another or the same?

He doesn't say anything, so I carry on.

"According to what criteria can you say, This thing ends there, and here's where another thing begins? What exactly is 'being' anyway? Unless you go down to the atomic level, there seem to be no spaces between things. Even empty space is teeming with particles. But when you look at atoms closely you realize there is hardly anything but space. You must have heard that analogy that an atom is like a sports hall with one tennis ball in the middle? Nothing is really connected to anything else. But we create connections between things in language. And we use those classifications and the spaces between them to create a culture such as the one we're now in, in which we both understand that it would be wrong to sleep together in a priory in which I am a guest."

Adam's eyes are hard but his voice is now soft.

"Why is it wrong?"

"Come on, you know why. We'd offend everyone here if they knew what was going on."

"But surely that would be their fault for not understanding about the atoms?"

"Would it? That's not what culture says. Imagine using that as a defense for murder. *But judge, I didn't really stab her because the atoms in the knife never touched the atoms in her body.* We can't just exit culture because it doesn't suit us. Well, we could—or we could tell ourselves that's what we'd done—but we'd feel guilt, anyway." I sigh. It's so easy to talk like this but it's not easy to explain what I'm actually feeling. What would I say? *Adam, I want to see you naked. I want to suck your cock and lie back and let you fuck me but not in a priory because it makes me feel dirty and evil and I'm probably going to die soon and even though I'm not sure I believe in heaven, I have seen an entity that claimed to be a god recently and so I don't want to mess up my chances at the last possible minute.*

And then I think of Derrida again. It's as though I'm in some kind of auction and my last bid for purity is this: I'm *thinking* about his cock in my mouth but I'm not speaking it and I'm not doing it. I'm not letting the atoms get too close.

Adam turns to the window again. This time he opens the curtains and looks out.

"Is it still snowing?" I ask. That reminds me of some quote: *Tell me, my dear, does it still snow?* But I can't remember where it's from. Maybe in the quote it's not even snow. Maybe it's rain.

"No." He sighs. "I should have stayed at your flat on Tuesday."

"I wouldn't have slept with you then, either."

Are you listening, God?

He nods. "You don't find me attractive."

"It's not that. I think it's more that I don't find myself that attractive."

"That sounds like shit to me."

"Sorry. You're right. But I just can't. I want to—but I just can't." Now he turns around again. He doesn't look me in the eye, though. There's no connection—whatever the hell that connection is when someone focuses on your eyes and you focus on theirs and for a second it feels like you're machines plugged into the same socket, or even that one of you is the machine and the other is the socket. Machines, sockets, electricity, lines of force . . . Our eyes might not connect, but all the other lines of force are still there, pulling me towards him.

"But you do want to? You do want me?" The way he speaks is as if he's been told that he's got a terminal illness but a year to live. Is it possible to take sex this seriously? Is it possible to take sex with me this seriously? Patrick says I "do" things to him but all I really do to him is implicitly promise to provide what I always provide: dirty sex with no strings. But if he never saw me again I don't think he'd care. Do I want Adam? Well, that's easy.

"Yes. But I can't have you. I'm wrong for you."

"You know that I've never . . ." He lets the sentence drift away, like a snowflake that melts before it lands.

"I know. That's why as well. The thing is that I have. Thousands of times, with hundreds of people."

"Ariel, for God's sake."

"What?"

"Why are you saying it like that?"

"Like what?"

"Like you're trying to make yourself seem . . . I don't know."

"Like a bit of a slut?"

"I wouldn't put it like that."

"No. You're too nice." I bite my lip.

"Oh, fuck off. You think I'm nice because I used to be a priest. I don't want to be nice. I want . . ."

"What? You want to be like me? You want to be *un*nice? You want to be dirty? Well, come on then." I start undoing my dressing gown. "Let's fuck in the priory. Have a little bit of what I've got. Look: Here's some of what I've got." I hold up my arms, wrists facing outwards as though I'm pushing something away. "That's what happened last time someone fucked me."

Adam walks forwards and for a second I imagine that he's on his way to rip open my nightdress and push me down on the bed. Is that what I want him to do? Or do I want him to feel sorry for me with my fucked-up wrists and my hundreds of sexual conquests? But his eyes are as still as fossils as he walks right past me and out of the room. Whatever I do want I'm not going to get it. He's gone.

Half an hour later I'm under the covers in my bed in the cold, still room, alone. Adam never came back, not that I expected him to really. Oh well. I achieved my objective, even if it wasn't in the most elegant way. It's like when someone fills a whole blackboard proving something in mathematics and then someone else comes along and shows that it can be done in one line. I could have just told him I wasn't interested. It would have been a lie but it would have been elegant; more elegant than the maybe/never I've ended up with. Now I don't know if he'll ever want to speak to me again.

But I'm still here, at least: no blond men. I still exist.

Now I can go into the Troposphere.

This time it doesn't take long to go through the tunnel at all. But when I get out the other side it's different. The street I am so used to isn't there anymore. Instead I am in a cluttered town square with gray cobbles, which looks tiny compared with the mansions and castles crowded around it. There must be hundreds of these buildings, although objectively I can see that this should be spatially impossible. Nevertheless, they are "there." Some of them are built in pale stone, others are rendered in a dark, rusty-looking brick and have gothic spires and turrets that seem to reach into the clouds, as if they were trying to claw their way to heaven. *Clouds*. That's bizarre. There haven't been clouds in the Troposphere before. But it's still nighttime here; maybe I can only see the clouds now because of the full moon. But then I realize that the moon hasn't been here before, either.

There's a statue in the center of the square, shining in the moonlight. It seems to be a copy of Rodin's *Le Penseur:* a man sitting on a rock with his chin resting on the back of his hand. But as I walk closer

I see that this man has a mouse face. It's a statue of Apollo Smintheus without his cape on. An owl hoots and I jump. Last time I heard sound in the Troposphere it wasn't a good sign at all. But nothing else happens so I decide it's just an owl. How many buildings are there here? An impossible number. It's very hard to describe what is in front of me but there does just seem to be too much stuff: too much information, all packed into such a small space. As well as the scramble of turrets and spires, I can see drawbridges and moats, mounds, smoke from fires, a rainbow bridge, and various flags; behind the buildings are mountains and cliff tops and lakes, all jumbled together like a bunch of landscape photographs overlapping on a crowded wall. In between these grand buildings are other, more familiar places: a couple of tea rooms, a small bookshop, and a shop selling magic tricks. They all seem to be closed, though. One place seems especially compelling, but it's not a building. It's an overgrown garden with high walls and a wrought-iron gate. Inside are a bench and several trees. I want to go in there, but it's locked. The other places here are also closed. Anachronistic neon signs glow pinkly all over the place. *Closed. Fermé. Closed for Renovations. Closed. Shut. No Vacancies.* What kind of place has gothic castles and towers with pink neon signs everywhere?

Console?

The thing comes up.

You have no choices, says the female voice.

Oh, great. This again. Has the whole thing crashed? Did those men do something to this place that means I just can't access anything anymore?

You have one new message.

What?

You have one new message.

Can I get the message? There's no response. Where's the little envelope that you click on? What is the equivalent here? How do I retrieve a message in the Troposphere? Who would have left me a message, anyway? For a second I imagine some brown paper package with red, green, and black wires coming out of it: a bomb from my enemies. But this doesn't make me feel anything at all and I remember that this is what I like so much about this space: no hot, no cold, no fear.

Something now glows in the console and I notice that's it's Apollo Smintheus's mouse-hole. I didn't notice it before, but it's there now: sitting between what looks like Valhalla and something called the Primrose Tea Shoppe. Am I supposed to go in there? I do want to see Apollo Smintheus. I switch off the console and walk through the white archway and into the room I recognize from before: the empty tables and shelves and the nest in the corner. There's no sign of Apollo Smintheus. I walk through to the other room. The fire is out and there's no one here. But there is a booklet lying on the table.

A Guide to the Troposphere, it says on the cover. *By Apollo Smintheus.*

Is this the message? I open the booklet.

You now have no new messages, says the console.

So the booklet is the message. OK. I sit down on the rocking chair and begin reading. The whole document is only about three pages long, but the script is large.

The Troposphere is not a place.

The Troposphere is made by thinking.

(I am made from prayer.)

The Troposphere is expanding.

The Troposphere is both inside your universe and outside it.

The Troposphere can also collapse to a point.

The Troposphere has more than three directions and more than one "time."

You are now standing in the Troposphere but you could call it anything.

The thought is all thought.

The mind is all minds.

This dimension is different from the others.

Your Troposphere is different from others'.

You achieve Pedesis via proximity in

> Geography (in the world)
>
> Tropography (in the Troposphere)
>
> Ancestry (in the mind)

The choices the Troposphere gives you relate to proximity alone.

> (Except when information is scrambled.)

You can jump from person to person in the physical world (but only if the person is at that moment vulnerable to the world of all minds.)

You can also jump from person to ancestor in the world of memory.

This is all memory.

The Troposphere is a different shape from the physical world to which it (loosely) corresponds. For this reason it is sometimes more efficient to travel in the Troposphere and sometimes more efficient to travel in the physical world (see diagram).

Time passed on return from y (not you) to x (you)

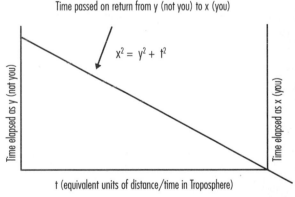

$$x^2 = y^2 + t^2$$

Time elapsed as y (not you)

Time elapsed as x (you)

t (equivalent units of distance/time in Troposphere)

Disclaimer: This diagram is a scaled-down version of a higher-dimensional calculation. It will be correct for journeys of a short or noncomplex nature. Pedesis that takes the ancestral route over many generations will (probably) lead to inaccuracies.

Note: Units of distance/time in the Troposphere work out as roughly 1.6 times that of their equivalent in the physical world. An "hour" in the Troposphere will last for 1.6 physical-world hours, i.e., ninety-six minutes.

Converting time to distance should be done in the usual way.

Distance is time in the Troposphere.

You cannot die in the Troposphere.

You can die in the physical world.

"You" are whatever you think you are.

Matter is thought.

Distance is being.

Nothing leaves the Troposphere.

You could probably think of the Troposphere as a text.

You could think of the Troposphere that you see as a metaphor.

The Troposphere is, in one sense, *only* a world of metaphor.

Although I have attempted it here the true Troposphere cannot be described.

It cannot be expressed in any language made from numbers or letters except as part of an existentiell analytic (see Heidegger for more details).

The last point could have been clearer. What I mean to say is that experiencing the Troposphere is also to express it.

　　End.

Chapter Eighteen

Back on my bed and it's only just gone midnight. I have to try to write down as much as possible of Apollo Smintheus's document before I forget it. I have to be able to think about it in the real world. What does it all mean? *The thought is all thought. The mind is all minds.* Is that what the Troposphere is? All minds? Perhaps I already knew that. Perhaps that's what I suspected. If that's the case, is the city in my mind so big that it has a little shop or house or, indeed, castle for every consciousness in the world? What were all those castles about, and why were they all shut? What is consciousness? Do worms have it? They must, if mice do. If I wanted to get in the mind of a worm in Africa, how would I go about that?

One thing is clear. Time does work differently in the Troposphere. I don't quite understand what distance/time travelled in the Troposphere is, but it seems obvious that when you come out of it, more time has passed than when you were inside. The first thing I do is draw out the diagram as I remember it. It's basically Pythagorean theorem. It's Pythagorean theorem but applied to space and time. I struggle to recall all the popular science books I've read over the years. Gravity works in a similar way, doesn't it? Isn't that what Newton said: The force of gravity is inversely proportional to the square of the distance between two objects multiplied by their masses? But there's nothing in Apollo Smintheus's document about mass. It's all about distance and time. Indeed, he seems to be suggesting that, in the Troposphere, distance is the same thing as time. I know that's true in the "real" universe as well. It's called space-time. But you don't notice it in your normal life. You can't mess around with time by taking a trip to the shops, or even a trip to the moon. If you want to mess with time you have to fly away from Earth very fast in a spaceship, and keep travelling at something close to the speed of light without accelerating or decelerating. Then, if you come back, you'll find that "more" time has passed on Earth relative to you in your spaceship. What seems to happen in the Troposphere is the opposite of this. Or is it in fact the same? My stomach grumbles. I'm going to have to eat again soon.

But I can't stop thinking about the castles and towers with their ornate spires and heavy drawbridges. As I write out the lines *You could think of the Troposphere that you see as a metaphor. The Troposphere is, in one sense, only a world of metaphor,* I wonder what the castles, if they are metaphors, represent. And then I also wonder: When you go into the Troposphere, do you immediately get access to the consciousnesses "closest" to yours? And if so, did all the castles belong to the religious people in this building? And who decided that they would be castles? Did they; or did I?

I finish writing out the document. I think it's almost right. It's easier than I thought to remember, but then I think about what Apollo Smintheus has told me and it becomes clear that my Troposphere (because it's different for everyone) is in my mind. This document is now a memory. But then memory isn't that reliable and I do need this to be a document in the real world, a text I can go back to. Memory is already decaying it, though. I look at one line I've written: *You can jump from person to person in the physical world.* It doesn't look right. Have I left something out? I scrunch my forehead, as if this will make my memories rub together and create a kind of friction of remembrance. It works. *You can jump from person to person in the physical world (but only if the person is at that moment vulnerable to the world of all minds).* OK. I don't know what this means but at least it's there on paper.

I yawn. My body wants to sleep—and eat—but my mind wants to keep doing this: to keep answering questions until there aren't any more questions. I glance back over my list. I have to smile when I see the reference to Heidegger. What's Apollo Smintheus doing thinking about Heidegger? But some instinct tells me that Apollo Smintheus knows how to explain things to people in their own personal language, and my language does include terms like *existentiell* and *ontical*, as well as their grander counterparts: *existential* and *ontological*. I've never forgotten what I read of *Being and Time*, although not finishing it is one of the big regrets of my life. I remember those terms because they're the ones I wrote so many notes about, all in the margins of the book.

When I read *Being and Time* I always thought of it as *Being and Lunchtime*: It was my private joke with myself for the month it took me to read the first one hundred pages. It took that long because I read it only at lunchtime, over soup and a roll in a cheap café not far from where I was living at the time in Oxford. That house had no heating at all, and it was damp. I spent the winters with chest infections and the summers with a house full of insects. I tried to spend as little time there as possible. So every day I'd go to the café and sit there for an hour or two reading *Being and Time*. I think I managed about three or four pages a day. As I remember this, I can't help wondering: Does Apollo Smintheus know this, too? Does he know about the day the café closed for renovations and I stopped going there? Does he know that I started having an affair with a guy who wanted to meet me at lunchtimes, and that I left Heidegger for him?

I wish I'd finished the book. I wish I'd brought it with me. But who takes *Being and Time* with them as an essential object when running away from men with guns? I get out of bed. There's a freestanding antique bookcase by the wall. It has a glass front and a little silver key. I look through the glass and see lots of texts written by Pope John Paul II, including a book of his poetry. There are thick brown Bibles and thin white Bible commentaries; all dusty. No thick blue books. No *Being and Time*. As if I thought there would be.

My stomach makes another peculiar noise, as though it's a balloon being blown up. I need to eat. I need fuel. I also need to start trying to find Burlem. How the hell am I going to do that? I wouldn't even know where to start. Except . . . Shit! Of course. I've still got the contents of his hard drive on my iPod. Does it need charging up? I walk away from the bookshelves and look through my bag. It's there, and it has almost a full battery. Fine. But *I* don't have a full battery: If I'm going to stay up doing this then I need to eat.

The corridor is dark and cold. I can't believe I'm on my way to steal food from a priory kitchen. Is it actually stealing? I'm sure that if anyone else was awake and I could ask them they'd tell me to help myself. That's what people usually say to guests, isn't it? At least I haven't had sex here; I haven't had sex in the priory with an ex-priest.

I wonder where Adam is. Is he in one of the other guest rooms? I imagine bumping into him in the corridor and taking back everything I said earlier on. But I'm not sure you can take back everything I said. My insides spiral into themselves as I briefly imagine touching him; touching him anywhere. It doesn't begin as a sexual thought, but it soon becomes one. I imagine licking his legs and scratching his back. As my mind spirals more tightly, everything falls away. There are no men with guns; there is no priory. In an impossible half hour with Adam, a half hour without context, what would I want to do? We could do anything. How far would I go? How far would be enough to smother this desire? Jagged, violent images dance in my mind like broken glass and I sigh as the fantasy breaks down. Perhaps nothing will ever really satisfy me.

The kitchen door is closed but unlocked. Inside it is dark, but some heat is still coming from the range, and there's an orange glow of fuel burning in there. I don't switch on the light; the orange glow is just bright enough to see by. The smell of stew that was so savory before has lost intensity and become something more like a memory of a meal: that plasticy food smell you often get in institutions. I try a couple of cupboard doors before I find the pantry. There are large red and silver tins of biscuits, all stacked on top of one another. There are about twenty catering-sized tins of baked beans. There is powdered milk and condensed milk. There are several loaves of bread. What can I eat? What should I eat? What will actually give me energy I can use to stay in the Troposphere? I recall advice columns from several years' worth of my ex-housemates' women's magazines. Complex carbohydrates. That's the kind of thing I need. Whole wheat pasta, brown rice. But I can't cook anything. There are lots of cereals but, I'm guessing, no soya milk. There's a box of fruit. Bananas. I'm sure I remember that bananas are a good source of something or other. I take three and then, after thinking about it, I take the whole bunch. I can take some with me when I go. What else? Hurry up, Ariel, before you're caught raiding the bloody pantry. A small loaf of brown bread. A jar of Marmite. A bottle of lemonade. For Christ's sake. I'm going to travel to another world on Marmite sandwiches, bananas, and lemonade. The thought is absurd. Just before I close the pantry I see something else: several huge tubs of Hi-Energy meal replacer. I take one just in case. It's a brown cylinder, with pink, cheerful lettering.

Back in my room I stash all the food items in the bottom of my bag, except for three slices of bread and three bananas and the lemonade. It doesn't take too long to set up my laptop and connect my iPod. I close iTunes as soon as it opens up and instead go to My Computer and scan through until I see the iPod showing as Removable Drive (E:). I transfer Burlem's files to my desktop and then unplug my iPod and hide it in the bottom of my bag with the food.

Outside I can hear the wind picking up and I imagine a blizzard, something like the LUCA numbers gone viral, even though Adam said the snow had stopped. I eat three bananas, each wrapped in a slice of brown bread. I sip lemonade. I browse files. I learn that Burlem's CV is out of date, even though he seemed to go through a phase of applying for jobs in the States about three years ago. I learn that he was halfway through a novel when he disappeared (and, I wonder, did he take the file with him? Did he ever finish it?). The first chapter is quite good, but obviously doesn't have anything in it that will help me find him. I can't help reading the rough plan as well before I move on. It's only a page long. The novel is about a young academic who has an affair with a colleague who then gets pregnant by him. His wife finds out about the affair (but not the child) and divorces him, but the colleague's husband believes the child to be his. When he dies, the child is told the truth about her parentage and begins a tentative relationship with her biological father. The narrator lives alone with only books for company, and wishes he could see more of his daughter. After I close that document, I keep searching through the files. I find all the parts of the application process Burlem had to go through to get his professorship. I find letters to his bank manager. But there's nothing at all that suggests that he planned disappearing, that he planned to leave the university and never come back. There are more letters. There's one to a Sunday newspaper, complaining about a cartoon that mocked Derrida the weekend after his death. I smile at that, remembering seeing the cartoon and hoping someone would write in. There's a letter to someone I don't recognize. *Molly*. There's no surname. It's written in a strange style, the kind of style you'd use to talk to a child. Then I realize it *is* to a child. It's written to a child—or perhaps a teenager—at a boarding school. Burlem's promising to go and see her soon, and to give her money. What would Burlem be doing with a schoolgirl? My mind fills with unpleasant thoughts.

Then I open the file of the novel again. The kid in the book is called Polly.

I read the letter again. This is Burlem's daughter; of course it is. Shit. He never mentioned this to me. I just thought he was an unmarried—or, I guess, possibly divorced—guy in his fifties. I didn't know that he had a troubled past, although I should have realized. He certainly always looked like a man with a troubled past.

There's no address on the letter apart from Burlem's. But now I find other letters—a whole list of them below the ones to the bank manager—that make sense. They are all to a Dr. Mitchell and are on subjects such as fees, bullying, and extra tuition. Then I look at the bank manager letters and find instructions to set up a direct debit to a school in Hertfordshire. The reference is *Molly Davies*. Now I get it. Burlem's paying for his daughter to go to boarding school. There's an address on these letters. The address of the school.

My mind's buzzing. Could I get to Burlem through her?

Now I need to go back into the Troposphere. I need to find Apollo Smintheus.

When I get there I realize that the town square has more than four corners. The same castles are standing around with the same neon pink signs, still looking like impossibilities. The owl hoots again.

"Apollo Smintheus?" I say.

Nothing.

I call up the console.

You have no choices, it says.

"Can I still use the Apollo Smintheus card?" I ask it.

The Apollo Smintheus card has expired.

Fuck. I thought he said I'd have it for a couple of days.

I wander around the square but everything really is shut. There's a road leading out of the square and I take it. With each step I think of Apollo Smintheus's "rough calculation," that each unit of distance/time in the Troposphere is worth 1.6 in the "real" world. So what is a footstep? How much time does this take me? If I take a hundred steps, and it takes me, say, two minutes, when will I wake up in the priory? How far would I have to go to miss breakfast? How far would I have to go to be pronounced dead? I walk on, past a couple of car parks and a jazz club. On the other side of the road there's a run-down strip club with black oily streaks down its white façade, as if it recently caught fire. Neither of these places has a name, but the strip club has silhouettes of girls on poles, and the jazz club has a picture of a saxophone. The jazz club is on a corner, and there are concrete steps leading down towards an alleyway, at the end of which is a cinema and another car park. None of these buildings seems to be closed. There are no pink neon signs here. Without really thinking about it, I enter the jazz club. But there's no music and no smoke.

You now have one choice.

You . . . I'm cold and I need to take a shit. But it looks like we're going to sit here all night. Ed's got the heat on full but my feet are still like blocks. There's snow on the ground outside and the wind's picked up, too. The sign on the church across the street rattles back and forth. Who is Our Lady of Carmel? The word makes me think of caramel; a lady made out of caramel or something. The car smells of coffee and junk food. There are sandwich wrappers all over the floor. I kick one of them and it makes a thin, plastic, broken noise.

"What's that?" says Ed.

"Sandwich wrapper," I say. "Sorry."

Ed says nothing. His eyes are pure pupil.

"Maybe she isn't in there," I say.

"Look, the priest knows about the churches and she's screwing him, right?"

"Yeah, but . . ."

"And he 'comes here when things go wrong.' Why wouldn't he ask her to come, too? They'll know that as long as they stay in there we can't do anything. Maybe she knows, anyway. Who knows how long she's had the book? She could have been surfing MindSpace for years."

"I say the book's on its way to Leeds."

"Where is Leeds, anyway?"

I shrug. "Northwest? It's not close to here."

"Shit."

"We'll get the book."

"We didn't get it last time."

"We'll get it."

I'm . . . Oh fuck. I'm in the mind of one of the blond men. Martin. Martin Rose. OK, Ariel. Don't let him know you're here. But how do you tiptoe around in someone's mind. *Shhh.* Do I stay or do I go? *Console?* The thing appears like a slide transparency and now, as I/ Martin look over at Ed, his face is busy with an overlay of images. Someone's baking something. Someone else is driving on a freeway. Another person is looking up at a blue sky. What are these images? I remember Apollo Smintheus's document:

You achieve Pedesis via proximity in
Geography (in the world)
Tropography (in the Troposphere)
Ancestry (in the mind)

OK. So if you get close to someone in the world you can get into their mind (but surely only via the Troposphere?) This kind of makes sense. These guys are right outside the priory, and I had to walk down a street to find them. I don't understand what Tropography might be. But *Ancestry*. Is that what I'm seeing now? Are these images something to do with Martin's parents and grandparents? There are only three of them. That's not much ancestry. In the mouse's mind there were hundreds of images. Come on, Ariel. Think . . . But I don't want to think too loudly in case I alert Martin to the fact that I'm here. I am almost intrigued enough to try one of the images in the console to see what will happen, but something tells me that this would be a big mistake. When I last did this, with the mice, I managed to jump from the cupboard under my sink to the backyard. Who knows where I'd end up if I jumped here. Maybe somewhere in America. How would that translate in the Troposphere?

"Ed?"

"What?"

"If she just stays put in there there's not much we can really do."

"Right."

"Does she know that?"

Ed shrugs. (There's been a doorway hovering faintly over him the whole time, but now I can see another image in the console. It's an image of the interior of a car and a blond man. . . . It's me. It's Martin. So I could choose to be Ed now? Is that right? Shall I jump? Shall I do it? No. Stay safe.)

"We could burn it down," I say, not really meaning it. I didn't come here to burn down churches—or shoot priests. We've been given a second chance to take the book and OK, we've gotten a little crazy. But on the other hand we don't have much formula left and so this whole thing feels urgent. Our CIA cards will only get us so far; especially if someone chose to actually call the number and speak to our ex-boss. What would he say? *No, haven't seen those boys since they joined Project Starlight. Haven't seen them since I signed the form releasing them from their duties. CIA? Not anymore.*

"That's not a terrible idea," says Ed. "At least we'd warm up."

"It is a terrible idea. Forget I ever said it."

"Why? Smoke them out. It's a great idea."

I look out through the windshield. I'm thinking that I have a problem with shooting priests, but I could hurt her: Ariel Manto. I guess she'll be expecting it. That makes it easier. The first time it wasn't so easy: I remember vomiting into the toilet in some pale blue diner out West. I held on to the bowl and there was blood on it afterwards; blood from my hands. The next person I killed was a piece of scum anyway and was expecting it. That made me realize that there's the possibility of impersonality in doing these things, and after that I found I could do it without really being there. As though you're there but you're not there. You have a haze in your mind and afterwards you just wipe it. Then again, all this time in MindSpace makes you empathize with people more. But still, we need to get rid of the people who know the secret—once we know the secret ourselves. I kick the sandwich container again and Ed glares at me. Every so often the wipers go off and more snow accumulates in these minidrifts on the edges of the windshield. On the right, just in front of us, there's the priory: the little red-brick building. Could I get out of the car and set it alight? How do you set fire to something? Isn't it hard, especially in the snow? We'd need gas to do it, and some kind of kindling, and a lighter.

"I don't think it's that easy to set fire to a place," I say.

"So how in God's name are we going to get them out?"

"I don't know."

A long pause.

"I'm cold."

"So am I."

———

So how do I go into Martin's memories? That's what I want to know. The console's still there, and I recognize the "button" for Quit. I switch off the console, just by thinking it closed. Now I'm just sitting there in Martin's presence, haunting him without him knowing anything about it. I can't let him know I'm here. But I want his memories. I want to know what he knows. Mr. Y did it in the book, so I should be able to do it, too, now that fiction has become truth and my world is so closely connected to the world of the book.

Childhood! I think, experimentally. I try to give it the kind of jaunty, authoritative exclamation mark I give when I think *Console!* Nothing happens. I try to merge a little more with Martin. I feel what he feels. I stop trying to be me at the same time as I am him. I focus on all the shit in my gut, and how I'm not even sure if I want the formula as much as I want to be in a clean, air-freshened bathroom, with my bare feet on a cream shag pile carpet, taking a dump, clearing all the waste from my system. I try it again. *Childhood!* And suddenly there it is: an image of a plastic toy; this thing that changes from a robot into a car and then back again. *Project Starlight!* I think . . .

Now I'm in a white room with electrodes on my head and chest. This is weird. This is different from the early parts of the study, where I had to hold pictures of triangles, circles, and squares and try to transmit them to Ed in another room. This feels more like the remote viewing experiment—not that I was any good at that. Other guys were travelling to Iraq in their minds and drawing out pictures of weapons dumps and biotech factories, deep underground. I couldn't find any of that shit when I went to Iraq in my mind. A couple of camels: They said I imagined them. But this is something completely different. They've given me some formula from a clear test tube, and now they've plugged me into this machine. I'm sitting on something that looks like an electric chair crossed with a dentist's chair. But . . . Then I'm in another world.

When I come out and finish filling in the questionnaire, they tell me I've been to a place called MindSpace. I'm like, *What the hell is MindSpace?* No one wants to tell me. But pretty soon I'm running errands for them; taking trips to Iraq but not looking for weapons this time. Not that there are any to find—not according to Ash, the guy in charge of that part of the program. I remember he once said to me that the skill of remote viewing is twofold: 1) find what's there and 2) find whatever they tell you to find. So I don't look for weapons in Iraq. I read people's minds. No one lets me go close to Saddam, though. I'm not good enough for that. Plus, my security clearance is a little uncertain. After all, Ed and I were recommended for this after things got out of hand in New Orleans and we shot right to the top of the transfer list. And a transfer into a wacky paranormal project? There's no better way to relieve yourself of a couple of crooked agents. Anyway, once the project was in full swing, my missions involved people much farther down the pack of cards than Saddam. Two of Diamonds; Three of Spades. I'd go out there, come back, and then some guy would come in from the military to question me. That became my job. Ed and I joked that we should get new titles: Mind Agents—something like that.

The skill of operating in MindSpace is to be able to plan your journeys. That gave me pleasure; knowing that I could find the most efficient way of getting to Iraq and then back home, without having to navigate the whole of goddamn MindSpace to do it. Of course, this was a classified project, so no one told me anything about what I was doing, or how it worked. But it's a real thrill, surfing on minds: riding memories out to oblivion and then coming back. I wish I could have told my friends—but once you're on one of these projects you can forget about even talking to your mother anymore. Ed's more into the philosophical side than me; I think that's fair to say. And I guess I had my own questions about reality, dreams, the past, the future. But mostly we didn't dwell on that. We talked about pussy, mainly. Yeah— like the time I was in some lady's head, on a plane to Baghdad (it's kind of weird that you're given this power to travel around the whole world in people's minds and you still find that the most efficient way to go is on an airplane) and she suddenly went off to the lavatory and pleasured herself. At first I always chose to be women whenever I could, although after a time it stopped being so appealing. One time I had breast cancer, and I knew I was going to die. *That* was a headfuck.

Another time I was in this reporter's head supposedly getting information on the gang who'd kidnapped her. I ended up getting raped by three of the men. Most times I'd come out of the trance and tell Ed about my latest tits-and-ass escapade. But it started getting old and in the end I just used men to surf through, and I just pretended to Ed that I'd stroked my own pussy, or done myself with a dildo or whatever. Maybe he was doing the same thing by then. Who knows?

I think the project was actually working when they brought in the KIDS. It would have carried on and who knows where we could have ended up. Although, to be honest, I'm sure it's still running somewhere, in someone's mind. Enough people must have known the formula when they told us we'd been decommissioned. But the KIDS were a bad idea (the acronym stands for Karmic Interface Delineation System but it's generally regarded as a load of crap and just an excuse for a neat acronym that spells "kids"). It all started when the head of the study put his semi-autistic kid into MindSpace. This kid was seven years old and he got in there way faster than most of us. Then they found out that this kid could stop a chimp eating an ice cream just by willing it. Then they did more studies on more autistic kids. They borrowed a few of them from the NSA—took them off the prime numbers study. It turns out that these kids can influence people's thoughts. They can actually change things. So then they got in a whole bunch of these kids and hooked us all up: one adult operative and one of the KIDS working together. The way it worked was pretty simple. First the kid got into your mind. Then you went into MindSpace. Wherever you went, the kid went, too. But the kid could actually manipulate reality or, at least, he could change people's minds. If no minds needed changing, the kid could do other things as well, such as retrieve your lost memories. All you had to do was look at a document once and it was recorded in your mind. OK—so not many people can retrieve documents from their minds like that, even after they've read them two or three times. But these kids could read them to you as if your mind was just an autocue.

We took our KIDS when we left. No one knew they'd stayed with us. They're dead, of course. All the KIDS are dead. That's why the project was decommissioned. Any project that kills a hundred children can't go on, either with government funding or without it. The KIDS simply stayed in MindSpace too long. No one thought it could kill you if you got lost in it. No one knew how to wake the poor little bastards up.

And now we have only one bottle of formula left from the twenty we took from the storeroom when we went. And what can I say? Surfing in MindSpace is something you just can't stop doing. So we need the recipe and the recipe's in the book. Of course, we don't just want it for ourselves. Can you imagine how much money there is in this? If we had the recipe we could sell it for thousands of times the amount they're planning on charging businessmen to fly to the moon. This is the only time I've ever been close to anything of any value. I have to get the book. I have to get the book. . . .

I . . . Actually, I have to take a dump. The urgency is like a voice in my head.

"Ed?"

"Yeah."

"I have to take a dump, man."

"For Christ's sake. Can't you hold on?"

"I've been holding on for a couple of hours and I really think I'm going to shit my pants. And how long are we planning to stay here, anyway? It's almost three A.M."

"Jesus Christ." Ed's hands are on the steering wheel even though we haven't been driving for hours. Now he moves it back and forth as if something is happening; as if we aren't just sitting here. The steering locks and he curses. "Fuck. *Jesus*."

"Sorry, but you know . . . We could wait here forever and she might never come out."

Ed hunches his shoulders forward. "If she's in there."

"Yeah. If she's in there. I still think maybe Leeds."

"We can't lose the book."

"I know. I want it as much as you do."

Ed rubs his face. "OK. New plan."

My breath's coming out all ragged, like a shredded ghost. "Go on."

"How about we leave here now? Go get some sleep. But we'll give it to the KIDS as a mission. We'll send them to trail her."

I almost ask him how exactly he sees that working but I need him to agree to give this up now, so I just say, "OK." I think of the pale shag carpet in my imagination and the real chipped linoleum at the motel. Either way we have to go. I have to go. Something sure is insisting that I leave here now.

Part Three

In its factical Being, any Dasein is as it already was, and it is "what" it already was. It *is* its past, whether explicitly or not. And this is so not only in that its past is, as it were, pushing itself along "behind" it, and that Dasein possesses what is past as a property which is still present-at-hand and which sometimes has after-effects upon it: Dasein "is" its past in the way of its own Being, which, to put it roughly, "historizes" out of its future on each occasion.

Heidegger, *Being and Time*

A *whole* is that which has a beginning, a middle and an end. A *beginning* is that which itself does not follow necessarily from anything else, but some second thing naturally exists or occurs after it. Conversely, an *end* is that which does itself naturally follow from something else, either necessarily or in general, but there is nothing else after it. A *middle* is that which itself comes after something else, and some other thing comes after it.

Aristotle, *Poetics*

Chapter **Nineteen**

So how long have I got? Not long enough. I get dressed and fold up the priory nightdress and leave it on the bed. Oh well, I knew I wouldn't be able to stay in that costume for long. Of course, I don't want to go anywhere. I want to stay here in my brown dressing gown and eat hot food cooked by religious people. I want to see Adam again. But they know I'm here. They'll send those KIDS here first of all. Can they go into religious places? I don't know. But if those guys got desperate enough . . . I just don't understand the system well enough to know what they would or would not do. I just have to go somewhere they wouldn't think of looking for me. I have to go where Burlem is. Wherever it is, he's been hiding out there for over a year now.

Unless he's dead, like those poor kids. But I'll have to take the chance that he's not. And there's a problem. I don't know what to do with the book. Once I am ready to leave, I take it out of my bag and touch it, perhaps for the last time. I can't take it with me: There's too good a chance that they'll catch up with me. No. This place; *this* is where they can't go. So I'll leave it here, and maybe one day I'll come back for it.

Can I actually do this?

I run my pale hand over the cream cloth cover. I can't take it with me.

But what if someone finds it?

I look again at the small bookcase. There's even dust on the silver key. No one reads these books. They are there for show. I remember some English lit. joke someone told me once about why it's so easy to be a theology student specializing in any Old- or New-Testament faith. I don't remember the whole joke, but I remember the punch line: *Because they have to read only one book.* I'm not sure it's true, but it got a laugh from us all in the bar. So, do I take my chances and leave *The End of Mr. Y* here with the pope's poetry? I don't see what else I can do. I don't even know if I'm still going to be alive tomorrow. With my heart hammering like a heavy piece of machinery, I unlock the case and put the book inside. You really wouldn't notice it in there. I shut the glass front. Then I lock it. Shall I take the key with me? No, they'll find it when they strip me down, after I am dead. I'll leave the key here. But where? There's nowhere else in this room to hide anything. Knowing I have to go, I just slip it under the bookcase in the end. It's not ideal, but it'll do for now.

When I get outside, the black car has gone. The freezing air scrapes my face like a thousand knives. It's almost dawn and I want to be in bed, in the warm. What the hell am I going to do now? I'm going to drive far away before those fuckers realize I've gone. I'm going to go and find Burlem and work out how I can stop these KIDS from messing with my brain. And . . . Am I now so lost in a fantasy that I don't understand what's going on anymore, or is it possible that I made the blond men leave? That's what I was trying to do. I just focused on Martin, and his horrible, clenched feeling, and I told him he had to leave and find a toilet. Is it that simple? So why can't they do that? Is it just the KIDS who are supposed to be able to do that? So why can I do it, too?

Apollo Smintheus. Why did you desert me?

There's a part of the A2, just around Medway, where it looks as if you're driving into the sky. Most roads in Britain seem to be designed on the principle that they should be enclosed by something: hedges; fields; houses. But this road sweeps through the landscape like the broad stroke of an eraser tool on a computer, as if the pixel size has been set too high and too much has been rubbed out. It's pale gray and four lanes wide. The sky is still black and everything that isn't road or sky is covered with snow that glows in all the artificial white lights. For the second time this week I feel as though I'm living in a black-and-white photocopy. It's six A.M., and, apart from two gritter trucks, I'm on my own out here, driving towards Burlem's daughter's school, not knowing what I'm going to do when I get there. I need to try to find Apollo Smintheus as well. I have so many questions.

The car heater is on full and I have finally started to warm up. But it's freezing outside and I don't know where I am going to sleep tonight. I don't even know how or even if what I've got planned is possible. How am I going to get into the Troposphere now? I don't have a sofa, or a bed. What am I going to do? I can't exactly pull over into a lay-by and hope for the best. I'd probably freeze to death before I starved. Or I'd wake up in prison—or an asylum. At least I now know that the blond guys are fakes. They can't do anything official. But I'm not sure if that makes me feel better or worse. I'm pretty sure they won't burn down the priory at least. When I was in Martin's mind I saw just how impossible it would be. But they've got a motel room and two KIDS to help them. And I know that they're willing to hurt me: that they want to hurt me. All I've got is my car and £9.50 in the whole world. I can't go back to the university. I can't go back to my flat.

It's when I think that: that I can't ever go back—that's when it actually feels real, and a liquid sort of fear starts to pump around my body along with (or instead of?) my blood. I feel cold again, despite the car heater. And then I seem to black out, just for a second—or maybe a bit more than a second. When I come back to myself I can see a sign that wasn't there before. *I hate it when this happens on the motorway*, I think, quite deliberately, as if what I'm feeling is normal.

The sign is telling me that if I keep going I'll end up in London. That's what I want. There's another sign pointing to the various exits you could take if you wanted to go to any one of the various Medway towns. I haven't lived around here long enough for any of the names to mean anything to me. Except . . . One of them does mean something to me. It's the town where Patrick lives. Would he lend me some more money? Would he even be up at this time of day? My brain does some kind of quantum computation that's too fast for my conscious mind to keep up with. And then, right at the last second, I'm indicating and pulling off.

Five minutes later I'm parked outside a Little Chef off a run-down roundabout. There are half-dead trees everywhere, and bushes full of lager cans and old take-away cartons. This place has the feel of something that's been mis-designed on one of those city-sim computer games: a corner you'd forgotten to delete, or even arranged to have cleaned. It's half past six. Does Patrick get up this early? I can't piss him off, or alert his wife, so I send a text message: *Will do anything for cash*. I add the name of the town and three coquettish ellipses. This has to seem fun or he won't buy it.

The cold air stings my eyes as I get out of the car and walk over to the door to the Little Chef. It doesn't open until seven. I get back in the car and put the heater on full. Can you kill yourself sitting in a car with the heater on? Or do you actually have to turn on the engine and run a pipe into the window from the exhaust? Now I can't seem to warm up, even with the heater on. I close my eyes. *Apollo Smintheus* . . . I think. And then I wonder how you pray to an entity you've actually met. Is that possible? *Apollo Smintheus. Please be OK. Please help me, if you can. I'm doing something bad now, something I'll never tell anyone about. But I need to get back into the Troposphere and see you and for that I need a warm room*. Is this even working? Is this how you should pray? I don't even know any classic prayers. I used to be able to meditate. Perhaps that's more appropriate. For the next ten minutes I sit there with the buzz of the heater in the background and my eyes shut repeating the words *Apollo Smintheus* . . . *Apollo Smintheus* . . . like a mantra. I don't know if it has worked, but when I open my eyes the snow under the car park lights seems about a thousand shades lighter than it was before. Then the world goes dull again. The Little Chef is open. I need some coffee.

I'm about halfway through my second espresso when my phone buzzes.

It's Patrick. *U r an early bird*.

I start typing back: *I know.* Then I hesitate, trying to think of some joke about catching a worm that won't insult him somehow. Nothing comes. In the end I simply write *So . . . ?*

Where r u?

Little Chef. Off the A2.

OK. C u in 10.

Can I do this? I have to do this. There's no other way. I sip my coffee and wait.

When he walks in he's dressed for work in black jeans and a dark red shirt.

"Well," he says, sitting down. "This is unexpected."

"Do you want some coffee?" I say.

"I want something else," he says, raising an eyebrow.

"Oh, you'll get that."

"Where?"

"Ever done it in a seedy toilet?"

He smiles and shakes his head. "God, this is dirty."

I smile. "I know."

"I've never . . ."

"Never what?"

The waitress comes over. Patrick bites his lip. "Two more coffees," he says.

"Never what?" I say again as the waitress goes over to the counter, picks two white cups from a pile, and then places them, one after the other, under the spout of the coffee machine.

"Well . . ."

He doesn't have to say it. To him this is an affair with a downward spiral of logic—but it is logic. We start in hotels and end up in a service station café, drinking bad coffee and planning sex in the toilets. For him this is a story: Act 1—glamorous sex. Act 2—violent sex. Act 3—we're going to do it in a grubby toilet and he's going to pay me for it. I hope he realizes that this is it now. Act 3. Game over. There'll be climax and catharsis, sure. And then the story will end. Of course, in my world there is no such logic. For me this has been purely episodic and accidental, and this situation now means nothing at all. There is no game. I just need some money. But if something wants to be a story, it will be.

Ten minutes later we're in the disabled cubicle and it smells of pink dispenser soap and damp paper towels. Patrick's got hold of one of my nipples and he's pinching it through the material of my jumper. He's pressing me up against the wall.

"God," he says. "I can't believe I'm doing this. Take your top off."

"Wait," I say. "We have to do this properly."

"Properly?"

"Don't you want to know how much I charge?"

He nuzzles his head close to my face and bites my earlobe. "You dirty bitch. Go on then, how much?"

"A hundred."

"Your prices have gone up. What do I get for that?"

"You get to fuck me. As hard as you want."

"I got that for twenty quid last time."

"OK. So what's worth a hundred to you?"

"You know what I want."

Yeah. And he got it for free last time. "Money first," I say.

He takes out five twenties, cash-machine-clean, and gives them to me.

"Now take off your top and pull down your jeans," he says.

I do it.

"Now put your hands behind your back."

He takes something out of his pocket and ties my hands together. And I'm thinking that whatever he does next doesn't matter. It's only my body. I don't mind how fucked my body gets as long as my mind's OK. And my body is up for this, anyway. However scared I am; however much I want to be driving away from the blond men and the KIDS—my body recognizes this feeling and wants more of it. It wants the familiar pain that's coming.

"Bend over," says Patrick. He takes some of the pink soap from the dispenser and smears it on his cock.

It takes about a minute and a half for him to come.

———

I get to Hertfordshire at around eleven. I have a plan of sorts. I figure that the only possible chance I've got of getting to Burlem is through his daughter. He's her ancestor, after all, and Apollo Smintheus's instructions did say that you could reach people's ancestors via Pedesis. So I'm going to check in to a bed-and-breakfast near her school and then get into the Troposphere and see if I can find Apollo Smintheus and ask him exactly how I would go about this. If I'm near her school, then I'm near her. And if I'm near her, then it should be easy enough to find her in the Troposphere. That's my guess.

The school is in a tiny village a few miles outside Hitchin. I drive around for about five minutes after locating it. There don't seem to be any hotels or boardinghouses here. I drive around again. There's a large pub. I park outside it and go in. There's no one inside, just a thin, sleazy-looking guy drying glasses behind the bar.

"Hi," I say.

"Hello," he says back. "Not an escapee, are you?"

"What?"

"Not from the school?"

Surely I don't look that young? "No," I say. "Maybe about twenty years ago . . . Have you got rooms here?"

"Bed-and-breakfast?"

"Yeah."

"Hang on. I'll get the book."

I haven't seen another human being since I drove into the village. I can't believe that this place is going to be full up, but I wait while he flicks to the right page and then runs his fingernail down it.

"Yeah. We can do tonight," he says. "Just you, is it?"

"Yes."

"It'll be seventy-five pounds."

Jesus. For a room in a pub? "Have you got anything cheaper?"

"No, love. I've got one more apart from this one but that's eighty-five. It's up to you."

I sigh. "Is there anywhere else around here that might be cheaper?"

"You can go back into Hitchin," he says. "You might get something there."

Hitchin was about ten miles away. I have to be close to the school.

"Thanks. I'll take it," I say. "Oh—can I smoke in there?"

"Do what you want in there, love," he says. "Do you want to settle up now?"

He doesn't trust me.

"OK," I say. I give him the cash.

The room's better than I expected. The bed is soft and plump, with a red eiderdown. There are two bedside tables, each with an antique lamp. There's an en suite bathroom with soft but worn white towels. I need to have a bath, but I don't have much time. Can I get to the Troposphere from the bath? Would I drown? I need to make the best use of the time I've got here. What are my priorities? Food, then Troposphere. Maybe I'll ring down for something and have a bath while I'm waiting for it to arrive. A quick bath, just to warm up. Can I even order food here? Yes, there's a menu by the bed. Room service seems to consist mostly of dead stuff and chips. I need something substantial to eat. They do soup; I doubt it's homemade. I call down and find out that it's pea soup today and that it is homemade. I order a bowl of that and two portions of chips. Then I have a bath. After my bath I put on a clean pair of knickers, a clean pair of jeans, a thick black thermal top, and a jumper. It's warm in here, warmer than the priory. I dip chips in my soup and reread the document I wrote out last night. I still have so many questions for Apollo Smintheus.

I miss having the book. I miss *The End of Mr. Y.*

When I search my bag for the vial of fluid, it isn't there. Even when I dump the whole contents onto the bed: nothing. All I've got is the black dot on the piece of card. How am I going to go into the Troposphere? Shall I cry this time? Or maybe I'll just lie back on the bed and look at the dot and focus on the feeling of the jellyfish lights and the tunnel. Do I even need the fluid? Maybe there's some in my system already, because the tunnel is suddenly real, and . . .

The Troposphere looks roughly the same as the first time I entered it. I'm on another thin city street and it's still nighttime. Is there no sun here? I look around at the neon signs and the broken shop fronts. Is this what the inside of my mind looks like? Why would that be? I walk past a sex shop with big purple dildoes in the window. Another sex shop? Then I realize that this is how I see sleazy men. This place must represent the man downstairs, the one who gave me the room. So is it my mind that makes these images? It seems like it. Next door to the sex shop there's a pet beautician's with a blue door. Where's my mind got that from? Then there's a greengrocer's with plastic-looking fruit in baskets outside.

Console?

It appears. *You now have thirty choices*, it tells me.

OK. That's not big enough for a school population. I'm obviously not that close.

Can I play the Apollo Smintheus card?

The Apollo Smintheus card has expired.

Apollo Smintheus?

Nothing.

I keep going. Obviously I am going to have to do this on my own. So how would I best get to the school? In the physical world it's about a hundred yards down the road. But in this world-of-minds? I keep going. I wonder for a second how direction works here. Do I have to go the "same way" to find something here as I would in the physical world? It's very confusing. For a moment I think back to Lumas's story "The Blue Room." Would it be possible to go somewhere in my mind that doesn't work in four-dimensional space-time? Could I get trapped in here?

This road doesn't make any sense. The jumble of small shops has now turned into a boulevard of exclusive-looking department stores and jewellers. The window displays repulse me. In one fluorescently bright space, mannequins in glittery evening dresses stand around ignoring one another. In the next, a mannequin takes a metallic dog for a walk. Another window has two male mannequins fucking one thin, fragile-looking female mannequin. I prefer that: At least it was unexpected. I walk on, past a mirrored building on my right and an office block on my left. The road narrows again and now there are houses everywhere. But these aren't normal houses: They're life-sized doll's houses, all with the fronts taken off and placed to one side, each with a hinge dangling just below the roof. They are all painted in pastel colors: lilac, powder blue, lemon, rose. This represents the girls' school. It must do.

Console?

You now have four hundred and fifty-one choices.

OK. I'm not sure quite how this is going to work, but I approach one of the closest doll's houses and walk inside, straight from the street into the sitting room.

You now have one choice.

You . . . I'm fifteen and I've been smoking for two months and I think I'm addicted already. I'm addicted to Coke as well, and those rolls from the village shop. My biggest dream is to be so addicted to everything that people have to whisper about me. I want my stupid fringe to grow out and I want to sit on Hampstead Heath with Heather and Jo and the Highgate lot and talk about how out of control we all are but I'm not sure about this because they all smoke weed and I don't want to. I'm going to have sex at the next ball. I have to do it now or *all* my credibility is going to be, like, out of the window. I've lied about it so far, but now people want details. Jules asked me to draw a picture of a penis in maths the other day!

I take another drag off my cigarette.

"Do you feel addicted yet?" I ask Nikki.

"Yeah," she says. "Totally. And it's fucked my voice."

Nikki's in the choir. But really she wants to be a singer in an indie band. You need to fuck your voice to do that. It's why she started smoking up here with me and the others. Where are the others? Soph's doing drama, but what about Hannah and Jules? I haven't seen Jules since this morning when she gave me a dirty look over breakfast. I don't know what I've done. Oh, please, Jules, don't stop liking me.

Think about something else.

"Do you think Jim'll manage not to, like, tell everyone in the whole village that we used the fag machine?" I say.

"Soph's working on Jim. Don't stress, babes. She's got him *in hand*."

"She didn't, though . . . ? Like, not actually . . ."

"You'll have to ask her. But . . ." She giggles. "Oh God. I'm not supposed to say."

"Basically yes, though, right?"

"Yeah. *Totally.*"

"Oh, yuck."

Soph really is out of control.

The name Molly comes into my head from nowhere. Ugh. Why would I want to think about Molly Davies now? OK. *That* girl is way out of control. Soph might have messed around with Jim a little bit for cigarettes but Molly's reputation is, like, legendary. I can't go anywhere near her; she freaks me out. It's not just that she isn't a virgin. I mean, well, no one here is a virgin (well, apart from me—but we're keeping that one quiet) but Molly is about the least virginal person you could ever meet. Last year, when they had our common room and we had the lame one in the basement, she actually SUCKED OFF a VB on the sofa. VB = Village Boy. They're all chavs. The idea that there's chavvy spunk on the sofa . . . None of us can bear to think about it.

"Hey, you've gone quiet. You all right, babes?"

"Yeah. I was thinking about Molly and that lot."

"Don't get stressed thinking about the lower sixth. They're not worth it."

"Yeah, I guess."

"You got that deo?"

"Yeah."

We spray ourselves with deo and, eating sugar-free mints, walk back towards the school buildings. Soph won't have these; she says they give you cancer. One day Jules was like, "They give cancer to *rats*, idiot." Jules is hilarious, like *all* the time.

There's Helene, the slutty French girl, on her way up to their dorms. Don't look at her; don't look. Oh piss. Why am I looking . . . She'll think I'm a lesbian, which won't be good as everyone says she actually *is* a lesbian, when she's not being a slut.

A large doll's-house frontage flickers over Helene. But I don't try to jump. I remember what has happened before, when I've ended up right back in the Troposphere. I need to do this a different way.

Console!

The thing comes up. The screen swims with images. I can't make them all out. I can see a little image of a desk; another of what appears to be a gym. I can see a white cracked ceiling in another. . . . But there are about ten altogether and I can't pick one out. The French girl has gone. I continue down the corridor with Tabitha Young, aka Tabs, the girl who wants to be addicted to everything. As she walks along next to Nikki, her brain doesn't stop chattering about people walking past, her socks (which are too short), her skirt (which is too long), her breath (which may or may not smell of fags), and a constant undercurrent of fear of saying or doing the wrong thing. At the same time as this she's able to say "Mmm," and "I so agree" every time Nikki says anything to her.

I leave the console on. I wonder if these images relate to what Tabs's ancestors are seeing. Again I notice that there's not much actual ancestry here. There's nothing showing on the screen that I don't recognize. No cavemen; no Roman graffiti. But I thought Mr. Y used Pedesis to travel through time. Or maybe I just misread that part of the book. I wish I understood this. I picked up some information just from being in Martin's mind, but it isn't enough.

Another girl walks past, and Tabs recognizes her as a lower-sixth girl called Maxine and tries to think of something cool and witty to say in case the girl says anything to her. This time, when the door opens over the image of the girl, a new display appears on the console screen as well. I recognize this by now: It's an image of me/Tabs and it means—or it must mean—that I can jump from here to there, just like I did with the mouse and the cat. OK. I'm going to try this. Cross my fingers: Go, go. Come on. And—yes—I'm blurring, but hopefully not back into the Troposphere. . . .

You now have one choice.

You . . . I smell. I smell so bad. Those year eleven girls must have smelled me as I walked past just now. I can feel the dampness under my arms and between my thighs—my large, oversized, supermassive, chunky thunder-thighs. Wearing tights means that my legs don't rub together so bad, and my skin doesn't go red, but they make me hot and when I'm hot I sweat like an animal. But at least animals are meant to smell. No one minds if animals smell. No one else will ever understand this. I don't know how I can go on through life with this problem. If I died, would anyone notice? No one is going to want to go to bed with me, ever. I even revolt myself when I get undressed, and I know that Claire, Molly, and Esther notice but don't say anything. Well, they don't say anything to me, but I think they talk about it when I'm not there. I so hope they're not planning one of those stupid "interventions." They did it last term with Nicky Martin. They all swooped on her just after she'd got into bed and told her that her breath stank. Obviously they were supernice about it. Everyone's supernice about everything here. "We just thought you'd want to know . . ." Smile, smile, privileged teeth. "We'd want you to tell us if, like, we had any problems." If they tried an intervention on me I'd kill myself. I don't know how yet. I don't like blood and I can't tie a noose. Oh damn. There's Esther. I have to go and change but I can't if Esther's on her way to the dorm. Great.

You now have one choice.

You . . . I'm so much thinner than Maxine now. That diet is fantastic.

"Hey, Maxine."

I like saying "Hey" rather than "Hi." It's kind of American.

"Oh, hi, Esther."

But she doesn't stop and talk; she practically runs in the other direction. What did I ever do to her? Stuck-up bitch. Anyway, so what am I going to do if Miss Goodbody ("Call me Isobel") does make a move on me? I've had this crush for so long that it never occurred to me that she might feel the same way about me. But she was the one who suggested extra drama lessons, and she was the one who walked in while I was getting changed for the dress rehearsal the other day, and she was the one who commented on my tits. Seriously. I am certain I didn't imagine it. There was the "Whoops" after she pulled back the wrong curtain. Then the too-long pause. Then the little smile. Then—and I am ninety-nine percent sure this really happened—then she said, "Nice tits" before walking away. So that must mean something. She's not just trying to be cool and young, etc. She must be trying to tell me something. But it was so much under her breath that I can't be sure she said it at all.

Just because I want her, that doesn't make me a lesbian. Does it?

I am not a lesbian.

I am not a lesbian.

But I do want her to kiss me.

I turn a corner and start walking up the lower-sixth staircase. Usually I take these stairs two at a time, but my breathing feels tight today. What did I do with my inhaler? Shit. I think it's in my gym bag down in the changing rooms. I can't be bothered to go down there now. I'll be all right. I haven't had a real attack for over a year now. If only I knew what to do with this feeling I get when I think about Isobel Goodbody. It's as though . . . It's as though my stomach is a fish tank with thousands and thousands of fish in it, but the water's been drained out and now they're all flopping around like on that horrible documentary we watched in Biology. How do I switch this feeling off? I think kissing her might do it, but when am I going to get to do that? And is it worth getting expelled for? What if everyone finds out and thinks I'm a lesbian? I hope no one's in the dorm. Oh shit. Someone is in here. It's Molly, and she looks weird. What is going on with all that eyeliner? Has she even got a free period now? I thought she was supposed to be in philosophy.

The console stays the same as the frame of the doll's house hovers around Molly. Come on, come on. I'm potentially two steps away from Burlem now. Well, if this works I am. Why isn't this happening? Why am I not getting the image in the console that tells me I can switch over to Molly?

I think of Apollo Smintheus's document, the bit I didn't remember at first:

You can jump from person to person in the physical world (but only if the person is at that moment vulnerable to the world of all minds).

Vulnerable in what way? I don't understand. I stay with Esther, but with the console in my vision, too. If there's even a flicker I'm jumping over to Molly.

"Hey," I say to Molly.

"Hey," she says back.

"No philosophy?"

"Couldn't be bothered."

I go over to my bed and sit on it. So much for thinking about Isobel in privacy. Now I've got bloody Molly sitting here simmering. She's putting on makeup. I watch as she applies pink blusher and black mascara. Now she's back onto the eyeliner, smearing more of it on as though she's about to join a troupe of mime artists who worship the devil in their spare time.

"Are you going somewhere?" I ask her.

"Yeah."

"Where?"

"Out."

"Molly."

"What? It's Friday night and I'm not staying in this shit hole."

"But . . ."

"Just cover for me, Esther, yeah?"

"Yeah." I shrug. "Of course."

In fact, the sooner she goes, the sooner I'll be alone. Unless Maxine comes up as well. I don't know where she was going. She went off in the direction of the changing rooms—but she never does sport. I should have asked her to get my inhaler. I sigh. You can get a good education here but no bloody privacy. At least next year I'll have my own room. I was supposed to have my own room this year, or at least be sharing with only one other person. But there's a "space crisis" and mice in the old sixth-form wing. So here we are and it's like year eleven all over again.

"Hey, Moll?" I say to her now.

"Yeah?"

"Who are you going with?"

Maybe she's going out with Maxine. Although Maxine's being weird with everyone lately. But I can still hope that the whole dorm's going out without me tonight. Imagine being here on my own and having Miss Goodbody walk in and . . . I couldn't call her Miss Goodbody if I was about to kiss her. *Oh, Isobel* . . . That sounds downright stupid.

"No one. I'm gonna hook up with Hugh when I get into town."

And that's when it happens: the flicker in the console. I jump. I'm in. . . .

You now have one choice.

You . . . I ache for Hugh. Someone said he was the most dangerous guy in Hitchin the other day. Fine. Maybe I'm the most dangerous girl. He doesn't see that, of course. He sees, what? A private schoolgirl with all the privileges he never had? A teenager; just an immature kid? But he must see something in me, otherwise why did he spend the whole night with me last Saturday?

But he hasn't answered his phone since then. He hasn't texted me. So I'm faced with another night of wandering from pub to bar to club on my own, pretending to be doing something other than looking for him. But what? I look over at Esther. She's like a skeleton lately. That's one good reason not to ask her to come with me. Maybe she'd be more his type with her natural blond hair, and the way she's got those ginormous tits on that tiny body. Bitch. No, I won't take her. I just need to be with Hugh again. I don't care about his stupid housemates, or his mattress on the floor, or that he likes to drink vodka from the bottle while he's screwing me. I don't care that while I was whispering "Hugh, Hugh" in his ear he only grunted back some name that didn't sound like mine, and that when I said to him, "Fuck me hard" (like on that Internet porn story Claire printed out last term), he grinned and called me a little slut. I don't even want to change him. Maybe I just need to change me.

Or have I already changed too much? What's it called when butterflies come out of their cocoons? Whatever it is that's not what's happened to me. I'd be a horrible butterfly. Whatever I was before I've *hatched*, that's what it is: I've hatched into something else now. And it's not as though I'm a typical stuck-up rich girl, anyway. Everyone knows about the "blow job on the sofa" incident—even the teachers; not that they can prove anything. OK, so nothing happened really. I saw the guy's dick but I didn't suck it. I mean—*yuck!* But I like the reputation it's given me, even though most of the form still aren't speaking to me because of it. I could tell Hugh I'm going to be expelled because I have so much sex. That should impress him. After all, last time I saw him he did try to make out that we shouldn't see each other anymore because he's so much more experienced than me. "I've seen and done things that would really shock you, babe." That's what he said. So what, Hugh. I've had a lot of sex, too. We're both damaged. We're both sad, lonely people, which is why we should be together. Like in that Tom Waits song you played me.

Also, I know that he's had a tragic past and everything, but *so have I*. What about the fact that my dad died when I was nine, and then I found out that my real dad was someone else—some colleague of Mum's? Or does that sound hopelessly middle-class? It's not exactly a case for social services, is it? I haven't seen my dad—my "real" dad—for over a year now. No one's seen him for over a year. More eyeliner. But my school fees are still mysteriously being paid. So I can't even say he's dead. Maybe I will, though. I could say I've had two dads who have died, and that I think I must be cursed. It's still not as exciting as alcoholism or drug dealing. I could say my mother beats me up, but that would be a lie. She hit me only once, when I said I was glad Dad had died.

The console's been there all along and I've been watching the images float around. There are five, but I don't know which one I want. I keep looking at them while Molly keeps thinking about Hugh. This is probably the first time I've been in someone's mind and felt a connection greater than simply *I'm here and I understand you because of that*. I understand Molly on a much more fundamental level. But I can't stick with Molly; I have to work out where to jump next.

Here are my choices:

–A view of a desk in an office;
–A first-person view of driving a car along a narrow lane;
–A view of an old woman chewing something;
–An old man reading the paper;
–Another old woman, but this one has pink streaks in her hair.

I know that if I jump into one of these I could end up anywhere. I have to end up with Saul Burlem, because I just don't know how I'll get back to this point if I get lost first. I look through the images again. The desk has a fluffy toy on it. The hands on the steering wheel of the car are female, with fluorescent pink nail polish. These people aren't male. Now I'm left with three elderly people. Are these all the POVs of grandparents: images of other grandparents or grandparents' acquaintances? Where's Saul Burlem? Where's his POV? I glance over the images again. I can't choose. None of them seems right. Maybe he is dead. But my mind seems to want to rest on the woman with pink hair. In fact, I'm just looking at it and thinking that it's unusual when my mind, clearly translating this into "interesting," starts to jump me into this consciousness, anyway. Oh hell. I'm blurring. . . . I'm leaving Molly. Just as I go I try to leave a thought in her mind: *Forget Hugh. Forget him . . .*

Chapter Twenty

You now have one choice.

You . . . I'm coming down the hill in the dark, the lights from the town below sparkling like reflections on water. The dog, Planck, won't go any farther up: It's as if he senses a presence there that I'm not aware of. He doesn't seem to like this space for exactly the reason I do like it. He can't stand the . . . The what? The history? The ghosts? Nothing surprises me anymore. So we're walking down. Away from the old, shadowy gateposts; away from the crumbling gray stone wall. When I'm up here I imagine people walking or travelling on horseback in a time when there were no cars, and I sense that there wouldn't have been that buzz you get now: the buzz of electricity being generated and used, and car engines, and pop music. But I'll go where the dog wants to go; it's easier that way. And I'm pleased with myself, pleased that I can give up control like this. But being pleased with myself won't do. I should be nothing with myself. I want the void. Idiot: I can't *want* the void. I have to let it come to me. I have to let it slowly envelop me when I'm not thinking anything.

Now I know what thoughts look like, thinking is more difficult, anyway.

The dog really does want to get out of here. We're almost running now on the icy, hard mud. Frost. *No good for plants;* that's what my mother used to say. And Christmas is coming, of course. As we reach the bottom of the hill I see the lights in close-up: hundreds of white, tasteful stars hanging over the road, all within reach. The tree by the roundabout is strung with lights as well. What does Christmas mean now? Not really more or less than it did before. Lura's a vegetarian, but she will force us both to celebrate. She likes rituals. Our tree is up but we haven't decorated it yet. Lura doesn't want stars and tinsel: She wants to decorate the tree with black holes, wormholes, and quarks. She wants to drape it in the fabric of space-time. I laughed when she told me this. I said I'd see what I could find in the shops. At least I go to the shops now. I go to the shops and I walk the dog. And nothing awful has happened yet. It's better than being locked in the house all the time.

Console?

It comes up. There's only one milky image in the middle of the screen: a blurred view of lots of green leaves. I ask it to close the image down and it does.

Who am I?

I am Saul Burlem.

Thank God. Where am I?

Walking along Fore Street. I'm walking along Fore Street but Planck wants to turn left, past the cheese shop, and then right, towards home. He can't want to go home already. No, he doesn't. He trots right past our front door and onwards, his muzzle like an arrow pointing down towards the space where the walls meet the pavement. Ah, now here's my second-favorite place in town.

Where am I?

I'm standing here while the dog sniffs some weeds growing out of the pavement. Yes, here's the space I like. It really is a space, an absence, enclosed with four walls. Various signs have gone up lately explaining that this is a building site belonging to blah blah, and telling you the various bad things that will happen if you trespass in it. It spoils the effect somewhat. It was better before the signs went up. An empty space, enclosed by walls: a house with no rooms and no roof and a carpet of pinkish Devon earth. I like that. It reminds me of my favorite place in town: the castle. The castle is the same kind of thing—walls enclosing nothingness. I have a postcard of the castle above my desk. It's an aerial view, probably taken from one of the helicopters that are always throbbing in the air on clear days. You look down on it and it's like a gray stone ring left discarded on a hillside, ripped, perhaps, from a giant's finger. And you can go to visit it as well: You can pay money to go into a circle of empty space with some walls around it. I love it. You look at this empty space, fenced off, made special, and you think: *What am I supposed to be looking at here?* Are the walls there to keep the nothingness in, or the town out?

And now, bizarrely, I know exactly how stone is constructed. But I still don't know who made the spaces. Who invented absence? Who chooses to celebrate it here? Of course, people don't know they're celebrating absence (although they should; they really should). They think they're visiting something, something tangible—but it just isn't there anymore. They think that by visiting an empty space enclosed by walls they can travel through time. And I know about that, too.

Why won't Burlem think of the name of the town he's in?

Where am I?

Now I've crossed the road and I'm standing outside the church, the church we go to every evening, just in case. We don't pray, but what we do is perhaps a sort of prayer. We walk in and then out again, just in case. I've never known exactly what sort of church it is, even though I'm inside it every night. I assumed it must be C of E or Catholic, but it doesn't actually have a name: It's not Saint Anything's. But every Thursday evening happy people come here in homemade clothes and do something cheerful inside. Well, they always seem cheerful when they come out. I think they go door to door in the evenings they're not here, selling something invisible like hope or salvation. Lura obtained the keys and no one minds that we go in there every night. Do I believe in what they do in there? Yes. I have to, now. But I wonder if they'd still believe if they knew what I know.

Where do I live?

St. Augustine's Road.

But I know where that is: It's his boarded-up house. Why doesn't he think of his address here?

Where am I now?

Walking up the hill where the road sweeps around like a question mark and you can get run over if you're not careful. There's a sign at the top: *Torquay*, and an arrow pointing right.

So he's near Torquay; but I don't even know where that is. It's not enough.

What happened to make me leave my house?

Oh. Where to begin this story. Why am I thinking about this now? The dog snuffles onwards, up through the market square, but I'm not seeing that anymore. I'm seeing . . . What? How far back does my mind want to go? I see scenes on fast-forward: The first one is, predictably, that paper I gave in Greenwich on the curse of Mr. Y. Lura was there. The Project Starlight men were there, too. Of course I had no idea who any of them were then. The only truly innocent member of the audience was Ariel Manto, and she was the one I kept looking at: the girl with the tight gray jumper and the red hair. I remember Lura walking away afterwards, going back to join the Lahiri group without saying anything. Then I see myself drinking too much with Ariel, fantasizing about making love to her, and then—the horror, the horror—realizing she probably *would* go to bed with me. I left, of course, before I had the chance to actually go through with it.

Then a couple of weeks later, or maybe a bit more: an e-mail from Lura. She is/was a scientist. She was at the same university as Lahiri. But she'd seen the title of my paper and been intrigued. She enjoyed it. She wanted to meet me.

And I was thinking: *Two chances of sex in a month?*

And then realizing that as usual one of them is (potentially) a student and the other is too old.

Or: *I'm* too old. That's the main thing. And I know that they can't really want me; not now. Although Dani did. Bland Dani wanted me. That was the last time: me, shirtless, with my gray chest hair shining awkwardly under the fluorescent office lights, and Bland Dani, the weakest of all the MA students, saying, "I want to see you," with her dull eyes pointing at my trousers. Of course, when she said "you" she meant my cock. Why is it that women do that? *I want you inside me.*

No. You just want my cock, and you may as well ignore the large lump of flesh attached to it, the man who has a brain that will never be "inside you," and that you'll never understand. It was supposed to be a tutorial. I suggested blindfolding her, not because it turns me on but because I didn't want her to see me. It ended badly, of course. What's wrong with not seeing? Then it's all in the mind, and perhaps not even against the university regulations. But she threatened to report me anyway when I (literally) stopped seeing her. I didn't even desire her: She looked like a slab of melting butter.

I arranged to meet Lura at a café in a gallery in London. What she said almost floored me. She owned a copy of *The End of Mr. Y;* perhaps the only known copy: the one in Germany. That's actually why she'd come to hear my paper. The book had been her father's. He had been one of the first scientists involved in the theory of quantum mechanics, she explained. She clearly didn't want to talk about him very much, but she outlined the basics: that he had been a contemporary of Erwin Schrödinger and Nils Bohr, but had refused to follow many European Jewish physicists to America to work on the atom bomb and other, similarly diabolical projects. Instead he stayed in his university and continued constructing his earth-shattering theory— details of which are now lost. The week before he was sent to the concentration camp he had written a note in his diary about *The End of Mr. Y.* He was very excited to have ordered it from London and believed it to be one of very few remaining copies. One of his last diary entries talked about the possible "Curse of Mr. Y." Lura had been shocked, she said—but also intrigued—to see the title of my paper. She said she hadn't ever come across that phrase before except in her father's diary.

She explained all this to me without changing her facial expression once. But she kept running her hand through her hair, and pausing for a long time between parts of the story. Then, when our coffees arrived, she gave up on the hair and started on the handle of the cup, moving it back and forth and pushing her thin finger through the hole.

"So that's it," she said. "I thought you'd like to know some of the history of the book; or, at least, that particular copy."

"I'm very grateful," I said. "Thank you so much for taking the time to come and meet me."

Her eyes looked as though she was going to smile but she didn't.

"The book was important to my father," she said.

I didn't know what to say to that, so I simply asked, "Have you read it?"

"No." She shook her head. "But I know it's important—after all, people keep trying to buy it from me."

"But you won't sell?"

"No."

"Why not?"

She sighed. "Much as I hate that book, I can't sell it. I haven't sold any of my father's books. Plus I don't particularly like the people who are trying to buy it. They've become a little threatening lately. But they can't do anything about a book in a bank vault. Perhaps they're planning a heist?" Now she did smile. "Well, I shouldn't think they'll have much luck."

"Who are they?"

She shrugged, and sipped from her café crème. "Americans." There was a long pause. "Well," she said. "I expect you'd like to see it, wouldn't you?"

"Really?" I must have sounded like a little boy excited over someone else's collection of rare comics. But I couldn't stop myself. "I mean . . ."

"Of course. It will be of some intellectual value to you. I can see that. My father would have approved, and I think that's a good enough reason."

"Has anyone else seen it?"

"No. I've looked at it briefly, but I couldn't touch it . . ."

"Why not?"

She looked at the table. There was a minute speck of demerara sugar by her saucer and she squashed it with her finger. Then she looked up at me again and laughed weakly.

"Family superstition?" Her laugh shrank into a sigh. "I'm a scientist and of course I know that Hitler killed my father, not some cursed book. But even so . . . It was the day after he received it that they got him. The last thing he did as a free man was to put that book in a bank vault."

We talked a little more, and she explained that she was going out to Germany the following month and invited me for a long weekend. Of course I wanted to go: to see the book, to touch the book. But I made some polite objections—would she want all those memories brought up again? Would she want some stranger intruding on her family business, etc., etc.—and she politely rebuffed them all as I'd known she would. So I went. It was the first week of term and I welcomed getting away from all the admin and e-mails and meetings for a few days. I tend to work when I'm at home, and I am terrible at taking holidays. We spent the Thursday evening watching an absurd play, and then we went to the bank vault on the Friday. It was supposed to be summer, but the air was gray and damp, and everything around me seemed as though it was being slowly smothered by everything else. When I had the book in my hands she looked at the floor and almost immediately said, "I want you to take it. Take it away from here."

"You're selling it?" I said.

"No," she said. "Just take it away."

We had a sad kind of sex on the last night I spent with her. There was a mundane inevitability about it, like flu in winter. I didn't think I'd ever see her again. She hated the book and she'd given it to me. I wasn't even sure whether or not she wanted it back. I didn't really understand anything about what was happening, but I didn't question any of it. I needed that book: I wanted it more than I've ever wanted anything.

Then came the strange events that I wrote off at the time as a kind of self-undermining parapraxis. First I forgot to pack the book; then I forgot to collect my bag from the carousel in the airport. Somehow I did get home without misplacing it. That afternoon I had to attend a university event at the cathedral—but it passed in no time. I sat next to my research student, Ariel Manto, and I think I even managed to flirt with her a little (harmless, harmless). Then I made my excuses and rushed home. I sat there in my ancient conservatory, and, as the sun set and then rose again outside, I finished the book. Afterwards I couldn't sleep, so I drank a vintage bottle of wine and wept several times, just because of the utter beauty of the experience: of holding the book, of being able to read it at last. No one bothered me and all I could hear was birdsong.

And I immediately resolved to make up the mixture from the book and try going to the Troposphere myself. I did some fast, blurred research, and found out that I could buy some Carbo-Veg in the right potency from a shop in Brighton. I drove there and back that afternoon and, after taking some holy water from St. Thomas's, had my first experience in the Troposphere that night. Most of what I can remember of my first few experiences is a blur. I remember travelling through the tunnel, so familiar to me now, and arriving in what appeared to me to be a nostalgic-postcard version of nineteenth-century London, full of dark slums and fog and abandoned hansom cabs. And I explored, of course, and started understanding some of the rules of this place. I tried Pedesis on the milkman. I attempted—and failed—to enter the mind of the university's vice chancellor.

I got the first e-mail on the Saturday evening. It seemed to be from a university student at Yale, despite the Yahoo e-mail address, asking me if I would be willing to enter into e-mail correspondence about *The End of Mr. Y.* I politely declined. The e-mail was poorly written and my own students take up enough of my time. I thought it was a coincidence that this person had got in touch just as I had obtained the book, but at the time I thought it was genuine. The second e-mail came on the Sunday, at roughly the same time of day.

Please forgive this intrusion. I am the director of Project Starlight, a significant interdisciplinary study into the activities and potentials of the Human mind. We have been recently studying a method outline in the book *The End of Mr. Y.* Or, I should say my predecessor was doing this? Since I have taken over this study I am interested in pursuing this study but unfortunately all our systems have

gone down and I have lost everything.....including the in-structions for making the formula. This also explains why I am using a Hotmail account right now! Our systems will not be running again for another week but I do need that formula ASAP. Since you own a copy of the book I hope you will not mind sparing a few minutes to write it up for us.

I called Lura on Monday.

"Project Starlight?" she repeated, after I had explained.

"Yes."

"They're the people who offered to buy the book from me."

"Do you know anything about them?"

She paused. "Well, I did check them out."

"And?"

"Project Starlight closed almost a year ago. There is no Project Starlight anymore."

"What is—or was—it?"

Now she sighed. "It was a highly classified American project. I found out about it through a friend of a friend—a physicist at MIT. He had only heard rumors about the project—that it had started as a simple telepathy study and then mutated into something else. He mentioned a highly secretive desert facility, remote viewing, staring at goats, and the quest for the 'ultimate weapon.' He said he'd heard that something catastrophic had caused the study to close down, and warned me not to get involved in asking any questions about it. It certainly sounded sinister."

"So if the project is closed, why are people going around saying they're a part of it?"

"I don't know. I think I already said that they soon became threatening."

"And how do they know I have the book?" I didn't ask if she'd told them.

"I don't know," she said.

I paused. "Do you think they are actually dangerous?"

"I really have no idea. Do you know why they want the book? I assume you've read it by now?"

"Yes. I've read it."

"And . . . ?"

"I have no idea why they'd want it."

Why was I lying? Of course I knew they wanted the formula, and I also knew why: because it worked. All I could conjecture was that these people were some kind of breakaway group who had been given the formula but never knew what it contained. And I was already familiar with the sensation of needing to go back into the Troposphere. Imagine needing it and not being able to go there? I imagined something of what a drug addict might feel.

"Well," she said.

"Lura, I really think . . ."

"What?"

"I think I should return the book to you now. I think it should go back in the bank vault where they can't get it."

"But if there's nothing in it that they'd find useful . . . ?"

"I think it should go back," I said.

After our conversation finished, I walked into the conservatory and looked at my own reflection in the glass. It was dark outside and I could only see a couple of stars, hanging in the sky like a halfhearted attempt at decoration. An American classified study. Goat staring. The ultimate weapon. That sounded military to me. I walked back into the house and picked up the book. Of course I would send it back to Lura; I'd do it tomorrow. But I also knew that the men from Project Starlight—or people like them—would get it in the end. And then what would happen? My mind filled with unpleasant thoughts of world domination and thought-control. If a repressive regime—or any regime—got hold of this mixture then . . . What? I found I could imagine exactly what such an "ultimate weapon" would look like. I sent back an e-mail to the Hotmail address given my the last correspondent saying that although I had seen the book, it was already on its way back to its owner in Germany. I apologized and assured him that he must be mistaken: There was no recipe in the book. And I put it on the table, ready to go.

But I didn't really want to post it. What if it got lost? Damaged? On the other hand, I had no time to go to London to meet Lura to hand it over in person until the weekend. And would she even want to see it? Perhaps she'd suggest sending it straight to the bank and asking them to put it in the vault. There were too many possibilities and I'd had no more e-mails. I did nothing. I spent the Tuesday and Wednesday in meetings, including Max Truman's annual Health and Safety presentation—compulsory; although Ariel Manto simply didn't go. I've always quite enjoyed Max's eccentric annual presentations. This one was entitled "When Things Go Wrong." It was a tongue-in-cheek history of the old railway tunnel under campus, ending with a dramatic account of its collapse in 1974. Max had obtained lots of PowerPoint slides of gruesome images of the Newton Building crumbling and people running around looking confused. He made various connections between the collapse of the university and the collapse of student-staff relations in the mid-'70s. While the tunnel was collapsing, he said, some demonstrating students had stormed the Registry and were busy drinking the vice chancellor's port. We learned that our own building had been constructed in 1975—right over the newly reinforced tunnel. Max told us that there was still a maintenance route into the tunnel from our building. We needed to know this, he said, so we could take the necessary precautions. At this point Mary asked what the necessary precautions would be.

"Just don't fall into it," said Max.

"How would we fall into it?" she said.

"Well, you can't," he said. "But new Health and Safety advice says I have to warn you about it, anyway."

"But it's been there for almost thirty years," said someone else. "And no one's fallen into it yet . . ."

"Where is it?" asked Mary.

"Photocopying room," said Max. "Next to the machine."

"You mean that sort of hatch thing that we all stand on every time we do any photocopying?" said Lisa Hobbes.

"Yep."

"So we could actually fall into it?"

"No, don't be daft. This isn't Alice in bloody Wonderland. It's well secured."

"What's it like in the tunnel?" asked Laura, the creative writing tutor.

"Don't even think about it, Laura," said Mary.

"What?" she said. "I think we should go down there and investigate."

Everyone groaned.

"OK, OK. I'm only joking."

Laura had been in trouble the previous year for sending all her students on some kind of psychogeographical project in which they'd had to use maps of Berlin in order to walk around the city center. Three of them had ended up walking along the motorway and were arrested.

While the questions and answers continued, I simply sat there thinking about the Troposphere. I thought I already had a fairly good idea of how it worked. In fact, I hadn't got too much sleep in the preceding few days because of it, and while the others kept on talking about the railway tunnel and whether or not Laura was going to lead a search party down the hatch, my eyes started to close. I dreamed of a world in which everyone had access to everyone else's minds, until some government recruited men in deep blue uniforms to go around and brainwash everyone so they didn't know how to do it anymore. When I woke up, everyone had gone. It was a good thing: I'd been sweating in my sleep and my shirt was almost wet through. Even though I was on my own, I had a profound sense of being watched. I knew I had to give the book back to Lura, so I went straight home to ring her to arrange it for the weekend. As I drove through the heavy rush-hour traffic I wondered if it might be better to burn the book altogether, or at least destroy the page with the recipe on it.

But I am a professor of English literature. I couldn't destroy a book if my life depended on it. At least, that's what I thought then.

I got the last parking space on my street and walked the last twenty yards to my house. Then I went inside and considered what I had to do. I had it all planned out by then. My idea was that I'd re-move the page with the instructions on it—but I certainly wasn't going to destroy it. I planned to keep it or hide it. . . . I wasn't sure quite what I was going to do with it. Perhaps it was clear to me that I would have to destroy it at some point, but for then I thought remov-ing it would be enough. I'd remove the page, give the book back to Lura, and then feign ignorance if she ever asked me about it.

It was at exactly the moment that I had opened the book to the correct page that I saw the car headlights sweep up outside. Then I heard the steady throb of a diesel engine, and I simply assumed some-one had called a taxi. But I was jumpy and noticing everything, so I went to the window to look, still holding the book in my hands. And then I saw them: the two blond men I'd last seen when I gave my paper in Greenwich. They were trying to find somewhere to park in my street.

They wanted the book. It was them.

And worse: One of them was driving—looking for somewhere to park—but the other one? Well, he seemed to be asleep.

I couldn't think quickly enough. If one of them was in the Tropo-sphere, then he was one or two jumps away from my mind and every-thing I knew about *The End of Mr. Y.* I looked at the book and quickly ripped the page from it. My thoughts almost collapsed then, but what I did next took on the clarity and focus of a bullet-point list. I had to leave the book behind but I'd take the page with me. By the time I'd decided that, I'd already folded up the page and put it in my shoe. By the time I'd done that I realized I had to get away before the men ei-ther came in here and beat me up or—worse—jumped into my mind and took my knowledge, anyway. They were still trying to park. I hid the book behind the piano; then I grabbed my coat, wallet, and keys and left via the back door. Over the neighbors' fence, through their garden, down their driveway, and into my car. I thought I was going to have a heart attack. The conscious man didn't even look over when the car door slammed. I imagined a car chase, but no one looked at me as I drove past. And I drove—faster than I've ever driven—to the uni-versity. My thoughts were racing ahead of me at a speed I've never experienced before. And in the jumble of strategy, fear, and conjecture, one thought stood out. I realized that I would be the target of those men for as long as I had my memories. It wouldn't matter if I destroyed *The End of Mr. Y*. It wouldn't matter if I shredded the page concealed in my shoe. If they could get into my mind, they could get the instructions for making the mixture, just as Mr. Y had learnt the secrets of Will Hardy's Ghost Show. It would be as simple as that. They couldn't get it from Lura, who hadn't read the book. But as long as I remained alive and sane, they could get it from me.

As I parked in the Russell car park I felt much as though I had just been given a life sentence. When I'd been a teenager I'd fantasized about the life of a tragic hero. I'd thought there would be some sort of glamour in being Hamlet, or Lear. But now I could see death at the end; I could see it with more certainty than I could see tomorrow. I remembered a dissertation that I'd marked a couple of years before. In it, the student argued that American eighties and nineties gangster films are postmodern tragedies. He spent a lot of time on one detail: that no one in these gangster films ever escapes. In our society—connected up with bits and bytes—you can never become entirely anonymous. At that moment I realized that the Project Starlight men would track me down, wherever I went, and take what I knew. They were going to rape my mind, and there was nothing I could do about it. I also realized that I had one slim chance of preventing this. I could disappear now. But I didn't have much time. They'd come here next: I knew that.

It was too dangerous to wait for empirical evidence of what they were going to do. I had to work from a priori assumptions, namely:

–The men wanted my knowledge of the ingredients for the mixture.
–The men could get my knowledge in three different ways:
   –Torture
   –Pedesis
   –Taking the sheet of paper from me by force

I reasoned that I could eat the paper, or not give in to torture, but I could do nothing about Pedesis. What I knew of the logic of the Troposphere suggested that in order to get into my mind the man in the Troposphere would only have to jump into the mind of someone near me, or likely to see me, and then, at the moment this other person saw me, make the final jump into my mind and all my knowledge and memories. In theory, the sleeping man could simply get into the mind of his colleague and send him to see me.

So I couldn't let anyone see me. Once in my office I closed the blinds and the curtains and locked the door. I hadn't smoked for twenty years, but when I saw that Ariel had left a box of cigarettes on her desk I took one out and lit it. I pleaded with myself to find some way out of this situation. Where could I go where no one would see me? My mind filled with images of roads and shopping centers and supermarkets. On a usual day, how many people would see me? Hundreds? Thousands? Everywhere I cast my mind I saw these blobs of flesh-and-consciousness; the detail that is always left off any map. Even if I got back in my car and drove, I would travel past people. I wondered why I had even come to the university; why I had chosen as my hiding place a room with my name on the door, a room whose details can be found on the university Web site, which also contains handy maps: how to get to the English and American Studies Building from anywhere on campus; how to get to the campus by road, rail, air, Eurostar, and ferry. I smoked and paced. I felt safe at the university. That was it: that was why I had gone there. But only because there are always so many people there. You never feel alone at the university, and, usually, in dangerous situations you want to be around people. Not this time.

Three or four minutes passed. I heard laughter moving down the corridor: Max and the others, no doubt, coming back from the bar. It didn't matter that I'd locked the external doors; now they were bound to be unlocked. I looked at the heavy paperweight on my desk. Perhaps I could stop them with force? No. You can't use force against remote telepathy. I urged myself to think faster. Should I destroy the page from my shoe? I couldn't. I couldn't do it. Why had I not driven away to somewhere random when I had the chance? My thoughts pushed and shoved each other like desperate Christmas shoppers, and I reminded myself that I had only two decisions to make: what I should do with the page; and where to go next. Before I knew what I was doing I had reached up to the very top shelf for the fourth volume of *Zoonomia*. I used to hide money in books a long time ago when I was a research student and my front door was almost as flimsy as a curtain and anyone could open it with a credit card. I reasoned that thieves aren't interested in books, and anyway, books are bulky. If you were a petty thief you wouldn't be able to transport a thousand or so books. So you'd ignore them. You wouldn't select, say, ten to steal. You'd ignore them all and focus on the VCR and the microwave. For that reason I've always hidden things in random books. I've hidden love letters, pornography, credit cards. . . . Would this work now? These Project Starlight men did clearly know the value of books. Ah, I thought, but this is where the university will help me. I can hide the page and lock the door and no stranger is going to be able to come and look through my things. And even if someone did manage to do that, the book they want wouldn't seem to be here.

And then I thought, *How long am I going to be away?*

I had no idea.

But at least I would be carrying only one copy of the information I had: the copy in my mind. And, although I knew I'd be too much of a coward, I could always kill myself if the men got too close. That was my theoretical last resort. I got a chair to stand on to relieve myself of the second copy of the information I held: the page in my shoe.

Perhaps it was stupid of me; perhaps I hadn't thought it through—but I could not imagine anyone going through all the books on my shelf and shaking them until a mysterious page fell out. I thought that by doing this I was preserving an important page of an important book. Why *Zoonomia*? I wasn't sure exactly, but something in my mind told me this was the right book. Ariel Manto wouldn't be using it: I'd told her not to. And who else would be interested in *Zoonomia*? I inserted the page somewhere in the middle of Volume IV and replaced it on the shelf.

I knew I shouldn't have done it, but I did it anyway rather than destroy the page. Was this my fatal flaw? And perhaps I thought that anyone who knew *Zoonomia*—an academic, definitely—and who also had the wherewithal to make the connection between the page and the book . . . Well, good luck to them. Perhaps that's how I justified it to myself. Knowing what I know now, I would never have left the page behind. But I can't get it now. All I can hope is that it's been destroyed.

So the next thing I had to do was disappear. But how to disappear in a building full of people in a university campus full of people in a world full of people? Where could I go? Where could I go that no one else would go? Where could I be unseen?

The railway tunnel.

In two minutes I was out of my office and in the photocopying room, with the door locked behind me. It was surprisingly easy to lift the hatch, now I knew it was there. I had no torch; just a small key ring light. But it was enough for me to see a thin metallic ladder. Had I lost my mind? I wasn't at all sure. But, as I lowered myself into the gloom below, and carefully replaced the hatch above my head, I heard the sound of furious banging, and a male, American voice shouting, "Professor Burlem!" They were at my office door across the corridor. But I was gone. No one had seen me go into the photocopying room. I felt as though I'd broken some loop; some chain of seeing and cause and effect. If I didn't emerge, no one would ever know where I was. If no one could see me, did I even exist?

The tunnel was dark and cold, with a persistent drip, drip, drip noise. It was much bigger than I had imagined—but then, of course, a railway tunnel is big: big enough for two trains to go through. It was too dark to see any detail, but I got the impression of size from the way sound travelled through the space. I walked in a direction I believed to be south, towards the underneath of the Newton Building. My feet crunched on something that felt like gravel, but I couldn't see beneath my feet. I used the wall to guide myself, and hoped that I was moving far enough away from the Project Starlight men that the sleeping one wouldn't simply chance on me in the Troposphere. I imagined something like a dawn raid: If the men knew I was at the university, could the sleeping one just burst into all the dwellings in the Troposphere until he found mine? This was the thought that bothered me as I walked farther into the tunnel. I already knew that so much about tele-mancy and Pedesis had to do with proximity. But then again, there'd be so many consciousnesses here on campus, and the men couldn't even be sure I was anywhere near here. I didn't know what to do next. As if some vengeful god had decided to play a trick on me, the next thing that happened was that I came to a halt before what felt like a pile of bricks and rubble. I knew I would have to clear a path to get through to the exit. Did I want to get to the exit? I sank to the floor and began to think about what I would do next.

Ah. Enough reminiscing. There's the church. I'll tie Planck up out-side.

I'm . . .

Oh fuck. That's it. I'm out in the Troposphere: bounced out by Burlem going into the church. So Adam was right about that, then.

Chapter Twenty-one

I'm standing on a long, metal bridge over a vast river that rushes below me. It's still nighttime here, but everything is death-kissed with a silvery glow that seems like moonlight (although I can see no moon), and every structure, including this bridge, seems to be strung with lights that are reflected in, and then slashed up by, the violent black water below. In the real world I'd feel vertigo immediately, but here in the Troposphere it's just that syrupy nothingness. You have to get a lot more emotional than this for anything to register in the Troposphere (or, as it seems to have been termed in Project Starlight—MindSpace). Yet I can feel some things. I'm disappointed about being bounced out here when I was surely about to discover exactly where Burlem went after he emerged from the tunnel. But that's it: mild disappointment. Outside I'd feel a lot more.

Outside. How do I get out, exactly? Presumably I have to find my way back to the place I started: the end of the street with the doll's houses and the crazy mannequins: the Tropospherical (is that a word? It is now.) representation of the Hertfordshire village where my physical body is now still lying, crashed out in the pub.

How long have I been in here?

Console?

It appears. Where am I?

Your major coordinates are 14, 12, 5, −2, 9 and 400,340.

For fuck's sake. What does that mean? What's a major coordinate?

Coordinates tell you where you are in the Troposphere.

Yes, but . . . What do they relate to?

All points in the Troposphere are calculated relative to the position of your living consciousness in the physical world. I can provide the coordinates in binary notation instead if you require.

No thanks. OK. So I'm not far from where I should be? Or am I?

Distance is time, as you know.

I have a feeling this thing only tells me what I already know. Go on, I tell it, anyway.

You have travelled a great distance, relative to your previous journeys.

So how do I get back?

You return to coordinates 0, 0, 0, 0, 0, and 1.

How do I do that?

You travel across the Troposphere.

Is there any other information you can give me?

You now have three hundred choices.

Great. Can you give me any actual directions?

The screen flickers. I see something that looks like a ring doughnut made into a giant spiral, with lines and cubes hanging off it. But in less than a second this has gone and I am instead presented with something like an ordnance survey map with a blue dot and the legend *You Are Here*. I ask the console to show me where my target location is and a red dot appears, miles and miles away.

But I'm not even sure you measure distance in miles here.

And another thing. When I left Hertfordshire it was January. But in Burlem's mind it wasn't even Christmas yet. Did I actually travel back in time to get to Burlem? But why? How on earth would that work? I start walking across the bridge, a humid, gray wind blowing my hair around my face. Oh, no; not more weather. I can do without weather. I think it's a bad sign in here.

Apollo Smintheus?

Nothing.

It takes me about ten minutes (or whatever the equivalent is in here) to get to the end of the bridge. I look behind me and see something like a fan of bridges behind me, gleaming in the silver light. When I look, it quickly collapses back into one bridge. Ten minutes, I think. Ten minutes multiplied by 1.6 is sixteen minutes. Is that right? So in crossing that bridge I've just spent another sixteen minutes in the Troposphere? I have to get out of here. My body is just lying there in the hotel room. Come on, Ariel. Faster.

But something tells me that faster may not even make any difference.

I'm now standing on a wide road that reminds me, in some way, of the Embankment in London, except that it seems to go on forever in either direction. The other strange thing is that the road does not have big, grand houses and hotels. Instead there are little cottages everywhere, arranged in a haphazard way: some on top of the other, some with three-dimensional edges. What? Don't be silly, Ariel. Three-dimensional edges don't exist. *Except in four spatial dimensions*, my mind reminds me. Oh God. I turn left and keep walking. I notice smoke coming out of some of the chimneys, but the smoke doesn't curl upwards, like smoke should do. As well as expanding into three-dimensional space, the smoke also seems to be curling in on itself, out of itself, and moving in some other directions I don't have the names for. As I walk, the large Embankment turns, improbably, into a dust track, with caravans scattered around and cardboard chickens everywhere. Hang on. Cardboard chickens? What's happening to me? There's a flash in the sky, like lightning, and then dawn starts to break, but much faster than it would normally. I feel so tired. I could just crawl into one of those caravans and sleep for a while maybe. No. Don't be so silly, Ariel: If you go inside one of those things there'll just be another mind with more thoughts and more memories. For the first time, this knowledge makes me feel exhausted. Now the sun is up, and I'm walking in a bright yellow desert, with giant sand castles popping up everywhere and then disappearing again. What the hell is this the equivalent of? All this is a metaphor, right? Well, what—or where—is the fucking reality that goes with this?

The desert seems to last for hours, but I have no real sense of time in here. The ten minutes I sensed on the bridge could have been three, or one, or twenty. All I know is that each footstep may as well be the ticking second hand of some cosmic clock and the closer I get to myself the farther away I get from any chance of surviving this. I emerge from the desert and onto another dust track, which contains various diners in blue and pink neon. Is the neon a good sign? Should I be pleased that it's back? The sun is going down again, too fast, like the evening of the end of the world. There's a dusty petrol station on one side of the street. If only I could fuel myself there. The air is still humid, and nothing's happened as a result of the lightning: no rain, no thunder. And I'm walking in what must be my own mind, lost inside my ideas and assumptions about what and who everyone else is. I don't know where "I" am. And the red dot in the console isn't getting perceptibly closer.

Apollo Smintheus?

Nothing.

Apollo Smintheus? I'll do anything. . . . Please come and help me.

Another soundless crack in the sky. Now I think I know what praying is. I walk on another two or three steps, but I seem to be fading. I don't think I can go any farther. There's a rumble in the distance. Thunder? I fall to my knees.

Apollo Smintheus?

And then I see him, like a mirage. A mirage on . . . a red scooter?

"Well," he says as he pulls up next to me.

There's a cloud of pale brown dust, and then it settles.

"I thought you weren't coming back," I say.

"I wasn't."

"But you are back. You are here. I'm not just seeing things?"

Apollo Smintheus smiles. "Of course you're just seeing things. But that doesn't mean I'm not here." He looks at his watch. "You're in trouble. Let's have a coffee."

He leaves his scooter in the middle of the dust track and walks towards one of the neon diners. I follow him, but every step feels soggy, as though I'm moving underwater in all my clothes. As we get closer to the diner I realize that it's called Mus Musculus, and instead of a door it has the same arch as Apollo Smintheus's house. The inside is like an amalgamation of every American road movie I've ever seen: red leatherette booths, laminated menus, big glass containers of sugar with silver spouts that deliver one spoonful when you tip them up. The tables are white Formica. In one corner is the same nest I saw back at the place next to the pool hall somewhere, I imagine, on the other side of the Troposphere.

"Well," Apollo Smintheus says again.

I look over at the counter. There aren't any staff here. Above the left-hand edge of the counter there's a TV screen attached with a bracket. It's switched off. There's a big white digital clock on the wall just behind it to the right, but whatever time it's telling isn't familiar to me. First it reads 82.5; then 90.1; then 85.5; then 89.7. It pulses irregularly, which is why I assume it can't be a clock. When I look back to the table, there's a white cup filled with brown liquid. Oh well, if I'm going to die I may as well drink some Troposphere coffee first. And I don't have the energy for much more than drinking coffee, anyway. I want to delay this trip across the Troposphere as long as possible. I can't believe I've been this stupid. I can't believe I'm lost in my own mind. Is this what madness feels like? Probably best not to think too much about that.

"Thanks," I say to Apollo Smintheus. "I mean, for . . ."

What am I thanking him for? The coffee? Being here? Potentially rescuing me?

"Hmm," says Apollo Smintheus.

"Are you here because I prayed?"

He sips his coffee. His gray paw looks like a key ring I saw once, made of a lucky rabbit's foot: hard and gray and dead. But the rest of him seems so alive it's crazy. After all, eight-foot-tall mouse gods don't actually exist. But he breathes like a person, and his long gray nose looks as though it would feel hard and warm if I were to touch it. Not that I would ever touch it. Another odd thing about Apollo Smintheus is that when I sit opposite him I feel as though I'm sitting opposite a very distinguished professor.

"Not exactly," he says.

"Why are you here?"

"Because you're going to do something for me. Or—perhaps it's easier to say that you have already done something for me. But you don't know what it is yet."

"I'm confused."

"I know."

"Look. Can I just ask you some questions, really quickly? I think I'm in trouble and I've got to get halfway across the Troposphere before I . . ."

"You are in trouble."

My shoulders sag. "I know. I think I might not be able to get back to myself in time. In fact, I think I already know that I'm not going to make it."

"I agree."

"And I think there's a chance I might die."

"Yes, well . . ."

"Well, what?"

"Being in the Troposphere, as you call it. If you're here, you're already dead."

Something in my body tries to release adrenaline, but it doesn't work like that in here. The scene in front of me blurs and then comes back.

"Oh fuck. Oh fuck." I grip the table in front of me. "So I'm too late?"

"Too late for what?"

"To go back. To find Burlem."

"You can go back."

"But . . . You said . . . Being here." I close my eyes and then open them again. "Am I dead?"

"This world, the world-of-minds. It leads to death. You know that."

"Do I?"

"If you gave it any thought you'd realize." He laughs, and it's like watching a CGI animation, except that I can feel the warm, humid air around me change when he breathes into it. "I'm sorry. You didn't call me back here for riddles. Why don't you just ask your questions."

"OK."

"But you'd better be quick, because we've still got to discuss this little commission you're going to take on for me—and we've also got to work out how to get you out of here, which isn't actually going to be that easy."

"OK. Well I'll keep it quick then. Am I . . . Am I safe for a moment?"

Apollo Smintheus gestures to the TV screen. It flickers into life. In grainy black and white I can see the interior of a hospital. The camera is focused on a bed where a girl lies unconscious. There's a drip attached to her arm.

"Is that me?" I say. But I already know it is.

"The pub landlord was alerted when you didn't come down for breakfast and then failed to check out. He went into your room and found you unconscious. When he couldn't wake you he called an ambulance. You're in a coma, officially."

"Oh God."

"You've travelled a great distance here. That takes a long time."

"Apollo Smintheus?" I'm still looking at the screen.

"Yes."

"Am I mad?"

"No. Not in the way you understand the word."

"This isn't some coma fantasy . . . Like a dream?"

"Well, this is a little like dreaming, but obviously it's the reverse. Why don't you ask your questions."

I stop looking at the TV screen and look at him instead.

"Every time you say something I have more questions," I say.

"Like?"

"Well, how is this dreaming in reverse?"

"Dreaming takes you into your unconscious. This is not your unconscious."

Suddenly, things start click-clicking in my mind. I haven't really yet had the chance to think deeply about Apollo Smintheus's document, but I've obviously absorbed it, because now I start making the connections.

"This is . . . consciousness itself," I say.

"Indeed."

"Everyone's thoughts, everyone's consciousness. But made into an elaborate metaphor that I can navigate. But this space doesn't really look like this—like you said before. There's no coffee, no table, no TV. But presumably I wouldn't be able to see whatever it is made of . . . And . . . And I can jump into other people's minds because they're all connected. They're all made out of the same thing."

"Very good. What are they made out of?"

"Do I know?"

"Yes. You should do."

I think about everything I know about consciousness. I start with Samuel Butler and his idea that consciousness is something that evolves, and that there's no reason machines—or bits of plastic, or whatever—can't become conscious, as long as they inherit the consciousness from us. We evolved from plants, I remember him arguing, and plants aren't conscious. So consciousness can evolve from nothing at all, just as life must also have done, once. We can merge with machines and become cyborgs and eventually the machine part of us might become conscious. But how would that happen? And how did it happen with the animals that first became conscious; who made consciousness for us? There must have been a moment when the first flicker of consciousness happened. What caused that sudden leap into consciousness? I've always liked these questions best of all Butler's writings, but they're not going to help me here, I don't think. What else do I know about consciousness? I know I don't like the idea of the collective unconscious. I don't like the idea of primordial symbols that exist outside the more arbitrary system of signifiers and signifieds. I prefer Derrida's idea of a gaping absence being the thing that creates reality and presence—not a weird B-movie interface full of snakes and witches and creepy jesters.

I think about Heidegger again, and realize there's so much I don't know. From what I can remember, Heidegger's special word for consciousness (or, at least, the kind of consciousness that most humans seem to have) is *Dasein:* literally a kind of being that is able to ask questions about its own being. For Heidegger, being cannot be considered without the idea of time: You can only be present in the present, and you can therefore only exist in the sense that you exist in time. Dasein can recognize and theorize its own being. It can wonder, "Why am I here? Why do I exist? And what is existence, anyway?" And Dasein is therefore constructed out of language: *logos;* that which signifies.

Lacan made the psychoanalytic argument that consciousness is connected with language—that our jump from being unconscious, gurgling babies into being part of the "symbolic order" (i.e., having a conscious world) happens at exactly the same moment that we acquire language. This is the same moment that we realize that we are separate beings in the world. We are not our mothers (thank Christ). We become something called a *self,* that can exist only because *others* do.

But the world is made from language (or, at least, my world is made from language), and we know how unreliable that is. It's a simulacrum: a closed system just like mathematics, where everything only makes sense because it isn't something else. The numeral 2 only means something because it is not 1 or 3. House only exists because it isn't a boat or a street. I am only me because I am not someone else. This is a system of existence with no signifieds; only signifiers. The whole system of existence is a closed system floating on nothing, like a locked hovercraft.

Think, Ariel. This isn't a fucking essay.

No. I'm lost inside consciousness and trying to work out what the hell it is.

Which kind of reminds me of something. . . .

"We haven't got too much more time," Apollo Smintheus warns me.

I look up at the screen. I'm still lying there, just as unconscious as I was before.

"This whole place is made of language," I say. "That's why I come here down a tunnel made of language—all language from the beginning of time. People's thoughts get stored here somehow . . ."

"Very good."

"And you're made out of a special language: prayer."

"Yes."

"But I don't understand. Why can't I see the true Troposphere? Surely it's just numbers and letters? I mean, if it's language, it's made to be understandable."

"Language written on what?"

I shrug. "I don't know." For some reason I'm imagining a big tablet in the sky, like a cosmic version of the Rosetta stone. Every time someone thinks or says or does something, it gets recorded there. But if that's all it was I would be able to see it. I mean—we'd all be able to see a giant stone tablet floating in the sky. Maybe this really is all just imaginary.

"You're going to have to give this some more thought," Apollo Smintheus says.

"Yes . . . ," I start to say.

"But not now. Now we've got to get you out of here."

"I . . . ," I begin.

Apollo Smintheus looks at his watch. "What?"

"Why do you care?"

"Oh, because you're going to do something for me."

"And what is that?"

"I'll tell you on the way."

We're walking out of the desert and into a suburban space, with little white houses with blue doors. It's nighttime again, but the silvery light is back. Each house has a window box outside with blue flowers, and a neat front garden. Each garden is dewed with moisture and covered with shiny little cobwebs. Apollo Smintheus has been explaining to me what he wants me to do for him, and it's completely nuts.

"You want me to go back to 1900?"

"Yes. And there's no point in arguing because in a sense you've already done it. That's why I'm here helping you now."

I ignore as much of that as I can. "You want me to go back to

1900 and mess with the head of a retired schoolteacher who bred 'fancy mice'?"

"Yes, that's right. Miss Abbie Lathrop. As I just explained to you, she virtually invented the laboratory mouse. Go to any lab and you'll find mice there bred from her original stock. I'll give you an example. The C56/BL6/Bkl. This is a strain of mouse that you can buy from any distributor. They are all black, all inbred, and all originated from Miss Abbie Lathrop's stock—the mating of male 52 and female 57, to be precise."

"Why?" I say, as my brain tries—and fails—to process any of this. "Why do you want me to do this?"

"The boys in Illinois tend to pray to me to do something about the plight of the laboratory mouse. Well, I can't think of anything better than wiping out the woman who invented them, can you?"

"But I can't wipe anyone out!"

"Oh really? You're saying you haven't changed people's minds since you've been in here? Got people to do things they wouldn't ordinarily have done? Isn't that how you escaped from the men in the car?"

"But . . ." This is frustrating me. "That was happening in real time. You can't change the past. What about paradoxes?"

"Everything that happens in the Troposphere happens in the past, in your sense."

"And paradoxes?"

"Oh, at the moment everything's a bit of a paradox. It wouldn't matter."

I see images in my mind of men in white coats bending over tanks of mice. One minute they're examining some creature with an ear growing on its back, or a tumor; the next minute there's nothing in the tank. But if the woman who bred the mice had been stopped from doing it way back in 1900, then the mice would never have been there. The men would therefore not be there. The whole world would change. I try to explain this to Apollo Smintheus.

"Oh, no," he says mildly. "No. That wouldn't be a problem. The mice would all just dissolve into the air, I think. The world wouldn't change. No one would notice."

"But . . ."

"You've already done it, so there's no point arguing."

"If I've already done it, then why are there still mice in cages in laboratories?" I ask.

"Are there?" he says. "I can't see any."

"And what about you? If there were no lab mice, then maybe the cult in Illinois wouldn't ever have formed, and you would never exist . . ."

"Oh, I've been around since the Greeks. Anyway, part of being a god is doing things to destroy yourself. It's like being a human. We're all trapped in the same economy."

There are so many paradoxes here that I'm developing a headache. At least I have a little more energy now. That must be from the drip attached to my physical body in the hospital.

"She's called Miss Abbie Lathrop," he says again, "and she lives on a farm in Massachusetts. You'll need to get to her towards the end of 1899. I'll leave you a message with the full details when you come back."

At least he doesn't want me to do this right now.

"But . . ."

"What?"

"I do have one more rather important question," I say.

"Which is?"

"Won't it kill me? I mean, going back less than a month would have finished me off if you hadn't come to help me. And—no offense—I still don't know if I'm going to get out of here alive."

"I don't know why you're so fond of this 'life.'" Apollo Smintheus sighs. "But don't worry. I'm going to show you something I think you'll find useful."

"What is it?"

"The underground system. I think that's an OK translation."

"The underground system? What, like trains?"

"Yes. That is how your mind would see this. Yes, I think it will be trains."

The suburbs are getting more dense. We're walking down a steep hill and I can see a main road glowing at the bottom of it. There's still no traffic, of course. No traffic, no rubbish, no people. We turn right once we get to the road and walk along a row of brightly lit department stores that are interspersed every so often with large gray office blocks. We walk on a little more and I begin to experience the sensation of there being more edges than there should be on all the things around me. I can see large off-white tenement buildings that have multidimensional launderettes and jazz bars as their outsides. There is way too much stuff here, and I can almost feel the density of the landscape physically pressing on me. Just when I think I can't stand it anymore, Apollo Smintheus points to some concrete steps up ahead that seem to burrow down underneath the street. As we get closer I realize that this looks just like the entrance to a London tube station.

"Here we are," he says. "It's not the easiest way to navigate the Troposphere, but it's the easiest way to get back to yourself."

I start walking down the steps; then I realize he's not following me and I stop.

"Aren't you coming?" I say.

"Oh, I can't go down there."

"So what do I do?"

"You should have a timetable with you, on that thing . . . The interface . . ."

"What, my console?"

"If that's what you call it, yes."

"But where am I trying to get to?"

"Yourself. I would suggest alighting at yourself before coming into the Troposphere this time. Then you can avoid the unpleasantness of the hospital visit, and those men catching up with you and so on."

"What, you mean there's going to be a station marked *Ariel Manto, pub in Hertfordshire, five minutes before embarking on the journey by which she discovered the way to get back here in the first place*? I mean, the paradoxes . . ."

"When will you stop talking about paradoxes? Your whole world is a paradox. Officially it has no beginning and no end. Nothing about it makes any sense, but it's what you seem to have created."

But I'm not really listening. I'm thinking, *So the men do catch up with me, then, in the hospital scenario.* I have to get out of here. Is this going to work? I don't know. But I am totally lost here in this too-dense, dark place: a city at night that I've somehow created, that somehow relates to the minds of all the people "outside." We've walked for about, what, ten Troposphere minutes to get here? It's hard to tell.

Then I hear it: the squeak of wheels. Apollo Smintheus hears it, too. His gray face crimples into a frown, and his ears twitch.

"You'd better go," he says.

"What is it?" I say.

But then it's clear what it is. The two blond KIDS are coming down the hill: one on a skateboard and the other on a rusty bike. They're still quite far off, maybe only a quarter of the way down.

"Go," says Apollo Smintheus. "I'll do something about them."

"What if they follow me?"

"They can't go underground. Just go, now. Don't let them see you're here."

"But presumably they already know I'm here. I mean . . ."

"They're not following you. You're still lost. They've been following me. But I can deal with them. Just go, before they see you."

He walks off, towards the KIDS. I wonder what he's going to do to them.

"Apollo Smintheus?"

"I'll see you when you get back," he calls over his bony shoulder.

The sky is still dark, and there's another brief flash like lightning as I run down the steps. Am I safe now? I must be. But that was pretty close. I can't hear my footsteps; all I can hear is an echoey sound of dripping. The visibility down here isn't very good; every so often there's a dim orange light fixed to the concrete ceiling, but nothing other than that. As my run turns into a walk, I try to look behind me, but I can't see anything. There are more shadows than light down here. *But I created this space,* I think. *Why didn't I just give it more lights?* I try to think more light into the space, but nothing happens. It's as if this is what an underground station is, for me; and there's no way I can change my ideas about it. I keep half walking and half running through the tunnel, going deeper and deeper underground. But I can't hear anything behind me and, after several minutes of this, I conclude I am safe—for now. Now I am worried that long concrete tunnel will never end, or change. Then, suddenly, there are signs everywhere, and some dim, black-and-white computer screens presumably showing departures and arrivals. I notice that there are now stairs leading down on either side of the tunnel. The sign on the left says PLATFORM 365; the one on the right says PLATFORM 17. Where is the sense here? And how on earth am I going to work out how to get back to myself in this system?

Console?

It comes up.

What do I do now? I ask it.

Read the Departures Board, it tells me.

So much for the timetable existing on my console.

All the screens seem to be showing departures. Are there no arrivals here? I stop in front of one of them and read the information on it. And then I don't know what to think. There don't seem to be any times on the board; there are just lots and lots of platform numbers. And the train lines are called Fear, Love, Anger, Frustration, Disgust, Pain, Ecstasy, Hope, Comfort. . . . Every abstract emotion you can think of is there. And, oddly, there's room for them all on a screen the size of a portable television.

How do I use this system? I ask the console.

You find a platform and board a train.

But which platform?

Where are you trying to get to?

Myself. Oh—do I use the coordinates?

No. The coordinates only relate to your position on the Troposphere. I believe you are trying to get out of the Troposphere.

So . . . What do I do, then?

You join with a train of thought relating to the state of mind of the person you want to rejoin: in this case, yourself. And you alight when you get there.

The console is mildly annoying me, so I close it down. Trains of thought. It's obvious and frustrating at the same time. Who invented this weird system? And then I think, *I did. I invented everything here.* Except . . . I didn't invent Apollo Smintheus, and I didn't invent those KIDS. I sigh and look at the board again. If I am going to get back to myself, it looks as though I'm going to have to identify an emotion I know I was experiencing at the time I want to get back to.

And I'm thinking: Time travel, to the past, using *emotions*? Einstein wouldn't have approved of this. I'm not sure I approve of this. And I don't know how you really distinguish between emotions, anyway. I have enough trouble (intellectually) distinguishing between *things*. But emotions are not even things. They don't really exist outside the mind. But I'm going to have to do this, anyway. OK. When I was in the hotel room, what was I feeling? Hope? Sort of. I hoped that I'd find Burlem through Molly. But it wasn't a strong feeling. Does it have to be a strong feeling?

The console opens up in my mind, even though I didn't ask it to.

You have one new message, it tells me, and then it closes itself again. I open it back up.

Where is the message? I ask it.

There's a glow on the screen and I follow it over to a news kiosk just beyond the Departures Board. There is one newspaper in a small rack outside and I pick it up. It's not a newspaper.

A Guide to the Underground, it says on the front. *By Apollo Smintheus.*

I open it up.

You now have no new messages, says the console.

In my previous work I alluded to a vulnerability that a mind may have to the world of all minds. I feel that this now needs greater explanation. As you are aware, consciousness itself is a sprawling landscape with many open doors from one mind to another. The landscape and the doors are metaphors. The openings may just as well be tunnels through a coral reef, or wormholes in space. In most cases, information in the Troposphere is stored where it is created: in the "mind space" of that individual.

However, there are several cases of information, which is more dynamic and, you may say, "global" (not that the Troposphere is a globe, of course). What you call "emotions" are types of information that are *shared* among minds in the Troposphere. The human experience of emotion can be said to be like a wind blowing across an infinite, curved desert, or a planet orbiting its sun. (And it is only ever "like"; it never "is." Emotion is a whole world of metaphor itself, a type of being that shows itself only in not showing itself—as the symptom and never the thing.) You choose to "see" it as an underground train travelling along an infinite, looping track. Minds are not passengers on these trains: They are the stations themselves—sometimes open; sometimes closed. When the station is open, the train of emotion can roar through. When the station is open, it is also open to other things: other open minds or, perhaps, people attempting to achieve Pedesis.

Emotion could simply be termed "motion." Indeed, I remember that this word used to simply mean movement, or a transference from one thing to another. In this world-made-of-language, meaning never really becomes obsolete. In this case, the motion is of something that has no mass (motion itself) and so the meaning it carries can travel at incomprehensible speeds: speeds fast enough to take you backwards. All you have to do is get on a train and find the right station.

I look at the Departures Board again. I think myself back into that hotel room. I'd just had a bath, I remember: I was trying to wash Patrick's horrible desire away. I was trying to forget that I'd just had sex for money. I was . . . What? I was afraid, of course—although I think I knew I'd lost the Project Starlight men for the time being. What else? I was sad, because I knew I'd never see Adam again. But I'm so used to sadness and disappointment that they don't even register.

Which train do I get on?

The platform for "sadness" is number 1225. The platform for

"disgust" is number 69. I'm not sure I want to board a train of sadness, or a train of disgust. What about pain? But I wasn't actually in pain.

I think back to the moments I have been able to enter other people's minds. With Molly it was that moment—that pang—when she thought about Hugh, and the pain of having to go all over town looking for him. With Maxine it was easy: She was worrying the whole time about being fat and smelly. And now I think I understand this "vulnerability to the world-of-minds." You have a strong emotion and something in your mind opens, slightly, and at the moment of emotion your mind connects with all the others that are feeling the same thing. Or maybe I don't understand. It actually sounds a bit flaky to me, put like that. As an idea, it doesn't have the hard lines of Derrida or Heidegger. Oh well. I think harder, but I'm not sure I was feeling anything very definite in that room. But . . . Hang on. Surely it doesn't matter how far back I go, as long as I aim for some moment before I came into the Troposphere. So when did I last feel strong emotion? What about the fear I felt as I drove away from the priory? That tumbling-over-itself sick feeling as I waited for the black car to slither out of some side street and start following me. I look at the Departures Board again. *Fear: Platform 7.* I can't see this working, but I'll give it a try.

I start the long walk down the endless concrete tunnel, ignoring signs to Platform 31, Platform 57, and Platform 99. There's no order here. Eventually I find it: Platform 7. I walk down a set of aluminium steps and see that the train is already there; it's an old rusty thing that reminds me of the oldest and nastiest Northern Line trains that would always seem to grind to a halt just outside Camden. Isn't it a bit lucky that the train is already here? But from down here I can see all the other platforms, all with trains sitting in them. Just as the screens upstairs suggested: There are no arrivals here, only departures. And then I realize that the train isn't "really" here at all. It's just a metaphor—just like everything else here. I rotate the tarnished silver handle and pull the door towards me. Whatever the metaphor is—and whatever this experience "really" looks like—I am left in no doubt that I am now climbing inside fear itself.

Chapter Twenty-two

But so far fear just looks like the inside of an old London Underground train. The seats are covered in tatty green velveteen with a repeating orangy pattern. The floor has a layer of dirt so thick that the real floor could fall away and no one would even notice. The carriages are joined together with creaky mechanisms that you can see (or so I imagine) when you look through the window in the adjoining door. I sit down and a whistle blows. The train starts to move. It slowly creaks its way to the end of the platform and then, suddenly, we're going at what feels like three hundred miles per hour, through a long tunnel and then out onto a landscape I don't recognize. I absurdly think, *This must be a Circle Line train, since we're going above ground already;* then I realize what's wrong with what I'm thinking, and I stop.

I don't like this landscape. I don't like it at all. The syrupy feeling I have in the Troposphere is now gone, and I feel not simply cold and tired but completely hollowed out, as if all I am is skin. The train speeds up again and I can't help but look out of the window. Looking out of the window feels a bit like when you look on the Internet to find out if your symptoms suggest terminal illness: You know they will, and you know you shouldn't look, but you do. Outside of this window is just one big field. But it's not a green, hopeful field: It's basically mud. And on the mud, I can see burning houses. It should feel just like I do watching the TV news—that hyperreal sense that nothing you see in two dimensions on a screen can ever really happen—but it does not feel like watching TV. The houses that are burning outside aren't just any old semis from the news: They're all the houses I've ever lived in. And I'm inside, and I can't get out; my parents are inside, and they can't get out. I know my sister is already dead. But more than that. This is fear without hope: This is the image of me asleep in my cold bedroom back in Kent, wearing the thick pajamas my mother got me back in the days when we still spent Christmas together. In the image I am not just fast asleep; the smoke from the fire has already knocked me out and now, as I watch, the leg of my pajama bottoms has caught fire and the skin around my ankle is starting to melt. I won't ever wake up again. I am just going to melt, and I won't even know anything about it.

After the fires all I can see are floods: water creeping up and up the outside of the same houses—my houses—until they are completely submerged; until even the people on the roofs, and the people hiding in the attics, are soon dead. My whole family; everyone I've ever known. On one level I know I don't care too much about my family—when did I last see them, after all? But I'm there with them now as we wait for help that does not come; as we accept the moment when the water becomes too high and we all fall into it. There's nothing apart from the water: It's black and cold and it stinks like death. And I'm the first one to go, to stop trying to hold my breath and actually breathe in the black water. That's it. Blackness. My useless body sinks down to where the street used to be. And, in this train of fear, I'm sweating, and my heart's beating so fast that it's like one long heartbeat, or maybe no heartbeat at all.

The worst thing about the images outside is that there is nothing else apart from them. And it's not simply that I cannot see anything beyond the houses and the mud: I know with the deepest certainty possible that there is nothing out there beyond what I can see. There isn't any me here; there is no train. I will die in all those houses and there is nowhere else to escape to. There's no sense that this will ever exist "around the corner" or on TV or be happening to someone else.

This is what it must be like to open the door to a dead-eyed man with an axe. This is what it must be like when you haven't fought him off (after all, how could you?) and you're tied up and you know you're going to die. You're not watching this happen to a fictional character; you are experiencing it for real: It's me; it's the end of me. Or, worse: You are like a fictional character, but not one of the leads. You're just one of the victims along the way.

The train lurches on. The alleyways I'd usually never walk down after dark are all there now: a world of dead ends with rapists patrolling the thin dark passages like the ghosts on Pac-Man. I am stabbed a thousand times by people who don't know my name, or what books I like to read, or that if my life wasn't such a mess I'd quite like to get a cat. I watch myself bleed to death like a farm animal in an abattoir, while parts of my own body lie scattered around me, hacked off and discarded. I pray for unconsciousness, but it doesn't come. Oh Jesus. I can't stand any more of this. I feel what it is all like: I'm having an operation but the doctors don't know I'm actually awake. I experience a motorway pileup. I see Adam dying a million different ways. Then I'm killing Adam: I'm killing him in every possible way, and I'm killing everyone else, too. I'm in prison, and I'll never escape. I have no choice.

I have no choice.

I have no choice.

Every millisecond of this horrible journey is an epiphany in which I realize that this is it. This is my last moment of life, and any idea of free will disappeared long ago. And each epiphany is, at the moment I have it, absolutely irreversible. It's not the moment when you think *Shit! That was close*. It's the moment after that, in a world where you are the unluckiest person on Earth and there's no one to help you and no one to care, especially when everyone you know is already dead. . . .

I can't stand this.

Console? I say, weakly, although I can barely believe that such a thing still exists.

It comes up.

Where do I get off? I ask it.

You get off at your station.

Where is my station?

You have to be able to see it.

What?

You now have no choices.

Well, I knew that.

I want to stand up and go and ask the driver to stop the train, but I know that there is no driver and this isn't really a train. I'm surfing on a wave of fear that's moving faster than . . . What did Apollo Smintheus say? *Incomprehensible speeds.* Think, think. Don't look out of the window. Don't . . . I look.

And then I realize that I'm not alone out here. There's actually something worse than being alone with your own worst fears, and I'm just beginning to see what that might be. Faintly—not above, below, in front of, or behind my images of fear, but in some other relation to them—I now sense the howling spectre of something else: layers upon layers of other people's fear. There are misty representations of money burning, of someone being fisted by his own father, of toys that tell you to "fuck off" and then rip out your throat, of the idea that there is no such thing as reality, of someone being abducted by an alien and strapped to a table in a white lab, of nuclear war, of a child drowning, of hundreds of children drowning, of it being all YOUR FAULT, of choking on fish bones, of lung cancer, of bowel cancer, of brain tumors, of spiders—thousands and thousands of spiders, of a prolapsed uterus, of sleep apnea, of eating, of any kind of sex, of rats, of cockroaches, of plastic bags, of heights, of planes, of the Bermuda Triangle, of the live rail, of ghosts, of terrorism, of cocktail parties, of crowds, of the dentist, of choking on your own tongue, of your own feet, of dreams, of grown-ups, of ice cubes, of false teeth, of Father Christmas, of getting old, of your parents dying, of what you might do to yourself, of coffins, of alcohol, of suicide, of blood, of not being able to take heroin again, of the thing behind the curtains, of soot, of spaceships, of DVT, of horses, of fast cars, of people, of paper, of knives, of dogs, of redundancy, of being late, of being seen naked, of scabs, of leap years, of UFOs, of dragons, of poison, of accordion music, of torture, of any kind of authority, of being kicked while you just lie on the ground trying to protect your head until you become unconscious and can't protect yourself anymore.

You—why don't *you* look out of the window for a while.

My eyes are now shut. *Incomprehensible speeds*. What does that mean?

I can't breathe. The man with the gun . . .

There's no man with a gun, Ariel.

There is. The whole world is made only of men with guns. There's no one else in the whole world, just me and billions of men with guns. I feel sick.

Incomprehensible speeds. I can comprehend the speed of light. I can comprehend ten times the speed of light. The only thing I can't comprehend is infinite speed. . . . That's what Apollo Smintheus said, didn't he? Or did he just say that the train track was infinite? Anyway, what if we were moving at infinite speed? Although I can't really comprehend it (which is, I think, the point of "incomprehensible"), something travelling at infinite speed would actually seem to be at rest at every point that it travelled past. Something with infinite speed, travelling in a loop, should be able to be everywhere at once, surely? Maybe more than once: Who knows? So maybe I don't have to wait for my station. Maybe my station is simply there, outside, and I have to find it.

I don't want to look out of the window, but I do. Now my own fears are in sharp focus again. Everything I've ever written is on fire. Someone's rubbing my name out of every document in which it's ever appeared. I don't know where these images are coming from. They appear to be random, but maybe . . . I try to think of Adam again and, as if I'd ordered the memory in the consciousness equivalent of the most efficient fast-food restaurant in the world, there he is, outside the window, fucking my mother. He's fucking my mother and saying to her: "Who's Ariel? I've never heard of anyone called Ariel." He seems to turn and see me watching them. Then he laughs. He pokes her in the ribs and points at me and they both laugh. "I don't have time for this now, Ariel," my mother says. "You're not the center of the universe, you know."

Cars, I think. *Driving*. Driving towards London from Faversham. Come on. I'm escaping from the priory; from the Project Starlight men. And then I see/feel it. I'm in my car and I'm zoning out into the fear. In the image through the train window I can see the men racing behind me in their black car, driving down the almost-empty motorway with the gray sky above and the snow lying in fields, on rooftops, and alongside the long, curving hard shoulders. I can see them behind me and I know this is the end. In a film, I'd shake them off. But they're going to run me off the road and no amount of gutsy driving or intelligence is going to save me. My life is going to end in a crunch of jagged metal, with my blood spurting onto the windscreen. I don't want to go there, to this place, but I have to. I have to get into that place from this one. My mind is open at that point, I instinctively know that. And the men aren't really there: That's just the fear.

At least—I hope it's just the fear.

How do I get off? Not knowing what else to do, I walk towards the doors.

The image is still the same one outside the windows. I focus on it, and then I press the button to open the doors. The train's still moving but the doors open and . . .

It's six A.M.—just gone—on the A2 and the sign is telling me that if I keep going I'll end up in London. That's not what I want. Or maybe it is? No. I need the M25 and then a road to Torquay, wherever that is. I glance in the rearview mirror: still no black car. There's another sign ahead of me pointing to the various exits you could take if you wanted to go to any one of the various Medway towns. I haven't lived around here long enough for any of the names to mean anything to me. Except . . . One of them does mean something to me. It's the town where Patrick lives. But—oh shit. I'm having déjà vu. I remember being here before and taking that exit and getting Patrick to come and fuck me in the toilets for a hundred quid.

Except it wasn't déjà vu. *It happened.* It happened and then I went to Molly's school and then I got lost in the Troposphere and then I time-travelled back here, in a train full of fear and . . . So much for paradoxes. I pull over to the hard shoulder and take out a cigarette. At the same time I check my purse to see if I still have the rest of Patrick's money. No. I've got the £9.50 I set out with and very little petrol. I light my cigarette and pull back onto the road. I'm going to Torquay. And I can't help smiling. I've no idea where I've actually been but—oddly—for the first time since I first went into the Troposphere, I don't feel at all mad. I feel absolutely fine about what just happened. *I'm not a whore after all,* I think as I drive off again. I got what I wanted without actually doing anything. Or did I actually do it and then overwrite it with something else? Oh, whatever. I put all thoughts of Abbie Lathrop—and the KIDS—out of my mind and, as I drive towards the M25, I try to make myself vow never to try Pedesis again.

It's just gone midday when I park in a big, anonymous car park next to Torquay Library, about 250 miles from the Shrine of St. Jude in Faversham. There's no snow in the southwest, but the sky is as gray and flat as the one back home, as if January has been reformatted in two dimensions and broadcast on a cheap black-and-white portable TV. The Troposphere always seems flat to me, but this is worse; I'm not sure that the real world, with its dirt and its people, is exactly where I want to be. But then I'm not sure the Troposphere is a good place for me, either. I still have half a tank of the petrol that I "forgot" to pay for, but now I need food, and coffee. There's a café just across from the library, next to a big slablike church of a denomination I don't recognize. I decide to go into the café before using the public Internet terminals that I hope are in the library. I'm going to search for local castles and see what I find. I remember Burlem's memory of the one in his town: the one he thought of as being like a giant's ring, ripped off, and left on a hilltop. If that doesn't locate it, I'll try something else, but I'm not sure what.

Even though I have my plan, I still sit in the car for about five minutes before I do anything. What a journey. I drove about two hundred miles before I stopped looking in my rearview mirror for the police (who I assumed would want to ask me questions about the petrol), and the Project Starlight men. Some time after that I lost track of where I was. I pulled into a town I thought was Torquay, but there was nothing at all to distinguish it from every other town I've ever seen in Britain, and I couldn't be sure that I'd actually reached my destination. There was a large roundabout with various signs to industrial estates, and a Sainsbury's supermarket off to the right. I pulled into the Sainsbury's car park and got out of the car for the first time since the petrol station on the M25. My legs felt shaky. I walked in and went straight up to the kiosk and bought a cheap packet of tobacco.

"Where am I, exactly?" I asked the woman, after she'd given me my change.

The way I said it made it sound like a completely normal question. But the woman looked at me as if I were completely odd.

"You're in Sainsbury's, dear," she told me.

But after some further conversation I realized that I was not in Torquay and got some pretty good directions that led me straight to the library.

So now I'm in a car park that is indistinguishable from any other car park in any other town, and I watch as people unload buggies and small children, or pack away large, shiny carrier bags with the word SALE on them. Two women go past, both in those new mobility scooters that look a bit like bumper cars, and they seem to be arguing about something. The gray concrete is smeared with old fag butts, familiar take-away wrappers, and polystyrene coffee cups. I look beyond all of this, towards the thin line of bare-branched trees up a small hill separating this car park from the road above. The trees are the only things that stand out in the grayish-whitish smudge of official buildings and the sky. And then I see something in the trees: six or seven squirrels all moving at once; one in each tree, or so it seems, moving and jumping and rearranging themselves constantly, like pixels on a screen. Their bodies are silhouetted by the pale light of the sky behind them. It's winter, and I can't imagine what they find to eat in a place like this. Aren't squirrels supposed to hibernate? Do they have a god looking after them or does nobody pray for squirrels? I shiver. What if Burlem isn't in this place anymore; or what if I can't actually find out where it is? I imagine what it's like to live as a squirrel—or any animal—in a concrete, urban space, where everything costs money. What will I do if I can't find Burlem? I can't go home; I think it's fair to say that I have no home anymore.

I wonder if the book is still safe.

I wonder if the men have got to Adam yet.

And I feel a pulse like a fist, hitting me first between my legs and then somewhere in my stomach. Is it possible that I'll ever see him again?

I stop thinking and get of the car. There's a billboard layered with rained-on, peeling posters, most of which are advertising a pantomime starring someone from an Australian soap that I've never heard of. Above that there's a sign: NO OVERNIGHT SLEEPING. Shit. I never realized that you could be stopped for just parking your car somewhere and sleeping in it. I walk over to the ticket machine, the cold wind jabbing at my face as if I've stolen something from it. As I'd feared, it's extortionate to park here: about a pound an hour. I pay for half an hour and then use my fingernail to smudge the time on the ticket as I walk back over to my car. Then I prop the ticket in a hard-to-see place on the edge of the windscreen, so only the date is showing, before locking the car door and walking across the road and through a tinkling door into the café.

It smells of soup, plus something sour that I can't identify. It's almost full up, but I manage to get a seat in the corner by a display of greeting cards, jewellery, and Fairtrade muesli. There are various pictures on the walls depicting slim white women in Africa leading choirs of small, brightly clothed children; or helping equally brightly clothed women pull water up from a well. I realize this is a Christian café just as a late middle-aged woman in a yellow twinset comes to take my order. As I ask for the carrot and parsnip soup and a black coffee, I notice the leaflets that are scattered around, and the poster on the wall advertising the times of the service in the church—presumably the one next door. And I wonder: What kind of god is created and sustained by the hundreds of people who must pray here? Apollo Smintheus is the result of six people's prayers and he seems real enough. What does more prayer do? What sort of god does it make? And is this god—the one made by the people here—the same god created by the people in the church near Burlem's house? Is it the same god created by the people in the Faversham priory? What would a god like that look like? I suppose if I met him in the Troposphere, he'd look exactly as I'd want him to look—probably an old man with a white beard: the atheist's view of a Christian's view of God. And what does he do for these people? What must it be like to have millions of people telling you what to do? And I also wonder: What does he ask in return?

While I'm waiting for my soup, I study one of the leaflets. It talks vaguely about "joy." But I haven't seen anything joyful since I've been in this place. I haven't seen anything joyful since . . . I can't actually remember when the last time was. And that's why I like reading Heidegger and Derrida and Baudrillard. In that world life isn't a matrix of good and bad; happy and sad; joy and failure to achieve joy. Failure and sadness are there to be examined, like a puzzle, and the puzzle is open to anyone. It doesn't matter how many people you've slept with, or whether or not you smoke, or whether or not you get something out of damaging your own body. You can have a go at the puzzle that assumes imperfection and never asks you for anything.

I look down at my wrists—the pinkish, silvery marks—and then I glance around the café. Most of the other people here are middle-aged and dressed in respectably unstylish catalog clothes. They scare me a little; not because of what they might do to me (these people never do anything: They're benign) but because of what I am in their thoughts. These aren't the middle-aged women I remember from the estate I grew up on—women who'd cackle and smoke and discuss the benefits of giving blow jobs without your false teeth. Neither are they like the social workers who'd come round every so often to check we weren't being sexually abused by these women's husbands (it was more usually the sons). No. These are of the same species as the women I remember from the bakery and the corner shop: the ones who don't bother to stop talking about your crazy mother when you walk in because they think you're too stupid to understand. They're the school secretaries who could have simply told me I needed to wash my clothes more often, rather than talking about it behind my back and, eventually, reporting me to the head teacher. They're the kind of women who would never wear flattering clothes—or anything black—because looking attractive equals sex. There's only one other young person in the café: a blond guy with shabby clothes who looks like the sort of RE teacher who'd spend a long time talking about world religions and not so long on Christianity. He looks at me for a moment and I see a familiar desire in his eyes. It's not romantic desire: It's for sex, raw sex, and it's because I look like I'd be up for it. Compared to everyone else in here I look like a whore. But, of course, that's the point of these women. By being what they are, they make you a bad person by comparison, even if all you're doing is wearing lipstick. I try to give him a look back that says "Not today, thanks," and then I pick up the leaflet and pretend to read it again.

The woman with the yellow twinset comes with my soup.

"Six thirty is the next one," she says to me, in a crisp voice.

"Sorry?"

"The next service is at 6:30."

I don't want to appear rude, so I just say, "OK. Thanks."

"Are you local?" she says.

"No. Not really."

I don't mention that I could easily become local: a local bum with nowhere to go—except, I'd guess, the library and the church.

"Oh."

"I'm just passing through," I say.

But respectable people don't have hair like mine, and they don't pass through anywhere. Passing through is the kind of thing men do—truckers and cowboys—and we all know what happens to women who act like men. The woman walks off, making a tutting noise.

When I've finished my soup I look around in my bag for a notebook, so I can write a list of things I'm intending to look up in the library. I take out the tobacco as well. Obviously I can't smoke in here, but I'll roll one to have while I'm crossing the road. I've rolled my cigarette and put it to one side on the table when the woman comes back to collect my bowl. I drain the last of the coffee and offer her the cup, too.

"You can't smoke in here," she says.

"Oh—I know. I wasn't going to, don't worry," I say, smiling.

"Yes, well, just as long as you know." She doesn't smile back. In fact, her body stiffens, as if she thinks I'm about to attack her or something. As if I'm *bad* enough to do something like that.

What is it about these people that makes me feel as though they're damning me to hell all the time? Or maybe it's not them: It's me. I should tie my hair up; my hair can offend people. I should pretend not to smoke. I should always use my nice quiet BBC voice, not my loud, confident one. I should always offer to help. I should always tell people exactly what they want to hear . . . I should join in with people who pretend that meaning exists and makes people like me bad in order to make them good. I should feel absented by their presence. I should lie all the time, because the truth just isn't nice. It isn't holy.

"What's your god like?" I ask the woman, before I can tell myself to shut up.

"What's *God* like?" she says.

I should never have asked this question. "Yes," I say.

Although all I've done is ask about her god, I've broken social convention and my eyes start to water and itch, and I can feel myself blushing slightly. I don't want a row; I really don't. I only asked the question because I was interested. And I meant to say "Yes" in a timid way, but I don't do timid very well, and it didn't quite work. Nevertheless, I expect the woman to be polite back—or even to answer my question. But instead her eyes harden further.

"He looks after the people who believe in him," she says.

And then she walks away.

As I leave the café, light my cigarette, and sit on a wall to smoke it, I remember the various times in my life when I've tried to find out about religion. It often starts with a logical idea: that so many people around the world believe in a god, or a way of life, that there must be something in at least one of these approaches. So I go to the local library, or the university library, and there's always that moment—perhaps similar to the moment before you choose the bread you want in the bakery—where there seems to be so much possibility. So many books; so much "truth." Surely it can't all be false? Surely it won't all be the same? But all the books do just seem the same to me. They all have the same hierarchies. They all have leaders. Even Buddhism has rules over who can really "belong" and who can't, who is in charge, and who is not. And all the leaders are men.

I remember once flirting with Roman Catholicism when I was seeing a guy who'd been a choirboy as a kid, and who seemed to get something out of the whole thing (and had worked it all out so you could be a Catholic and still have dirty sex). I got a couple of books and magazines from the local church and started to read up on it. I'd kind of bought all that stuff about the Virgin Mary and was in the process of trying to convince myself that a religion that took a woman so seriously must have something going for it. Then I read a humorous anecdote in one of the magazines about a time when Pope John Paul II was visiting some town, and the nuns who were supposed to cook for him messed it up and ended up giving him fish fingers. Obviously the point of the story was that it was funny that the pope had eaten fish fingers, but I couldn't get over the detail that the pope had nuns to cook for him. Surely religious leaders are supposed to be somehow wiser than the rest of us? But I realized then that there was nothing special about this system at all, nothing that made it more profound and extraordinary than the rest of society. If someone who had given up his whole life to thinking about goodness and rightness and truth still expected nuns to cook him his fish fingers (because after all, nuns haven't got anything else better to do, and none of them are ever going to be priests or become the pope, because women aren't good enough for that), then something was very wrong. How could he have missed the bit about everyone being equal in the eyes of God? If this was the wisest Catholic, I certainly never wanted to meet the stupidest one.

Perhaps this is similar to the anthropic principle, but I am a woman, and after a lifetime of experiment I know I am capable of everything men can do, except things that specifically require a penis (like pissing standing up). I mean it's so obvious it even sounds a bit silly to repeat it, a bit like saying "All humans have heads." So what does religion know about me that I'm missing? Am I worth less in an a priori sense? But that would be utterly nonsensical. How is it possible that religion, which claims to be more profound than anything else, still has less of a grasp on humanity than any personnel department in the country?

It's not just Christianity, either: How could the Buddhists have missed the bit in their thinking about freedom from desire, when most of them seem to desire to be reincarnated well, and in such a way that they can be a man, and be called a "venerable master" and tell other people what to do? Why is religion so disappointing? You expect it to tell you something you don't know, and all it ends up telling you is the stuff you've known for years, and that you long ago decided is wrong.

Over to my left is the big gray wall in front of the church.

ARE WE THE THOUGHTS OF GOD? a poster asks.

No, I realize. It's the reverse.

I put out my cigarette and stop thinking.

The library is a large square space with two floors. There's a checkout desk in the middle of the ground floor, and bookshelves all around it. The second floor is basically just a gallery with a big hole in the middle, so you can stand up there and watch what's going on downstairs, or sit at one of the small desks and try to work, if you don't mind all the noise. I remember the library I went to as a kid. It was always deadly quiet and, at least in my memory, everything in it was orange, including a little sunken bit in the kids' section that to me felt like a huge abyss, and that I would beg my mother to let me go and sit in.

I walk up to the counter.

"Hi," I say, when a bearded librarian walks over to me. "I want to use the Internet."

"Are you a member?"

"Of this library?"

"Yes."

"Oh, no. Sorry. I'm not."

"Are you a foreign student?"

"No."

He smiles. "We can give you a day pass. You'll need to fill in this form . . ."

He gives it to me. But I'm wondering whether I can lie on it, and if so whether they will check. I certainly don't want to leave any written record of myself.

"Maybe I'll see if I can find the information I want in a book first," I say. "But I'll try this if that fails." I did want to look up the Web site of the cult of Apollo Smintheus as well as look for the information on the castle, but maybe I won't bother. After all, I am vaguely in debt to these people.

"Fine with me," he says. "Can I help you locate a book?"

I think this is the most helpful librarian I've ever come across. All the university librarians just act as though you're getting in their way. That's not to say I'm not missing the university, though, and I don't know where else I'll ever find a secular green space with no take-away cartons on the ground. For about the thousandth time today I have a pang: I'm not going back; I'm not going back.

"Um, I'm interested in local castles," I say.

"Ah. Any in particular?"

I smile. "No. Just generally. I want to look at the shapes of castles." That sounds mad. I think quickly. "It's research for a book."

He looks impressed. "And it's Devon castles you want?"

"Yeah, I think so."

"Well, you'll need the local history library then."

Oh shit. "Where's that?" I say.

"Oh, it's that little room over there," he says, pointing to a door in the corner. "You shouldn't really go in if you're not a member, but I should think it'll be all right. Obviously you can't take any of the books out. And I'm afraid you can't take your bag in with you."

He signs me in and takes my bag. Then he gives me a laminated pass.

"Just go straight in," he says.

———

The local history library is a dusty, low-ceilinged room split into three distinct sections by the layout of the shelves and the position of several desks and one microfiche reader. I instantly feel comfortable in here, around the musty smell of old books. There's no one else here but me, and I wonder if I'd get arrested for just crashing out here at the end of the day. Probably.

I drift around looking at faded old spines of parish records and biographies before I realize I'll need the computerized records to find what I'm looking for. There's a terminal in the corner, just under a CCTV playback of what's going on in here. I sit down, but it feels odd seeing myself on TV, and I'm a vague shadow in the corner of my eye as I type in the keywords "castles" and "Devon."

There are several books on Devon castles, and I choose a couple with pictures and take them to one of the desks. I flick through the largest book, which contains line drawings of all the major castles in the area. Exeter Castle and Powderham Castle are too grand and rectangular, as are Berry Pomeroy Castle and Bickleigh Castle. Gidley Castle and Lydford Castle are both too square. There are several castles by the sea. But the castle Burlem was thinking of was on a little mound. Finally I find pictures of two castles that are on mounds. They're both circular. My heart is like a machine that's been turned up a notch. I've now got two choices. I almost know where I need to go. I have to look at another book—this one with more recent photographs—before I see that one of the castles is now really just a ruin, like a tooth left in a giant's mouth.

But the other one looks exactly like Burlem described: like a giant's ring thrown on a hilltop. And I can see what he meant about the absence, as well. The picture I've got here in this book, this aerial view, certainly does make it seem like the space—the thing that isn't there—is more important than the walls, which are. If you look at the castle for long enough the walls blur, and it's as if they don't have any point at all, except to keep all the nothingness in.

Chapter Twenty-three

By four o'clock I'm standing outside the house from Burlem's memory: the one he lives in with Lura (or, at least, the one where he lived in December); the one you get to by walking past the cheese shop and turning right and walking up the narrow cobbled street. It's a tallish, thin gray stone cottage with green wooden shutters over the front windows. It looks cozy, but it also has an air of the fortress about it. Maybe that's the effect of the shutters, or just my paranoia. I'm not actually sure I should be here at all, but I'm fairly certain no one's been following me. Well, at least, no one in the physical world. I realize suddenly that I should have gone into a church just in case one of those Project Starlight guys (or the dead KIDS) is in my mind. It's too late now, though. It was probably too late almost from the moment I set off this morning. If they've been with me at any stage, they'll know where I'm going. But if they've been with me at any stage they won't need to know where I'm going: They'll have their recipe.

But I don't think they are here, anyway. I think I'm on my own.

In fact, I know I'm on my own. I don't think I've ever been so alone in my life. I hesitate before lifting the heavy brass door knocker. My eyes are filling with tears, but I don't want to seem unbalanced when, and if, someone opens the door. When did I last cry? I didn't cry after Patrick fucked me at the university, or in the service station toilet; I didn't cry when my parents finally abandoned me for good; I didn't even cry when I left Adam at the priory, probably hating me, probably gone forever. But now, standing here in the early twilight, in the cold air, with seagulls squawking above me, and stars already beginning to prick the sky, I want to cry more than I ever have before. I gulp it back. But if this doesn't work then I'm totally fucked. I have no home. I have no money. I have no family.

I lift the knocker and bang it twice against the door.

Please be there, please be there, please be there.

I see smoke coming from the chimney: Someone is in.

After two minutes or so I'm just about to knock again, but then a woman opens the door. It's Lura. I recognize everything about her, from the flowing clothes to the gray shoulder-length hair streaked with pink. I suddenly realize that I haven't worked out how I should play this. I know what it's like to make love to this woman; to lie to her; to live with her. But I should probably pretend I don't know her at all. As long as I remember I am me, that's perfectly true.

She doesn't say anything.

"Hello," I say. "I wonder if . . ."

"Sorry?" says Lura. "Who are you?" Her voice, which I recognize anyway, is educated and low-pitched, with just a hint of a German accent.

"I'm sorry to bother you, but . . ."

"Yes?" She's trying to hurry me up. Maybe she doesn't like people pissing her around, wasting her time. But I'm not sure she's going to like what I've got to say, either. Although she has to. She has to, because I've got nowhere else to go.

"I'm looking for Saul Burlem," I say.

Lura's face looks as though it's been freeze-framed in one of those movie special effects that lets the rest of the world just carry on as usual around the frozen object. Then she's normal again, except for the fear I can now see in her eyes, like the beginning of a storm.

"You're looking for whom?" she says.

"Saul Burlem," I say. "I need to see him. Would you mind telling him that Ariel Manto is here? Tell him that I found the page and I have to speak to him."

As I speak, the fear in Lura's eyes hurricanes outwards and now she reaches a hand up to her face, as if to steady it: to stop this; to confirm, perhaps, that she's imagining it. This must be the last thing you need when you're in hiding. This, if you're in hiding, must be your worst nightmare.

"Who are you?" she says.

"I'm Saul's Ph.D. student."

"You're . . . *No*. I know where you've come from."

"I'm not with them. I'm not part of Project Starlight."

"How do *I* know that? If you aren't with them then why the bloody hell did you come?" She takes a deep breath and touches her hair. "Saul isn't here, anyway. He moved on, about two months ago. He went . . ."

"Ariel?"

It's Burlem. He's standing behind Lura.

"Saul," I say, "can I . . . ?"

"Let her in, Lura," he says, in his gravel voice. And then, leaning against the wall in the hallway while I walk in: "Oh fuck."

The downstairs of the house is an open-plan space with wooden floorboards and oak beams that you access by walking through a wide hallway and through an arch. A fire is burning at the far end of the large room, and there are red, brown, and dark yellow rugs everywhere. There's a large dining table on the left-hand side of the room. At the moment it has a newspaper spread out on it with a half-finished cup of coffee on a wicker mat. Just beyond the table there's a black-and-white dog asleep in a cane basket, and then, at the edge of the room, what must be a set of patio doors covered with heavy curtains. As if the dog knows I'm looking at it, it glances up at me sleepily and then falls asleep again. There's a mantelpiece over the fireplace with an assortment of items on it: a couple of rosettes, a framed black-and-white photograph of a man and a woman, a hairbrush, a set of knitting needles, and a vase of blue flowers. The closest thing to the fire is an armchair with some knitting balanced on the arm. There are two sofas—big, deep, and yellow—and they face each other across the fire but set slightly back from the armchair. One of them looks more used than the other, and there are books and papers scattered on it. There's a coffee table—a polished section of tree trunk—between the sofas, with books and old crosswords and Biros all over it. There are tall piles of books on every surface, and the whole right-hand wall is covered with thick pine shelves, a bit like the ones from Apollo Smintheus's apartment, but stocked with what must be hundreds and hundreds of books. There's no TV.

I'm not quite sure how I feel to be here. I'd expected something like relief, the emotional equivalent of having come home after a long wet journey, or having a drink when you are thirsty. But I still ache for that kind of safe, fulfilled feeling, the feeling that I've achieved something by coming here. At the moment I feel rather as if I've dropped in on one of my university professors at home, on the weekend, when his wife is there. And worse: I know, and Burlem must suspect, that I read his mind to get here. What felt like a necessity at the time feels somehow wrong now. I didn't really come here for him: I came here for me. Then again, he must understand that I didn't have any other choice. But I know too much about him now, and we're both aware of that.

The kitchen area is around to the left and runs adjacent to the hallway.

"I'll make tea," Lura says, walking off towards the kitchen. I hear water running and then the click of the kettle being switched on.

Burlem motions for me to follow him to the large dining table. He folds the paper and puts it to one side. Then Lura comes and picks up his mug and takes it away. For a whole two or three minutes now no one has said anything.

"I'm sorry . . . ," I begin.

"How did you find me?" Burlem says.

"Through Molly," I say.

"Molly doesn't know where I am," he says. "No one in my bloody family knows where I am. That's what you give up when you go into hiding like this. One of many things."

"Pedesis," I say. "I used Pedesis. I'm sorry. I've got the book."

He closes his eyes for a couple of seconds and then opens them again; then he runs a shaky hand through his dark hair.

"Fuck," he says again.

"I'm sorry . . . ," I say again. There's a long pause. "They came after me and I didn't know what to do. I realized that the same thing must have happened to you, and so I logically thought that if I came to where you were I might be safe."

"The curse," says Burlem.

"Yeah," I say.

And I think we're both remembering his paper in Greenwich, where we both agreed that we'd read the book if we could, regardless of the curse. I know I'd do it again, but I don't know about him. His face looks rougher and more lined than when I last saw him, and he now has several streaks of white-gray in his hair. Or maybe he used to dye it and now he can't be bothered. What must it be like to have to leave your job like that? To leave behind a daughter?

"How is Molly?" he asks.

"She's doing normal teenage things," I say.

"But she's OK?"

I weigh this question in my mind. All right, so Molly's fucking an unsuitable guy, but then we all do that. When I was in her mind I didn't detect any obvious anorexia, self-harm, or drug abuse. But then, of course, she has the potential for all of that: I knew that from the connection I felt with her.

"She's fine," I say.

Burlem sighs. "Are you still smoking?" he asks.

"Yeah, why?"

"Can I have one?"

"Sure." I take my tobacco out of my bag. "Roll-ups," I say. "I'm a bit skint."

"Can you do it for me?" he asks. "I've lost the knack."

And his hands are shaking too, I notice. I roll two cigarettes and give one to him. We both light up.

"Oh, that feels better," he says. "Fucking weird, but better. Why don't we go over by the fire. You'd better tell me what's been going on. Let me know how terrified I should be."

We get up and walk over to the sofas. He takes the messy one and I take the other. It does feel amazing, sitting in a warm, comfortable room after everything that's happened. But somehow I don't feel quite comfortable. I don't sit back in the sofa, although it's soft and vast. I perch on the edge as though I'm having an interview. There aren't any ashtrays, but I notice that Burlem flicks his ash into the fire, so I do the same.

"You shouldn't have come here," he says.

I think I'm going to cry again. "I know . . . But I . . . I had . . ."

"But, well, it's good to see you again." He smiles now for the first time.

"Oh. Thanks, I . . ."

"And I'm sorry about the book." He sighs. "I feel responsible."

"Don't be," I say. "I'm sorry I freaked you out by coming here. But I honestly couldn't think of anything else to do. I mean . . . Just to be in the same room as someone who has had the same experiences as me is . . ."

Burlem cuts me off. "How sure are you that you weren't followed?" he asks.

"A hundred percent," I say. "Or, well, maybe ninety-nine. But they only want the recipe, don't they? They can get that from me now. They wouldn't need to use me to get to you. They'd only need to get into my head. I've got all the information they need. I can promise you that after the last time I met them in the Troposphere—or MindSpace, as they seem to call it—I've got no intention of letting them anywhere near me, my mind, or my body. That's why I ran. That's why I came to find you. I can't go anywhere anymore. I can't go home; I can't go to work . . ."

"That's neat logic," he says. "That stuff about only needing to get into your mind for a few minutes to get the recipe. But they want all of us dead. You do know that?"

"No. I didn't know that. Well, I mean I know they're violent and they'll use force to get the recipe . . . And maybe even for fun. But I thought that once they had the recipe they'd go away."

Burlem coughs and takes a drag on the roll-up. "When they sell the patent for the mixture—or cook it up illegally; I don't know what they've got planned—they won't want people like us coming along and undercutting their price. They'll want to get rid of any competitors. Well, I don't know for sure, but I expect they do want to sell it; that seems logical."

"They do," I say.

"How do you know?"

"I . . ."

Lura comes through the large room carrying a yellow tray with a teapot and mugs on it. Burlem quickly shifts some magazines and newspapers out of the way and she puts it down on the coffee table between two stacks of books. Then she sits down in the armchair and looks at me.

"Are you all right?" she asks me, peering over her silver glasses. "I'm sorry if I was rude at the door. We've been hiding for so long, and . . ."

"It's OK," I say. "I'm fine."

"Ariel knows about Project Starlight," Burlem says to Lura. "She knows what they want."

"Yes, I overheard that," Lura says. "How do you know? I couldn't find out anything about them on the occasions when I tried—well, beyond the very basics."

"I got into one of their minds," I say. "Martin Rose."

Burlem half laughs and half snorts. "How the fuck did you do that?"

"They were waiting for me in their car. I was in a priory and they couldn't come in, obviously, so they were kind of staking me out. I got into the Troposphere from inside the priory and ended up in one of their heads by accident. I didn't even know they were there before that."

"What were you doing in a priory?" Burlem asks.

"Hiding from them. It's a long story," I say.

Burlem pours the tea, spilling at least half a cup onto the tray.

"I think maybe now's the time to tell us all of it, if you don't mind. How you got the book, what happened next, and so on," he says.

"No, that's fine," I say. "But can I stay here, tonight at least? I don't want to impose, but . . ."

"It's all right, Ariel," says Lura, but she doesn't look happy about it.

"Yeah," says Burlem. "You're fucked in the outside world, just like me."

Lura shakes her head. "How long is this going to go on?" she says softly. Then she looks at me. "You're more than welcome to stay as long as you like," she says. "We've got a room for you." Then she looks at Burlem. "But we're going to have to stop this before we wake up and find that there are ten of us, and then twenty, and then that the whole bloody world knows about the Troposphere."

"It's OK," Burlem says. "Ariel won't have told anyone else."

"No. I haven't," I say. But I don't mention that I've left the book—intact again—in the priory. I think that will make more sense as part of my whole story.

I sit back in the sofa and start telling them about the day the university started falling down, and the secondhand bookshop and everything that happened after that. And as I speak I finally realize that I didn't imagine any of this: As much as anything can be said to be real, this is real.

Telling the story takes hours. At first Burlem keeps interrupting to ask me things, but after about half an hour of intense conversation about the university, and then even more speculation about how Burlem's books ended up in the secondhand shop (his ex-wife, he thinks, claiming the house), Lura steps in and forbids any more questions until after I've finished. At some point she gets an A4 notebook and starts writing things down in it. I get the impression that although Burlem has obviously spent more time in the Troposphere, she's the one who possibly understands how it all works. Which means I'm going to have plenty of questions for her, too. She scribbles most furiously (and has to shut Burlem up again, too) when I talk about Apollo Smintheus, and also when I get to the detail about the underground network, and how I travelled on a train of fear to get back to myself before I made the mistake that was surely going to kill me. At the point when I explain that I was able to change things in people's minds, they both seem to freeze and exchange a look, but neither of them says anything to me about it, and Lura doesn't write anything down.

At about eleven o'clock I'm almost done. My throat hurts from all the talking and the cigarettes I've smoked. My mouth feels dry; that hangover mouth you get when you've only had a couple of hours sleep. We've drunk about four pots of tea since I got here, but I haven't actually eaten anything since lunchtime and my stomach is audibly growling, although I don't feel hungry.

"We need to eat," says Lura, after my stomach makes the noise again.

"I'll phone for a curry," says Burlem.

But he waits until I finish my story before he does. The story isn't complete. I've left out the detail about fucking Patrick in the Little Chef toilets, obviously. But I haven't made it clear that the book is in the priory, either. So I'm not surprised when the first question Burlem asks is about the book.

"Where is it now?" he says. "You've got it with you, presumably."

I shake my head. "I did what you did," I say.

"What *I* did?"

"Yeah. I left it behind, thinking it would be safer than carrying it with me."

"Tuck" is all Burlem says before he goes to collect the food.

While he's gone I am left on my own with Lura and the dog, who has now woken up properly, stretched, slurped some water, and then come to sit on the sofa next to me. Lura hasn't said anything at all since Burlem left, and I feel I have to say something.

"What's his name?" I ask.

But I know already: *Planck;* presumably after the quantum physicist.

"He's called Planck," she says. Then she sighs and shakes her head. "You've had some lucky escapes," she says. "I can't believe . . ."

"What?"

"Oh, nothing. There's even more to the Troposphere than I thought. Although it all makes sense, of course."

"Sense?" I laugh. "Please tell me how it makes sense."

"Oh, we will," she says. "But not now. It's late."

There's a silence for a few seconds. I'm not sure Lura likes me. I scratch the dog between his ears and try to think of something simple I can say that doesn't simply amount to "Tell me whatever it is I don't know—that no one knows—about how the world works, now! Tell me what could possibly make sense of the experiences I've had, because I haven't got a clue."

"How did you come to be here?" I ask her in the end. "How did you make it so they couldn't find you?" I remember that when Burlem cut me off by walking into the church, he was still in the railway tunnel. I have no idea how he came to be here, with Lura, and how they remained undetected for so long. "How did Saul even get out of the tunnel?" I ask.

"He shifted the pile of rubble," she says. "Brick by brick. From the sound of what you've said that tunnel was unstable anyway, and I'm surprised it took another year to collapse after he disturbed it."

"Oh—you think he made it collapse, then? How weird," I say, thinking that the tunnel collapsing was the reason for everything starting: that if the tunnel hadn't collapsed then I wouldn't have got the book, or found the page. Or maybe I would; maybe I would have found those things eventually, anyway.

And I realize that someone will find the book in the priory eventually, as well.

"Anyway," she says, "he got out of the tunnel and got on a bus to anywhere. He just travelled randomly until he was far enough away to get his thoughts together. He went up to Scotland and lived in a bed-and-breakfast for a while, during which time he explored the Troposphere—and was very lucky not to get killed. He sent me a mobile phone and asked me to go into a church on a certain date, at a certain time, and said that he would phone me." She smiles. "It was a bit like being in a film. He was completely paranoid and didn't trust me at all at first, and we kept having to have these coded conversations with me standing in a church talking on a mobile phone—which did not go down well with church people at all. But we got through it. I'm retired now, as you probably know, so I wasn't tied to London when all this happened. We came down here temporarily at first and then ended up staying. It's actually my brother's place, but we have an arrangement." She shrugs. "He needed a place in London, and we've sorted out all the paperwork so we are officially renting this place from someone else entirely, under assumed names. It's complicated, but we thought it was quite solid."

"I have to ask," I say. "What is the logic behind the church detail: You know, that no one can jump into your mind if you're in a church?"

"You don't know?"

"I know hardly anything beyond what I've worked out, and what Apollo Smintheus has told me." I shrug. "I can make a guess, but . . ."

"What's your guess?"

"That all the prayer in a church—all the extra-charged thought and hope—somehow scrambles the signal, if that makes any sense. You know, like interference."

She smiles. "That's good. That's exactly what I think as well." Now the smile goes. "I'm assuming you know about my book?"

"No." I shake my head. But the way she says it—I realize that this is why she has a problem with me. She thinks I know her as intimately as Burlem does because I've been in his mind. She thinks there's a possibility that I know everything about her. For the second time I get the feeling that she's the wife and I'm the mistress, and she knows her husband hasn't just been screwing me; he's been telling me things about her as well. I remember when I used to have affairs with married men whose wives didn't know, and wouldn't have approved, and those marriages were always in crisis. Inevitably the guy would tell me things about his wife that I didn't want to know—and didn't feel I had any right to know. The special dinner she arranged to try and get their marriage back on track (and during which he called me on his mobile, from the toilet); the special dress she bought to try and get him interested in her again (and which he told me made her look old and fat). I shudder to remember these exchanges. I don't think I've ever felt so bad in my life as when I heard those things, and I stopped sleeping with men like that because I didn't want to be a party to anything so sad.

I want to say something to make this all right, but I can't think of anything.

"Hm" is all she says in response to my not knowing about her book.

A couple of seconds later the dog's ears prick up, and he acts as though something's about to happen. Then, two or three minutes after that, I hear the sound of Burlem's key in the lock and feel the blast of cold air as the front door opens and closes again.

The dog knew, I think. *The dog knew that Burlem was almost back.*

How does that work?

For the first time since all this happened, I feel my understanding of the world start to shift, as if it's only now—now that I know this is all true—that I can allow myself to start answering all the questions I have: to start adding up all the pieces of information and all my experiences. The dog knows, I realize, because we *all* potentially know everything about what other people are thinking and doing. We all potentially have access to one another's thoughts. I wonder properly where the Troposphere is, and what it is, now that I'm convinced it isn't just a figment of my imagination. Is it hovering less than a particle away from us, perhaps in another dimension to which we have access only some of the time? Or does it work in another way entirely? But I am suddenly sure that the moment when you catch someone's eye, or the moment you think someone's looking at you, or the moment when you think of someone and then they ring, or the moment when you start getting lost in a building you know so well because most other people in it are lost—these aren't accidents. They relate in some way to the structure of the physical world, to the fact that all our minds are as connected as everything else.

I wonder what Lura's book is about? I was lying, of course, when I said I knew nothing about it. It was sitting there in the back of Burlem's mind the whole time I was with him. *Lura's Book. Lura's*

Book. It's important, but she hasn't taken this opportunity to tell me anything about it. I wonder what would make her trust me.

We eat vegetable curry and rice at the table with a bottle of white wine from the fridge. Planck goes back into his basket and falls asleep as we all start questioning one another on the Troposphere, and what my experiences in it could possibly mean.

"I'm intrigued by this god, Apollo Smintheus," Burlem says.

"Yeah," I say. "I thought I was going mad."

"Maybe you were," he says. "I never met any gods in the Troposphere. In fact, I've never met any other beings in the Troposphere. I didn't think it was possible."

We talk about Apollo Smintheus some more and all the questions of religion I was thinking about earlier today. It seems that neither Burlem nor Lura has thought about the Troposphere in a religious context, apart from noting the detail about the interference caused by churches. Lura seems vaguely—but only vaguely—impressed by my feminist analysis of all major religions, but Burlem seems uncertain about me lumping Buddhism in with everything else.

"Zen," he says gruffly. "Zen's different. And the Tao."

And I remember his desire for the void, tempered by his need to lose desire altogether. And that makes me think of Adam and what happened to him. I hardly know Adam, but I miss him more than I thought possible.

"We've all got our own ways of aiming for enlightenment," Lura says. "I'm writing the book, but he's meditating all the time, trying to see outside everything we already know. There's still so much . . ." But she doesn't finish the sentence. Instead, she yawns. "Oh. What a day."

Our conversation has meandered around so much. We've discussed Pedesis, and the possibility of time travel using people's ancestors, and Burlem has confirmed that the milky images you get in the console when you're in someone else's mind relate to all their living ancestors: That's why the mice had hundreds and he only had one (his mother). The way you can most effectively go back in time is to use living ancestors until they run out (presumably, for example, Burlem's mother has none, so, if you got to her, you'd have to jump into another person rather than pick another image from the console, and then go back as far as possible using that person's ancestors). We discussed this point for some time, as I couldn't quite see how you'd ever get beyond people who are living now. But then Lura reminded me that distance is time in the Troposphere, and that by jumping across the world using ancestors, you also go back in time, sometimes by years rather than months. When I jumped from Molly to Burlem, I was jumping from Hertfordshire to Devon, and that's what got me back to before Christmas. If Burlem had been in Scotland, I may have ended up in August or September; if he'd been in Australia, I may have gone back three or four years. If you're lucky (or if your journey is well planned), you'll eventually find living ancestors who were dead when your journey started, and each time you jump, you'll go farther back in time. It sounded like a slow process, but Burlem reminded me that the jumps themselves are very quick. He also pointed out that this is obviously what Mr. Y was doing when he died. Mr. Y is a fictional character, but Lumas isn't. Burlem made it clear that this was also how Lumas must have died, and everyone else who was "cursed" by the book. Pedesis is dangerous, just as I discovered when I did it to get to Burlem.

I've also learned that Burlem's Troposphere is indeed the Victorian city he was thinking about when I was in his mind. Lura gets a little cagey when we start comparing our personal Tropospheres. When I ask her how she experienced it, she tucks her hair behind her ear and says, simply, "Oh, a scientific matrix kind of thing. Not something anyone else could visualize, really." And then she gives Burlem a meaningful look.

"We'd better all go to bed soon," he says. "We can pick this up in the morning. There's still so much to talk about. And Lura, why don't you make use of Ariel. She may be able to help you in some way. She's better with science than I am."

"I'm really not," I say.

And Lura looks at me for a second as though she's sizing me up, and then her eyes drop as I clearly fail. Whatever Burlem thinks, we're not just going to settle down together cozily to work out a theory of the Troposphere, or whatever. Not unless I can convince her to stop disliking me.

All night I dream of Adam. In my dream he's telling me that he loves me; that he will never leave me. Dreams are so cruel sometimes. I'm never going to have that life. In fact, these shreds of life that I'm left with—I'm not sure they add up to anything very much.

Chapter Twenty-four

Saturday and Sunday pass by in the same sort of way, with haphazard discussions and my growing sense that there's a lot I don't know, and that Burlem and Lura are trying to work out when to tell me something. We punctuate each day with tea, coffee, and sandwiches, as if our lives are just one long conference. Each evening we all go into the church across the street before having our last cup of tea before bed. I get the impression that Burlem and Lura discuss me when I'm not there, and that Burlem's still trying to persuade her to trust me. They are obviously still jumpy about me being here and pretty much put me under house arrest, apart from the visits to the church. Burlem tries to explain to me about his meditation and Lura mainly avoids me. In the evenings I sit up with Burlem and try not to flirt with him. I'm not sure what is going on with the two of them, but I don't want to get in the middle of it. Every so often the phone goes, but Lura always lets the machine get it. I have the impression that they have a friend whom they've only recently fallen out with, but I don't get any more details than that.

My room is small, white, and cozy, with exposed beams and a short, fat, four-poster bed with a pink blanket over a white cotton duvet. I spend most of my time sitting on the bed, writing notes about the Troposphere. I mainly do this to keep my mind off my desperate need to go back there. But Burlem and Lura have forbidden me from going back in, at least for now. They're worried about this mission that Apollo Smintheus has in mind for me, as am I. And it's so clear that getting lost in it is a danger, although I'm sure that I can now get back anytime I want using the underground system. But Lura and Burlem seem unconvinced by this system, even though it must definitely exist. I wish they'd just tell me things directly instead of whispering in the kitchen and then stopping when I go in to make coffee. I know they want to get the book back from Faversham, but I don't know how we could ever do that.

And I'm not sure exactly how I feel about everything. I'm warm, comfortable, and well fed for the first time in ages, but in another sense my life is over. Not over, maybe, that's a bit dramatic, but every-thing I thought I "had"—my job, my Ph.D., my few friends, my flat, my possessions, my books—I'm pretty sure they're all gone now. And unless Lura changes her mind about me, I'm not going to be able to stay here forever.

On Sunday night I am having the same dream I have had since I got here, in which Apollo Smintheus is standing in front of me saying, "You owe me." I am awoken by the rain pounding the skylight like an industrial machine, and the clock says that it's four A.M. On Monday the sky is drum-metal gray and the morning is broken up with sudden pulses of strip-light yellow lightning. At about midday there's one crack of thunder, and then it stops raining. Burlem has the radio on for a while, and it warns of some huge storm coming, with winds of eighty miles per hour. But the storm doesn't come.

On Tuesday morning the sky is as blue and sharp as a reflection in metal. I'm thinking, *Is this the calm? The eye?* Lura decides to do some gardening and I just sit there smoking at the dining table while she locates her gardening gloves and goes outside without saying any-thing to me. Through the window I can see what looks like a falcon perching on one of the telegraph posts behind the house. I wonder if Lura's seen it. It's so beautiful; it's more like something from a book than from real life. It's more like a picture or a word than a thing. And I wonder: Does language distance us from things so much that we can't believe in them anymore? Or is it just because I've been in the Troposphere so much that I'm in the habit of looking at things like that, like the falcon, and assuming that I invented it, and that it's a metaphor for something else? I put out my cigarette. Maybe I should go and try to make peace with Lura. I haven't had any fresh air for days.

She's on her knees by one of the flower beds, turning the soil.

"Hello," I say, walking towards her. "Can I help?"

"No, it's all right," she says without looking up.

I should just go away, but I persist. "Please," I say. "Let me help for a bit?"

She sighs. "Trowels are in the shed."

I get a trowel and a piece of tarpaulin similar to the one Lura's using to kneel on. I walk over and place my tarpaulin next to hers, and start copying what she's doing. We stay like that for five minutes or so before I realize I'm going to have to start any conversation I want to have.

"I'm sorry for turning up the way I did," I say.

"Hm," she says back. The same short closing-down sound she always makes.

"And . . . Look. I've been wanting to say this for a few days. I really am sorry that I went into Burlem's head to get here. I do know things about you that you probably don't want me to know and I'm so sorry I've intruded." I take a deep breath. "It's one of those problems with the Troposphere that you don't think about until it's too late and you've already done it. I mean, all my experiences in there so far have really been experimental." I think again; that's not quite true and she knows it. I have to be honest if I want to connect with her at all. "OK, I guess the one time I did use it in a deliberate way was when I wanted to find Saul . . ."

"Why do you call him 'Burlem' sometimes?" she asks me, still turning the earth.

"Er, I just do," I say. "I think I picked it up at the university. A lot of people there call him 'Burlem' rather than Saul."

"Surely they call him 'Professor Burlem,'" she says, frowning.

"Not the other members of staff." I shrug. "Does it bother you?"

"Yes. But I don't know why."

"I'll stop doing it. I really am sorry, you know."

We both carry on turning the earth. I find an earthworm, which I carefully pick up and move somewhere safer. Lura watches me do this, but I have no idea what she's thinking.

"What did you find out about me when you were in Saul's head?"

"Hardly anything," I say. "I know you slept together in Germany—that's the only intimate detail I do know. There were obviously a lot more details about the two of you, but remember I was just trying to find out where he was, not how he felt about anything, so I followed one set of memories rather than another."

"Hm."

"I really am sorry. Look, you're welcome to go into my head if you want, anytime you want. I've got some pretty sordid stuff in there, including some details I left out of my 'story so far' I told you the other night."

"It's OK. But thanks," she says, and goes back to turning over the reddish earth with her trowel. What I've said seems to have made no difference at all.

But then she smiles.

"I always like to garden when I've got something to turn over in my mind," she says. "It's repetitive and relaxing, don't you think?"

My God. Has she actually just started a conversation with me?

"Yes," I say. "It is, actually."

"Saul has to do everything in a 'Zen' way, at the moment. So he puts his whole being into turning the earth, if that's what he's doing. Not that he ever does the garden. But sometimes when he paints a fence, or wires a plug, you can see him doing it: giving up himself to the activity and not using it as an excuse just to think about something else."

I wonder what she's turning over in her mind. Probably how she's going to ask me to leave. I don't quite know what to say next. But I don't want the conversation to end, either. For the first time since I've been here I don't feel as though Lura despises me.

"Oh, there was another answerphone message earlier," I say.

"Ah. The writer. Again."

"The writer?"

"Yes. This is the problem I'm turning over in my mind." She sighs, and there's a long pause. "Saul tells me you know a lot about thought experiments."

"Yes," I say. "I am—or maybe I should say 'was'—doing my Ph.D. on thought experiments."

"Hm. Would you say that a story can be a thought experiment?"

"Oh yes," I say immediately. "I'd say all thought experiments are stories."

"That's interesting. Why?"

"Well, because all thought experiments take the form of a narrative. Well, the ones I understand do." I realize I'm talking to a real scientist and suddenly see I need a disclaimer. "I'm sure you can tell me about thought experiments that aren't stories. But . . ."

She's frowning. "No. I like the idea of thought experiments being stories. I suppose if they're not stories then they're actually hard science and not thought experiments at all. Einstein's trains . . . Schrödinger's cat. Hmm."

"Yeah—they're two that I'm studying quite closely."

"Well, we'll have to talk properly about them at some point. But, for now, you agree that a thought experiment could be a story?"

"Yes, definitely. Why?"

"How about if I ran a thought experiment by you? It's concerned with the Troposphere, and although it does exist as a story—with characters and so on—I haven't actually seen the story, so I'll just tell it as a kind of story but with no characters, if that makes any sense."

It doesn't really, but I nod. "Go on. I'm intrigued."

"What have you already worked out about the Troposphere?" she says. "And I mean the very basics."

"Um," I say. "It's a place made of language."

"More specifically?"

"Well, thought," I say. "And it's made in metaphor and . . ."

"Thought," she repeats. "Excellent. Yes. It's a place made out of thought. So we might want to pose the question: *What is thought? Would you agree?"*

"Yes."

"And our experience of the Troposphere shows us that thoughts aren't just invisible, imaginary nothings. They are inscribed as soon as they happen, and in that sense they become entities. Would you agree with that?"

"Yes. I'd agree with that."

We're still turning the earth, although this bit is really done now.

"Right. So we want to consider this idea that thoughts have substance."

I remember something from Apollo Smintheus's first document.

"'Thought is matter, perhaps,'" I say.

"Yes! Exactly. But it's hard to visualize how thoughts are matter exactly."

"Yes. I must admit that I haven't been able to see it."

Although the sky is still completely blue, a couple of raindrops fall on my face. I look up to see where they're coming from, but there aren't any clouds.

Lura smiles at me. "All right," she says. "Here's the story. The thought experiment. What would you think of the following scenario? Imagine a computer, with a vast hard drive memory. There's a program running on the computer—maybe a little like a game, with characters and locations. Now, the little characters in this program are written in binary code. Say they're part of a simulation game. You must have seen the type of thing I mean, where you create, say, a little town for them to live in and then the software generates effects like rain and droughts and wars?"

"Yeah. I know the kind of thing you mean," I say.

"All right, well, this next bit takes a leap of faith. What do you know about artificial intelligence?"

"I know that Samuel Butler was concerned that machines could become conscious as easily as humans did," I say. "That machine consciousness is as inevitable as human consciousness."

"This is interesting. Go on."

"He argued that consciousness is just another part of evolution. It's a random mutation that could happen to anything. And after all, machines are made out of the same stuff we're made out of . . . And we feed machines all the time. We feed them fuel, and language . . ."

"Yes!" She taps the soil with her trowel. "Good. But don't jump ahead."

Since I don't know where this is going I'm not sure how I can stop myself jumping ahead by accident. But I turn over some more earth and just say, "OK, sorry. Go on."

"Imagine that some mutation happens in our computer simulation. The little characters become conscious. Now. What would their thoughts be made of?"

I visualize my laptop sitting on a desk, with this game playing out on it. I imagine what it would be like to be one of these digital, binary characters. How many dimensions would you be aware of? How would you interact with other characters? I think about what this world is made of—basically zeroes and ones—and then I realize that in this little world everything would be zeroes and ones. The little characters may not be able to see them, but everything, including their thought, would be made from the same thing.

"Their thoughts would be made from the same code their world is made from," I say to Lura. "Zeroes and ones."

"Yes, very good. Yes—if it was a contemporary silicon machine, which would obviously be coded in binary."

"So it would be up quarks and down quarks, if it was a quantum computer."

Now she smiles. "You do know something about science," she says. "Except you're not quite right. Up and down quarks are still a binary system. The whole point of quantum computing is that the quarks can be in a combination of different states, and can therefore carry out more than one calculation at once."

But I'm already feeling sick, because I think I know where this is going.

"Now tell me," she says. "The grass and trees in our binary world. What are they made from?"

"Zeroes and ones," I say.

"And the houses, and the water and the air?"

"Zeroes and ones."

"And what happens to thought in this world once it has happened? Does it disappear?"

"It gets stored on the hard drive." I pause, thinking about temporary caches and the difference between RAM and ROM. "Does it?"

"Yes. It's information rendered in zeroes and ones just like everything else in this world. So would you agree that the hard drive is expanding at the rate that these beings think?"

I think about this. I've stopped using the trowel, so I put it down and sit back on the tarpaulin. Another couple of raindrops fall from nowhere: the same invisible cloud in the sky.

"Yes?" I say. "I'm not sure about this one. It sounds like it's potentially a trick question."

"Yes. It is. The hard drive itself doesn't expand, or change, or gain mass, or anything like that. But the information on it changes. It gets written on all the time. If you thought the hard drive was just empty space to be written on, you'd think it was expanding. But if you realized that it was just information being coded so it made sense—but not more or less information altogether—then you wouldn't think it was expanding. You might argue that there is no empty space in this scenario."

"OK."

"So. What do you think so far?"

"I think I feel a bit sick."

"OK. But why?"

"Because what you say makes perfect sense. The Troposphere is like a hard drive that we wouldn't normally have access to although in theory we could, as it's on the same machine . . . And. Oh shit. We're living in a computer simulation. Is that what you're saying?"

"Ah," she says. "Good. That's interesting. No. I don't believe we are living in a computer simulation. The computer is a metaphor."

"A metaphor for?"

"That's what I want you to think about for a while," she says.

"You've already helped me with my conundrum about the writer. But now I want you to think about something else. In this computer simulation, if thought and matter are made of the same thing, then how is matter made?"

The rain starts coming down more heavily now, even though there are still no clouds. Lura gets up.

"Maybe it's this famous storm," she says. "Let's go in."

Once we're inside Lura goes off towards her study.

"Think about it," she says to me again.

So I do. I sit on my bed and I think it all through. I spend all day doing it: playing the thought experiment to the end with a little more detail each time. If thought and matter are the same thing, then how is matter made? I think about matter, and what it is—just quarks and electrons—and I wonder how quarks and electrons are really different from zeroes and ones. In both of these possible worlds they "make matter" in the same way. Or, at least, they *are* matter: The rest is just shape and perception. Or perhaps shape and perception are the same thing. The universe, just like the computer world, comprises the same amount of matter. Quarks and electrons can be combined to form anything you like in the physical world: a seed, a tree, carbon. And then things rot and get made again, out of the same stuff.

In the computer world you could make something from zeroes and ones—a pornographic picture, for example—and then you could overwrite it with something else entirely if you had the right software that let you fiddle around with the memory on the level of zeroes and ones. You could make it look as though the image had never been there: that it was unwritten space all along, or a document about a tree. But you might leave a trace; fossils, for instance, are traces. Quarks and electrons frozen in time, refusing to be broken down and made into something else.

So, how is matter made?

Later, over a dinner of mushrooms on toast, the discussion starts again.

"I told Ariel about my book," Lura says to Burlem. "Or at least that thought experiment about the computer."

"That's the only bit I really understand," he says. Then, to me: "The rest is mostly maths."

"I haven't answered your question yet," I say to Lura. " 'How is matter made?' "

Burlem laughs. "That's a nice conundrum to set someone for a rainy afternoon."

The sky has been darkening all day, and by three o'clock I wasn't sure what was happening outside: whether it was night, or the storm. At about five o'clock I was making a coffee and I saw Burlem trying to entice Planck out of the door. But all the dog would do was reverse back into the house. It was the quickest way to get out of the rain, but it looked faintly comical.

"I didn't expect you to," Lura says, with a friendly smile.

"But I get that quarks and electrons are just like zeroes and ones," I say. "And it seems obvious to me now that thought is matter . . ." Except I have a bit of a problem with this. If thought is matter, then everything is real. But I thought that nothing was real. Derrida's différance; Baudrillard's simulacra. If thought is matter, then *everything* becomes real. But if you turn the equation around—if matter is actually thought—then nothing is real. Can both of these ideas be true at the same time? Can this equation work in the same way as 'energy equals mass'?"

"Although thought doesn't make *more* matter," Lura says, "neither thought nor matter can come from nowhere."

"No. I can see that, I think. But thought kind of . . . shapes . . ."

"*Encodes,*" Lura says. "Thought encodes matter."

"Which means what?" I take a sip of red wine and my hand trembles.

"When you think, you potentially change things."

I think about this, and everything she's said. I imagine the little binary people in their world where all the stuff they see around them, and all their thoughts, are made of the same thing. Presumably in this world you could create things just by thinking them. There'd be no difference between a thought of rain and rain itself. But surely that doesn't follow in this world.

"Are you saying that if I think a tree, I can make a tree?" I say to Lura, unconvinced.

"Not in this world," she says.

"But in the computer world? In the thought experiment?"

"Sort of," she says. She looks at Burlem. "She has a very good knack for simplification," she says.

"Not a skill you really need in an English department," he says. "But yes."

"Why 'sort of'?" I ask Lura. "Why can I only *sort of* make a tree by thinking it if I'm one of these beings?"

"Because it depends on what sort of code you're thinking in," she says. "Whether you can think in machine code or just within the software program."

"I'm having trouble with this," I say, frowning.

I can barely taste my food. I'm so aware that this is reality we're talking about: This is the room I'm in, and the chair I'm sitting on, and my mind and my dreams and everything that makes me exist. I have the bizarre sensation that if I get any of these questions wrong, things will start melting around me: that the existence of everything depends on this.

And then I think, *Don't be stupid: It's just a theory.*

But I've seen the evidence for it. I've been in the Troposphere.

But the Troposphere could mean anything, surely?

"Trouble?" Burlem says, laughing. "Oh, join the club."

"I mean, it's as though the whole world is turning, I don't know . . ."

"Upside down?" Lura says.

"Yeah. But in more dimensions than just four. I can't . . ." What do I want to say? I'm not sure. "So what is machine code?" I ask. "And why can't I think trees?"

She takes a sip of wine. "My whole book is about what this 'machine code' possibly is. I'm not sure myself yet. I've got my hypothesis that it exists, but I'm still looking for the mathematics that completely explains it . . . I think I'm probably seventy-five percent there." She puts her wine down. "You know, of course, that in the real world you can't make something just by thinking it. You can't create a ten-pound note when you're poor, or a sandwich when you're hungry. The mind just can't do that."

"It's a shame," Burlem says.

"But we also know—or we've agreed for the time being—that thought *is* matter. Thought is encoded; thought never goes away. Everyone's thoughts exist in another dimension, which we are experiencing as the Troposphere."

"Yes," I say, putting my fork down.

"We know thought is matter because it is happening in a closed system, in which *everything* is made from matter. Just like in the computer program in our thought experiment. There's nothing in there that isn't written in code, because, well, you just can't have something on a computer that isn't written in code. Anything outside the system by definition couldn't exist within it."

I imagine my laptop again, and the little binary beings in their little world. I'm outside of their program—their world—as is the plastic case that holds the screen and the hard drive, and the computer screen itself, and the desk the laptop sits on, and the whole of this world. And the beings would never, ever be aware of those things. Even if we did decide to tell them about it—we'd have to put it into their world using their code. And then, somehow, it would be part of their world.

"But we also know that thought doesn't create more matter," Lura says.

"I can see that," I say. "The computer beings couldn't just will more RAM into existence, for example."

"Good," Lura says. "But the matter that is there can be manipulated."

Where have I heard the term "spoon-bending" recently? This is what comes into my mind, but I don't say anything. I'm not even sure spoon-bending really happens, and there don't seem to be any examples of people thinking of a goldfish, for example, and making one appear. Magicians who seem to turn silk scarves into doves don't really do it: It's just an illusion.

"I'm not sure I can see how matter is manipulated," I say. "I mean, well, maybe I can just about see how it *can* be . . ." And then my brain cartwheels around and I think I can see it all. "Hang on," I say. "Do we just see what the majority of people see? Like, I could think a tree and it wouldn't be there, but if lots of us thought a tree, that would be enough?"

"That's intriguing," says Burlem. "That's what we thought of last, before Lura started working on the book properly. But the world is not a projection of the Troposphere."

"Yes—that's very good," Lura says. "But I think it's got more to do with this idea of the machine code. Machine code is the code that makes the machine run, rather than the software. The machine code tells the software what to do. The machine code sets the rules for everything in the system: how the trees are invented in this computer-program world, for example."

"OK," I say.

Now, on my little image of my laptop I can imagine two layers of code: the stuff that makes the program and the stuff that makes the machine work. I can see that the two would be closely related, but that one—the machine code—is operating on a deeper level than the other.

"So in our world, what is written in machine code?" Lura asks me.

"Um," I think quickly. What tells our world how to work? Do we even know? "The laws of physics?"

"Yes. Excellent. And?"

"And . . . ?"

"This is impressive," says Burlem. "It took me longer than this."

I think for a few minutes. While I'm thinking, Burlem finishes eating and tops up everyone's wine; then he clears the plates away and stacks them in the dishwasher.

"What about philosophy?" Lura prompts me. "Metaphysics?"

I nod slowly. "OK. So . . . What are you saying? That some people think in this machine code?"

"Possibly," she says. "Who do you imagine would think in machine code?"

"You mean as opposed to the more 'ordinary world' kind of code?"

"Yes."

"So the code of the ordinary world is basically language, and machine code is the thoughts of . . . um . . . scientists? Philosophers?"

"Yes. Now think of a historical figure. Someone who would be capable of this."

I sip my wine. "Einstein?"

"Good answer. But now I've got the hardest question of all. When Einstein came up with his relativity theories, was he just describing the world as it was already or . . ." She raises her eyebrows and leaves a space for me to finish her sentence.

"*Making it work like that,*" I say. "God."

"Do you see it?" Lura asks.

"I think so. You're saying that Einstein came up with relativity theory as an explanation for the world, but what he was actually doing was constructing it? So when he said that nothing could go faster than the speed of light, he wasn't observing nature's speed limit but actually *setting* it."

"Yes."

I roll up a cigarette for Burlem and then one for myself. I do it almost in slow motion, my brain using 99 percent of its processing power to think over what Lura is saying, and most of the remaining 1 percent just keeping me alive while I do that. There's very little left for self-destruction. But still, I manage to light my cigarette, and Burlem lights his.

"Have you ever thought just how fucked-up twentieth-century physics is?" he asks me.

"Yeah. Obviously. You know that's one of my interests."

"It's odd, don't you think," Lura says, "that Einstein found exactly what he was looking for, even though it shouldn't have made sense. It was a brilliant theory, of course, but so outlandish compared with Newtonian physics. Then Eddington went off to look at the eclipse and

Einstein's predictions were proven. They keep being proven. You can't build a GPS system now without taking relativity theory into account. And even the cosmological constant, which Einstein rejected and said was his biggest mistake—even that refuses to go away completely. And then there's quantum physics . . ."

"Which Einstein didn't like," I say.

"Hmm. Yes. Well, what's the one main thing we know about quantum physics?"

"It's absolutely crazy?"

"Yes." She laughs. "And?"

"Um . . ."

"It's the study of things you shouldn't be able to see," she says. "It's the study of things no one has ever looked at, or thought about very much. And what happened?"

"They found that everything's messed up and uncertain," I say.

"*Uncertain.* That's the key word," she says.

I frown. "How do you mean?"

"No one had ever said what this tiny stuff should be doing," Burlem says. "So when they looked at it, they found it was doing whatever the fuck it liked."

"Oh you do paraphrase in an awkward way," Lura says. "Matter doesn't 'do what it likes.' Quantum matter just had no laws. No one had decided whether or not light was waves or particles. And then people were surprised when they found that it was both at once."

"But didn't Newton's laws apply to everything?" I say. "I mean, once they were invented."

"Ah," says Lura. Then she doesn't say anything else.

"Sorry?" I say.

"This is where it gets complicated."

"In what way?"

"Well, I'll tell you in a minute over coffee. But for a moment, think about this. There is a possibility that the quantum level is fundamental: that when you look at subatomic particles you are actually looking at the most basic parts of the physical—and mental—world. I suppose you might call them the basic building blocks. And in terms of my theory, perhaps it's not a surprise to find that on that level the electron is everywhere at once until you decide where it is—and therefore what it is. It fits the theory. Matter has to be coded before it can mean anything. And thought is what encodes matter. Thought decides where the electron is."

We move onto the sofas with a *cafetière* full of coffee. Lura knits as she speaks: pale green cashmere turning from something that looks like string into something that looks like the sleeve of a cardigan as the gray needles click-click-click in her lap. She explains to me the way in which she believes the laws of the physical world are constructed. She says that there was never any a priori existence: no sense that matter was anything or obeyed any laws until there was consciousness to perceive it. But, because consciousness is also made from the same matter, the two areas that we always think are distinct—the human mind, and the world of things—started working together to create, refine, and mold each other. Conscious beings started looking at things and deciding what things were and how they worked. Thus, the first fish didn't just chance upon the weed it needed to survive: It created it. And no one "found" fire by a lucky accident. Someone just had to think fire and, as long as the thought was in this "machine" code, there it was. And, for a while, things worked exactly the way everyone assumed they did. And there were no competing laws, so everything was simple. Earth *did* revolve around the sun, and magic *did* exist. But then other people came along—also people able to think in this machine code—and decided that the world worked differently. The sun became the center of something called a "solar system" and the stars stopped being the burn holes of the saints. Magic gradually faded.

We talk about chaos theory, and how butterflies suddenly acquired the power to cause hurricanes; and we talk about evolution. Lura explains her theory—part of her whole project—that once someone has thought something into being via this machine code, that theory has to survive. Some do and some don't. Newton's theory had some small glitches that were worked out in Einstein's theory. Einstein's theory was a mutation, but it was stronger. It survived.

"So knowledge or, at least, its *effects* are democratic?" I ask.

"Yes, but not in the way you might think from what I've just said."

"What do you mean?"

"Well, it's not belief that keeps things in the physical world—the Enlightenment took care of that. You can see only what can be proved. Everything else just haunts the Troposphere. This mouse god of yours must be one of many. I've been thinking about this since you got here and told us about what you'd seen. Everything's recorded in the Troposphere, of course, and if enough people believe in one thing, then the energy seems to come alive. I think that there are conscious beings in the Troposphere made out of this energy. Ghosts, gods . . . And they have omniscience because we've given them that power. But they can't act in the way we can. They are not agents. Omniscience implies infinite knowledge—but not necessarily the possibility for any action. That's why, when Apollo Smintheus's cult prays to him, he has to get you to do his task for him. You see, you just can't have gods in the physical world. In the physical world you have to be able to prove things exist."

"But if Apollo Smintheus was standing right here, we'd have proved that he existed," I say.

"No. Think about it," Burlem says. "All you could prove is that you could see him. Even if you took a photograph, people would say it was a forgery."

"Whoops," I say, smiling. "I forgot all about phenomenology there and almost became an empiricist."

Burlem smiles back. "Indeed."

"And the question isn't whether or not Apollo Smintheus exists, but what existence is."

"Exactly, and, for now, Apollo Smintheus isn't consistent with the laws of physics, so he's consigned to the Troposphere. He can't exist in the physical world because he wouldn't make sense here."

"Which probably isn't a bad thing," Lura says.

"But didn't Einstein's theories go against Newtonian physics?" I say. "I mean, they were probably more against the laws of physics than Apollo Smintheus."

"Yes, but he thought them in machine code," she says. "Or, to put it another way, in *mathematics*. Einstein was able to think relativity into existence because he could think it into the very fabric of the universe. And of course his theories were plausible. They went with what had come before, even if they seemed counterintuitive."

I make a little gasping noise. "*Mathematics*. Of course." That's what machine code is made from. That's what makes the laws of physics.

"Yes."

"And that's what *you* see when you go into the Troposphere, isn't it?" I say.

Lura doesn't catch my eye. "Yes," she says.

But my mind is racing on.

"So what if someone who could think in this code thought about God?" I say. "I mean, didn't Einstein even say that he was trying to read the mind of God? He believed in God—so how come that didn't make God a physical being?"

"Because you can't create your own creator," Lura says simply.

"You can't create anything outside the system," Burlem says.

"But . . . So how come God exists in the Troposphere? I'm still not sure I get that. I can see how an entity like Apollo Smintheus would end up there. But God with a capital 'G': He's supposed to be the creator—just like you said."

"God has other functions," Lura says. "As you pointed out the other day, God is simply a collection of people's thoughts about how we should live and what the world means. I expect that if you met God in the Troposphere he wouldn't claim to have created the whole thing. You have to sit outside something to create it. And we just don't know what's outside."

I think about Jim Lahiri's book again, and the argument I got so excited about when I was talking to Adam and Heather. I can't help thinking about those questions about the beginnings of everything. Is there a multiverse? Or is God sitting beyond the laptop; the entity that switched the whole thing on?

"What about time?" I say.

"What about it?" says Lura.

"Well, no one thinks that relativity only existed from 1905, or whenever it was. People think that there was *always* relativity, but no one noticed it before."

"What do you think?" says Lura.

"I'm not sure," I say. "But there does seem to be the possibility that these theories have backwards effects . . . Or am I going nuts?"

"No. That's very sophisticated," says Lura. "You could give that some more thought. Of course, the other possibility is that the way the world works is always changing." She doesn't say anything else for a minute or so, and when I look at her lined face, it seems tired.

"Who's the writer you were talking about before?" I ask. "The one who keeps leaving all the messages."

"Ah," says Burlem.

"Oh," says Lura. "She's interested in my theories and she's condensed some of them into a short story. She's having it published in *Nature* magazine, but I wasn't sure I wanted her to. She offered to put my name on the piece, but I'm not sure I want to put my name to all of this just yet. And as for my book . . ."

Lura's eyes drift away from mine and settle somewhere on the table.

"What's your book called?" I ask her.

"*Poststructuralist Physics,*" she says. Now the click-click-click noise stops. She sighs and puts her knitting in her lap. "It will never be published, of course," she says.

"Why not?" I say.

"Because there's no evidence for anything I've said tonight. There is no such thing as poststructuralist physics."

She shrugs: a small, almost imperceptible movement.

"What about the Troposphere?" I say.

"The Troposphere is going to be gone," Burlem says.

"Gone? But . . . How?"

"You're going to destroy it," he says.

Chapter Twenty-five

I'm sitting on my bed with my thoughts flapping in my mind like chaotic butterflies.

Oh fuck.

Now I understand why Apollo Smintheus took a special interest in me.

So I can change things in people's minds—just like the KIDS can. I can make people like Martin Rose want to go to the toilet so badly that he leaves his stakeout. And I made Wolf refuse to tell Adam where the book was when the Project Starlight men were surely in Adam's mind, listening in. But I thought everyone could do that. I didn't think there was anything special about me. Now it turns out that there is. Lura also thinks I could probably think in machine code; that I have that potential. And that's why Apollo Smintheus wants me to seek out Abbie Lathrop and, through her, to change history. So now Burlem and Lura want me to go even farther back and convince Lumas not to write the book at all. They say I can have as long as I want to plan my journey—after all, once the book is gone then the knowledge is gone. The Project Starlight men will never find the book in the priory because the book will not be there anymore. There won't be any Project Starlight. But I am bothered by paradoxes again: They are pinning me down by my wings. If I had already done this and been successful, then I wouldn't need to go. And I don't have all the time in the world, really.

Martin and Ed could come here tomorrow and blow my brains out. The fact that they're here, in this world, and they want to do this—surely that implies that I have already been unsuccessful.

Except . . . I'm not sure that time works in exactly the way we all think.

But maybe I'd better not think about that too much . . . I'm actually a bit scared of thinking anything, now I know what my thoughts potentially are.

So I wanted knowledge, and I got it. But did I ever want this kind of knowledge? Did I ever want to know that there is no God: that we *are* God? That there's not necessarily a creator or a reason? We *make* reason and only dream of creators: That's all we can do. But I knew this all along, right? Maybe. But how awful this is: How awful to be proved right; for someone to demonstrate to you that yes, there's no Daddy up there who's going to approve of you because you got the puzzle right. No supreme being is going to clap and give you a special place in heaven because you understood some of Heidegger. God might be up there in the Troposphere, but the Troposphere is simply our thought. And there really is nothing outside of that. Our thoughts spin quarks up and down and smear electrons into whatever we want them to be.

Newtonian cause and effect suggested that someone wound the original clock and set it ticking and that every single action in the universe could be predicted—if you had something powerful enough on which to do the prediction. There's no free will in that world: a world where everything can potentially be known. In that world I'll get up in the morning and do what I have been programmed to do: as though all my actions are just computer-game dominoes, triggered by other computer-game dominoes. It's what happens when you try to combine God with science. It's narrative, pure and simple. There's a beginning, a middle, and an end. And the middle is only there because the beginning is; the end is only there because the middle is. And in the beginning was the word, and the word was with God, and the word was God.

Take away that cause-and-effect narrative and you have the quantum world, disturbing enough in its own way, with all the possibilities of multiple universes and infinite probability. But if you don't take it too seriously, and if you factor in evolution and economics and everything else that's taken for granted in our world, then you have at least the illusion of free will. You can decide to become rich. You can grow up to be president. Improbable, but possible.

But in this new world of poststructuralist physics I have so much free will that nothing means anything anymore.

But you believed that before, Ariel. You've read Heidegger, Derrida. You got a thrill out of it all: no absolutes. It's what you believed. Everything depends on everything else.

But I didn't want it to be true. Or, I wanted it to be true for the closed system of language in which nothing is ever absolutely true, anyway. I wanted uncertainty. But I didn't want the world to be made only of language and nothing else.

Maybe that's why Burlem's heading for the void.

And that's where I'd be going, too, if I didn't have to go into the Troposphere again, with a real possibility that I'll never come back. But I suppose that Burlem and Lura's reasoning is clear enough. If I'm going back to change Abbie Lathrop's mind for Apollo Smintheus, why not just keep going and change Lumas's mind for the human race? And of course what they said made sense. The Troposphere shouldn't be there. If enough people knew about the Troposphere, we'd have the worst possible scenario: no God—and no free will, either. People would simply be able to control other people's minds. Those with power could simply manipulate the rest of us to think what they want us to think. Any "bad" or "revolutionary" thoughts could be erased.

Yeah: like I'm going to erase the thoughts of Abbie Lathrop and Thomas E. Lumas.

Later that night, I can hardly sleep. And when I do drop off I just find I'm dreaming of Apollo Smintheus again. Most of the dream is the same as the one from the other night, with him saying, "You owe me," over and over again. But the other half of the dream is about everything he said about time travel and paradoxes. I'm asking him, "But how can I go back in time and change a world that is not already now changed by what I did?"

And he's saying, "You already have."

I get about an hour's sleep in the end.

When I get up in the morning the rain has stopped and Burlem's cooked me porridge. I'm not sure I want porridge: I think I want to smoke a lot and then go through the kitchen drawers until I find the sharpest knife, and then I want to spend a few hours alone convincing myself that I'm real and I'm human and I mean something. But in the end I just eat the porridge and then smoke one cigarette with a glass of water. Lura comes down from her study at about ten o'clock.

I'm sitting on one of the yellow sofas finishing my second cigarette of the day. The fire is dead and I flick the stub into it. Burlem is out walking Planck. Lura makes herself a cup of herbal tea and comes to sit in the armchair.

"So," she says.

I cough a little. "So," I say back.

"What a night," she says. "How do you feel?"

I look beyond her and out through the patio doors. The grass is still damp from the frost last night. I can see the patch of earth that we dug over yesterday, and it looks redder and fluffier than the rest of the garden.

"I feel completely wasted," I say. "All that thinking . . . And I didn't sleep very well."

"Oh? Because of the thinking?"

"Mainly because of bad dreams," I explain. "Time-travel paradoxes."

"Ah."

"And the human foot."

She smiles and sips her tea. "The human foot?"

"Yes," I say. "No one knows exactly how it works—well, not well enough to be able to replicate one. And then there are things like junk DNA and cognitive processes, and the way quantum theory doesn't match up with gravity, but everyone thinks it must . . . How does that work?"

"You may have to explain more clearly," she says. "How does what work?"

"Well, clearly no one's been able to 'think' these things into existence, but they do exist. I suppose what I'm trying to ask is how poststructuralist physics accounts for things that exist in the world without explanation, if the explanation is what creates them."

Lura's nodding. But she doesn't speak yet.

"I mean," I say, "in the scenario you've described, how is there any mystery at all?"

"Good question," she says. "Very good question."

"Is there an answer?"

She sighs. "Yes. I think so. It's interesting you were thinking about time-travel paradoxes, because . . ."

"What?"

"Well, all these questions are really about creation. What is a creator? What does a creator do? When does creation take place? Of course, scientists hate the word *creation* and *creationist*. Science says it is against creationism, or intelligent design—or at least, it's against them being taught alongside science, in science classes. But science is itself a form of creationism. It is the scientists, after all, who create the world." Lura sips her tea and then puts it down. "And we're so used to the idea of creation as something that happens in the beginning. First the world was created, then we were created; then things started to happen. That's the way the story usually goes. But what if it's the future that creates us, not the past?"

"Shit . . ." I say. "But . . ."

Lura laughs. "But how does that work? It doesn't; not according to classical physics."

"So . . . This is connected to that question I asked last night, about thoughts having 'backwards effects,' isn't it?"

"Yes."

"So you're saying that in the future someone will come up with a theory that, for example, reconciles quantum physics and gravity, and that this theory makes the world work the way it does now? So scientists are just discovering things that have already happened?"

"Yes to the first bit, but no to the second. Einstein still created relativity by thinking it," she says, picking up her tea again and taking a sip. "But someone in the future will do the next bit, and someone else will do the bit after that, and it will all trickle down through history."

"So we're living in a world that has had infinite people in the future thinking about it already," I say.

"No. Because the future hasn't happened yet. And the future may not be infinite."

"But . . ."

"It's not a cause-and-effect universe anymore, Ariel. Nothing really happens before or after anything else. You could say that in some way everything happens at once."

I think of the train of fear, and the way I was able to return to myself at any point I wanted. But that was because I was moving on something that had no mass, that was able to travel infinitely fast. I was travelling on emotion, not on anything real.

But is thought real? Does thought have mass?

It must. We've already agreed that thought is matter.

Or have we? I'm still not sure about all this.

"Sorry," Lura says. "This is a lot to take in."

"No," I say. "Don't be sorry. I want to know it all now before I go back into the Troposphere. I want . . . Lura?"

"Yes?"

"When—and I suppose if—I get back, the book won't exist, right?"

She nods. "I hope that's what happens."

"So you don't actually know?"

"No. I don't know what is going to happen."

"It's possible that I'll never have met you," I say. "After all, Saul will never have given his talk, and therefore never met you, and therefore never found the book, and therefore never had to run away. And the Project Starlight men won't be chasing us all and . . . I won't actually even know Saul, because I met him at the conference. So I won't be doing a Ph.D. anymore and . . ."

"That's a cause-and-effect universe, though," Lura says. "I don't think we are living in a cause-and-effect universe."

"So what do you think will happen?"

"I think the book will go, but everything else will stay the same."

I remember Apollo Smintheus. *The mice would all just dissolve into the air, I think. The world wouldn't change. No one would notice.* I just don't get it. How can you go back to edit the past and expect it only to change the future a little bit?

"You *think*. You don't know?"

"Sometimes thinking is knowing," she says.

And then I wonder what this is. Is my last trip in the Troposphere an experiment or something less or more than that? But I have to go. I know all the reasons why. And I am glad Lura is telling me all this before I do. Presumably my thoughts won't change? I hope not. There's still so much to think about.

My stomach churns. I've made a decision. I'm going to do it this afternoon.

I tell Lura.

"Yes," she says. "I think it's the right time."

When Burlem gets back we all have another cup of tea, and they ask if I want lunch before I go, as if I were a weekend guest about to take a train back to London. I should have some lunch, but I don't have any appetite at all. I don't want to say good-bye, exactly, and it's clear that they don't want to, either. Saying good-bye would be a bit frightening, and it's not even clear that we *are* saying good-bye. Perhaps I will be able to find my way back, and perhaps I will still know who they are when I get here.

The black circle on the card. Perhaps I don't even need that. But I take it out of my bag anyway. And so I find myself lying on my bed just as the sun starts to fade in the sky like a dissolving tablet, wondering if I'll ever see anything in this world again. I'm sure I no longer need the liquid; so now all that remains is for me to lift the black circle up above my eyes. And I'm blurring away from here. *Good-bye*, I think. I didn't want to say it before. But suddenly I have to. I have to end this properly. *Good-bye, Lura. Good-bye, Burlem. Good-bye . . .*

———

It's nighttime in the Troposphere, as usual. I'm standing on a famil-
iarly cluttered street, with too many edges and outsides and insides.
But I can make sense of it. There are cobbles beneath my feet, but on
either side of me there are great looming gray buildings set behind
rows of shops, casinos, herbalists, brothels, sex shops, pawn shops,
and toy shops. There's a tiny antique bookshop on the corner, and
I think: *Burlem*. But I can't see anything at all that relates to Lura.
The neon flickers everywhere. OPEN. OPEN. GIRLS, GIRLS, GIRLS. Some of
the signs are just arrows, and when I look at them they seem to be
pointing at other arrows. One of them says YOU ARE HERE. Another
points to a doorway that, when I approach it, looks like the entrance
to a mouse hole. Do I want to see Apollo Smintheus? I suppose I have
to see him. I have to find out exactly where to find Abbie Lathrop. I
walk towards the mouse hole.

And then the sky darkens.

There's movement. What's happening? I catch a glimpse of
brown, and then blue. That color blue: Where have I seen it before?
But I don't have too much time to speculate because the next thing
that happens is that both the KIDS walk out of the mouse hole.

"Aha," says one of them, the one in the cowboy suit.

"Too fucking easy," says the other one, his blue cape moving in a
nonexistent breeze.

They both giggle.

Oh God.

"Well, there's her mind. There's the gate. Let's go in and finish
this job," says the first one.

"It doesn't look like everyone else's minds," says the boy in the
cape. "It's all full of weeds."

"Yeah, well. Who cares, right?"

"Wait," I say.

"*Wait*," says the one in the cape, mimicking my voice.

"Yeah, right," says the other one. "*Wait*."

They giggle again.

"We never get to have any fun in here," says the one in the cape.

Shit. Shit. What do I say now?

"This is going to be the most exciting thing we've *ever done*," says the one in the cowboy suit. "Woo-hoo!" He makes a little whooping sound as if his parents have just told him that he can have that toy, or that they are going to the zoo, or that he can stay up late and watch the film with everyone else.

"I know what happened to you," I say. "I'm really sorry."

"Why? You didn't kill us," says the one in the cape.

"No, but . . ." I want to say something about how I understand; about how I think I might be one of them. But nothing comes.

"Shut up, Benjy," says the cowboy. Then, to me: "Don't try to psychoanalyze us, bitch."

The other one opens his eyes wide, and then laughs.

"OK, coming through," says the other kid. He pulls a skateboard from under his cape. "Come on, Michael."

I've got to do something. But what could I possibly do? There aren't even any weapons here. No metal bars or anything like that. Although I get the impression that those things wouldn't work so well on these two.

Where is Apollo Smintheus?

Please help me, I think.

"We've already taken care of your lover boy," says Michael, the cowboy.

The other one stifles another giggle. I don't know why he tried to hide it: It's not as if I can do anything about it.

"He's really lost his mind," says Benjy. He rotates his finger around by one of his temples. "Cuckoo. Cuckoo," he says.

Oh God. What does this mean? Did they get to Adam in the priory? I imagine them sneaking in there somehow, despite everything being closed, and finding him: creeping into his mind like deranged little goblins. What would they do then? Perhaps they tried to persuade him to come out with the book. *But they didn't know the book was there.* So what would their motivation have been? Just spite? Or maybe they thought he knew where I'd gone. Maybe they wanted to find that information. And then, for whatever reason, they turned his brain into spaghetti. Just as they'd promised to do to me. Just as they are now going to do to me, because there's nothing I can do to stop them.

And then I see another shape moving down the street towards us. It's a man, walking alone. At first I think it's Apollo Smintheus, but this figure isn't quite as tall. And then the shape comes closer and I realize that it's a man running.

It's Adam.

"Are you sure you succeeded with that?" I ask the boys.

And I'm grinning now. Adam's carrying two rocket launchers, one slung over each arm. Where on earth . . . ? And then I see that he's carrying something else, too. A white paper bag with twisted edges, like a bag of old-fashioned sweets. What is happening? Am I dreaming this? No. This is real. As real as anything can be.

The KIDS turn to see what I'm looking at.

"Oh. It's the priest," says Benjy.

"Bor-*ing*," says Michael.

"Hello," I say, as Adam hands me one of the rocket launchers.

"Ariel," he says, taking a deep breath and closing his eyes. "At last."

"Where the . . . I mean how did you get these?" I ask him.

"Oh, I met God," he says. "It's great in here, isn't it?"

"Um . . ."

"Well, apart from these little fuckers."

"Oh *no*," squeals Benjy, stamping his foot. "We got the wrong guy."

"Whoops," says Michael.

Wolf, I think for a moment. They saw me with *Wolf.*

"I told them you were involved with Patrick," Adam says.

"How do you know about Patrick?" I ask.

"I'm afraid I know everything," Adam says. "I'll tell you how in a moment."

He raises the rocket launcher and aims it at Michael.

"Adam," I say, aiming mine at Benjy, but more shakily.

"What?"

"We can't. They're just kids."

"Yeah," says Benjy. "It's not fair."

He begins to cry. Then Michael starts crying, too.

"You said you were going to get us some sweets," says Benjy. "But instead you're going to hurt us. You're just like all grown-ups. I hate you."

I notice they don't say *kill*. And I remember what Apollo Smintheus said. Nothing can be killed in the Troposphere. So how are we ever going to get rid of these kids? And why is Adam here? I don't understand anything about what's going on.

"Do you want some sweets instead?" Adam asks, lowering the gun.

Michael's lip is trembling. "Yes," he says. "Yes, please."

"Me, too," says Benjy. "Me, too."

Michael is now wringing his hands together. Benjy seems unable to stand still. He's jiggling about like a toddler who wants to go to the toilet.

"OK. Well, don't eat them all at once," says Adam.

He walks over and hands Michael the white bag.

"Share them," he says, as Michael immediately dips his hand into the bag.

"Ow, get off," says Michael, as Benjy tries to force his hand in at the same time.

"Boys," says Adam.

They both manage to take a fistful of pink, yellow, and green sweets from the bag. They stuff them into their mouths until their faces look so inflated they might burst.

"Why are you giving them sweets?" I ask Adam.

"Watch," he says.

As the boys eat the sweets, they seem to fade, slightly. At first I think I might have something in my eyes, and so I rub them. But of course your eyes can't go wrong in here. They boys really are dissolving into the landscape.

"They're disappearing," I say.

"They're on the way to God," Adam says. "The guns would have done the same thing. They're just, um . . ."

"Metaphors," I say. "Like everything in here."

"Yeah."

The boys have now almost completely disappeared. Another minute passes and they've gone, and all that's left is the empty white paper bag.

"What exactly is God going to do to them?" I ask.

"Free them," Adam says. "Make them properly dead."

"Can God do that?" I ask.

Adam nods. "He may not have created everything, but He's good as a manager."

I laugh. "That sounds like the kind of thing you'd read on one of those fluorescent posters they have outside churches."

"Yeah, well," says Adam, laughing, too.

And then I realize: We're together, alone, in the Troposphere. Adam is actually here. Or at least, it certainly seems that way.

"Adam," I say softly.

He walks closer to me. So much for not feeling anything in the Troposphere. The syrupy feeling intensifies to a point where it's almost uncomfortable, but only in the sense that an orgasm is uncomfortable. And everything in me seems to slow down. This doesn't feel like it would in the physical world: There's no racing pulse; no sweaty hands. My body feels like a misty landscape, melting into its sky.

"Ariel," he says.

We put the weapons down and embrace. It feels as though a million years pass, with us standing like this.

"I found the book," he whispers. "And this vial of liquid. I came to find you."

"How did you find me?" I ask. "The Project Starlight men couldn't do it. I thought I covered my tracks quite well. I . . ."

"Shhhh," he says, into my hair.

"Really," I say. "I have to know. Did God help you?"

"No. God doesn't approve of what we're doing."

"Then . . . ?"

"The mouse god. Apollo Smintheus. He said he'd show me where to find you. But those boys seemed to want to tag along as well, and everywhere we went, they went, too. I thought I'd be able to do something about them before you came back in and opened up the gateway. I was almost too late."

"What do you mean?" I say. "What gateway?"

"They can only get into your mind by themselves when you're actually in here. Otherwise they have to go with Ed and Martin. You know that already, but you've probably forgotten."

"So you've been inside my mind," I say. It's not a question. I know the answer.

"Yes. But you bounced me out when you first went into the church. But I just jumped back in when you left the church. I just waited in the Troposphere in between."

"How did you find the book?" I ask.

"I dreamed it," he says. "I dreamed everything."

"What?" I say. "What do you mean?"

"Just that," he says. "I dreamed you putting it in the bookcase, and I dreamed you accidentally letting the vial roll out of your bag under the bed. Later, when I was in your mind, I saw it all again, like déjà vu."

"Oh . . . ," I say. I'm not exactly sure what I want to say next. "So . . ."

I don't want to let go of Adam, but I do.

"Have you seen Apollo Smintheus?" he asks me.

"No," I say.

"I don't know what happened to him. He was supposed to be watching out for those KIDS."

"His mouse hole is just there," I say, and we walk towards it.

And inside me two things are happening. One is that my whole body feels like a smile. I'm not alone in here anymore. I can actually talk to someone. Not just that: The someone I can talk to is Adam, the person I thought I'd never see again, and the person I think I love. But the smile keeps warping into a question mark. And I can't bear to ask, or even think about it. *How long has he been in here?*

Chapter Twenty-six

Apollo Smintheus is tied to a chair, and he looks very pissed off.

"Oh, thank you," he says, when we untie him.

He stands up, sways a little, and then sits back down again.

"Oh," he says. "Those little brutes."

"They've gone now," I say. "Well, I think they have."

"And you two are reunited," he says.

I'm wondering whether Apollo Smintheus has told Adam about the dangers of staying in here too long: whether he's shown *him* a screen of himself in the physical world, like he did with me. Where is Adam's body? Is it still in the priory? I wonder if anyone has found him and saved him. I remember those images of Apollo Smintheus in my dreams: *You owe me. You owe me.* And I wonder if it was Apollo Smintheus who got into Adam's dreams, and why he wanted him to come in here as well.

It's a horrible thought, but for a second I imagine that it's a punishment: because I took my time coming back; because I haven't yet completed his mission.

"Where's the address?" I ask him. "I need to know how to get to Abbie Lathrop."

"Don't you want coffee first?" he asks.

"No. I just want to go. I'm going to see Adam back to the physical world, and then I'm going to go straight off and do this. I don't have much time."

Apollo Smintheus seems to narrow his eyes slightly.

But Adam's quicker to speak. "I'm coming with you," he says to me.

"You can't," I say. "Don't you know . . . ?"

"Know what?"

I look at Apollo Smintheus, who doesn't seem to want to catch my eye. Then I look at Adam again. His big eyes are as warm and clear as a midsummer morning. They're so deep, I think again. But here they don't look like fossils from the past, they just look like a promise of the future.

But what do his eyes look like in the physical world? I think.

"You're not supposed to stay in here too long," I say.

"Did I not mention that . . . ?" Apollo Smintheus says.

Adam looks at me. "I've been in your mind, Ariel," he says. "And, on the way back to your mind, Saul Burlem's and Lura's. I know everything."

"But . . ."

His eyes leave mine. "I wasn't going to talk about this now."

"Talk about what?"

"I think it's already too late. There was a very big storm yesterday. Apollo Smintheus said that when you get weather in the Troposphere . . ." But I'm not listening properly. Why didn't Apollo Smintheus save Adam? Why didn't he tell him to go back?

Sadness in here feels like a warm flannel. But it's still sadness; the warm flannel is over my face and I can't breathe properly.

"It can't be too late! Apollo Smintheus must have told you about the trains?"

"I did," says Apollo Smintheus. "Well, sort of."

"He told me there was a way I could get back to where I'd started. But I didn't want to go back there. I wanted to find you."

"But Adam . . ."

"What?"

"Adam, you can't . . . You didn't . . ."

"I think I'll leave you two to it now," says Apollo Smintheus. "Here's that address for Abbie Lathrop." He produces a slim white business card, very similar to the one he first left for me: the one I found on the street after I'd done Pedesis for the first time. I take the card and look at it. When I look up, he's gone. I'm here on my own with Adam.

"I don't like it in here that much," says Adam. "Let's go outside."

There is no outside, I think. *Not anymore.*

But I follow him down the jumbled-up street, anyway. We pass a car showroom and a small haberdashery. I want to cry but it doesn't work. I don't think you can cry in here. But raindrops start falling softly from somewhere above me, and when I look up, the night sky seems wet and glossy.

We end up in a meadow by a river. The bright moon seems to touch every part of the black water, and moves through the tall yellow grass like gentle fingers. There are benches that face the water, and Adam sits on one of them. I sit on one, too. The wood isn't cold. Like everything else in here, it doesn't seem to have a temperature. Tiny drops of rain still fall from the sky, but they don't feel wet.

"Ariel," says Adam, taking my hand.

"Why did you do this?" I ask him.

"I wanted to know . . . ," he says.

"Know what?"

He shrugs. "Just to know. I couldn't go back."

"But . . . Why did you want to find me?"

"I just had to. And I missed you."

I breathe in for a long time. Then I sigh. "I missed you, too. But . . ."

"What?"

"Shit. Adam. *Why?*"

He shrugs again. "Apollo Smintheus told me you needed me."

"I would have found you when I got out. I'd . . ."

Adam looks away from me and out onto the river. An owl hoots.

"Fuck," I say. "So it's all too late. Nothing means anything anymore. Everything's . . ."

"Don't say it," Adam says. "Just come with me."

He takes my hand and we stand up. We walk down the path, past thousands of trees that seem to reach up into heaven. Moonlight strobes on their leaves, and bats flicker in and out of the trees like shadow puppets against the black of the sky. Soon we come to a clearing: a circle of thick, soft grass, surrounded by trees. We walk into the clearing and Adam immediately pulls me towards him.

"Ariel," he says. And he kisses me.

But what's happening? This kiss is a million kisses. This kiss is every kiss. Our lips seem to press together with the force of ten thousand hurricanes, and when his tongue meets mine it feels like the softest electricity: a million-volt shock happening in slow motion, one electron at a time, where each electron is the size of the sun.

And in the sky, there's lightning.

The rain starts to hammer the ground, but I can't feel it.

Adam is pulling me down onto the grass.

As I close my eyes I can see that there are tornadoes everywhere, but I can't even feel a breeze. All my clothes have gone. I'm so naked it's as if I don't even have skin. Adam's taut body moves down onto mine. And when he enters me it's as if I'm being turned inside out, and the whole world is penetrating me; and that means I contain everything.

Afterwards we both lie there on the ground, shaking. I know everything about Adam now, and he knows everything about me.

"Oh . . . ," says Adam.

"Yeah."

"Oh . . . Is that . . . ?"

"No."

"You don't know what I was going to ask."

"Yes I do. You were going to ask if that's what sex is like usually."

He takes my hand. "Well, something like that."

"And the answer is no."

"But *we'd* never done it before," he says, and I can see him smiling in the moonlight.

I imagine tornadoes around the Shrine of St. Jude. But maybe he's right.

I put my head on his shoulder and he puts his arm around me. I feel so small and warm, like I'm an acorn he's holding in the palm of his hand. But at the same time I feel as if I'm the one holding on to him. He only exists here now. And if I do this and then go back . . . *Don't think, Ariel. Just have this moment.* But if there's no Troposphere, I won't be able to see Adam ever again. Perhaps I'll go back and find that I don't even know who Adam is. Perhaps I won't miss him, because I'll never know I knew him.

But if the book is the only thing that disappears? If I make it so it was never written?

Then maybe I did know Adam. Maybe he did move into my office. Maybe the railway tunnel did collapse. But not because of Burlem. And maybe I became a Ph.D. student, anyway. Maybe Burlem still did the conference in Greenwich, but on another subject. Maybe he talked about Samuel Butler. I would have gone to that. We still would have talked and we still would have got pissed together and we still wouldn't have had sex and everything would be more or less the same.

I can sort of see how that might work.

But Adam would still be dead.

Perhaps I'd wake up from a scary dream about men chasing me and there'd be a knock at the door, and a policeman would be telling me that he just passed away in his sleep. A tragic mystery. But don't be stupid. No policeman would come and tell me anything. They'd tell his relatives, and I wouldn't even be invited to the funeral because no one would have known we were involved. Perhaps I'd read about it in the university newsletter, or in one of those "Sad news" e-mails.

I sit up.

"Where are you going?" Adam asks sleepily.

"I've got to . . . Well, basically, I'm going to 1900," I say.

"And I'm coming, too."

"Are you sure you want to?"

Adam sits up and shakes his head. "We've just shared the most amazing experience that I've ever had," he says. "And I'm not leaving you. Not ever." He pauses. "Not until you have to go back."

I don't know what to say next. *Until I have to go back*. I didn't have any lunch. Who knows how much time I've got? You can only use the underground system if you are alive. But does it even matter now whether I am alive or dead? I really don't know.

"So what do you think? Should we aim for America and then go back in time?" Adam asks. "Or the other way around?"

"Hmm?"

We're walking hand in hand back towards town, the moon racing us down the river and winning. The way I feel with him now is hard to describe. It feels as if we've already grown old together. I know, already, that we're going to die together.

But he's already dead.

"Pedesis," he says. "How shall we do it?"

"I think we're going to have to go back and forwards around the world in order to jump the time," I say. "We can aim for Massachusetts later. In fact, maybe we should be aiming for one of Abbie Lathrop's descendants and then carefully jumping backwards from there. I'm not actually sure what would happen if we missed her. Say we jumped back ten years too far or something. You can't exactly go forwards in time here—well, you *can*, but it has to be in real time. We'd be stuck in Massachusetts for ten years."

Adam sighs. "I think you know more than me about doing this."

"I'm not sure. I mean, I managed to find Saul Burlem, but only because I found out about his daughter and found her in the physical world. I don't really know how to approach this problem. It's over a hundred years. It's huge."

We walk through a gate and then the river goes off to the left while we walk towards the right, past some old boat-building sheds towards the city.

I frown. "Surely you know as much as I do about this?" I say.

"Why?"

"You've been in my mind. You must know everything."

"I'm not sure I do know everything," he says. "Your mind is very complicated. Everything I know about you . . . It's real and unreal all at once. No . . . That's not a very good description. It feels ghostly in some way. As if I thought I was there—I thought I was you—but now it's just a dream. I remember it all, but it doesn't make sense yet. That's the only way I can describe it."

I think about the moment when he penetrated me in the clearing and how I knew then that what we were doing wasn't physical. It was as if I was the void and he was everything real, and the sensation of him entering me was like the largest presence filling the smallest absence. Our minds were making love, and in the moment when I came I saw his whole life as if I was him and I was dying.

I felt the humiliation of my father's belt.

I knew what it was to be hungry.

I walked in bare feet over brown, dusty earth.

I kept worms as a science project, but really I thought of them as my pets.

My father smashed up my wormery when he was drunk.

My mother never said anything.

(They're both dead and I don't miss them; I miss what could have been.)

Those hot, wet evenings when my cousins would stay over.

The ghost stories that frightened me.

The little bell I would ring during Mass, when I was an altar server.

The cold echoey church, and the way it comforted me because the violence in the Bible was on such a large scale that it made my father's actions seem small. I inverted my life, so what was real became unreal, and everything that was said in church was the truth and everything else was a lie.

My father never saying he was proud of me, even though I joined the church for him, because it was the only thing I could see that meant something to him, the man who didn't like rugby or cricket, who said that sports were for "poofters" and arts for "nonces" and school didn't prepare you for the real world and that men should work and pray and do nothing else. The excessive alcohol consumption was somehow never factored into his philosophy of life.

The night I told my cousins about the Holy Ghost, to scare them.

And on another occasion I told them all they'd go to hell.

When I decided to go into the seminary for all the wrong reasons.

The morning my father discovered me in bed with Marty, my cousin.

The hollow look in his eyes when he looked at me after that.

Trying to make myself holy. Blank. Blank. Blank.

Adult life: I'm trying to be a father for everyone . . .

But I look at women. I try masturbation but I hate myself.

I try self-flagellation. It just makes me feel more aroused.

When the priest from the village rapes my sister I feel as though I did it.

My father abandons the church.

My father is God now.

I am going to eliminate all desire from my life.

(. . .)

I know him, but I don't know it all: I wasn't connected to his mind for long enough. I don't know what's in the gaps. There's still an eternity of knowledge of him that I don't have. And I want it now as much as I want to breathe.

We're in the city again now, walking towards the place where Apollo Smintheus's mouse hole was. It isn't there anymore, but the street is still exactly the same apart from that. This was where I emerged into the Troposphere from Burlem and Lura's house. All I'd have to do to get back to the physical world would be to carry on walking. I could go back and tell Burlem and Lura that I simply failed. Then Adam could live in the Troposphere and I could come and visit him.

But that's not possible. That would be the same as only having him as a memory.

"Why don't you hate me?" I say, even though I already know the answer.

"What do you mean?"

He's holding my hand so tightly that it might break. I don't care.

"Well, you know everything now. All the sex. All the . . . everything."

"I understand it all, though," he says. "I *know* you."

"Yeah. I know what you mean." We stop outside a pawnshop. I'm not sure why. Then I see the café glowing somewhere inside it. It's the dimensional problem again.

"Shall we have coffee before we go?" Adam asks.

"Troposphere coffee," I say. "How can I refuse?"

We sit at a table outside, and after a couple of tries we realize that all you have to do is think coffee for it to appear. Well, actually it takes a bit more effort than that. You have to think coffee and believe it will appear, and then it does.

"Why did you come looking for me?" I ask. "The last time I saw you I really pissed you off; I could see that. I shouldn't have said . . ."

"It doesn't matter."

"Maybe not. But why?"

"Would it be stupid to say that I thought I'd fallen in love with you?"

I look down on the table. "Um . . ."

"Sorry. I'm not that good with words. Well, I am good with words, but not these sorts of words. Oh, that actually does sound stupid. Why did I fall in love with you? On reflection, it wasn't a great move—well, objectively speaking. But . . ." He sighs. "I couldn't help it." Now he runs his hands through his hair. "Oh. I can't explain."

"It's OK," I say. "I don't understand why you feel that way but . . ."

"What?"

"I was going to say I'm glad you do. But I'm not sure. You'd be alive if it wasn't for me—and *The End of Mr. Y.*"

"Yeah. *But.*" He closes his eyes and then opens them again. "I wouldn't have this." He opens his hands as if he's holding the world, but there's nothing in them. He just means that I should look around and see what he would be holding, if his hands could hold ideas, and metaphors, and multidimensional buildings.

"Why do you see the same thing I see?" I ask.

"Hmm?"

"You see the same thing I see. The same Troposphere. I thought this was the inside of my mind?"

"It is."

"Then . . ."

"I died inside your mind."

"Oh." I get that Troposphere pain, briefly, like a dull blade cutting me up inside, slow and dirty. I can't think about this. "What was your Troposphere like?"

"Very similar. A city. But it was daytime. There were more parks. But it did have a graffiti problem that yours doesn't have."

"It was daytime here once as well," I say. "I don't know what happened to that."

"Oh well. I like night. It's romantic."

"Like that meadow and the river," I say. "That space was very romantic. But I'm not sure those came from my mind. It's funny . . ."

He tips his head over to one side for a second. I think we both know what happened when we made love by the river. His mind is inside me. "Hmm. Yeah. Both our minds at once. And all the minds in the world are in here with us . . . We could do and see anything."

"Adam . . ." I reach for his hand across the table. "I want . . ."

But that sounds wrong here. This isn't a place for wanting.

"What?"

"You. But *wanting* sounds wrong. I wish we were still in that meadow . . ."

"Mmm. Why don't we go back?"

"No. I owe Apollo Smintheus. I'd be dead if it wasn't for him."

"We'll do his mission, and then Lura's mission and then . . ."

"Yeah." *And then.* "OK." I finish my coffee. "Let's go."

Adam finishes the last of his coffee.

"Mice," he says, suddenly.

"What?"

"Why don't we use mice?"

"For what? Oh . . . I see. Go back to Abbie Lathrop using mice. Wouldn't that take ages? I mean to get back a hundred years using Pedesis we'd really need to be crossing continents every few jumps. Remember that time is distance in the Troposphere. The more distance we can cover in the physical world, the more time we can jump through in here."

As I say the phrase I feel something like déjà vu. That expression: *Time is distance in the Troposphere.* I keep hearing it and I keep saying it, but I don't know what it means. The Troposphere is made from thoughts. Distance in the Troposphere is just the arrangement of thoughts. What do I already know?

Distance = time.

Matter = thought.

So what if there's another equation to add:

Thought = time?

Then, I guess, thought really is everything. And it makes sense: Time isn't measured in anything other than thought. The only thing that separates today from yesterday is thought.

"What are you thinking?" Adam asks.

I laugh. He can see what I'm thinking: It's all around him.

"What?"

"I'll tell you on the way," I say.

"Hang on. We don't even know where we're going yet."

"Oh. Yes. You're right. OK—do you understand about the distance thing?"

"Yeah. I think so. If I'm in someone's head and I can see all their ancestors, I can jump to any of them. If one of them lives in Norfolk, and I'm in Kent, I'll go back maybe a couple of weeks at the same time as I do the jump. But if one of them lives in Africa and I'm in Kent I could maybe go back a couple of years."

"That's right," I say. "So maybe we find a well-travelled family to go back through."

"Look up," Adam says.

I do. I can see the black sky hanging there like something I just clicked on, with the moon like a big digital button. But its light is still real, draped over the buildings and the street. Just beneath the sky I can see the gray tower blocks that seem to be everywhere in the Troposphere, just rising out of the ground and pointing upwards.

"What am I looking at?" I ask.

"The tower blocks," he says. "Where the animals live."

"Why do the animals live in tower blocks?"

"I don't know: This is your metaphor."

"Oh. I suppose I wouldn't think of them as shops. People are shops. People are part of an economy in a much more direct way . . ." I shake my head. "Oh, I don't know."

"Well, let's find some mice."

"But the *time* . . . ?"

"We'll see how far we have to jump before we get into a lab mouse, and then it should be just millisecond jumps all the way back to Abbie Lathrop, surely?"

"I don't think all lab mice are descended from her stock," I say. "I can't remember what Apollo Smintheus said. Damn."

Console? It comes up.

"Can you see that, too?" I ask Adam.

"Yeah," he says.

"Hmm. I wonder if it's possible to send messages on this thing?"

But we don't have to. There's the broken sound of a small engine struggling to fire, and then a red scooter comes around the corner.

"Good plan," says Apollo Smintheus, getting off. "Mice. I like it."

"So where do we start?"

"I'll take you to a descendant. But that's all I can do."

I want to say thanks, except that I'm doing this for him, anyway. But I do owe him.

"Thanks," I say.

We all walk towards an office block. There's an entry phone, but Apollo Smintheus manages to get us buzzed in by saying something I don't understand in that unfamiliar language of his. While we walk up a set of concrete stairs, I try to plan this, but there isn't too much time.

But surely what Adam said is right. Apollo Smintheus said before that all of these mice are inbred. We should be able to go back to Abbie Lathrop directly. We should . . . Apollo Smintheus has stopped outside a door. And Adam is opening it.

You now have one choice . . .

You . . . I . . . We're walking quickly over bare floorboards and our claws are going click-click-click as we move. It's like the sound of Lura's knitting needles, but in a much larger, more bare space.

"Adam?" I say.

"Yeah."

"I don't think we're a lab mouse."

"I know."

I become aware of the mouse registering our voices—or, actually, only my voice—and I immediately know that we shouldn't communicate with each other like this. *The mouse* . . . I can hear sounds in my mind and I try to run away from them. Faster, along the wood. I haven't eaten for several hours and I remember that if I run down here and then follow my own scent through the large gap in the wall I will probably find something.

Console!

It appears. I can see lots of images. Most of them are moving, but one is still.

"I'm going to let you do all the choosing," Adam says. "I'm not even going to look."

"OK. But *shhh.* I think we're disturbing the mouse."

"Sorry."

Voices, voices. I can hear a person but I can't see her. I remember another time when I heard voices like this and there was pain. And then hands on my back, but hands gloved with something that wasn't shiny and smooth, and then sickening movement in the dark, and then freedom: Something I had never known before.

This new voice sounds like that one, a little. But all voices are danger.

I fix my mind on the static image in the console. Something tells me that this could be the lab animal. The mouse we're in now was freed. I can sense that from his memories. But . . .

We switch. And . . .

You now have one choice.

You . . . I can hear something muffled and distant.

"No!" It's Adam screaming. "Ariel, no . . ."

But I can't hear him because I am screaming, too. But I can't even hear that properly because the pain stops me registering anything very much. I want to die. . . . I don't know what death is, but there's something in my mind that does, and understands that I should be able to move and that there shouldn't be metal spikes in my eyes, that if they weren't there I would have less pain in my head, and maybe I'd be able to see. What is seeing? The world is a black slab and I have never known anything apart from this. Each day it takes an effort to draw air into my lungs, and that's what I spend my life doing, just trying to breathe. . . .

"Jump again," Adam's saying. "Oh God . . ."

The pain is like nothing I have ever felt before.

The console is still there, faintly.

I don't think I've got any legs. I don't think I have ever walked. Everything is black. I pick an image from the console: any image.

You now have one choice.

You . . . I . . . We are standing at the entrance to a maze. A new world! How exciting. Maybe this is finally going to be the way out. I've been down this passage before. And this one. I can smell the food at the end. It's the same stuff again, but it keeps me alive, and it keeps me doing this. I'm only halfway down an unfamiliar passage when a gloved hand picks me up, and the feeling of the material against my fur smells the same as the walls of my world, and all my life I have been comforted by these smells. Now I am being placed down again: my feet touching the glass. Where's my reward? This is the wrong tank. Where's the sawdust? This doesn't smell like my tank. I can see the same symbols on the ground (and which I can now read, and which say HappiMat™) but something is terribly wrong. Fear pierces me like the needles my carers use on me every day. My brothers and sisters are lying around me, but they're not trying to fight me or mount me. They smell different. I walk over and look at them. I nuzzle one of them with my nose: He's cold. They are all just lying there like the wet cloths our carers sometimes leave in the tanks when they have finished wiping off some of the smell. I walk over and sniff them. . . . They're not right. They're . . . *Ow!* Get off. Another gloved hand takes hold of me, but this one isn't gentle. . . .

"Ariel!"

"Sorry."

We jump.

You now have one choice.

You . . . I . . . We're being injected again. I don't know what is worse: the sensation of the cold, sharp needle going in, or the sensation of it coming out again. Once it's in I want it out, but once it's out I feel dizzy, and I can't make my nest properly and . . . I don't actually care about my nest. I feel something warm and wet creeping down my legs. I just want to sleep. My nest smells sour now but I need to sleep. I can't even be bothered to lick myself clean.

You now have one choice.

You . . . I . . . We can't breathe because of all the smoke. I can't move my head.

You now have one choice.

You . . . I . . . We are flying through the air and then landing with an awkward bump, and then flying again. My friend is flying as well, and another mouse I haven't seen before, and all around us people are laughing; although I can't understand the language, something in my mind can hear the carers saying, "Stop juggling the mice, Wesley." I am very dizzy and I want to go back in my tank.

————

You now have one choice.

You . . . I . . . We can't understand why this keeps happening. I keep making my nest in exactly the way I like it (the way my mother taught me), and then I find it's gone. The hand takes it away. And then the hand gives me more nesting material and I start building again. Every night I sleep on bare glass, despite all the nests I have made.

You now have one choice.

You . . . I . . . We can't sleep with these lights on all the time.

You now have one choice.

You . . . I . . . We

You now have one choice.

You . . . I . . .

You now have one choice.

You . . .

You now have one

You now have

You now

You

You

You

You

You

We're now jumping so fast that it feels like a fluid journey, just as Mr. Y described in the book. It takes a lot of concentration, although it is hard to concentrate when you're essentially surfing on a wave of pain, fear, humiliation—and the constant simple desire for a warm, quiet nest. This is a wave of death: a wave of dead black bodies and dead white bodies and gloved hands and bony fingers and the pain of the needle and the pain of the tumors and the blindness and trying to lick off your own blood when it's still pouring out of you, and being left with your legs and back broken in a pile of other broken bodies and still thinking that there'll be food at the end, and that the carers will put you back in your tank just as they always do after something bad happens.

While I surf, Adam tries to locate details.

Most of the labs have calendars on the walls.

And I notice that as we go back the lights become dimmer and the tanks become smaller. There are no more HappiMats. We hear sirens and explosions, and we travel through labs that all smell of metal and gunpowder. But each tiny jump is a new kind of pain. By the time we reach 1908 I have bled thousands of pints of blood and vomited and pissed myself and fallen asleep in my own shit, and each time—every moment—I have just wanted to crawl into my nest, because something I am born with tells me it's good and comfortable in my nest, but all the time I have known that there's something not right about my existence. I either don't have a nest, or someone has taken it away, or I simply know that there shouldn't be glass walls around it.

We slow down as the calendars start showing 1907, 1906, 1905. . . .

And then there she is. She's lifting our friend out of a box full of sawdust.

In the console the black mouse she is holding is blurred.

And we jump. We're in.

Chapter Twenty-seven

You now have one choice.

You . . . *I* . . . We are taking one of the best mice—one of the black ones—and putting it in a box. Does it need sawdust? No, it's not going far, and the dumb animal probably wouldn't take any notice, anyway. Everyone knows that mice don't *feel*. They don't have a soul, as my friend Dr. Duncan MacDougall will prove just as soon as his experiment in Mass. General Hospital is conducted. The human soul weighs something: He will prove that. Animals do not have souls to be weighed. The mice squeak when I pinch them but it's just a physical reaction. They have no real minds. And the creature shouldn't get used to luxuries, anyway. There won't be much comfort where it is going. But if the scientists like this one, then I feel sure they will order more. Will sawdust make the mouse look better, perhaps? Like a little black chocolate in a box? I can't decide. I take another look inside. The dumb thing is quivering in the corner as though a cat is after it. But it does appear pathetic there on the bare wood of the box. I'll add some sawdust, and then I will get changed.

This is going to make my fortune. Can it? I'm darned unsure that anything I do will ever go quite right, but with God's will, we all just carry on—the pioneer spirit, just like Mama said. What am I going to wear? I think. . . . My most fancy formal skirt and that black shawl, although I don't want to look like a widow in mourning. In that case it should probably be the green jacket.

I'll tell him I can supply him with all the mice he needs for his experiments. And then they'll earn their keep at last. The waltzing mice—what a *disaster*! Why did nobody want the waltzing mice? I thought they'd be exactly the kind of thing that children would adore: little mice that danced around. But then that awful woman pointed out that there was something wrong with them: that they danced because of an ear defect. Well, it didn't take a genius to work out that there was something wrong with mice that danced instead of walked— but it was fun. Why didn't the children love them?

It sure is difficult working with fancy mice. It was worse working with poultry. Was it easier working with the children in the school? I can hardly remember. No, now I come to think of it, that was the worst of all. Being a schoolteacher was the worst of all the dead-end paths in my life. The children did have minds, and that made a difference, somehow.

I look at mouse number 57, twitching in his cage. He'll be the next to go.

I think I am a good mouse breeder.

I want to be rich. . . .

"Adam?"

Who is Adam?

"She can hear us."

"I know. Stupid bitch."

Oh my. Oh my. I'm hearing voices. Well, one voice.

"Let the mice go," says Adam.

"I don't think she can hear you. Let me do it. Open all the boxes, Abbie Lathrop, and let the mice go."

Oh my. I feel a little faint. I'll just sit down for a moment. But . . .

"Let the mice go. You don't know what you're doing. You have no idea of the pain you're causing by your actions. Let the mice go."

Adam is being a little kinder than I feel, but she can't hear him: I'm the one they can hear. I'm the one who can change minds. Of course, now we're in this woman's mind we understand exactly why she's doing this. But that doesn't make it right, and it's going to take a lot more than a little bit of empathy for a lonely, miserable woman to cancel out the crushing waves of torture we had to surf to get here.

"Do you know what happens in a lab, Abbie?" I ask her, inside her head.

"Oh, shut up." I clap my hands over my ears. "Go away. Demons!"

"Let the mice free and we will go away. Otherwise we will stay here forever, telling you what a worthless piece of shit . . ."

"Ariel!"

"Do it for God, Miss Lathrop."

"You're not a demon?"

"We are not demons. We're your conscience."

"My conscience?"

"Let the mice go. Let the mice go. Let the mice go."

And then Abbie Lathrop gets up and, with a shaking hand, releases the wooden catches on all the cages.

That could have been more subtle, but it worked.

The console is still up. I look at the Quit button and then we're out on the Troposphere. Adam and I fall into each other's arms immediately, knowing we don't have to say anything about the experience we've just had. I feel as though something has been lifted from me because I don't owe Apollo Smintheus anything anymore. But the weight of what I know about suffering makes that lifted weight feel like a speck of dust I have just brushed off myself. And I still feel haunted: not by Apollo Smintheus, of course. Something has replaced that, but I'm not sure what it is.

The Troposphere looks exactly the same as usual, except that when I bring up the map in the console we seem to be thousands and thousands of miles from where we started. There's something different about the map now and I realize what it is: There are little yellow circles dotted here and there, and I understand that these represent train stations. These are the way I could get out of here, if that was what I wanted to do.

We only have to get back to the early 1890s to find Lumas, and we're already in 1900. We cross from Massachusetts into New York via a travelling salesman, and then we find a newspaper editor whose grandfather still lives in England. Once we're in his mind, we don't have to make too many more jumps to get to London in 1894, a year after *The End of Mr. Y* was published. We make the next jumps quite steadily. First we cover most of the time and then we do the last of the distance, working our way across London until we are standing outside Lumas's publishing house. And the person whose mind we are inside is a Mr. Henry Bellington, age twenty-two. He is holding a thick manuscript under his arm.

We've agreed not to talk when we are inside people's minds, so I am left to make my own impressions of the things around me. The first thing I notice about Victorian London is how wonderfully quiet it is. Mr. Bellington doesn't agree. He finds it chokingly oppressive, with the beggars and thieves and all the thick black smoke. But then he isn't used to a world of air traffic, car engines, mobile phones, and the constant thick drone of electricity in the background.

Bellington is shown into the publishing house.

And then it's only two jumps into the mind of Lumas's editor.

I only need his address. Do I know it from memory? Yes I do.

And then it's out of the building via a pigeon on a window ledge, and then into a hansom cab with a young accountant, and then off again once we're on the Strand. And then I simply hop from person to person until I'm standing outside Lumas's front door. But the people whose minds I am inside don't want to stop and after I've jumped a couple of times simply with the purpose of standing still, I choose Quit in the console and end up on the Troposphere again with Adam.

"That was good," he says.

I look around. My mind has done something odd—and rather tacky—to this part of the Troposphere. Although it still feels like a futuristic city, this district is like the film set for a Hollywood film that needs to briefly depict 1890s London. Everything seems to have the volume turned up. Abandoned hansom cabs lie everywhere, just as in Burlem's version of the Troposphere, but these seem hastily drawn, as if I want them here but don't really know what they look like. There's a Dickensian fog everywhere, although I've never properly read Dickens, so it only seems to halfheartedly hang over everything, set in an uncertain state somewhere between actual fog and coal dust and the smoke from all the London chimneys. There's also a pennyfarthing leaning against some wrought-iron railings.

The street is cobbled and all the buildings are made out of red brick. There are lots of shops here, all with ornately designed frontispieces. On one side of the street they seem more familiar than on the other. There's something called the Musical Bank, and a vegetarian restaurant, among various other things. I recognize these buildings: They're from stories and novels I've read. The Musical Bank shouldn't be in London, though: It's from *Erewhon*. But the vegetarian restaurant is from Conan Doyle's *The Red-Headed League*. The other side of the street has shops with just as extravagantly designed signs, but these are places I don't recognize. There's an ironmonger, a jeweller, a bank, a tobacconist, and a bookshop. Farther down on the fictional side of the road is a pub that's glowing in the console in the same way that Apollo Smintheus's mouse holes glow, and all the various coffee shops. I've never seen a pub on the Troposphere before.

I point it out to Adam.

"Shall we take a break before doing Lumas?" I say.

He shrugs. "OK."

But I'm stalling for a reason, and I think he knows what that reason is. Once I convince Lumas not to write *The End of Mr. Y*, everything is going to change. And I'm not even sure I want to change Lumas's mind.

The pub doesn't look that different inside from the dives I used to drink in when I was a student in Oxford, or even from places I've gone on a Sunday afternoon in London. The place is done out in bottle green and brown, with a long curved wooden bar, and plush green seats. All the fixtures and fittings seem to be familiar, except that there are oil lamps instead of electric lights, and the tables seem more polished. There is no one behind the bar, and there are no customers, although there are half-finished drinks on one of the tables, along with a book of matches, a packet of playing cards, and what looks like a manuscript for a book. What's that all about?

Adam and I sit down at a table in the corner.

"If we think of alcohol, do you think some will appear?" Adam asks.

"Let's try it," I say.

A couple of minutes later we have a small glass bottle of vodka and two glasses.

"Were you thinking of vodka?" Adam asks.

"Yes," I say. "How about you?"

"Yes. It's my 'trauma' drink."

I laugh. "Mine, too. I thought yours would be Communion wine."

"No. I've discovered vodka since then. It's the only thing my father refused to drink, which gives it a special sort of appeal."

"Yeah." I nod and look down onto the table.

"I'll open it then," he says. He picks up the bottle. "Ow, it's cold."

"Good," I say.

He pours a glass for each of us. And when I put mine to my lips I find it smells of bison grass: my favorite sort of vodka. I knock it back in one gulp. I'm trying to drink away the mice, and I'm trying to drink away what's happened to Adam, and most of all I'm trying to drink away the responsibility of being here, and being able to change things. But I'm not sure that Troposphere alcohol actually gets you pissed. Mind you, I do feel a little more relaxed. I pour another glass and drink it slowly while Adam keeps sipping his first one.

"I can't stand this," I say.

"Ariel?" he says. He reaches for my hand across the table. "What is it?"

I sigh, as though all the air is leaving my body. "Can't you see it?"

"See what?"

"The mice . . . What we've just done for those mice. We should do that for everything. We could go and prevent the Holocaust. We could stop the atom bomb from being invented. We could . . ."

"Ariel."

"What?"

"We can't edit the world. We can't just go and rewrite it, as if it was just a draft of a book we weren't happy with."

"Why not?"

"Well, aren't you here to stop the possibility of that? Lura and Burlem sent you back here to take the book away so that people wouldn't even have the option of doing that. It's important. It's important that people can't change history."

"I know. That's why I'm not sure about changing Lumas's mind," I say, drinking more of the vodka. Amazingly, it is working, and the syrupy feeling intensifies the more of it I drink. "I mean, who made me God? I shouldn't get to decide any of this. But since I have been put in this position, and I do get to decide, I want to go and erase Hitler."

"But you know you can't."

"Do I?"

"Yes. Think about it. If Hitler were in your position, he'd erase something else. If the pope were in your position, he'd edit the world differently again. You've got to close the loophole that lets people do this."

"What if I know I'm right?"

"Come on. I know your mind. You can never know you're right."

"Hitler thought he was right," I say. "But everyone agrees that he wasn't."

"Of course he wasn't right," Adam says. "I'm not just saying that every opinion is as valid as every other . . ."

"Moral relativism," I say. "It's a trap."

"Yes, but you must still realize that you can't decide. We can't decide. It's not up to us. History has to make itself. And it probably will anyway, whatever we do. In erasing Hitler, we could just open the door for someone worse. I'm not even sure that what we've already done will have actually changed anything. Abbie Lathrop could decide to just get some more mice. If she doesn't, someone else will. We've helped *those* mice, but not *all* mice."

I drink more vodka. "I'm glad you're here," I say. Then I realize what I've just said. "I mean with me. I'm not glad you're here in the way you are." I put my glass down. "Adam?"

"What?"

"What do you think will happen to the Troposphere once I've been into Lumas's mind and stopped him from writing the book?"

"I don't know."

"I don't want you to disappear."

"Even if I do, it's worth it."

"Is it?"

"Yes. Now, we should hurry up and do this. You'll need to get back."

I don't say anything.

"Ariel?"

"Yes, I know. I just want to . . ." I get up.

"Where are you going?"

"Just over here."

I walk over to the table and look at the manuscript on the other table. Just as I thought, the title on the front is handwritten, and it says *The End of Mr. Y.* I turn away and walk out through the doors, with Adam following me.

"Will you come in with me?" I ask him.

"Of course," he says.

That way, I think, there's less possibility of him disappearing once I've done what I have to do.

We walk to the bookshop down the street, and I look in the window. There are various Samuel Butler novels there, as well as *Zoonomia.* I know who is behind the door, I just have to actually open it. I can't think about it anymore. I'm here now, and I know I'm not going to decide not to do this, so I may as well just do it now. I kiss Adam before we walk to the door and I open it and go in.

You now have one choice

You . . . I . . . We are sitting at the old desk in the draughty sitting room, writing, as usual. This book . . . I have to write it; I have to finish it. Is it possible that people who do not write can ever understand quite how this feels? I have set poor Mr. Y going like a top, and now I have to keep him spinning until he reaches his end. And then I have to stop him spinning and put him back in the toy chest, limp with death. Oh, what a cruel God I would make! Can I have him live? No, don't be ridiculous, Tom. To have him live would break all the rules of tragedy, and more than that: It would not be the truth. So Mr. Y will die, and he will die by my hand. And then . . . *And then*.

My hand trembles when I think of that. *And then*, of course, I must die as well.

I have made the most solemn oath, with myself as a witness, that I will not visit the Troposphere again until this novel is completed. But when I go back, I am never coming out again. This cough will be the end of me otherwise; I understand what the doctor told me. As well as that—I want to be free of my right leg and these eyes. Of course, I am also cursed to suffer the most grievous impecuniosity, and I have known for many years that I shall never fuck again. Oh, when will this book end! Each time I dip my pen into this ink bottle (the sixth this month) I wonder if this will be the last bottle of ink I shall use and if this will be the last pen nib I wear out, and if so—in both cases—I wonder if I should frame the damn things or burn them. I am now obsessed with endings: the ending of this novel, and the ending of my own life. Can I be content now that I have a title? Perhaps. *The End of Mr. Y* has a pleasing double meaning, although I am convinced that most reviewers will be far too dull to notice anything like meaning and, if they review my book at all, will simply reference that awful business with Darwin.

Oh, I feel weary. This lamp oil smells toxic.

Perhaps I should just toss the whole book in the fire.

What am I thinking?

I can hear the coarse clip-clop of hooves outside, as men younger than I take to the clubs for an evening of entertainment and cunt-sucking. But mine is a more lofty purpose. Oh, it is so very cold in here, and I have only a little more coal.

When I began this long, arduous composition, I admit that I was seeking revenge. I desired that every man should hold the knowledge that I had been given. For I *am* Mr. Y—in spirit, if not in precise detail, and I, too, paid all the money I had in the world for another taste of this medicine that has since become my most demanding mistress.

The man who sold it to me will have nothing of value once I have completed my book.

And then I shall end my life, just after I have ended the life of Mr. Y.

But . . . What thoughts are these? Am I now to have a crisis of conscience? Am I now, when the whole novel is more than seven-eighths complete, to wonder what the results of its publication will be? Oh, curse these introspective nights. But now that I can see the narrative taking shape on the page I wonder: Will others try the recipe as I have? And how many will die that I may get my revenge? And . . . *No!* This is an absurd thought. But it insists on petitioning me, any-way. What would happen if those who read my book not only discover the Troposphere, but find some way to alter it?

I will burn the book.

No! No . . . Not my book.

My hands are someone else's as they grasp my most precious manuscript and, with me as their unwilling assistant, toss the pages into the fire. The warmth is brief but intense as all two hundred pages crackle and pop. The fire cares not what is ink and what is white space. The book is gone.

What have I done?

What have I done?

I fall to my knees and begin to weep.

Quit.

Back in the Troposphere, it has started to rain.

"I wanted to spend so much more time with him," I say to Adam.

"No. Look at the weather. You need to get to the station."

The night sky looks smeared, as if it were a windscreen with all the night and all the rain happening behind it.

Adam calls up the console.

"There's a train station just around this corner," he says. "Hurry."

But I am not moving. I am not following him as he starts walking.

"Adam," I say to his back.

"Come on."

"Adam."

He turns to face me, water dripping down his face. "What?"

"I'm not going back."

"Ariel . . ."

"There's nothing you can say to change my mind. I don't want to go back."

"But you've got your life to live. You heard what Lura said—you've got the potential to become the kind of thinker who can change the world. You could be the next Derrida, or . . . anything you want."

"But I know what I want."

"I'll always be here. I'll always be in your dreams," he says.

The rain is bouncing off the pavement like tears on a table.

"That's not enough," I say. "That's not enough in so many ways."

There's a crack of thunder in the sky. I think this may be the end for me.

"Ariel!"

Adam has to shout now because the rain is so loud. Lightning fissures the sky, ripping it open so that more rain and darkness can fall out. I can hardly see in front of me, but I can feel Adam's hands on my arms. I can feel him pressing me against the wall and kissing me hard.

"You have to go," he says.

"Don't stop," I say. "I want to be making love to you when it ends."

He pauses. Nothing is happening except for the rain falling down.

"Adam, please," I say. "I can't get what I want outside of here, I know that. And I also understand that this is the curse. But I want the knowledge I can find in here. I want us to go to the very end of this together. I want us to go back as far as we can go, to find the edge of the Troposphere. I want to know how it all started, and what consciousness is. I'm staying."

The thunder stamps all over the made-up sky as Adam and I sink to the ground, our clothes melting off by themselves. But I can feel the rain on my face and dripping in my hair. This time, I can feel the rain.

And this time when he enters me I black out.

But when I wake up, the sun is shining.

Epilogue

It's impossible to say how long it takes us to get to the edge. There is no time anymore. We've been camped here for days now, at the edge of consciousness, wondering what to do next. It's like being on the edge of a cliff, but the edge is thinner than any cliff I've ever seen.

It doesn't feel like the edge of something: It feels like the middle.

But somehow there is an edge. You can walk to it and it seems as if you can look down, but you can't. And there's something that looks like an electric fence: a wavy line crackling around the whole thing, like electricity.

We've made love here at the edge of consciousness; we've done it thousands of times. And we've told each other everything we know. And sometimes it feels as if we are in fact on a cliff top, and that there may even be sea down below, and the ground is sandy underneath us, and little wildflowers grow in clumps. But other times it feels as though we are stuck here on the head of a pin, and the void isn't just below us, but all around us, and it's impossible to turn back because there is no back. There's no forwards, backwards, up, or down.

Today, we've decided (although this place is one long day), we'll actually make the choice, because the problem when you go to the very edge is that the console seems to break down, and there's static and crackle when the voice says, *You now have infinite choice*. And when we hear that we retreat, because we can't make that choice.

It's as if we're looking at something that has never been looked at before.

You now have infinite choice.

We've already been everywhere in the Troposphere: We had to, to get here.

So we look at each other and, holding hands, we walk towards it.

And today, yesterday, whenever this moment is: We walk through it.

And now I thought we'd be falling (and I hoped for the void).

You now have infinite choice.

But we carry on walking, anyway. We don't have to say anything.

And all the choices are there in front of me. Every single one.

But what we walk into is a garden. The most perfect garden that I have ever seen, with more trees than I have ever seen, and a river shimmering like a mirror running down the edge of it. I think that this makes sense, for consciousness to have begun in a garden, because consciousness evolved from plants, after all. And I look at Adam, but I can't speak anymore. I'm not sure I can even think. And there's one tree, standing by the river, and we walk towards it.

And then I understand.

Acknowledgments

Thank you to Jenna Johnson, a wonderful editor without whom this book would not exist. Thanks also to others who believed in this project in the early stages: Tom Tomaszewski, who makes everything possible; Simon Trewin, my agent and friend; Sam Ashurst; Hari Ashurst-Venn; Emilie Clarke; and Sarah Moss. I'd also like to thank my fantastic American agent Dan Mandel for all his support, and my mother, Francesca Ashurst, for always being there.

Thanks also to Rod Edmond, Jennie Batchelor, David Herd, Abdulrazak Gurnah, Jan Montefiore, Caroline Rooney, David Stirrup, Peter Brown, Donna Landry, Sarah Wood, David Ayers, Dennis Borisov, Deborah Wright, Stuart Kelly, Sam Boyce, Tony Mann, Andrew Crumey, Mel McMahon, Jason Kennedy, Mick Owens, Suzi Feay, and all my other friends and colleagues for their moral support.

Several friends, relatives, and colleagues were kind enough to read the completed manuscript and provide feedback, and I am very grateful to Tom Tomaszewski, Sarah Moss, Jennie Batchelor, and Hari Ashurst-Venn. I'd particularly like to thank Couze Venn for his insightful and thought-provoking comments and suggestions. Ian Stewart also took the time to read and comment on the manuscript in detail, for which I am very grateful. All errors remaining in the text are, of course, my own.

I would like to acknowledge the influence of some ideas I first found in *Parallel Worlds* by Michio Kaku and *Big Bang* by Simon Singh. The idea of the primordial particle in chapter 11 was directly inspired by Kaku's work; and most of the material, including the Gamow quote, on page 120, comes from Simon Singh. The quote on page 106 is from *Frankenstein* by Mary Shelley. The quote on page 118 is from *Lectures on Homoeopathic Materia Medica With New Remedies* by J. T. Kent. *Literary Portraits of the Polychrests*, on page 118, is fictional, but was inspired by *Portraits of Homoeopathic Medicines* by Catherine R. Coulter.